FALLEN

THE FOUNDER'S SEED BOOK 1

FALLEN

DREMA DEÒRAICH

NIVEYM ARTS LLC

For
Becky S
Dylan W
John C
Liliana A
Lillith T
And Vince G
who read every draft as if it were the first.

Iridos

Segregated Landing Bay
Night Side (ne'ani)
Storage and Supply Dome
Science Dome
Mechanics, Scientific
Central Dome
Daily Business
To surface
Sand buildup
Pyramid
Spring fed fresh water
Greenhouse Dome
North Ritual Site Access
Rites of Mourning
Guildhouse Dome
To Temple Cavern
Hematium mines
Day Side (ha'ani)
N
Pulsar Landing

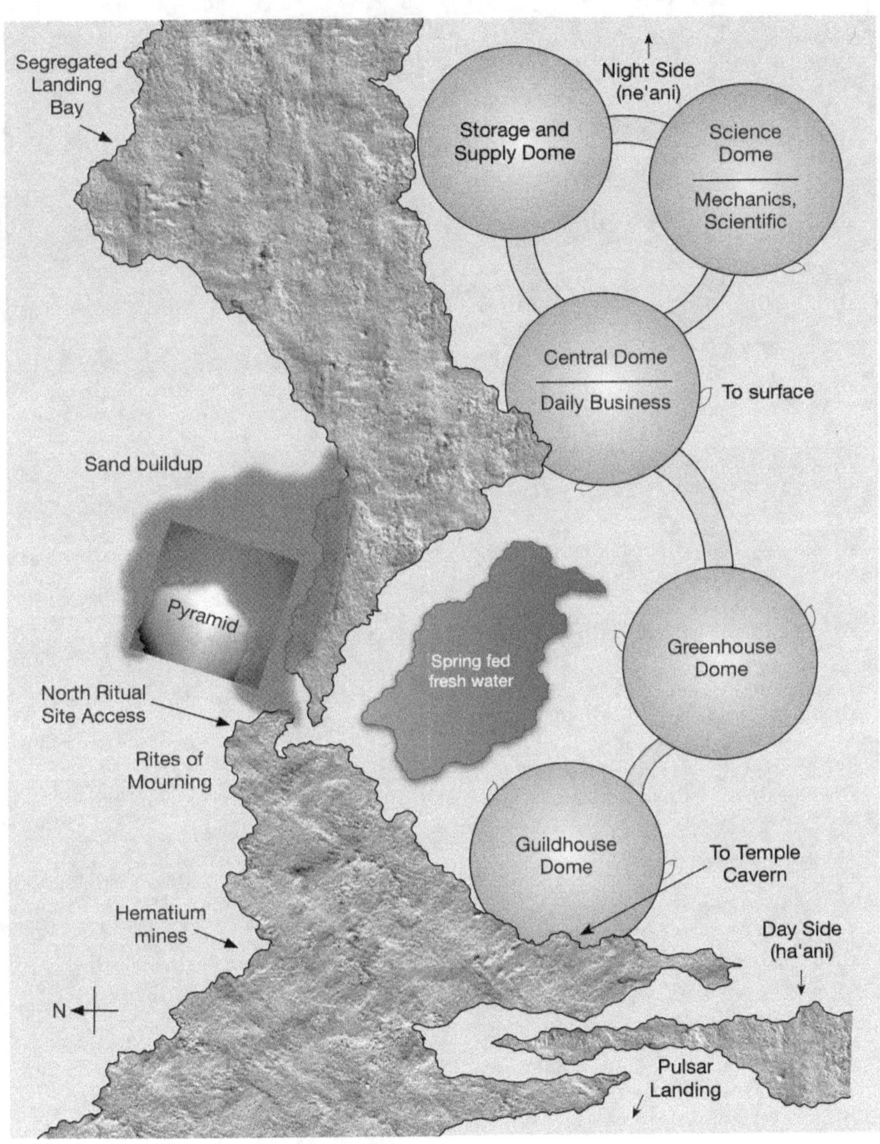

New Canaan, Harajüd

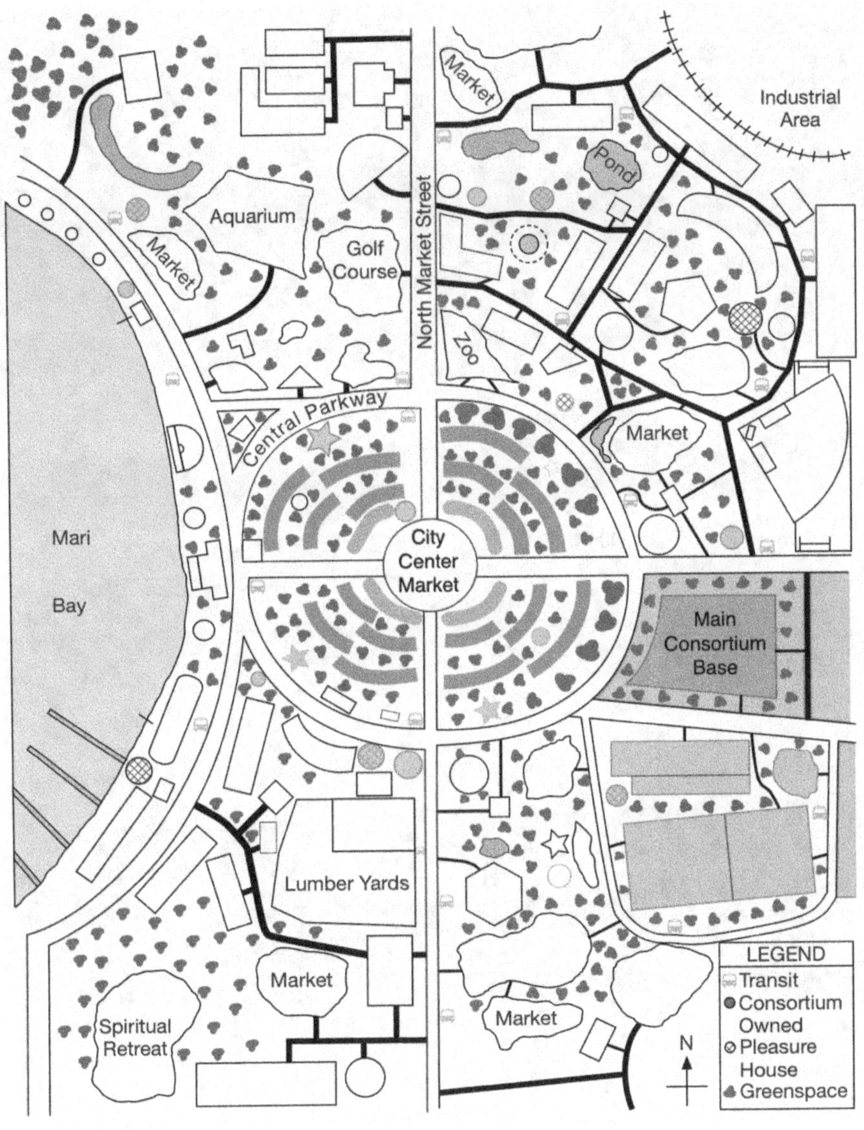

Bejami

Canyon
Stawanel Mountains
BREGAINA
Dairnen Bay
BEL-RHOVAN
Baisken River
Dorucuin
LEGEND
Bog
Ice, Snow
Inland Water
Jungle
Land (undefined)
Mountains
Open Water
N

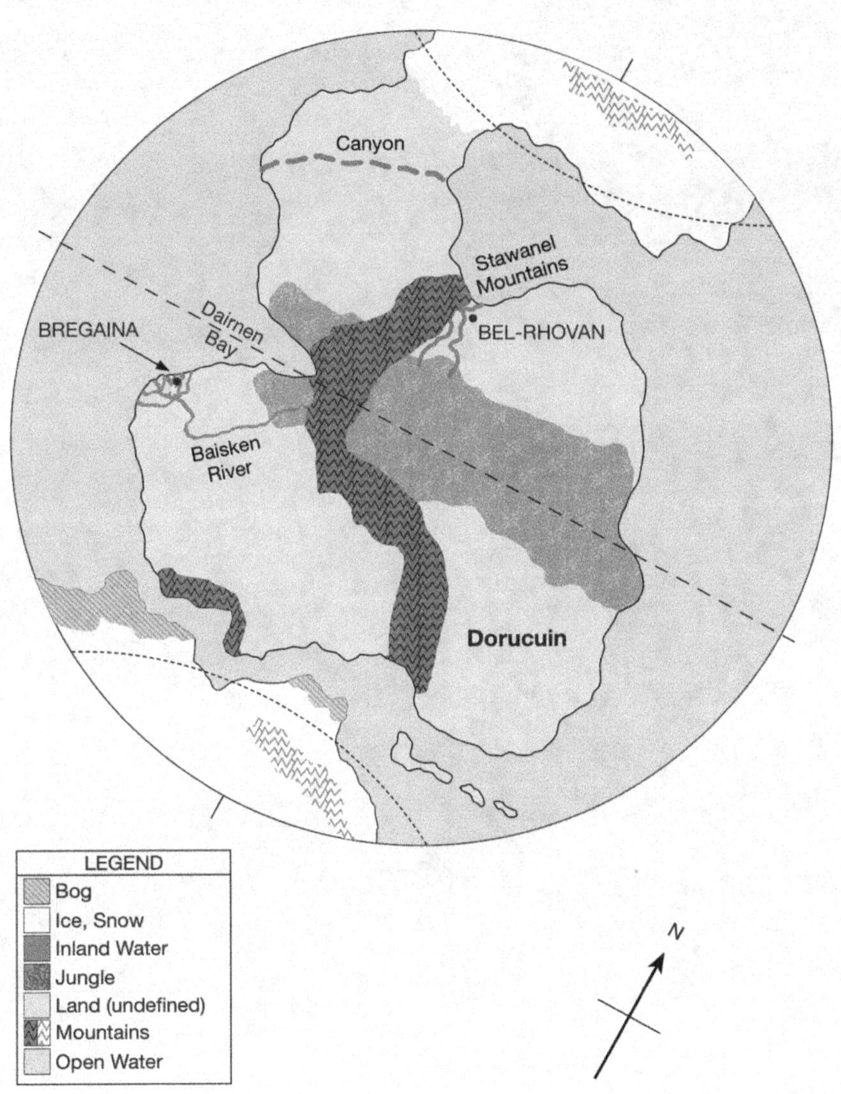

Rubene

SYCHANOLFAN
YNYSBEDD
LEGEND
Bog
Ice, Snow
Inland Water
Land (undefined)
Marsh
Mountains
Open Water
N

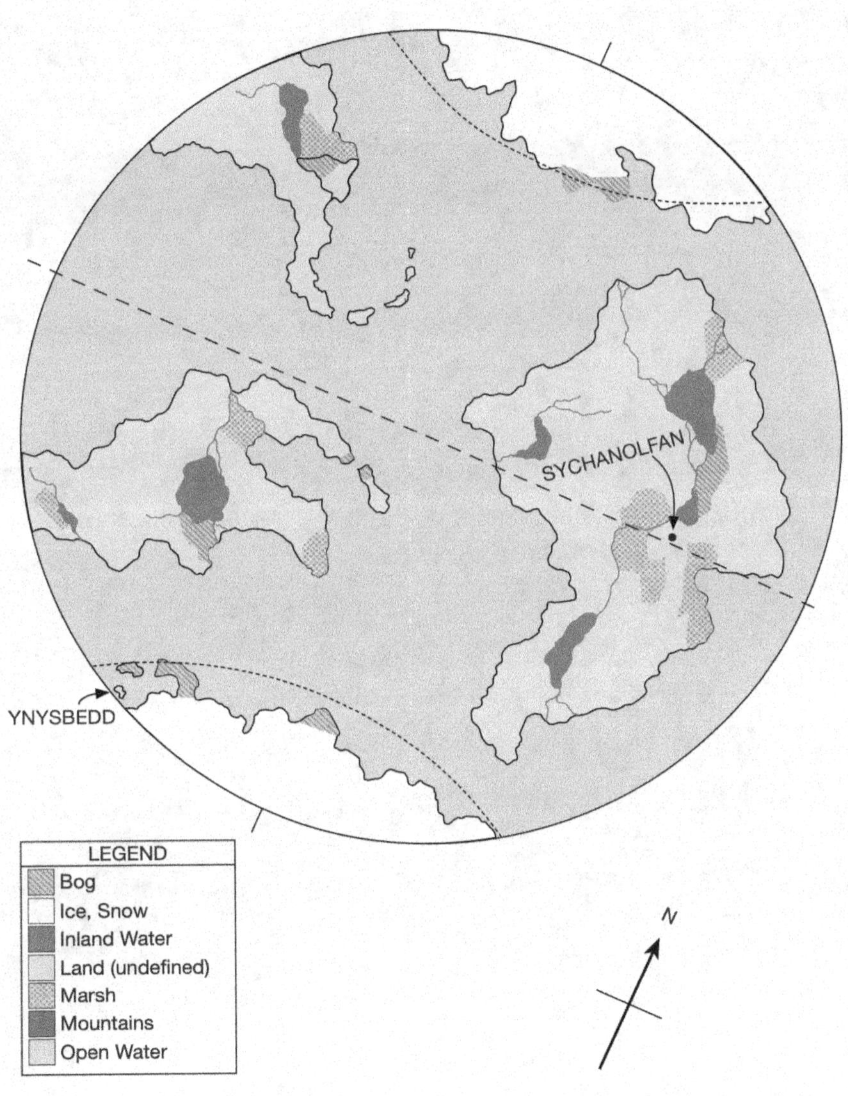

Part One

chapter 1

<u>Iridos</u>

ALIRA STABBED HER DIGGER INTO the ground, throwing clods of soil about as she gouged a hole with a fervor beyond her love of this spot or her gratitude for a moment alone. Frustration sparked patterns of colorful luminescence along the pale blue skin of both her arms and drove her stick deeper among the roots.

Surrounded by the rich smell of peat and the muffled sound of the wind, Alira's tension drained. This copse felt like her own personal sanctuary. Its peace kept her sane in a community where she would never belong. Here, no one thought her strange. Here, she could be more than a cleric. Here, she could violate the sacrosanct guild boundary and imagine herself a forager. If she didn't stay too long, the council would never know. Her mother would never know.

Another jab of her digger speared a rufesh tuber. She brushed away the dirt, squeezed the peel to pop it into her mouth, sat back on her heels, and chewed the starchy flesh. Outside the grove, wind rushed howling across the plain from ne'ani, where their star's light never shone, toward ha'ani, where it always did. Inside the grove, towering trees, thickets of fern, and tangles of dozhan weed muted the din enough that she could track sounds in her surroundings. Only deep in the belly of the city, where tunnels burrowed far below the surface, did the unammi escape all vestiges of the wind's wail.

Blue flickers from her dermal display lit the shadows around her and reflected like watershine on the boles and foliage nearby. A scurrying sound accompanied by waggling ferns a short distance away hinted at some minor drama playing out among the ground-level wildlife. It didn't concern her. No carnivores to worry about other than the rare serpentine atlish grown large enough to swallow a squat unammi youngling, but that hadn't happened in many generations.

She drew a deep breath, tightening the band of cloth wrapped around her chest, and let her head fall back. Far above, scaly muñise trees sprouted branches that reached so far as to touch surrounding trunks. Each tree's lower limbs twined among those of their neighbors to form a strong support for the canopy's abundant life. Nearer the top, above the winds, they reached up instead of out, purple leaves turned to capture as much of ha'ani's light as possible. Alira closed her eyes and imagined the insects, worms, and other small creatures that thrived there above the winds. Elevated so, they had few predators besides the delicate white niveym, large birds rarely glimpsed by surface dwellers, and atlish that slithered with ease from canopy to surface and back within the thickets.

She drifted, lost in thought, until voices snapped her eyes open. A group of other unammi approached—too late for her to flee unseen. Alira's shoulders tightened. Pink annoyance and sprinkles of white alarm raced up and down her arms. She bent to her task once more to lend an appearance of validity to her presence. Gathering food for the unammi couldn't—shouldn't—be wrong. If it fed workers in the city, what did it matter who did the digging?

The voices approached, then all stopped at once. Alira began a silent count. One…two…three…four….

"What are *you* doing here?"

Faster than she'd expected. "Digging for rufesh."

"Aren't you supposed to be teaching spiritual fundamentals to the younglings?" another said. "Grinding some muñise resin for incense or leading a ritual?"

"I'm on my own time," Alira muttered. "I'm allowed to do as I like."

"Hobbies are fine," the first said, "but you take it too far. How many guilds' crafts are you studying now? Eight? Ten? More? If you were normal, you'd stick to the one you chose at your rite."

Alira kept digging, red streaks joining the riot of color on her skin, racing down both arms and onto all ten fingers where the color disappeared beneath the dirt caked there. "At least I have more than one skill. If our people ever faced the loss of any guild, you wouldn't know how to survive on your own."

"That's insane. Stop inventing excuses for your behavior," a male said. "You're scaring the younglings."

Alira looked up. The wildcrafting class spread out in a semi-circle before her. Frem adults stood with seven students and Sufamel, the most experienced elder in the horticulture guild. The younglings' skin showed speckles of white, and Alira chided herself for not thinking before she spoke. Still, it rankled to be rebuked in front of the entire group. Some of these little ones were in her own classes. Lavender unhappiness flooded out the red in her dermal display and she sighed.

Two of the frem herded the students away from the confrontation as one teacher pointed at various plants and identified each. When they were out of earshot Tisalan, one of the remaining frem, stepped closer.

"You're a disgrace, Alira. I heard you're learning to weave, and that you asked a miner to teach you the differences between minerals they extract."

"Don't worry," Alira said. "He refused."

"Thank Na'Staani for that. Think of the trouble had he agreed. I'm told you're even working in the landing bay with the mitigants! The *mitigants*! You go beyond odd, cleric! Why won't you respect our boundaries?"

Alira stabbed her digger into the dirt with half-hearted enthusiasm. Why indeed. Her life would be much easier if she could. "I don't like living in a box."

Tisalan scoffed. "That box you scorn was designed by the Founder because it benefits all unammi. We've thrived inside it for generations, yet you think your own ideas are superior?"

Alira glared at her. "I don't believe for a heartbeat that the Founder would have established laws to limit his people so."

Tisalan's display flecked with red and pink atop the green of duty, her colors racing down her neck and under the chest wrap she wore. "I suppose we shouldn't be surprised at your attitude. Human interaction corrupts. You're a walking example. Just seeing those aliens on the trade guild holovids has sullied you."

Red flooded Alira's own skin as she surged to her feet. "What would you know of the humans?"

The other female stepped closer, her features tight. "Everyone's seen enough of the training vids to know humans are disgusting. Their feet are so tiny they look deformed, especially at the ends of such thin, fragile legs. With that flat, dull skin, how can you tell what they're thinking? And all those fibers on their heads like they'd stripped dozhan of their filaments and sewn the strands to their pates. What purpose do those serve?" She shuddered. "It's enough to give one nightmares. You're the only one who liked those vids. It's no wonder you're aberrant. You should have chosen the trade guild at your Rite of Decision. Then you could be a pilot and live with your freakish humans. You'd fit in better with them than you do with your own people."

"Because I think for myself?" Alira asked, closing the distance between herself and Tisalan. "As far as I'm concerned, that's better than reciting council rhetoric for lack of anything better to say."

"Basu'tao." Sufamel's quiet voice cracked the tension as she stepped between the two females. "Tisalan, you have work to do. Alira, walk with me."

The two remaining foragers moved away toward the younglings, glancing back as they went. Sufamel shifted her attention back to Alira. "What will we do with you, chithe?" she said, her skin a confusion of tan affection and pink annoyance.

Chithe? Alira brushed the dirt from both legs of her loose pants and flushed blue with angst. "I haven't been a youngling in seasons of seasons."

"Then stop acting like one." Sufamel started back toward the city.

Alira sighed and fell into step beside her. "I'm sorry. I—"

Sufamel sliced a hand through the air. "Stop giving me words that don't agree with your actions. Why did you choose the clerical guild?"

"My ama has driven me toward it all my life."

"Shame on Lurien for influencing you so. It should have been your free choice." The elder walked on. "It's clear you regret your Decision, but it's too late to change now. Why do you fight it?"

If only she knew. "I love being a cleric. But I also enjoy doing other things. It's wrong to force us to choose when we're so young. The council should at least allow a longer period of experimentation so we can be sure of what we want before we commit our entire lives to a single guild." She sighed. "I keep hoping my actions will entice others to follow my example so the council will see how wrong it is to confine us so."

Sufamel nodded, her jaw working. Probably chewing a leaf or a piece of root. "How can an uprising among the unammi help us?"

Gray surprise flooded Alira's arms. "I never said—"

"If you divide the unammi, if you tear down the guild structure that's been in place throughout our history, you'll break our people. Our civilization. How will you bind us back together then?"

The wind's roar rose as they approached the border of the grove and Sufamel stopped, her aged profile so calm, so patterned with green veins. An occasional pink speckle touched that dutiful display.

"Why do you think your way is better?" Sufamel asked. "Have the Iri told you this?"

Alira frowned. "No, of course not. You know they don't speak to us."

"But they do." Sufamel bobbed her head. "The Iri have always whispered guidance and wisdom to the high cleric. They speak to Lurien, do they not? That's why she is the first voice on the council." The elder chewed her leaf a moment, a twinkle in her eye as she peered at Alira. "They'll speak to you one day, assuming you settle enough to take on your mother's role. The people expect the same of you."

Alira fidgeted. She'd heard her ama say as much, but Sufamel's words added weight to the admonition. Life would be so much easier if Alira could be content with her Decision like everyone else. She plucked a twig from the knotted shoulder of Sufamel's wrap.

"Do you think I'll ever be ready?" Alira murmured.

"That is between you, Lurien, and Na'Staani," Sufamel said. "But you know what it means if you do not resolve this conflict. Mitigation wouldn't suit you, Alira. Don't press the council. You won't like their decision any more than you liked your own." She took Alira's hand and leaned closer. "Open defiance makes you a target. Quiet rebellion satisfies almost as much but with fewer troublesome side effects. If you really want to play in the dirt, come to my quarters. I've plenty of seedlings there and can put you to work where no one can see." She squeezed Alira's fingers and went back to her class.

Sufamel was right, but that didn't make it any less complicated. It was still so surprising that no one thought to investigate deeper reasons behind Alira's discontent. They always chose instead to assume she enjoyed causing problems. But that was the least of her worries. Far more pressing was the fact that one of the others was sure to speak of this encounter. Word would get back to Lurien.

Alira worked on an explanation as she closed her inner eyelids against blown sand and stepped outside the shelter of the trees. Walking into the wind, the trek to the protected canyon and the city beyond always took longer than the trip to the wood. She was almost at the mouth of the canyon before she remembered she'd left her gathering sacks in the dirt.

chapter 2

New Canaan, Harajüd
<u>Consortium Trader Base</u>

ADMIRAL SKALAR EXITED THE CLEAR plaz holding cell and stood far
enough away that the prisoner wouldn't be able to see him in the shadowed
corridor outside. He looked her over again. Most curious, that broken and
badly set nose, that scar along the bottom of her jaw. Now why didn't she
get that fixed? All colonial worlds provided free medical care. It didn't
make any sense for her to have a badly set nose and a scar anywhere on
her body. Unless she couldn't go to the medfacs because....

Because what?

His adjutant, Andrea Sweeney, stepped up beside him. "Sorry, sir, but
the DNA swipe was a bust. No records."

High-level connections, then. Who sent this troublemaker? This
netzyl? One of the other factions, maybe, given the human cargo she'd
been carrying. Surely not a bigwig from another colony world, despite the
prisoner's claims that corporate would burn him for holding her.

He'd almost laughed at that. Civilian governments did dip an
occasional toe into Trader business, but they were far more likely to hire

a Trader faction to do work they, as respectable governors of their various worlds, could not. Skalar had no compunctions about breaking colonial law or even violating the Intercolonial Charter. Those rules didn't apply to Trader business.

But slaving? Never. Nor had he ever known a colony world to trade in slaves. For them, it was too reminiscent of a past they wanted to leave behind.

For Skalar, the issue was far more personal.

His little sister's image swam through his thoughts, Rugrat's laughing, childish face followed by her petite form so wracked and abused her kidnappers had dumped her on the docks like a broken toy. The last time he'd seen her alive, she'd shied at every sound. Her haunted expression highlighted the pain etched into every line on her skin. She never would've been taken in the first place if their recalcitrant mother hadn't refused his support. Skalar clenched his fist and shoved it into his pocket.

"Should we bring the prisoner some water, sir? It's been almost two days. She can go a bit longer without food, of course, but she's gonna need something to drink soon." Sweeney shifted on her feet. "Unless you're finished with her. Did she tell you anything?"

He spared her a glance before looking back to the cell. "No. She's not ready to talk. Yet."

Sa'abah, captain of security, approached the cell. "Sorry to disturb you, sir, but Captain Crow is on his way to your office with Jarod."

"Acknowledged. Sa'abah, have your teams prep the blackout cell," he said. "When it's ready, tranq and transfer our guest there."

"You want the full system setup?"

"Same as last time. Wait, belay that. Amp audio volume by six."

Sa'abah nodded. "Right away, sir."

Skalar gestured for his adjutant to follow, then swept out of the brig and into the main lift.

Sweeney hesitated, pointing at the private lift behind the security desk. "But…aren't you going to your office?"

"Via the scenic route. There's a guest in my office. I'd rather not draw attention to the lift there." He flashed a quick smile he didn't feel. "I want to know who this prisoner is. Keep checking. Send every tidbit you find to my TICS pad."

"Yes, sir. Do you know who's behind this?"

"I have my suspicions. Any other questions?"

"No sir." The lift stopped at the administrative level, and Sweeney hurried off to her tasks.

Alone in the lift, Skalar brushed at his immaculate trousers and crisp shirt and tried to fend off dark childhood memories.

Forget it. Can't go back.

On the top floor, crewmen along the wide corridors stepped back to give the admiral space and he swept past them. Up here, thick windows formed outer walls offering stunning views. On any given day, Skalar stopped at one or another of these to survey his domain. That's how he thought of it. *His* domain. Never mind that HHU, Harajüd House Unlimited, governed unchallenged on this colony world, or that they owned every resource, every scrap of dirt outside Consortium land. They didn't own his Trader faction, and they didn't own him. On the contrary, the HHU board of directors—and Chairman Logan Roucharde in particular—owed a great deal to the Consortium. To Skalar. Trader factions stood outside the law. They could do what colonial security forces, neutered by the Charter, could not. In exchange, HHU left Skalar alone to run the Consortium's many business interests and fatten his personal credit account like any other member of Harajüd's colonial elite. The sole difference between him and them was that Skalar didn't sit on the HHU board of directors and couldn't influence planetary policy.

At least, not yet. But that was a problem for another time.

The office door slid aside and Skalar entered the comfortable, familiar room. Outside his private residence, this workspace best supported the image he wanted to portray: simple, refined, elegant. One floor-to-ceiling window stretched from the north wall around the northwest corner overlooking markets, sculpted skyscrapers of the city center residential district and, in the distance, Mari Bay. Two of Harajüd's seven moons shimmered low in the afternoon sky beyond the bay. An enormous nanopanel, now set to exhibit an ever-changing swirl of blue and green, filled in the remaining window space. Pearl gray walls stood unadorned save for a preserved Jolly Roger, a tribute to the pirates and privateers on whom all early Trader factions were modeled, which hung above a table halfway across the room. A bar and seating area before the door invited visitors to relax. Those familiar with the admiral knew better than to fall for that trap.

Skalar poured a drink while he sized up the setting. At the other end of the room his second, Captain Crow, stood near the spartan desk with arms crossed over his wiry chest, green eyes in that lined brown countenance. Even from behind, Skalar would have known who he was, given the captain's standard choice in clothing—dark, utilitarian shirt and pants, and those heavy, steel-toed boots he seemed to favor. Salt-and-pepper braids hung to his shoulders and swung with his movements.

Jarod, the Consortium's chief metalsmith, waited near the nanopanel, his lanky form tense inside his artsy trousers and loose tunic, his silver-shot black ponytail slightly askew. At his sandaled feet lay two square metal plates, each about thirty centimeters to a side. Skalar glanced his way. "Why are you here?"

Jarod shifted his weight. "I've been at the hematium again."

Skalar took his brandy to the desk and sat. "We discussed this."

"I was on my own time, Admiral."

"You work for me," Skalar said. "All your time is mine. Hematium wastes it. That metal is fit for nothing but ship parts."

"I think this might change your opinion, sir. If I may?" He inclined his portable TICS pad toward Skalar.

Skalar nodded.

Jarod touched the pad and threw a small holovid, which hovered above Skalar's desk. In the vid, a panel like those Jarod brought hung in braces at one end of a test room. "This is playback at 1/1000th speed."

He started the vid. Seconds later, a small projectile crossed the holo in slow motion and punched through the plate. Jarod paused the playback and picked up one of the panels. Its surface, scorched black, sported a hole more than seven centimeters across. "This is that same outer hull segment," he said, "which came off a personnel carrier, XL class. A ship part, if you will."

"Where'd you get the test panel?" Crow asked.

"Faction shipyard. Recycling."

Crow grabbed the piece, examined it, then passed it to Skalar. "That ain't even a bug bite."

"Big enough to be disastrous in space. That," he said, pointing at the hole, "came from a projectile the size of a typical meteoroid, maybe three centimeters in diameter, discharged by a rigged pulse cutter at one hundred percent strength. Larger debris in space packs a bigger punch."

Skalar laid the damaged metal aside and squinted at the metalsmith. "Standard risk for space flight. So?"

Jarod restarted the vid. The hologram switched to a new panel of slightly different color, same size, same braces, same sized projectile. This time, however, the panel deflected the nugget.

"That's one hundred percent," Jarod said.

A few seconds later, a bigger chunk flew across the vid and bounced off the panel.

"Two hundred percent."

The third time, a large hunk of metal flashed across the vid and shattered against the panel, its pieces careening in every direction. One fragment raced closer to the holocam, increasing in size until it impacted the camera and the vid vanished. Skalar set his drink down hard and surged to his feet.

"Three hundred percent. I would have tried more force, but that was the best I could coax out of improvised gear. Also, we lost the holocam and a bit of the ceiling to collateral damage in the last test." Jarod lifted the other panel off the floor. He tilted it one way, then the other. Turned it around, back. No marks marred the light gray surface. "This is the panel from the second test."

"Hematium?" Skalar said.

"Yes, sir. The whole panel." He exuded that smug excitement of scientists everywhere when revealing a new discovery. "Ships made from this would be nigh impervious."

Crow barked a laugh. "Big boats confined to space, maybe. A hematium hull would be too heavy for atmospheric craft."

Jarod tossed the panel at Crow.

Crow scrambled, bracing himself, and caught it mid-air. His eyes widened, then narrowed. He scowled at Jarod.

"Hematium, my ass. This ain't heavy enough. What is it really?"

Skalar leaned over and snatched the panel from Crow, hefting it with one hand. He raised a brow at the metalsmith. "Well?"

"It's hematium with a honeycomb core. See for yourself." Jarod threw a new visual to the holodisplay. "Here's a bottom-line analysis compiled by your own chemists."

Skalar passed the panel back to Crow and scrutinized the breakdown. The numbers were close. "Trace elements are off."

"Temperature accounts for that."

"Temperature."

Jarod nodded. "Yes, sir. Extreme heat."

"I thought that would shatter it," Crow said.

"It does if you do it fast. This took a long time."

Crow squinted. "So, if it breaks…."

"No second chances, Captain. If it breaks before the process is completed, or if it's fired more than once, the finished product will never reach this level of integrity. But, once it's worked in this way and cooled at a controlled rate, tensile strength is enhanced beyond belief."

Skalar sat down. "Every hematium part in every ship's energy chamber is heated and cooled in production. Why has this never been noticed before?"

"It isn't the heating and cooling alone, sir," Jarod said. "It's a multi-step, specialized process. I'll show you if you want."

"Later." Skalar sipped his brandy. "Did you try this on a normal piece of hematium scrap?"

"Yes, sir," replied Jarod. "Without that sequence in its initial construction, the panel's as vulnerable as any other to hull stress or damage."

"Why?" Skalar said. "No other metallurgy results in magical effects like this."

"It's part of the allotropic phase transformation. And the timing, of course. This new process evokes a stronger reaction in hematium than in any metal I've ever worked with. The difference is off the charts. It's as if the molecular bond—"

Skalar held up a hand. "Thank you." He swiped away the holo, retrieved the undamaged plate, and hefted it again, considering the panel and all the implications of this discovery. "How long did this take?"

"Not counting the trial and error in the learning process, start to finish, that one piece took about two days."

Two days! "At that rate, it'll cost a fortune to build even one ship."

"Not if we refine the process, sir. Automate it. Mass production at our shipyards would bring the cost down."

True. "I want to see this for myself. Set up a series of off-world trials."

Jarod squirmed. "I can do one, sir, then I'm out of material. I used up most of my spare stock to produce this," he said, nodding at the plate.

Crow smirked. "Scrap yard's full of it. Pick up all you want."

"No, I told you," Jarod said. "That won't work. Scrap's already been fired. It has to be raw ore."

Skalar laid the panel on his desk and leaned back. "How much do you need to set up five additional tests?"

"Depends on how big you want them to be," Jarod said.

"Say we convert one quadrant on each of several junked ships," Skalar said.

"Yeah," Crow said. "Then we haul 'em off-world and use 'em for target practice."

Skalar nodded. "Just so. This shows the material's effectiveness against ballistic damage from space debris. It doesn't guarantee its effectiveness against energy weapons. We'll test for that, as well, and include a comparison between new and old panels."

Jarod's eyes darted back and forth as if he were reading calculations on an internal screen. After a moment, he said, "Fifty tonnes might be adequate."

Crow whistled.

Skalar pursed his lips. That would raise Roucharde's brows. "Very well. Set up the first one with what you have. Keep me informed of your progress. TICS," Skalar said to the air above his desk, "attend."

A chitter sounded in response.

"Send Lieutenant Sweeney to my office." The system responded, and he picked up the panel again, examining its webbed construct. "Has anyone else seen you working on this?"

"Sure. I had to use the shipyard to do it. But I didn't advertise my medium. I figured you'd wanna hold this close to the vest."

"That's correct," Skalar said. "Tell no one. This is your new priority." The door chime sounded, announcing Sweeney's arrival. Skalar smiled at Jarod. "Good job. My adjutant will see you to the gate."

Skalar pointed at a chair. Crow sat.

"TICS, attend."

The system chittered.

"Comm Logan Roucharde."

Soon, the chairman's smiling image hovered above the desk.

"Hello, Skalar. What can I do for you?"

"Logan, I need a favor." Skalar liked calling the directors by their first names. "The Consortium needs an additional quantity of raw hematium."

"How much?"

"Fifty tonnes."

Roucharde winced. "Damn! That's nearly twice your annual allotment. Building some new ships?"

"I'm testing a new prototype."

Logan leaned to one side in his seat. "We only delivered your regular shipment two months ago. I don't have that kind of quantity lying around. Have you tried buying it from our competitor?"

Skalar lowered his brandy. "Come now, Logan. To buy from Saacharis Aggregate would breach our contract with Harajüd House. I would never violate the Charter that way." Not and admit to it, anyway.

Logan seemed to consider the issue. "Is this a one-time thing?"

"I'm not sure. It may be."

"If not, let me know. We'll work something out. In the meantime, I won't take it amiss if you don't buy from us this once. Will that work for you?"

"Indeed," Skalar nodded. "Please have your staff draw up an agreement and transmit it to my TICS right away. I'd like to have your permission on record as soon as possible. Oh by the way, that interference job you asked me to run...."

"It's done?"

"Yes." And Roucharde better not forget who did this for him. "Should I expect the price to go up on Gadney livestock?"

Logan leaned forward and dropped his voice. "There's no… evidence?"

Skalar's free hand went to his heart. "You wound me."

"No offense. I'll transfer payment in installments over the next week, as agreed."

"Of course."

The chairman sat back. "Was that all?"

"Yes. Thank you, Logan. I'll keep you posted on the other deal you asked about."

"Sounds good."

The visual winked out.

On the other side of the desk, Crow grinned. "You sure know how to make Roucharde dance."

Skalar sipped his brandy. Damn right. He'd been doing it since Logan took over as chairman almost twenty years ago.

Crow slid down in his seat. "So, what are you thinking? Use it on our own ships? Take over the other factions? If the tinker's right, we'll be undefeatable."

"If it works as Jarod claims, we'll use it for our newer ships as an edge in our favor, not to issue a statement of intent. There's no sense courting a shooting war."

"Why not?" his captain said. "The other admirals wouldn't hesitate, especially Rizzo."

"They're stupid. I'm not." Skalar frowned. "Have you forgotten the Triad Wars?"

Crow's expression went blank. "Of course not."

Skalar shook his head. Crow was never a student of history. "The Unions destroyed what was left of the ecosystem on Earth, exacerbated the spread of the virus that killed the remaining population. No, we will not fire the first shot in a new war. It isn't worth destroying the six surrounding colonies to take over our competitors. And what would I do with crippled factions? I want them whole. Functional. Profitable. There are better ways to assume control. More insidious, perhaps, but less destructive to the worlds we all require."

He rose and turned toward the window, his mind working at an alternate plan. If Jarod was right, Skalar could sell the plating to Harajüd House. Not the formula for its production, of course. No way he'd part with that, but he would be more than happy to fabricate the parts required to replace the hulls on their space stations. For that matter, all the colony worlds would buy such advanced protection. Small orbital debris did a share of damage from time to time.

When it came to HHU, he could sell the parts for fewer credits if a seat on the board came as part of his payment. As a director, he'd be in a unique position to benefit the Consortium, as well as Traders on other worlds. Leadership of the other five factions seemed a reasonable next step. Those admirals wouldn't thank him at first, but they'd come to see the benefit of an alliance with a Trader admiral who could influence laws, loosen trade restrictions, and manipulate influential administrators, not only here but on all the colonies.

Of course, it would be a simple matter of time before the other admirals wanted the same kind of shielding for their own ships. Even at an exorbitant price, he'd lose his advantage if he sold to them. He made a mental note to set Jarod the task of breaching the hulls, too. No sense in having the shield if you didn't also know how to defeat it.

Skalar finished his brandy, then went to the bar. "TICS, record communique, destination Iridos." He filled his glass and returned to his seat.

"I am Admiral Skalar of the Harajüd Consortium. I wish to purchase fifty tonnes of hematium to be delivered as soon as possible to my main base in New Canaan. What is your asking price? Do remember that I can also assist you with acquisitions you might find difficult to secure through either of your other corporate connections. Further considerations are possible. I await your reply." He paused with an amiable smile. "TICS, end communique. Conclude and transmit."

Momentary silence filled the space before Crow broke it. "Colonial security isn't used to seeing direct dealings between squibs and Consortium crew," he observed. "You think they'll kick up a stink?"

"Logan blessed it. Who's going to argue with that?"

Crow blurted a sarcastic laugh. "He meant his colonial competitor, not the squib source. HHU will have words."

"He didn't specify any particular seller." Skalar shrugged. "I'll have his written agreement as carte blanche."

"What makes you think the squibs will deal with you? If I recall correctly, it was hard enough to get them to deal with humans in the first place."

"Indeed. But it has been almost twelve hundred years since anyone new tried. Who knows? Maybe they're tired of their exclusivity with HHU and Saacharis Aggregate. I could offer them more than both put together."

"Worth a try, I guess. It's not like we could get it anywhere else," Crow muttered. "At least not unless we find it on some other rock."

Skalar sipped his brandy.

Crow frowned. "Are you gonna want me to deal with them when they come?"

"Is that a problem?"

"No. I can handle it if you want. They're just so weird-looking."

"They're humanoid," Skalar shrugged.

"Sure, one bald head, two arms, two legs. But they're blue. And their parts are mismatched. Huge eyes, big-ass feet on squat pissant bodies. Hell, I never even saw a squib that stood as tall as my chest."

"Evolution, Captain."

"What?"

Skalar gestured with his snifter. "The core of Iridos is denser than any colony world. Higher gravity means a different body shape."

"I guess. But they light up. Like bugs."

"Iridos is tidally locked with its star."

"So?"

"So, it's a safe bet they live in permanent shadow. We already know they trade glowing pigments and plant fibers. I expect bioluminescence is common there." Skalar shrugged. "You'll have at least three days to get used to the idea, time for them to get the message and deliver the shipment. But if you don't want the job—"

"I didn't say that." Crow looked almost offended. "Don't worry. I can deal with ugly."

chapter 3

<u>Iridos</u>

YOUNGLING VOICES REACHED INTO THE tunnel outside the classroom. Alira slowed, listening.

"You can't be a raneal," one said. "You're too big."

"Can, too," another said. "Watch me."

Alira crept to the door. Kipa's small body melted into a horizontal position, his limbs retracting and reforming as four thick legs. Skin raised into pebbled bumps along his back and down the tail that grew from his spine.

Alira freckled with tan affection. Youngling classes always raised her spirits. Everyone encouraged Kipa with shouts and bright colors of excitement. Everyone except Trumo, who observed in silence.

She stepped into the room, clapping. "Good try, Kipa. But Enfili is correct. An actual raneal lizard could sit in the palm of your hand. Your approximation will always be too large. Pick something closer to your own size. Like a fealle sprite. Watch."

The younglings around her shimmered and wavered as Alira shrank to half her normal size. She couldn't see herself, but she knew how it appeared to them. Luminescent hues in her skin flattened into subdued dun fur. Her shifting form dropped to all fours, hindquarters raised over a wide, stumpy tail and back legs built for power. Huge, double-lidded eyes dominated an exaggerated head with a fuzzy snout pointed to dig under the sand. A sudden leap carried her morphed body into the air and she landed in the same spot. Snorting and huffing, she pushed her muzzle toward the younglings, eliciting squeals and yellow flashes of delight. Then she expanded and straightened until she stood upright wearing her own face.

"You see?" she asked.

Bright features shone back. "Shifting makes me tired," one said.

"It gets easier as you get older," Alira explained, "but even frem can't hold an unnatural configuration indefinitely without rest."

Another chimed in. "Why does everything look so weird and shiny when I'm morphing?"

"Because your eyes are changing their shape. You get used to it."

Trumo leaned forward. "Can we mimic something that's bigger than us?"

"Sure," she said "to a point. What did you have in mind?"

Trumo drew a breath to respond, but the others nudged Kipa.

"Do it," they challenged.

Kipa hissed back. "No."

"Do what?" Alira asked. "Show me, Kipa."

Blue sprinkles danced across his chest. "I shouldn't."

"Why not?" Alira said. "Practice is a good thing. We won't tease you. Will we?"

"No," the younglings said in unison.

Kipa glanced at the others and back at her. His silver eyes dimmed to a startling gray before he expanded to almost half again his normal size. His torso lengthened, drawing up from the waist until his too-small head towered above his overlarge feet. Sparkling colors died into wan, dull skin stretched taut over exaggerated bones. Alira gaped up at him.

He'd come close. Too close. The other younglings waited, hands at their mouths, for her response.

Her breath snagged, drawn tight on a barb of fear. Had she neglected to secure the trade guild vids the last time she'd been in that classroom? "Kipa, where have you seen a human?"

He resumed his own form. "I don't remember."

"Was it the holovids?" she said.

"No. I—" he mumbled to his feet. "One of the pilots in the dining hall was thinking about the humans. I saw it."

Alira blinked. Kipa was telepathic? Already? Such gifts normally surfaced after fifteen or sixteen seasons. He was no more than twelve. "You saw it in the pilot's thoughts?"

He nodded, meeting her gaze.

"Did you ask permission first?"

Kipa paused. "No, Na'ama. It just came to me. I didn't mean to peek."

Alira took in the tense coloring of the other younglings. "Who else have you told about this?"

"Only my friends."

"Kipa."

He looked up. Lavender veins of uncertainty streaked his small face.

"Your other teachers should be told. And not by me, do you understand? This must be considered in your training."

He nodded.

"Good," she said. "Now, take your seats."

"But morphing's fun, Na'ama Alira. Can't we do that a little longer?" Enfili pleaded.

Alira weakened. "We have other studies today."

"Can you at least tell us if Kipa got the human right?" another chimed in.

She eyed them. "Very well—*if* you can answer my questions about the Founder."

Excited assent greeted her suggestion as if she'd offered to play a game. Perhaps she had.

"Who was the Founder?"

All spoke at once. "Elisul."

"Good! Why did he and our ancestors come to Iridos?"

Everyone clamored to answer, and Alira pointed at one youngling.

"Their world was unstable. They needed a new planet."

"That's right. Did Elisul send founders to other worlds?"

A young female shook her head. "No one knows."

"No," Alira agreed. "We don't. It's strange, isn't it, wondering if there are other unammi out there somewhere?"

Everyone nodded.

"One more question. What sorts of things did Elisul pass down to us? Call them out."

"Our social structure," one said.

"Our culture," another said.

"The rites."

"The taboos!"

Alira winced.

"Elisul didn't like outsiders," another added. "I don't think he would have traded with the humans if he were still alive when they came."

Alira sighed. Indoctrination ran strong in her people. The council saw to that. The students took advantage of her pause.

"Can we talk about morphing now?"

"Yes, Na'ama Alira, was Kipa right?"

"He was close," she said, choosing her words. "Humans' feet are smaller, their legs thinner. And they have hair."

"What is 'hair'?"

"Questions first," she said. "What are the Iri?"

No one jumped to reply.

"Anyone?" She waited, then went on. "They're microorganisms too tiny to see without technology. Where do they live?"

"In the irolium," several students called.

"Not exactly," Alira said. "They live in the rock at the base of the irolium. It's the Iri that produce the crystals, right?" Many younglings nodded. "Do you know why?"

"Na'Staani made them sensitive to us," one said, "so as long as we live with them, they could grow the crystals and make us special."

"Special how?" Alira said.

"The Iri give us healing," one began.

Another broke in. "And morphing and all our other skills."

"And without it, we'd be ordinary. Like fealle sprites. Or the humans."

The humans again. "That's speculation, Kipa," Alira said, "not fact. We don't know what would happen without the irolium. Let's hope we never find out."

"Na'ama Alira, what's hair?"

"Yes!" another said. "Mimic a human for us!"

All their voices joined in the plea.

Alira sighed. She shouldn't. Her better judgment told her to say no. But as the younglings matured, frem would expect them to put aside silly games and take on added responsibilities. Once they took on frem roles, duty would define their lives. Could she deny them the occasional fun?

Before she could change her mind, she reached into the molecular structure of her clothing and her body to transform both at the same time. While they watched, she stretched her body taller, slimmed its torso, and widened her shoulders to match her hips. Midway between, she pulled in her waist and shrank her feet to uncertain foundations beneath legs thinned to slender reeds. Her clothing shifted to darker pants of a coarse fabric that hugged her shape, while her arms, neck and face faded to dull brown beneath a loose, thin shirt that scooped deep to show off her chest. Cheekbones pushed out against her skin. Her growing jaw pulled at her chin. Coarse filaments, short and shaggy, pushed out of her scalp and tickled her ears. What color should she make it?

The younglings' shocked expressions and their unanimous wash of gray snapped her out of it. She resumed her normal form and stood once more in her wide-legged pants and loose drape across her chest. "That's what a real human looks like. Hope it's the last one you ever see. Now it's my turn. If the Iri are so small we can't see them, how do we know they are there?"

"We can see them with special equipment."

"Well, yes," Alira said, "but how else do you know?"

No one spoke.

"You know this answer," she encouraged. "Here's a hint: close your eyes and listen."

Her words prompted a unanimous reply and sparkling yellow flashes in their displays. "The song!"

"Yes!" Alira clapped. "The Iri sing to us in what are called 'low frequency tones' that comfort and soothe us, right?"

Heads nodded.

"Does anyone want to give one word to describe how the song makes them feel?"

They thought a moment, then began to offer replies.

"Happy."

"Focused."

"Hungry." Several others flashed amusement at this.

Alira peered at Trumo. He'd been quiet throughout the discussion.

"Trumo, do you want to share?"

He shook his head, and she sighed. "Very well."

"Na'ama Alira, did the Iri tell us the humans are dangerous?"

Alira cringed. "Would someone else like to answer?"

Kipa spoke up. "They didn't tell us. They only show us pictures in our minds or make us feel a certain way to let us know things." He swallowed hard. "But they do talk to the high cleric. Did they tell her we should be afraid of the humans?"

"No!" Alira said, leaning forward to emphasize her words. "The Iri told us no such thing. We don't fear humans, not exactly. But they do threaten the unammi."

"Why?" asked another.

Why indeed. Alira remembered the first time she'd asked her ama that question. "They aren't like us," she said, her rote response echoing her mother's. "The elders tell us they worship chaos, that they're unsettled, contentious. Exposure to them makes us question our established traditions."

"But I thought asking questions was a good thing," Trumo said.

"To a point, it is," she said. "Right now, for all of you in the educators' house, questioning helps you learn. Later, when you become frem, questions lead to discontent and uncertainty." She couldn't believe she was telling them this. Her questions fed her own unease, true, because the council and unammi elders offered no answers beyond repetitive rhetoric and dogma. When she mentioned this, the councilors treated her like a grain of sand in their eyes.

Kipa's voice broke her reverie. "That's why they Adjust us at our Rite of Decision."

The other younglings fidgeted, blue and teal sparkles flickering across their skin.

Alira frowned. "Correct. The Adjustment helps you to be content with your role. A frem's life purpose is to serve the people. You can't be effective if you doubt your choices." Oh, the hypocrisy. Of all the clerics who might teach this subject, she had the least right.

"But isn't the Adjustment like being mitigated?" Enfili said. "I don't want to be a mitigant."

This had gone far enough. "No," Alira said, forcing her display to calm. "The Adjustment nudges the initiate's mind only enough to remove any confusion. Mitigation is a much deeper process to reprogram the entire brain. It's a rare thing, chithe," she said, touching Enfili's cheek. "Don't worry. None of you will have to endure that. Now, we need to get back to our studies. Take your seats, please."

They scrambled for the best cushions. This wasn't over. Younglings didn't let things go as easily as the frem.

As easily as *most* frem.

She shelved the conversation in the back of her mind to simmer for the rest of the class.

chapter 4

ALIRA ROUNDED THE CORNER ON her way to the temple and almost ran into her ama, who pivoted on her heel, skin suffused with angry red veins and patterns. Nearby, a group of nervous dedicants waited with their teacher.

"Where have you been?" Lurien snapped.

Alira shot the listening dedicants an embarrassed glance.

"Never mind," Lurien said. "We'll discuss it after ritual."

She moved ahead and Alira trailed behind, her mind churning over the younglings' questions. How could she cope with thousands in a ceremony now? They passed the teacher and students before Alira touched Lurien's shoulder. "Ama."

Her mother stopped just outside the entrance. "What?"

"I'm preoccupied with another matter. Can't you do the ceremony without me?"

"Alira, at this moment, the dedicants are your duty. Whatever your distraction, put it aside."

"I'm not sure I can, Ama."

Lurien's expression flickered with momentary hesitation, then resumed its usual stoic set. "In spite of everything, daughter, you inherited my strength. If you set your mind to a task, you can achieve it."

She resumed her progress.

Alira followed, marveling at Lurien's exquisite control as they entered the crowded temple cavern, leaving the dedicants and teacher in the tunnel. Few red veins now marred the green of duty in the high cleric's skin. Alira's own traitorous display splashed blotches of lavender across her limbs. Strength, indeed. She'd get an earful after the ceremony, no doubt.

Glow globes hovered throughout the packed temple, their light softened by the blue emanating from irolium crystals that encrusted the ceiling and every wall in the cavern. Here, the Iri's song resonated through her bones and blood, warming her. Alira loved performing rituals here in this sacred place. Habit guided her motions as she approached the central altar and added resin to the censer. Smoke twisted up and around her and she straightened to meet her mother's gaze.

Lurien waved her fingers to beckon the waiting teacher forward. Behind, bound to him by ribbons, followed his small clutch of students, each between twenty-seven and twenty-eight seasons and all flushed green and yellow with a brush of white fear. Their passage drew a hush across the enormous space like pulling a drape across a doorway.

When they reached the altar, Lurien turned to the witnesses.

"Aes te nalya!" We are One! Her voice carried through the air and vibrated through the unammi joinedmind, the shared awareness that connected them all.

Spectators shouted the response. "Nalena t'staani, Na'ama." One is all, respected elder!

Lurien dragged out the moment, her deft touch playing the gathered thousands like a well-tuned instrument. Everyone knew what would happen next, yet anticipation danced on nearby faces. Lurien's rituals never failed to thrill her participants, as if she could reach into their connection with the all-encompassing Na'Staani and strum that thread to a fever pitch with the mere tone of her voice, the movement of her hands, the tilt of her head.

Erect and proud, Lurien circled the stone altar, facing outward, sweeping one arm toward the dedicants. "We come here to honor the achievements of our young!"

The cavern reverberated with chanted response. "Ae'staani te Musjuva." We are in the Flow.

Lurien paced with slow, deliberate steps, her arms out to encompass everyone present. "We come here to separate them from the past and free them to brave their futures!"

"Ae'staani te Musjuva!"

Alira's quickened breath parted her lips. Throughout the temple, collective dermal displays flashed and winked yellow with excitement. Every single witness leaned forward, features alight. How did Lurien *do* that?

"We come here to isolate them from distraction and to promise our encouragement and support!"

"Ae'staani te Musjuva!"

The high cleric spun toward the dedicants.

"Pithin basu'bilen." You have been dreaming.

The dedicants answered. "Pithin bi'tiche." Dreaming of choices.

Lurien thrust her hands high, eyes wide. "T'oeran horeste opahla!" The time has come to wake up!

"Tae'be opahles!" cried the dedicants. Awaken to our duty!

Alira plucked the long blade from the altar and passed it to her mother, who swept its edge through the ribbons to sever the ties between teacher and students. Freed, the dedicants spread out and the teacher stepped back.

Cheers of elation roared through the chamber. Alira's stomach fluttered. Shivers climbed her spine. This noisy crowd, their ceremonial and ecstatic recognition of special honorees, the pulsing blue glow from the walls—she had seen holovids of enormous assemblies where the humans celebrated athletic prowess. Would those raise the same tingle of excitement?

Lurien's voice rang out again, drawing her daughter's attention back to the altar and quieting the crowd.

"My people, you are their kin. Will you stand in witness of their achievements?"

Golden pulses rippled across the gathered bodies. "Te tu, Na'ama!" We will!

"Will you offer them guidance and support if you are asked?"

Alira joined in. "Te tu, Na'ama!"

Lurien nodded. "So be it."

Alira scooped up the i'betser—fiber neck cords strung with three beads each: gold for debt to their teachers, copper for duty to their people, obsidian for connection to Na'Staani—and gave one to every dedicant as Lurien delivered the final lines of the rite.

"To each a role. May yours find you capable, willing, and strong."

As the last word fell from Lurien's lips, drums burst into rhythm, joined by the swell of musical instruments that overwhelmed even the Iri's song. No one came forward to offer congratulations. Each dedicant donned their i'betser, alone in the midst of thousands at the beginning of their momentous internal quest to choose between the guilds and set their futures in unammi society. Once declared, their choices could never be changed. Alira longed to extend words of encouragement or support, but unless they sought her guidance, speaking to the dedicants before the Rite of Decision was forbidden.

She caught her mother's waiting eye. Lurien jerked her chin toward the tunnel and gestured, leaving Alira to follow.

chapter 5

ILLUMINATION FROM TUNNEL GLOBES GAVE way to the wider reach of hoverlights glowing blue beneath the guildhouse dome as Alira and Lurien emerged from the underground passage. Pathways crossed the surface between buildings and tunnel entrances, curving between plants, large stones carved into intricate forms, and other works contributed for exhibition by various guilds. Other frem dotted the walks on their way to carry out some dutiful task. Alira met the eyes of the few who passed but exchanged no words of greeting. Most were too busy to socialize, even for a heartbeat.

What would it be like to live her life as they did, without doubt or question? She pushed the thought away. Again. No sense wasting energy on circumstances beyond her control. She glanced up, as she always did, as if in search of answers beyond the dome's transparent shell. The dun sky, filled with grit from windblown sands, revealed no more than it did any other cycle.

Alira sighed and followed her ama into the guildhouse, up the stairs, and through the maze of corridors to the frugal office of the guildmaster and high cleric. Muted blue lighting swelled at their entrance. One woven hanging and a single painting lent glowing color to the walls. Two low tables marked the side and back of the space, one large enough to accommodate the entire council, the other for solo use. Across the chamber, cushions waited in a comfortable pile before an altar. Alira tried to imagine it her own space, as it would be when she assumed her mother's mantle at some point in the distant future. Far distant. Far, far—

"Sit," Lurien said.

Alira blinked away her reverie and lowered herself to a cushion.

Lurien deposited the ritual items on her desk, then squatted before the altar. Soon a thin line of fresh smoke rose from the censer, spicy fragrance wafting throughout the chamber. Satisfied, she sat.

"Tisalan tells me you were foraging in the grove."

Well. That didn't take long. Alira looked down at her fingers.

"Were you?" Lurien pressed.

"Yes, Ama." Alira met her mother's gaze. "I like it there. It's peaceful."

Lurien scoffed. "I wouldn't call anything outside the domes or tunnels peaceful, not with all the noise and the wind blasting sand across the plain. You were hiding." She peered at Alira. *Into* her. Ama was good at that. "The others again?"

Alira examined her fingers once more. Blue flickers shot through her skin. "Yes." She almost couldn't hear her own voice.

"Daughter," Lurien began, then stopped and tried again. "As long as your actions give fodder to gossip, they'll never stop. You'd make a fearless head cleric. Na'Staani knows the people need such a role model, but they also need someone they want to follow. Why can't you be that for them?"

Alira almost told her. The words trembled on her lips like dew on the moisture traps, but she licked them away and swallowed hard. "I try, Ama. I do."

"You and I have different ideas on what that means. I hear regular reports from frem about your irrational behavior. Two cycles ago, I heard you were in the kitchens—in the middle of your sleep period, mind— digging through the supplies. Whatever for?"

She considered saying she was hungry, but Ama would see the lie. "I heard two nutritionists talking about a difficult dish they'd tried and failed to master. I wanted to try it myself."

"You meant to take on a kitchen challenge with no experience whatsoever?" Lurien leaned closer and placed her tan and pink hand on Alira's knee. "Make no mistake. I don't agree with your…exploits. But if you *must* pursue these other interests, at least keep them small. If you had damaged any of the implements or wasted food, the council would haul us both before them in a heartbeat."

Relief wound through the colors in Alira's display. "Yes, Ama."

Lurien exhaled, long and slow. "I assume you had another dream."

Alira's breath caught in her throat, tightening it so she couldn't speak. Instead, she nodded. *Here it comes.*

Disappointment splashed colorful patches on Lurien's arms. "Bejhe asal."

Alira winced. "I can't help it. They come whether I want them or not." This discussion always devolved into an argument. She risked a peek at Lurien's profile. "I'm sorry. I know how you hate them."

"I don't hate anything. Emoting is your foible."

Alira sat up straighter. "Don't do that. We all feel emotions."

"Feeling them is one thing. Flaunting them is quite another."

"Then what is that pink on your face and neck?"

"Stop twisting my words," Lurien snapped.

"We just came from a ritual," Alira waved in the direction of the tunnels, "where ten thousand unammi shone yellow with excitement. No one doubted their state of mind, yet the temple echoed with their revelry."

"That's different. Ritual touches us on every level. Limiting emotional expression during ceremony diminishes our spiritual connection to Na'Staani."

"That's true outside the rites, too," Alira said.

"No. Secular exhibition invites conflict and discord. It's vulgar. Shameful."

"Suppressing our natures shames us all."

Lurien lurched to her feet and strode past her daughter. "You have an answer for everything."

"I am who I am."

"Choices determine identity. Yours lead toward an ominous path."

Alira sighed. "You never ask about my dreams. Aren't you curious?"

"No. It's folly to encourage you."

"So you've said. Ama," Alira eyed the corridor, "there was a human in this one," she said, her voice lower than before. "It frightened me."

"Good."

"Humans are so fascinating," Alira said. "Outside the Iri, they're the one other intelligent species we've seen—"

"Intelligent? Humans?"

Alira sighed and stood. "I didn't say many humans," she said as she refreshed the censer. "I said one, but he was strange. His form wavered and shifted from human to unammi to other types of beings I didn't recognize."

"What did he say?" Lurien asked, her tone tremulous.

"I don't remember him speaking." Alira frowned. "At first it was the usual images, the ones that churn my stomach, the surface of our valley ravaged and burned, all the domes flattened and melted. And the smell...." Her words dragged out as she recalled the dream. "Then I stood in the Flow of Musju and the human stood on the river's bank while the water surged and boiled around me." Alira shuddered, sprinkling white across her skin as the vision rose again in her mind.

"I've seen similar dreams," Lurien said, "where a shifting figure hovered in the background projecting watchfulness like a Teacher or offering comfort like a spiritual Companion." Her pinched voice and white display sparked a thumping dance in Alira's chest.

"Is it the Iri? Are they warning us?"

Lurien focused inward for another moment before she began to pace. "It was nothing."

"Then why are you frightened?"

"No, not...I'm just surprised," her mother said.

Surprise would have given Lurien a gray face, not a white one, but Alira knew better than to question it outright. She rubbed her chilled arms and tried a sideways approach. "Isn't it unusual for people to share the same repetitive dream?"

"Not enough to concern me. We're both clerics...." Lurien's fingers played with the glass bead strung on a silken cord around her neck. Only initiates wore such an odd adornment, and then no longer than their period of isolation. Yet Lurien wore hers all the time. Alira had made it for her over a hundred seasons ago, one youngling craft among many.

"A literal interpretation makes no sense," Lurien said. "Your dream describes the aftermath of an attack. Who would do that? Not the humans. Cesar says the historical guild knows of a single conflict early in our association with them. They are unpredictable, but they have no reason to harm us now. We're already trading everything we have to offer. I do believe we've grown too complacent where they are concerned, too reliant on their goods. The council agrees." She shook her head. "The problem stems, I think, from too many pilots."

Alira stepped closer, bright yellow veining her skin. "You're bringing some of them home?"

Lurien turned away with a groan. "You know that's impossible."

"Why? They serve, the same as any other frem. They deliver our resources to the humans and bring back curiosities in return, but rather than thank them, we cast them out to live among the aliens. Why can't they stay here between trips?"

"Human contact—

"—contaminates them. Yes, I know." Alira gestured at her pacing mother. "So, all things human are bad?"

"Yes." Lurien passed her again.

"What about this?" Alira touched the silk wrap Lurien wore, made of imported textiles. "Or that?" she added, pointing to the crystalline decoration on Lurien's small desk. "What about the human foods on the feast table in the temple cavern right now? Are these things harmful too?"

"Yes." Lurien stopped, speckled with confusion. She closed her eyes, drew a deep breath, and turned toward Alira. "I'm not suggesting we stop all at once. Weaning takes time. We'll reduce the number of pilots through attrition. As their interactions with the colonies diminish, our risk of human corruption will drop as well. We need to get back to who we are. Who we were. Before they intruded."

"Ama—"

"Forget your fascination with humans. Spend more quality time with others of your own kind."

"I do."

"I don't mean the pilots," Lurien said, "especially that one you favor so."

"Don't disparage Galen. He's my i'shin, my mate."

"He's a trifle. Find an i'shin who isn't outcast."

Alira flushed pink. "I don't want another. Galen is creative, sweet, intelligent. What more could I ask for?"

Lurien paced away and whirled back. "Why do you refuse to conform?"

"I feel like I can't breathe in the tiny space those restrictions allow. And I don't think I'm alone. There must be others who feel the same. That's why our people want human foods and trinkets and clothing. Some of them want to explore new things. Some of them want change."

"No one says such things, daughter," Lurien said, speckled with red again. "No one but you."

The image of bright younglings alight with curiosity rose shining in Alira's thoughts. Despite their current queries, those from her class would at some future ceremony announce their Decisions and serve in one guild or another. Would they be content, as she had promised them? Or would their Adjustments fail as hers had, leading to a life of uncertainty and doubt?

"They say nothing because they're afraid," she murmured, almost to herself. "I mean to set an example for them. If every unammi with a question spoke it aloud, together their voices might awaken the rest."

"Zhachi!" Lurien hissed, darting a white-faced glance at the door drape.

Alira stepped toward her mother, reaching with her hands and her heart. "Don't you see, Ama? As long as we isolate ourselves from change, we'll never know if we could evolve into something more."

"What does that even mean?" Lurien said, pink spots of annoyance surfacing in her display. "You speak of change with no specific goal. How can you expect anyone to consider such a vague notion?"

"I've submitted plenty of precise suggestions to the council, all aimed at enriching our society, making it more sustainable," Alira said. And more secure. Images from her dreams flashed through her mind.

"So I've heard," Lurien muttered. "Cross-train the healers with the food handlers. Allow the miners to craft the materials they dig." Her features puckered into knots of white flesh. "The council believes you've built a fantasy in human terms from human concepts. I'm inclined to agree."

"I don't. Those ideas could help our people." Alira pressed a hand to her chest. "I *feel* it in my bones."

Lurien's white lips moved, but no sound arose. She took a trembling breath. "Are you *trying* to get mitigated? Because that attitude will guarantee it for you."

"Even if I remain silent, others may not. Sooner or later this will need to be addressed."

Voices sounded in the corridor outside. Mother and daughter stared at each other through wisps of smoke in the blue light.

"Cautioning you is like shouting into the wind," Lurien snorted. White faded to green and blue swirls tinged with red across her skin. "Remember that personal agendas carry a price. Be sure you are willing to pay for yours."

chapter 6

A GALE MOANED AT THE tunnel entrance ahead like breath puffed past holes in a musical canara. Alira loved that haunting lament! Its hollow, melodic voice echoed down the corridor to reach her ears in the north passage, growing louder as she went until she emerged under the dusty sky, facing the northern plain. This was her favorite spot in the city, sheltered as it was from the howling wind by the slanting western facade of the Founder's monument on her right and the ridge at her back. Few people came here except for ritual purposes. Until someone intruded or demands sifted through the joinedmind to drag her back, she could find a few moments of peace.

She breathed deep the plain's dry smell and took in her surroundings. Behind her lay the underground city and the sheltered valley with its domes. To the east lay ne'ani, where the traps captured crucial moisture blown in from the frozen lands. The western vista split between craggy stretches of the city's shield ridge and an open landscape rimmed at the horizon by the ever-present red glow of ha'ani. Ruddy layers painted random stripes on the slopes, a sharp contrast to muted shades of dun sand in the semi dark distance beyond.

Alira stepped away from the tunnel and squatted in the crook of the lee, peering upward. Nothing there to see except the perpetual dim glow reflecting off the dry windblown dust in the atmosphere. Galen had once described for her the twilight sky above that fog, but she'd never see it. She lowered her chin once more. The lee of the monument blocked most of the blown grit, yet no plants thrived here. Infrequent as it was, the passage of many feet in ritual uprooted any seeds and sent them flying into the winds.

Outside this sheltered spot, she'd seen evidence of erosion's toll in worn lines and folds on the escarpment. Yet the harsh sand also created. On the opposite side of the monument, generations of fine granules had built up and hardened into a new ridge, connecting the Founder's legacy to the planet's backbone in a seamless line. Alira had trekked past it a few times, in part to get out of the city for a while, but also to try and detect the edifice hiding beneath the sandy ridge—a pointless exercise. Unless you knew it was there, the introduced structure disappeared into the landscape, just another finger of the creeping mountain chain.

What shape had that ridge held when the Founders first arrived? History and details from the before-time were passed down in oral traditions like the Tellings that followed feasts on Founder's Day or most rites of passage. It was said that none of the Founders remained on the uninhabitable unammi home world. Still, was that true? Did some still linger there and if so, did they ever dream of their kin who'd left to live among the stars?

Movement caught her eye. One of Lurien's acolytes beckoned from the tunnel and Alira rose, then moved into the tunnel, beyond the wind-song.

"Lurien calls you to Sufamel's quarters," he said.

Spots of gray colored Alira's arms. "Did something happen?"

The acolyte motioned for her to follow him.

"I know the way. Go back to your duties." Alira hurried past the acolyte, moving toward the dormitories. Sufamel could have any number of reasons to call for Alira's presence. But why would Lurien do so from Sufamel's quarters? And why had she sent a messenger, instead of calling through the joinedmind? Unless....

A sense of dread sped Alira's pace into a trot, then a run. Others moved aside as she raced through the corridors and caverns, through the dorms toward Sufamel's rooms. The door drape, dotted with hollow seed husks that gave it a shushing sound whenever it moved, had been affixed to one side to grant easy passage. Others came and went as Alira approached, and her dread blossomed into grief.

Ah, no!

Alira slowed as she entered the cluttered room and threaded her way through the steady stream of others. Lurien, shaded in purple sorrow, sat by Sufamel's bed. Lurien looked up.

"I know you called her friend."

Alira traced the lines of fresh clay beneath the elder's fingernails. So, she'd been digging when Na'Staani called her home. Good. It's what she'd loved most.

A memory sprang to mind—Sufamel teaching her to pot wild plants.

No, Alira, don't yank it out of the dirt. You'll hurt the poor thing. How would you like it if someone snatched you up with no warning? Dig your fingers down into the soil like this, get beneath the roots before you pull. Be gentle, now!

Sufamel chewed a stem while Alira sank her small hands into the cool loam, felt the living rootlets anchoring the plant to its spot, sensed the connection between her own life energy and that of the plant.

Sufamel's body flashed and rippled in deshtant, the death display, its riot of color lighting the entire room. Patterns, spots, splashes, and veins in all the hues of the spectrum danced across Sufamel's skin and reflected on the walls and furniture around the bed. Only ten cycles had passed since Sufamel offered to let Alira help with the seedlings. If she'd come sooner, if she had been here when Na'Staani came for the elder, maybe she could have helped. Maybe....

Alira laid a hand, purple with grief, against Sufamel's bright skin. The first time Alira had witnessed the deshtant, Ama had explained it happened when the pithasia, the part of the person that was eternal, pulled away from the physical shell to reunite with Na'Staani. It's a sort of goodbye, she'd said then.

Alira sat on the edge of the bed and touched the elder's face. Heady fragrance from the nearby censer made it hard to think. She lifted Sufamel's hand and touched it to her cheek, then leaned close. "Goodbye, Sufamel. I'll miss your lessons." Her voice sounded small in her own ears.

Lurien pressed herself against Alira. "She was old. It was her time."

A councilor's arrival stopped Alira's response. "Rakalesh," Lurien said in greeting. "Sufamel would welcome you."

"Na'Staani grant her peace," Rakalesh said. "I'll pay my respects later. There is a human ship in orbit and a shuttle on its way to the surface."

White peppered everyone nearby. Lurien stood. "How long until they land?"

"Maybe long enough for us to meet them in the canyon. Kobe is evacuating the domes. He'll meet me outside."

Alira exchanged a glance with her mother, their shared dream resurfacing. "Why would the humans come here?" Alira said.

"I don't know." Rakalesh shook her head. "I thought our silence was a clear communication that we wanted nothing to do with them, but—"

"Our silence?" Alira asked.

"They want to contract with us for hematium." Lurien paced away from the bed, gesturing to visitors to stay back a moment.

"But we're already trading that."

"Yes, with colonial governments on Saacharis and Harajüd. This comm came from an individual human, someone named Skalar." Rakalesh gestured to Lurien. "You might want to call the council together."

"I can't leave Sufamel yet. The deshtant isn't finished."

"Then we'll come to you. Send word to gather here and I'll report for the trade guild when we finish." Rakalesh started for the door.

"Wait." Lurien pulled Alira away from the bedside, then pushed her forward. "Take Alira with you."

"Why?"

"Because she needs to see firsthand what humans are like."

Rakalesh hesitated, then waved. "Come on, then."

Alira hurried to keep up as they wound through the underground. Rakalesh's plan made sense. Humans couldn't know about the unammi landing cavern in the northeast ridge, nor did their city's small valley offer adequate space to accommodate ships of any significant size. Imposing ridges rose on all four sides. The one reasonable surface access was the western gap, its confined space narrow enough to limit the intruders' movements. She dared a peek at Rakalesh, who was testy in the best of situations. Now her skin pulsed red over white. Alira didn't envy the aliens she was about to meet.

The two of them moved against the stream of evacuees. The earlier bustle of regular activity had shifted to one of sharp focus. Everywhere, residents clearing the city retreated into the tunnels. By the time Alira stepped out under the central dome behind Rakalesh, the grounds were empty.

Just in case.

The impending encounter squirmed to the forefront of Alira's thoughts and fluttered in her chest like a captive raneal struggling to free itself. Humans! Here! The thought of seeing one in person shot yellow sparkles through her dominant white and purple display. They could be violent, or so she'd been told. But if they were all savages, they never would have survived. Everything she'd seen in the trade guild vids suggested the aliens were like immature younglings—eager, arrogant, unthinking in their pursuits. Like this folly, for example. What in all the worlds made them think coming here was a good idea?

She'd heard recounted stories from generations ago of the early encounters with humans who'd come here. Their initial visit, a needful landing to repair their ship, introduced the two races. Despite the language barrier, Alira's ancestors helped the crew and sent them on their way. The next human ship brought communications tech, a gift from humans in that first encounter, as well as many wonders new to the unammi. Translation specialists among the crew helped begin negotiations to trade for hematium. A third visit brought the unammi a special ship all their own that they were taught to use. If the humans had left it at that, things might have been fine.

But word spread among the aliens. More and more of them came, threatening to overwhelm the unammi until the elders had enough. The council instructed the newly formed trade guild to tell the humans they were no longer welcome on Iridos. The unammi would purchase more ships and send their own pilots to the human colonies to continue trade relations with two worlds—the two they'd first met—and no others. Later, the trade guild relaxed that two-world restriction on everything but hematium, as long as the humans honored those boundaries.

Only one human ship came to Iridos after that, landing almost a full season later despite warnings. Its crew went home with nightmares courtesy of the joinedmind, an unammi defensive response intended to discourage repeat visits. Those humans must have shared the experience with the rest of their people because the aliens stayed away ever since.

Until now.

Kobe of the security guild waited at the surface access and Alira felt the subtle buzz as if the air around them had been charged by static, which signaled his connection with Rakalesh in the joinedmind. Whatever came next, they could act as one without the need to speak to each other. Prickles ran up Alira's spine. If this encounter became contentious, Rakalesh and Kobe would widen their network and send a call for everyone to link and assist. For the unammi, the ability to work together in such an integrated way was a blessing, an extension of their sacred connection to Na'Staani. But if the humans ever realized what the joinedmind could do, to minds or to matter, the aliens would live in constant fear and the unammi would have worries greater than a single ship. Hopefully, there would be no need for such a risk now.

Their trio passed beyond the dome's protective cover. Soon the chill wind at their backs hurried them west to the canyon where high cliff walls offered shelter from the grit and cold while the winds keened high above. Under normal circumstances, Alira would have slowed to enjoy the stark beauty of this gorge, lit here and there by vegetation. Now, she hurried past, her mind racing to the confrontation ahead. The similarity between atmospheric gasses here and on human worlds meant the aliens should be able to breathe. But were they fit to endure this world's winds and robust pull? On the vids, their physiques appeared frail like that of the dainty alien she'd demonstrated for the younglings cycles ago. Not at all like the solid unammi. It hardly mattered. Rakalesh would send them away and nothing would change. Nothing ever did.

The three of them rounded the ravine's bend and moved toward the plain. A tall figure stood in the canyon's mouth, silhouetted against ha'ani's dull glow. Rakalesh and Kobe walked faster, and Alira trotted behind. Yellow and white competed for space across her body as the two parties closed the gap between them. Rakalesh stopped at the canyon's narrowest point.

There, they waited.

All five aliens looked exactly as Alira expected. She eyed them with distaste. They would never last here. A single hard run would shatter those fragile bones.

The human in the lead, far taller than Rakalesh, spoke first.

"I'm Lieutenant Commander Vandana Walker. Admiral Skalar, of the Consortium Trader faction, sent me to negotiate for hematium."

Alira squinted at the sound of human speech. She had heard it plenty of times on the vids, understood the words, and could speak them well enough, but this female's speech seemed harsh. Forced. Breathless.

Rakalesh's red flickers intensified. "Humans aren't welcome here. We made that plain in the past. Is this admiral of yours slow to understanding?"

The human stiffened. "Of course not. Why would you—"

"Your presence is offensive. Take your people and your ship and begone."

The alien stepped closer. "Admiral Skalar asked politely eight days ago but received no answer even after a second request two days later. You left him no choice but to send an envoy."

Alira felt the brysedu, the unseen push from Rakalesh and Kobe in joinedmind, gentle at first.

"Silence is a response," Rakalesh said. "Perhaps your species isn't clever enough to recognize that."

"The admiral knows everyone has a price. He wants to know yours."

Was she witnessing a touch of uncertainty, the first effects of the brysedu in the humans behind their leader? It was so hard to tell with these aliens and their flat, dull skin! Why hadn't the educators touched on this in their lessons?

A surge ran up Alira's back and tingled at her neck, physical confirmation that her elders had increased their efforts, nudging the unwelcome visitors toward the desired response. Lieutenant Commander Vandana Walker blinked, but the others with her stepped back.

"Go home." Rakalesh pressed forward. "Tell your admiral we will do no business with such presumptuous humans."

The alien tried again. "I'm not…."

The brysedu peaked in an enormous burst of energy manifesting in the humans before Alira. They squirmed, ready to flee. Lieutenant Commander Vandana Walker faltered, mouth opened as if to say more, then she led her party back the way they'd come. When they were out of sight, the elders eased toward the canyon's far end, pushing until the shuttle lifted off toward the larger craft in orbit.

Alira felt the joinedmind cease. Rakalesh and Kobe passed Alira on their way to the city.

Her gaze went from shuttle to elders before she jogged to catch up. "Na'ama, what are 'days'?"

"The human version of cycles, but longer."

"Oh," Alira said. "Do they have seasons, like we do?"

"No," the elder huffed. "They have years."

"So it is similar in nature." Alira frowned. "I wonder what other commonalities we might share?"

Rakalesh ignored her.

"What about guilds?" Alira pressed, keeping pace. "Is that what a trader faction is? One of the human guilds?"

"Traders are privateers who operate outside colonial control and break their taboos with impunity," Rakalesh said.

"If they were all Traders," Alira asked, "then why did you only have trouble enforcing the brysedu on one of them?"

Rakalesh, bright red, whirled.

"I tire of your endless questions, Alira. These things have no relevance to a cleric. Leave it alone."

Alira worked moisture into a mouth gone as dry as the plain. The moment drew into an odd intensity of awareness. As if from a far distant place, Alira heard the wind above the ravine, and saw with crystal clarity the pebbles at her feet. Sand, its dry acrid scent filling the narrow space, danced along the canyon floor around them. Nearby, a luminescent acusjal plant snatched its breathers back inside its crusty tube. She should be quiet now.

"It might help me to learn from this experience," she said.

Rakalesh muttered under her breath, her color shifting to shades of pink.

"Kobe, set up a special watch," she said, glaring at Alira. "I don't expect them to accept my refusal."

He nodded and left them alone.

Rakalesh squinted. "One more question, Alira. Make it count."

Alira raised her head in gray surprise. How best to phrase it? The vids indicated the persistence of these humans. After all this time, now that one ship had come what was to stop others? That might not be a bad thing, in Alira's opinion. But this was the wrong time to address that issue.

"Hurry up," Rakalesh snapped. "I have work to do, and so do you."

"What will the council do if the humans won't accept our response?"

"We've tried civil. If that doesn't work," Rakalesh's red flared again, "we'll introduce them to our direct approach."

<h1 style="text-align:center">chapter 7</h1>

ANY OTHER DAY, AN INTERROGATION would cheer Skalar up. This prisoner, though, resisted every effort to question her. Even his trademark methods had taken eight days to chip her shell. Hours in the brig had soured his mood beyond saving until he'd stalked out before pique drove him too far. He didn't want to kill her. Yet.

His skimmer passed the base gate and its crew, then turned toward home. Overhead, bloated clouds brewed their spring payload of rain. He could smell it coming. Rising humidity snugged the sticky air around him and Skalar opened the skimmer's top to take advantage of the breeze. The whine of other skimmers mingled with the crackly buzz of ground cars and snippets of conversations from pedestrians as he whizzed by, sounds blurring as they always did into a background hum. His focus lingered in the brig and on the techniques he would employ next. He still didn't even know her name, much less who'd sent her, but it wouldn't be long now. Her facade had begun to crack. Soon, Skalar would know which of his competitors had brought this scourge into Consortium territory. Once he had that tidbit—

Well. This kind of infraction called for an unmistakable response. If he let one person get away with such an offense, his other competitors would think he'd weakened. Test his boundaries. He could lose all the ground he'd worked so hard to gain, bounce back to the bottom, powerless and dependent on corpgov for his living. Worse, loss of the faction could force him back to his family, to his mother who had wanted no contact with a Trader son.

No. That part of his life was over. He refused to go back.

His jaw began to ache, and he realized he'd been grinding his teeth. He needed to relax. Soon all the factions would be under his control.

A corner of his mouth curled up at the thought. All his life, his "betters" had vowed he would never amount to anything. Nothing felt quite so good as proving them wrong.

At the intersection, he veered right to skirt the city center. Chic high-rise residences surrounded the central marketplace. Landscaped grounds dotted with greenery and water features bespoke the influence of colonial officials who rated these flats. Trendy public houses and cafes—including several Consortium businesses—nestled into the manicured settings, their fare priced high enough to keep out the riffraff. Laughter and tantalizing aromas wafted from the sidewalk tables. His stomach growled. He hadn't eaten for hours, but he was in no mood to sit in a cafe just now, even one of his own.

At the waterfront, he took another right and drove the skimmer along Bayside Parkway. Salty air blew inland with a distinct cooler edge, and he glanced past the amphitheater toward the ocean. Far beyond the bay and its barrier island, the sky darkened to a threatening gloom. Rain, bearing down on New Canaan, filled the space between cloud and sea. The idea of getting caught in a downpour further soured his mood. Skalar drove faster.

Entering the Westside Landed Residential District always made him feel better. He could have lived on the base. Admirals for all five of the other factions did so, according to his spies. Irrelevant. Even the best faction housing wouldn't give him the same air of respectability as home ownership, nor would a suite in the finest high-rise in New Canaan. Skalar stopped in his driveway and leaned out, eyes wide, to allow the retinal scan. The gate opened and he drove the short distance to his house.

Minutes later, his skimmer locked in its stall, he stepped out and moved inside. Maybe time in his gym would distract him. Or a good brandy. He hadn't decided yet. He made it almost to the bedroom before the TICS addressed him in a crisp genderless voice.

"Welcome home, Admiral Skalar. You have twelve incoming communiques. One is marked 'urgent.'"

So much for the diversion. Skalar changed course and entered the great room. The brandy had won. "Point of origin?"

"Consortium corvette, designation Pulsar, high Iridos orbit. Message recorded twelve hours ago by Lieutenant Commander Walker."

Walker? Already? He frowned. "Receive."

Her upper body appeared midair in the back half of the great room, near Skalar.

"Admiral, the Iridosians never even gave me a chance to present your offer, sir. They met us not far from the shuttle and turned us away, wouldn't let us near the city. Their representative sent you a message, sir. She said—" Walker paused, a flush coloring even her dark skin. "She said to tell you that they would never do business with such a presumptuous human. I didn't try to force the issue. I don't read any planetary defenses, but we have no idea what their tech is like or whether the Pulsar's weapons will match theirs. I'm outside Iridos orbit, awaiting your orders. Walker out."

The image vanished.

The Iridosians refused him outright?

Like HHU Census Bureau did when Malcolm Skalar was third-born in a colony with a two-child limit. No extra amenities or resources. Sorry, but those are the rules. Too bad you exceeded your allotment.

Perhaps they mistook his order for a polite petition.

Like the little brats who'd harassed him in the day school, despite his requests to leave him alone, until weak little Malcolm beat the living shit out of one provocateur with no warning at all. That kid didn't walk for weeks afterward.

Or maybe they believed they were better than humans. Better than him.

Like the HHU security training academy, or that entry-level position in HHU marketing and shipping. They wouldn't even let young Malcolm compete for an opening.

"TICS, attend."

"Ready."

"Comm Captain Crow. Override privacy. Summon him at once."

The TICS chittered and fell silent.

Skalar moved to the bar and poured a double splash of his best brandy, his palm warming the bottom of the snifter and the golden liquor inside.

He'd change their minds, of course. This sort of persuasion was similar to interrogation. Only the stage changed. If a gentle nudge proved ineffective, shove.

Walker said she read no planetary defense. Maybe they had nothing. Hard to believe, but not impossible. Even if they did, there was no way their tech would measure up to a battlecruiser, or perhaps a squadron. That could be the incentive the Iridosians needed to revise their decision. If so, all the better. Of course, he'd want more than a mere fifty tonnes *now*. Resistance had to carry a penalty. If they acquiesced, he could forgive this little inconvenience and place a standing order over and above what he already bought from HHU. If not....

Skalar sipped the brandy. Use of force in general violated the spirit, as well as the letter, of Interplanetary Charter law. But Iridos wasn't under the umbrella of the Charter so, technically speaking, a show of strength there broke no rules. Still, the gray area surrounding such loopholes could stretch from here all the way to Old Earth.

He tapped the snifter against his lips. If HHU discovered and objected to a strong-arm tactic on Iridos, he would use the same logic he'd applied years ago when the Consortium located a fast-moving dark asteroid. Charter law proclaimed such wandering astronomicals the property of all twelve colonies. Any resources found thereon were to be divided equally among the worlds once the discovering colony took their finder's share of thirty-five percent plus expenses. But no one else even noticed this asteroid's presence. Skalar didn't wait. He sent ships, found it rich in platinum and other high-demand metals, and dispatched a mining crew on the spot.

After the job was completed, he'd approached Logan. There wasn't time, Skalar had explained, to share the news. He'd told Logan that the Consortium had managed to mine a decent quantity of ore before the resource traveled beyond reach, but equal shares for everyone else wouldn't have amounted to a single handful of credits for anyone. However, if they split the total between HHU and the Consortium, they'd both make a tidy profit. There hadn't been much Logan could say to that and, wisely, he'd agreed.

Skalar had never been to Iridos. Few humans ever had. The last time was centuries ago, long after first contact. The Iridosians didn't like outsiders. They must have seen Walker coming, which meant some level of tech. No telling what kind of force might be required to take the metal without the Iridosians' consent. It might get messy, and present problems he would rather avoid, but Jarod's two small tests had convinced him of hematium's unique value—and now that resource had become key to his plans. Besides, the whole deal was a matter of principle. Word would spread. He couldn't afford to let this slide.

Twenty minutes later his TICS a chitter broke the silence. "Captain Crow is at the front door."

Skalar moved back to the bar and poured a second drink, this one from a less expensive bottle. "Alone?"

"Affirmative."

"Let him in." Skalar moved past the shelving divider toward the front half of the great room.

Crow entered, expression crisp. "What happened?"

Skalar held out the cheap brandy. "I have a job for you."

"Okay." Crow downed half the drink in one gulp.

Skalar's lip curled. That's why he never gave Crow his good alcohol. Brushing past his second, Skalar sat. He raised the snifter close to his face, breathed in the liquor's delicate bouquet, then sipped. Let the captain see firsthand the proper ritual of fine drink.

"TICS, replay most recent incoming communique from the Pulsar."

When it finished, Crow took a seat and leaned back. "You want me to go mining."

"I hope you won't have to. I want you to convince them to sell me seventy tonnes of it."

Crow snorted. "You don't expect that to work, do you?"

"It would make this easier, less expensive."

The captain regarded Skalar. After a moment, Crow slugged back the rest of his drink, braids swinging. "If the Pulsar didn't convince them—"

"An armada behind a battlecruiser might be more persuasive. No matter what their defenses, they can't say 'no' to that."

"What if they still refuse?" Crow said.

"Then you take it."

"The squibs will make a lot of noise over that." Crow shook his head. "Harajüd will be all over our asses before Jarod can make a single panel outta the haul."

Skalar paused, regarding his second over the rim of his snifter, then sipped. "Not if you leave no Iridosians."

Outside the windows, a distant, low rumble punctuated the susurration of rain.

Crow scratched his jaw, mouth stretching into a thin line. "There won't be any hiding that."

"I admit there are risks." To Crow and his crews, anyway. Skalar knew Crow had his eye on the admiral's office. If they were discovered, or if Crow failed to return the haul to Skalar's control, the admiral could claim Crow and his task force crews mutinied and did this on their own to amass capital to take over the faction. "But they're minimal. Humans never go there anyway."

"Walker did."

"On my order." Skalar rose, grasped Crow's snifter, and went to the bar. "Use LADRAS."

"You want me to blow up their city?"

Skalar paused. "LADRAS has a low explosive yield. Detonations above the surface would suffice to kill those above ground and subdue the rest without collapsing the entire region. We don't want to bury the mines. Go in after, track down the survivors."

"Okay," Crow said. "But a few ships ain't gonna be enough. This will take a couple of frigates, haulers, and equipment and personnel carriers—I don't wanna be stuck that far from home without equipment I know my people can run—a supply ship, maybe more. You're talking about a big, sloppy op. No matter how careful we are, we're bound to leave some trace. The colony will find it. They'll know."

Skalar refilled Crow's drink and passed it to him. "They would need a reason to go there in the first place."

Crow started to respond, then paused. "You don't want a single load of hemi," he finally said. "You want us to scrape that fucker raw."

Skalar shrugged. "I would have been content with fifty tonnes of it when I first asked. But if they won't sell me the seventy I'm asking now, I want it all."

"And then you'll take their place." An appreciative grin spread over his second's face. "Selling that shit raw to the shipyards will net you a lot more income than Jarod's station hulls."

"Don't be so sure."

The glee drained from Crow's expression. "What about the crew?"

"What about them?"

"It's gonna take a big crew to mine so much ore, which means a whole lotta witnesses to shush. One drunk Trader at a pub could bring the whole thing down. It won't be limited to the ship or mining crews, either. You can't hide that much product. Somebody will see it and blab."

Skalar sat down. "Offer them each a fractional share of the action, say .001% of the total take. The more they bring back, the more they profit. As leader of the expedition, you'll get .005%. But if anyone talks, everyone forfeits their share. They'll police each other."

Crow nodded.

"Feel free to remind your crews that if the op goes public, they are party to genocide and every bit as culpable, assuming they make it in one piece to any trial. Shoot someone out an airlock as an example. Tell the crew they were a threat to the faction. Do what you need to do, as long as everyone understands this isn't up for debate. Don't tell anyone where you're going until the fleet's well away from Harajüd. Then, inform the captains. Secure the rest of your communications. We don't want any interruptions once you begin."

"Right." Crow downed his drink. "What about the squib pilots out in the colonies? If we wipe the city, you'll need to kill them, too."

"Then we can take their ships and use them to deliver the ore. That will be an issue only if the Iridosians won't sell. Razing the city would complicate things for a while—"

"Ya think?"

"—so I would rather avoid that if I can. Once it is decided one way or the other, send a report. If necessary, I'll round up stragglers on the other worlds."

Rain pounded the roof and hammered the windows. Outside, a bright flash lit Skalar's landscaped yard, followed by a crash of thunder.

Crow pursed his lips. "This is bigger than your original plan. If you start making deliveries outta squib ships, you're gonna have to use drones to deliver from orbit. No one would buy a human pilot on a squib ship."

Skalar kept his voice neutral. "Leave that to me."

"Where are you gonna stash the hemi?"

"Our outpost is far enough off the map to be safe."

"We haven't used the place in a while." Crow nodded. "Guess we'll have to send a crew to dust 'er off. Running shipments from there warrants a full-time crew on site."

"*If* it becomes necessary."

Crow tilted his head, braids swinging. "You've given this a lotta thought."

"I have."

"Don't you ever worry about—" Crow began.

"No. That base was never infected."

"You know this for sure?"

Skalar lowered his drink and glared at his second.

"Okay, no offense." Crow lifted a placating hand. "I'm sure you're right."

chapter 8

<u>Iridos</u>

"I KEEP TELLING YOU," NYROS repeated, "to channel your emotions instead of expressing them. Let them inform your intellect. Then you can respond from a more considered position. Your life would be so much simpler."

Freckled with annoyance, Alira swung her focus to her brother. "And your life could be more fulfilling if you would take an occasional chance. You're always so serious, so fearful of any temptation to rebel. Doesn't it bother you that your life isn't your own?"

"I chose this, sister."

She snorted. "I know what you gave up to be a pilot."

"It is what I wanted. It's a difficult choice, and every pilot does it for their own reasons. I made it to save someone else the pain of leaving home."

"And are you still happy with that choice?"

"I'm content to serve our people."

"Of course you are," Alira muttered. *His* Adjustment had worked.

She turned away. Across the hangar bay, a stone protrusion jutted over the cave's maw, muting the surface windsong into a low drone. A few mitigants lit with dutiful green crawled next to transport guild workers over her brother's ship, unloading his cargo, effecting repairs and routine maintenance. She didn't want to quarrel with Nyros. He had just gotten here. In three cycles, he'd be gone again.

They sat in silence for a moment. "Ama said you suggested to the council that frem should be trained in at least two guilds if not more. That they should be allowed to move back and forth between them." He glanced at her. "Haven't they rejected the same suggestion before?"

"Not that exact one, no."

"Then I come home to find you working in the landing bay alongside the mitigants."

"I'm living by my own advice. Setting an example. I've also learned to construct a level foundation for a building project and started reseeding nawhúd flowers in the canyon. Their numbers have dropped so low!"

Nyros shook his head. "These changes you want for us, you know they are impossible."

"No, I don't."

"If we adopted even two of them, our whole society would change."

"That's the point."

"It wouldn't be unammi."

"It wouldn't be *old* unammi."

"What would you have the council do?" he said. "We need an assurance of support in every area to sustain our infrastructure. That can't happen if frem are allowed to change their minds after guild elders have invested time in training them."

"I'm sorry I brought this up. You're asleep, like the rest of them," she said, waving an arm toward the city. "I hoped Galen would have opened your mind a little by now."

"He is one of your biggest problems, you know."

She threw her hands up. "Not you too. I thought he was your friend!"

"I'm reconsidering that relationship. Anyone who hurts you is no ally of mine."

"Galen's my lone supporter. At least he tries to understand me. He doesn't believe my proposals will work, but he dreams with me about what our society could be. How can that be harmful?"

"He's besotted," Nyros said, sounding annoyed. "He always speaks of you with devotion. The last time I saw him, he told me how much he enjoys your company. He likes the odd thoughts you provoke in him. And he loves your eyes."

Alira drew back with a frown. "My eyes?"

"He likes your thick lashes, that they are so long. He went on at length about how they are bronze instead of white or clear like the rest of us, how they make you more beautiful." Her brother drew a breath, held it, then let it out with slow precision. "You know the council is monitoring you, right? Yet you sprint as fast as you can toward their cure with Galen's encouragement. If they treat you, I'm holding him responsible, at least in part."

She leaned forward, flaring red, her retort interrupted by a sharp cry behind them. Brother and sister whirled in time to see a mitigant fall from the nose of Nyros' ship.

"Rashin!" Nyros leaped to a run, Alira right behind. By the time they got to the fallen worker, a small group of witnesses surrounded his broken form, its limbs bent away from his torso at gruesome angles. He lay unmoving, his breathing shallow, rapid.

Alira dropped to her knees at his side, laid one white hand on his smooth scalp and the other on his belly, and slid into muñara, meditation. Around her, the rocky landing bay melted into a damp riverbank behind her closed eyes. The crew's murmurs blurred into the babble of water coursing over stones while she stood waist-deep in the river Musju, the Flow of Things As They Are. Rashin floated before her, pain-free in this sacred place. Alira's awareness probed his body.

Fractured skull…broken bones…abdominal bleeding…. Ah, Rashin!

A touch on her shoulder jolted her out of the muñara. She looked up into Nyros' white face.

"Alira, stop! You're not a healer. We have to wait—"

"No," she hissed, shrugging him off. "They won't get here in time. He's dying, Nyros. Help me or get out of my way."

She dropped back into the Flow and straightened Rashin's limbs, pushing them into place. Nyros appeared on the bank, followed by the bay crew and the few other mitigants. One by one they splashed through the water to link hands around her and Rashin, their energy a ripe and ready resource. Alira drew it, channeled it into Rashin's own natural healing while she manipulated the damaged tissues, nudging their unique cellular consciousness into action. In his concussed brain, synapses reestablished electrical connections one by one. At each fracture or tear in skin, cells reached across the separation to mend the gaps. Internal bleeding slowed, then stopped as surrounding tissues opened pores to reabsorb the excess.

Power rushed into her, through her, from the workers, from Nyros, from Musju's rocky bottom and loamy banks, its passage a sharp advance of brilliant rippling orange that banished all vestiges of white across the conduit of her form and peaked her senses. Every object along the riverbank shimmered. Intoxicating fragrance from a nearby flowering vine wafted on the breeze. Trees arched their branches above, an offer of shelter and support. Water in the Flow whispered secrets more felt than heard, and Alira matched her efforts to its hissed guidance. Hope and faith lay beneath and within her every breath.

Soon her radiance bathed the circle's entirety, pervaded every participant, and shone through Rashin's injuries. Alira dissolved into the surrounding space. Boundaries between herself and the others vanished, transforming *her* and *them* into *we*. Time lost all meaning. Linked by water, hand, and heart, the surrounding vitality harmonized with the Iri's song in her ears and in her mind while the air cooled her skin and the fragrant land caressed her nostrils and the water washed away her fatigue.

At last, the glow surrounding Rashin's injuries began to fade. Rashin opened his eyes, and the swirling force began to ebb. Alira stepped back in the water, bringing the muñara to a natural end. When she returned to the landing bay, the others retreated and Rashin sat up. Even in the corporeal setting, pale orange lingered around his hurts, bright spots amid the dull green of his skin.

"Better?" she asked.

"Yes," Rashin said. "Thank you." With no sign of pain or difficulty, Rashin got to his feet and went back to work. The others followed suit.

Every cell in Alira's body still tingled with the energy she'd channeled. It always lingered like that. She made an effort to push it down, through her legs and feet, and back into the ground.

"That, right there," Nyros said, pointing at Rashin, "is why we do it."

His voice jarred her back to the mundane. "What?"

"The conformity you so despise conditions our minds to think as one. Without it, the muñara would be impossible, and the healing, and most of the other abilities we take for granted." He tilted his head. "Do you see?"

Her arm flared red as she waved toward Rashin. "That, right there," she spat, "is why we should train in multiple disciplines. If I hadn't known how to draw energy and channel the healing, Rashin would be dead right now. Do you see?"

Gray speckles dotted her brother's face before lavender uncertainty chased them away. His lips drew into a thin line. "Perhaps a rare circumstance would find it useful. Still, you're asking us to change the fundamental nature of our society to meet your ideas on propriety and expediency."

She threw up her hands. "I can't help it, Nyros. I can't be content as you are. I've tried. My ideas—"

"—are going to get you mitigated if you aren't careful."

"I'm aware of the council's threat. It disgusts me. We decry the cruelty of humans while we measure our own kind by standards that don't fit us all and force this horrific sentence on anyone found wanting."

"It isn't so simple and you know it," he said, his voice soft.

She knew. She still hated the idea.

"Besides, it doesn't happen often," Nyros said. "Mitigation is always the last choice of the council.

Alira winced. "It shouldn't even be an option. It's barbaric."

"Sometimes an individual is broken. They can't control themselves. Their minds aren't quite right, or they have a harsh reaction to the Adjustment." He lowered his chin. "There are maybe a hundred mitigants in our whole population. If they can't be content any other way, and the treatment gives them peace, isn't that better than a life of angst?"

She wasn't broken. *Her* mind was fine, yet the threat still shadowed her. Doubt wove its thread through her conviction. Were the mitigants she knew really at peace? Or were they just…empty, numb?

"At least we care for our misfits," Nyros said.

She twitched. Misfits, indeed.

"Humans treat theirs with chemicals," Nyros said, his voice saturated with distaste, "or isolate them from the rest in special facilities. A few get dropped from the humans' records and live abandoned in back alleys or in undeveloped areas outside the cities."

"They came here, you know. The humans."

"I heard."

"I still think the council should trade with them here," she said, "instead of sending you and the other pilots offworld."

He flushed gray, then white. "You don't know what you're saying. I live with these aliens. Believe me when I say they can't be allowed to know we can morph, much less heal or any of our other skills. At their best, they would cage us for entertainment. At their worst, they would want those abilities for themselves. They experiment on their own kind in the name of curiosity and greed. What makes you think they wouldn't do it to us? One or two or ten or even a hundred unammi would be nothing to them in their search for answers."

"They can't all be like that."

"Enough to be dangerous."

"So how do you hide your gifts from them?" she said.

"I have a flat for my human persona," he said, lavender and blue washing through his display. "I always morph out of sight and away from the flat, so no one will connect me to him. As long as I'm cautious, most humans are too caught up in their own drama to even notice I'm there."

"And no one has ever seen you?"

"Once," he said, his voice tight. He dropped his gaze. "A woman came across me in the park behind a thick cluster of shrubs in the middle of the day. I had morphed a hundred times in that very spot and never…." His words trailed off.

"She saw you change?"

He nodded.

"What did you do?"

"I killed her," Nyros whispered.

Alira flushed. Gray cascaded down her limbs.

He looked up, his eyes asking her for the forgiveness the human would never be able to give. "I didn't have a choice. We—"

"Shhhh," she said, touching his cheek. "I know."

He heaved a sigh as if to calm and center himself. "You asked me if I was happy with my decision to join the pilots. I'm glad to serve, but not a cycle goes by when I don't wish I could be here. Maybe then I could help you."

She sagged, weary of the topic. "You make good points. I always believed the humans were harmless, but I have to admit the ones who came here felt contentious. I didn't expect that."

He took her hand in his own. "If you were wrong about this one thing, isn't it possible you may be wrong about others, too?"

She frowned.

"Sister, our wants have been irrelevant since we left the birthing house. As frem, our purpose is to foster the good of the people." His colors calmed, his features softened. "Now do you see?"

Maybe he was right. "I'll think about it."

"Good." Nyros squeezed her hand and went back to work, leaving her alone with her doubts.

chapter 9

ALIRA PASSED OTHERS ON THEIR way out as she arrived at the door of Sufamel's quarters. Lurien still held vigil at her bedside and would do so throughout the deshtant.

Beloved memories arose and receded in Alira's thoughts, veins of purple webbing her skin. Sufamel had taught her about plants, how to interpret the auric signals given off by wild edibles as well as food crops in the greenhouse dome and, when they were sick, how to heal them.

Now Sufamel's lessons were done.

Grief twisted in Alira's throat, pinching her words. "Ba'riba asatu'lan, Na'ama."

"You won't be alone in that." Lurien spoke without breaking her vigil. "Many will speak her name. She will be missed."

Alira regarded her mother through slitted eyes. It was the closest Lurien ever came to admitting an emotion. Alira considered pressing the issue, but for now, Lurien's presence offered comfort. Alira sat beside her, recalling moments shared with Sufamel.

All at once, Sufamel's color pulses stopped. The deshtant was over. Lurien shifted to the bedside and leaned over to peer, tense and expectant, into the now dark face. Alira had seen this before but still didn't understand it. At last, her mother let out a breath.

"Thank you, Sufamel, for your knowledge." Lurien laid a hand against the body's smooth head.

"Why do you say those words?"

Her mother's skin flooded with sudden purple, then dimmed to lavender again. "Tradition."

It had to be more. Lurien always spoke that exact phrase at the end of a deshtant. "But how did it begin? What is the purpose of such a ritual?"

"Not now, daughter. When you're ready to lead, I'll tell you."

"I'm surprised you still want me to," Alira said. "Maybe you should just birth another daughter."

Sparkles of gray flickered in Lurien's display. "Why would you say such a thing?"

"I know how everyone feels about me, how they wonder if I'll ever be 'normal'."

"You're wrong," Lurien said. "Councilor Cesar believes you'll settle into the role someday."

"He must be the only one," Alira muttered.

"Not true. Yoloron agrees with him. And I have complete faith that you will fill the role meant for you."

Before Alira could remark on her ama's vague comment, Lurien returned to the bench and pointed to a nearby table.

"You should take that rock before it gets tossed outside one of the domes."

"I will. What will you do with her other belongings?"

"Don't start."

"I'm curious."

"We'll put the nawhúd flowers back, maybe in the canyon. Some of this can go to the greenhouse dome. The rest will be offered to her kin, as always."

"What about her door drape? It's so like her. May I keep it?"

Lurien shook her head. "I've never understood your fascination with such odd things. You keep rocks in your quarters. Dead leaves. Animal parts. I can almost understand why you'd keep niveym feathers. They're beautiful and rare. But why atlish hide or sprite whiskers? Only members of the supply guild need those."

"Why do you wear a bead on a silken cord around your neck, Ama? No other frem do so."

Her mother touched the bauble. Had she ever taken it off?

"We all have our quirks," Lurien murmured.

"Some more than others. I collect whiskers. Sufamel sewed seeds onto a drape. It must have meant something to her. Maybe she liked the sound. Maybe it reminded her of something from her life." Sufamel's dark body, lying on the cot, seemed a far cry from the lively elder Alira had known. "Who could tell? She lived so many seasons."

"Fuj bejhur churen," Lurien said. Her life was full. "Experiences enough to entertain Na'Staani for a long while."

A story trembled on her mother's lips. Alira could feel it building, an early start to the Telling that would follow their Mourning Rite.

"When I was twelve seasons into my life, Sufamel caught me picking a bashito blossom in the greenhouse dome."

"Why would you do such a thing?" Alira said.

"To eat it."

"Eat it? But—"

"I know. Can you imagine?" Lurien brightened with speckles of amusement. "I had seen one of the gardeners nibbling one, then watched his gait grow more and more erratic. I wanted to see for myself what the flower had done to him, so I intended to eat one."

"What did Sufamel do?"

The story paused, Lurien focused on that distant memory as she fondled her bead. "She hid with me inside a whorl of ralonga leaves and made me eat two of them while she kept me company."

"Wait. I don't think I heard you right. Sufamel got you inebriated when you were a youngling?"

"I was going to do it anyway. She stayed close to keep me out of trouble. One flower would have been plenty. Two made me sick like she knew they would. My body couldn't process it. Intoxicants are best left to frem. I never again ate one of those things."

"Is that why you scrape the seeds out of the melons before you eat them?"

"Yes. I know they aren't so strong as the flowers, but I don't ever want to feel like that again."

A rare, comfortable silence fell between them.

"She thought I was being too hard on you," Lurien said.

Gray flooded Alira's exposed skin. "She said so?"

Lurien gestured, a noncommittal response.

"Do you believe it's true?"

"No."

Of course, she didn't. Alira frowned, unsure what to say.

"I'm hard on you because I must be." Lurien seemed to search Alira's face. "I expect a lot of you because you expect too little of yourself. Already your oddities have delayed training you should have started long ago. I've always been able to hide you behind the ralonga leaves, shield you from the council with a promise that you would mature beyond this rebellion and follow your destiny."

"And now?" Small white dots appeared on Alira's arms below the confused tangle of colors.

Lurien closed her eyes for a moment as if searching for patience. "Some doubt you'll ever be ready. They are convinced you'll always question everything, that you'll go on flouting their guidance. Even with the support of Cesar and a few others, the council won't listen to me again. The best way to change their opinion is to comply with their expectations. Because if you are to carry all these—"

Lurien's jaw snapped shut, biting down on her words. After a moment, she began again. "If you are to be high cleric one day, you'll need a tougher skin and stricter self-control. The unammi expect the council to guide them, and the council relies on the high cleric—on me—for the same reason. This role requires discipline and restraint and I wonder sometimes if you will ever find it in yourself. Your weakness is inherited. Even though it isn't always in your best interest, I accept that about you. But the council won't. The unammi won't."

Strands of anxiety twined through her mother's affection while Alira sat bathed in gray at Lurien's revelation.

"Inherited?" Alira squeaked. "From you? From my apa?"

Lurien seemed sorry she'd spoken, reluctant to add to her mistake.

"It's from my apa, isn't it? You never speak of him. What is his name?"

"That isn't important right now," Lurien said. "My point is that I know I demand a lot from you. I do it because—" Again, she stopped the thought before it could flow out of her mouth. Her throat worked, lips locked tight until she found better words. "I do what I must to help this city and our people to function as best they can, as is my duty. But the council is aware of your activities, Alira. You need to try harder."

Lurien rose and left the chamber. Alira, still gray, followed.

chapter 10

MYRIAD COLORS LIT THE CROWDED space between monument and ridge, the darkened remains a sharp contrast to so many shining mourners. More came, and still more. Alira's respect for the deceased swelled. She'd never grasped the full magnitude of Sufamel's influence among her people until now.

She looked a question at Lurien, who nodded. Alira separated attendees into two concentric circles to better use the tight space. By the time the high cleric called the opening lines of the ceremony, they were ready. Sufamel's body lay in the center. Lurien paced around it.

"We come here today," she called through the joinedmind and over the wind's wail, "to mark Sufamel's passage through our lives, to mourn our loss, to celebrate her joyful reunion with Na'Staani, and to cut our ties to her pithasia so that we might learn to live without her."

Mourners waited.

Lurien turned to the center. Swirling with green and purple, her hands reached out to the elder's remains, leaning closer almost as if she might embrace the departed.

"Aes te nalya, Sufamel! Livuce'ba wenaes bujhul!" We are One, Sufamel! By your loss, we are diminished!

Her mother's words weighed on Alira's mind and tightened her throat.

Lurien's torso ducked low toward the body, then curled up in a graceful sway, arms rising and swinging out to encompass the whole sky.

"Na'Staani bu bale, Na'ama! Ba riba te'lan!" Na'Staani take you, honored elder! We will speak your name!

As one, the gathered mourners began to chant Sufamel's name in a whisper barely heard that grew in intensity until the wind could not be heard over their shouting. Chanters blended purple to gold and all the hues between, exhilaration swelling in Alira until she felt she would burst. She grasped the hand of the person next to her. Around both circles, hand linked to hand as all present entered the shared meditation on Musju's bank. This time, her kin stood with her on dry land while the water before them surged around the waist of a single individual who moved away, caught in the Flow.

Sufamel.

Alira led the procession thigh-deep into the river. Water pushed at the backs of her thickset legs as she stood among the others, connected to them by the Flow, by their fondness for Sufamel.

Connected to them by her similarity, Nyros would say.

Behind them, far off to one side and up to his ankles in the water, she spied her brother, allowed at the rite and in the muñara so long as he did not take a central role or intrude on the visions of the others. He nodded, acknowledging, and she scanned for the mitigants. None had come. *They* would not be welcome.

She focused again on Sufamel, farther away now. The water rushed around the elder's chest, her shoulders, her head, until she disappeared fully into Musju's embrace. Alira led the procession out of the water, back to normal awareness where Lurien pointed at the corpse.

"This is not Sufamel. She is gone, reunited with Na'Staani." Lurien paused, building energy among the mourners for what was to come. "She has no need of this shell now. Let the elements reclaim it!"

"Ae'staani te Musjuva!" shouted the mourners.

Lurien pivoted toward the remains, flinging her arms toward the howling sky. "Pidai'ba livitu, ba'riba t'ujendun!" Your body is dead, but your name lives on!

The crowd cried out in response. "We honor you!"

Lurien's voice, lower this time, intoned, "Pidai'ba livitu." As the words fell from her lips, her arms dropped to her sides, and she backed out of the center.

The others made room beside Alira. "We complete the task," they replied as one.

Tension vibrated through their shared space like the charged air beside their wind turbines. Prickles raised Alira's skin into tiny thrill bumps.

Howling wind faded into the background of awareness as the mourners connected one to another in the joinedmind. Together, they reached into the smallest particles of Sufamel's abandoned form and began to disconnect its composite bits. Piece by piece, the conjoined group separated the particles of the empty frame, freeing its raw materials. As they worked, the shell began to wither, to melt, to merge with the sand below, then the clay and rock beneath that. Wisps of wind snatched at the result, sweeping matter from their working up and out to join the atmosphere. Some, perhaps, might be carried farther to reunite with the stars.

Then it was gone.

Alira brought the mourners' union to a close and walked in silence to where the body had lain moments before. Memories tumbled over one another in their clamor to be recognized, each too vivid to express in words alone.

At last, Alira drew a deep breath. "Sufamel!" Her voice echoed off the rock walls. "You took me on my first windwalk, showed me the beauty of the landscape, and that putting my hands in the soil brought healing. You taught me things I didn't know I didn't know, and heard me even when I was afraid to speak. Sufamel! I remember you!"

She stepped back to make room. Another followed, then another. She listened to the tributes as joy and grief and affection washed over and through her fellow mourners while they spoke. Lurien had been right. Many called Sufamel's name.

Later, the temple's walls glowed blue as unammi crowded into its cavernous space, joined by the younglings and their caretakers to share a celebratory feast and recount memories of the deceased. Alira loved Tellings. Stories from humorous anecdotes to poignant revelations always deepened her understanding of the departed one whether she knew them or not. Yet this one hit her hard, and she sat near a tunnel at the periphery where no one would notice her shaky state. She heard none of the tales. Instead, her last conversation with Sufamel played through her mind. The elder's question echoed in her thoughts. *Why do you think your way is better?*

Looking out over the seated throng, Alira had to admit their traditions unified her people, bonded them with shared purpose and meaning. Mourning Rites, Tellings, and avowals of achievement, all offered nodes of connection where the people came together in recognition of their similarities. She took no issue with those. It was how unammi treated their differences that bothered her. She ached for the mitigants who had no opportunity to mourn. Some of them must have known and admired Sufamel. How would they adapt to her death without the support of their people? How could the council shut them out this way?

New horror edged in as a thought occurred to her. Did mitigants even feel loss?

She shuddered and hugged herself, rocking to and fro.

A sound from the corridor drew her attention. Nyros stood there. He'd loved Sufamel, too, though he would never admit it. Outcasts weren't welcome at the Telling, but at least he could stand outside the chamber and listen. He gestured, then moved back into the tunnel. Glad for the distraction, she caught up and walked beside him.

"Your ship was supposed to leave almost a cycle ago."

"Ama cleared my delay so I could honor Sufamel."

"But you're leaving now."

"Yes. It is Ijydin's time to come home."

Alira nodded. They walked in silence to the landing bay. "Do you ever visit the other pilots out there?" Alira asked.

He threw her a glance. "Sometimes."

"Maybe you could hold your own Tellings with them."

"No. Thirty of us in one place at one time would unnerve the humans. Far too risky for us."

"Why couldn't you do it dressed as humans? How would they know you were unammi?"

Nyros stopped them both. "What would be the use of that, Alira?"

She held a hand toward him. "I think you miss these traditions, that's all. I know I would."

His face softened, hues and patterns shifted to understanding. He touched his palm to hers.

Alira let out a long breath. "Three cycles isn't long enough for us to visit, especially when I spoil part of our time together by picking a quarrel."

"I'm never annoyed with you for long."

Lurien's sharp voice intruded on their moment, sparking blotches of gray in the siblings. "Why aren't you gone, Nyros?"

Nyros' hand jerked away from his sister's. "I'm going now, Ama."

"What are you doing here, Alira?"

"I'm saying goodbye to my brother." Pink surged as Alira stood her ground.

"Then make it good. This will be your last opportunity."

The confusion in Nyros' display reflected Alira's own feelings. "What are you talking about?"

"You are not to associate with Nyros again. Nor Ijydin, nor Galen, nor any of the outcasts or mitigants. You are not to spend another minute working on the ships or learning from the mechanics. I ban you from the landing bay."

"What?"

"You've left me no choice, daughter. So long as you have an alternative, I'll never convince you to seek companionship among others of your kind."

Red flooded Alira's skin. "You can't do that!"

"I can, and I have. I don't doubt the council's support in this, but you are welcome to appeal the matter to them if you wish." Lurien pointed toward the temple. "Go back to the Telling."

"You should encourage me to spend more time in Nyros' company. He supports your warnings for me to conform. Maybe he can convince me even though you couldn't!"

The high cleric stepped closer to her. "You—"

Nyros pushed Alira back as he stepped between mother and daughter. "Stop it. This will solve nothing." He turned to Alira and drew a deep, trembling breath. "Ama is right. I can't see you again."

Alira gasped. "Nyros, don't."

"If I as an outcast contribute to your problems after all I've said to you about Galen, then I'm no better than he."

She stepped toward him, hand outstretched, but he pushed her away.

"Don't let your emotions drive your actions. Remember!"

Choking on her rage, she rounded on her mother. "I will never forgive you."

Whirling, Alira ran.

chapter 11

New Canaan, Harajüd
<u>Space Port Station, Docking Slip HH1-889456SP</u>

CROW EXITED THE SHUTTLE'S DOCKING gangway and passed into the noisy concourse. Travelers filled the TICS seats down the middle of the corridor, their holodisplays clashing and combining in colorful array with the angle of his passing. Outside the thick windows, four of Harajüd's moons—he could never remember their names—hung suspended in the black. Past the big one, the Orbital Repair Station's albedo flashed in the light and made him blink. You'd think they'd paint that fucker another color besides white, but then some moron would miss seeing it and ram his ship up its ass.

A chuckle rumbled in his throat and curled his face into a fleeting sneer. He passed a pleasure den and eyed the females in the foyer: no, no, hell no, maybe, definitely. Wait, had he been with that one before? She smiled with those big pink lips. He winked but kept walking. No time to fuck today, babe. Maybe on the way back. Ahead, beyond the Consortium-controlled docks, a shitload of tourists swarmed out of a passenger transport and came his way.

He might wanna move before they ran him down, but to hell with that. He wasn't steppin' aside for nobody. Not anymore.

He plowed through the crowd of pissant sightseers and ducked into the concourse for his ship, his mind settling on the job ahead. Skalar wanted him to scare the squibs, if possible. Three frigates might do the trick, alongside the light cruiser and his own battlecruiser. If not, at least they would have plenty of firepower. Every frigate held several illegal nukes. Each cruiser carried six. Who would tell a Trader captain he couldn't have them, eh? The colonials were all happy crappy to lax the laws when they needed Traders to do their dirty work, so they could damn well shut the fuck up about it now.

Besides the shooters, he had three haulers in case they found a lot worth taking, a carrier for the mining crew Skalar hoped they wouldn't need, and a supply ship to allow them a longer stay. It took some convincing to get the admiral to approve the extra assets, but Crow had called bullshit. He'd told Skalar that night in the admiral's house over the cheap-ass brandy he always foisted on him—as if Crow wouldn't know, as if Crow hadn't been more sophisticated at age nine than Skalar would ever be—that they would need a shitload of assets to pull this off. Crow grunted. Skalar thought he was so smart, better than Crow or the rest of the Consortium crew. Well, fuck that shit. If Skalar knew Crow was already working to take over the faction, or how many of the crew would back him over the current admiral, Skalar's nose might come down a peg or two.

The fresh lieutenant at the main hatch stepped aside as Crow passed. Little shits were getting younger every year.

Crow'd been fifteen when he'd come here.

Besides, it wasn't the years that mattered, but the lightyears.

A lot had happened since then. Now he was second in command of the largest, most powerful Trader faction on any colony world. 'Course it was just a matter of time 'til he took over, but he'd get one shot at a coup. If he blew his wad too soon, he'd be dead, and somebody else would take what was his by right. No way he'd risk his chance. The detour that landed him here inflicted scars, visible and otherwise. Crow intended to pay back those responsible for each and every one. But as far as he was concerned now, admiral of a Trader faction beat his former life in the upper colonial echelon any day.

The lift brought him to the command level and he exited onto the bridge.

Harley jumped to his feet. "Captain on deck!"

"As you were," Crow said. "Report."

"Everything's ready, Cap, but there's an unfamiliar ship in hangar bay—"

"I'm aware. Contingency resource. Alert the rest of the fleet. Five minutes 'til go. Once we leave colonial space, disable the trackers."

"Yes, sir."

Crow scanned the bridge. Every surface, including the floor, shone in spit-and-polished shades of gray. In the last six months, he had updated every piece of equipment to top-end models except for holographic arrays, the one modern thing his ships didn't have. Those took too much space. Crow preferred a two-dimensional screen anyway.

"Flight, do we have vector and clearance from traffic control?"

"Working on it, sir."

"Very well." Crow took his seat in the middle of the space while his crew hustled around him. If they had worn uniforms, they might have even passed for an official arm of the colonial peacekeeping force or some such shit. To keep the distinction clear, Skalar never required Consortium crew to all dress alike, a detail on which he and Crow agreed. It paid for a Trader crewman to blend in with their surroundings. Plain clothes served that purpose well, though with the odd attire worn by some of them, "plain" was in the eye of the beholder. Crow frowned at one lieutenant whose pants were so tight they could have been painted on for all Crow could tell. How did anyone sit down in those things?

He shook his head. "Lieutenant Commander Walker!"

She stepped forward and stood at attention. "Yes, sir."

He took in her appearance. Dark eyes, dark skin, black hair, flat expression. The woman had some bulk on her. "You fought hard for a spot on my crew. Why?"

Her gaze flicked from his face to Harley's before going blank again.

"I think you know, sir."

Crow squinted at her. "You've been speaking to Commander Harley."

"The Commander is mentoring me, sir."

"Uh huh." He took in her stance, and her apparent attitude, and did the math. She wanted payback. The squibs made her look bad, so she hoped to return the favor.

"Commander Harley," Crow said, still watching her, "your opinion of Lieutenant Commander Walker's abilities?"

"First rate, Captain. I'd trust her in a pinch."

Now Crow swung toward his second, a big man with broad shoulders and a pot belly. "Even though her last mission failed?"

Harley glanced at Walker, then back to his C.O. "That could have happened to any of us, Captain."

"It won't happen to me."

"Of course not, sir." Harley offered him a broad smile. "But I'm sure the lieutenant commander learned from her experience."

Crow knew Harley was his man. It bought him a lot of slack sometimes. "You had better hope so. She is now your second," Crow growled.

"We're clear to depart, Cap. Vectors are set in flight control."

"Good. Get us off station and form up the armada."

"On it, sir."

Walker still stood at attention. Because it amused him, Crow left her that way. "Congratulations, Lieutenant Commander, but keep in mind this placement is temporary."

"How do I make it more permanent, sir?"

He shot a wink at Harley before he turned back to her. "Ballsy, ain't you?"

"So I've been told, sir."

Crow sucked his teeth. Good as her record was, Walker's previous assignments had been gravy compared to this one. He didn't expect a lot of trouble from the squibs, but the unknowns numbered too many to count. At last, he nodded.

"Convince me you're worth my time. While you're on this assignment, you will take your orders from Commander Harley or from me. You will not fuck up. Is that clear?"

"Yes, sir. Thank you, sir."

"Don't thank me yet. This job ain't done." He waved a dismissal at her and hailed the fleet. "All ships, move out."

chapter 12

<u>**Iridos**</u>

RASHIN'S HEAD LEANED CLOSE TO Alira's, both bent over an open panel atop Ijydin's ship. He pointed. "This is the connection you want. All the lighting for the control sector meets here. See how the surrounding compartment is shielded? Stronger than those around it? That's a protective measure. Unless the ship is hit hard in this very spot, these shouldn't be easily damaged."

She nodded.

"If there's a problem behind this panel, though, signs of trouble may not be visible. You'll need other means of detection. Lean closer," he said. "Smell the compartment."

Alira did as instructed, then wrinkled her nose. "It smells…I don't know, metallic?"

"Yes. That means all is well. If it smells hot, or if you detect a carbon odor, something is wrong behind the panel. You would need to pull this out to run a trace."

She sat back. "Thank you. This helps."

"I should thank you," he said. "I know what you did for me. I'm not sure the healers would have worked so hard for a mitigant."

Alira's throat tightened at those words delivered with such a flat tone. No other colors marred the dutiful green of his skin. Did he feel anything? "Oh no, Rashin. I'm sure they would work as hard for you as for anyone."

"If you say so." He reached for his harness and rigged it to lower him to the bay floor. "You asked about the communications system next. We should start inside the ship."

She followed and caught up to him on the ground level.

"I see you're up to your usual defiance."

Alira glanced around. Ijydin stood nearby, yellow and pink competing in her display and splashing blobs of light against the dark gray underside of the ship like the reflections of watershine in the reservoir cavern. "There you are!" Alira detached herself from the harness. "I tried to find you."

"I had to check in with Rakalesh." Ijydin looked up at the ship. "What were you doing up there?"

"Learning about the master panel for the control lighting. Rashin's been teaching me about ships."

Ijydin shot a look at the mitigant.

"We'll continue later, Alira." Without another word, he walked away.

"Couldn't you say something nice to him?" Alira waved toward his retreating back. "He's helping me."

"Is he? Nyros commed me about your fight with Lurien."

Alira kicked the harness out of the way. "And?"

"Why are you here? You were banned from the bay."

"You're my friend. I wanted to see you again. Tell you myself. Maybe get one more lesson on the ships. Ama's edict is fresh. I can squeeze out of trouble one last time."

"What about Galen?"

Alira drew her lips into a tight line. She had already assessed ways around that restriction. He was her i'shin. They would find a way to meet. Somehow. "I'll think of something. Let's sit inside your ship while we visit. Maybe Ama won't know I was here."

In answer, Ijydin gestured for Alira to lead the way. Together they climbed the steps into the ship and followed the dim, narrow corridor to the lift. Up three levels, then out and to the right.

Outside the command door, Alira stepped aside. "Your ship. You first."

Ijydin pushed past and ran into the door, which didn't open. She pounded it with a fist. "Why must you persecute me, sticky brat?"

Alira touched her friend's arm, her own hand freckled with amusement. "May I try?"

"It's no use," Ijydin muttered. "I've oiled it, I've replaced the mechanism, I've—"

Alira stood on tiptoe and reached past her to press the top left corner of the door. It slid open with a rasp and took all Ijydin's protests with it.

"What did you do?"

"The slot is bent. There. See?" She pointed. "Just pull it straight again."

Ijydin examined the bend. "How long have you been working on ships?"

"Not as long as you."

Ijydin muttered something under her breath and entered the command room. Two comfortable seats sat bolted in the center, one more set in a floor track on either side of the space nearer the black-and-gray manual controls. "I think you enjoy being in trouble with the council."

Gray colored Alira's response. "That's—why would you say such a thing?"

"Because you refuse to obey their mandates." Ijydin peered sideways at Alira, her colors betraying her query before she asked it. "The Adjustment is supposed to make it easier to accept frem life. Why is this so hard for you?"

Alira sighed. The same old question. She had never told anyone the answer. "I *want* to be content. I don't like feeling so alone all the time. But—" She hesitated. Should she confess? If anyone could keep a secret, it would be Ijydin. "The Adjustment didn't work on me."

It felt good to say it out loud, even if it was to someone who couldn't fix it.

Ijydin blinked gray. "Of course it did. Wondering 'what if' to a thousand possibilities is normal. You're no different from generations of unammi who went through their rites and had lingering questions, except you won't let yours go."

"No, Ijydin," Alira said. She leaned forward. "My Adjustment didn't work. At all."

"You're imagining things." Ijydin bent to poke around in a woven brown pouch on the floor. The rich smell of loam, disturbed by her digging, rose to drift through the small space. "No one ever said it would remove all doubt from your mind. It doesn't work like that."

It didn't matter whether her friend believed her. Maybe it was better if she didn't. It would have been nice, though, to have someone to talk to about it.

Ijydin extracted a few rufesh from the sack and sat, offering Alira a tuber. "Why do you think I chose the trade guild?"

Alira shook her head.

"Because I knew I'd never be happy living under the council's scrutiny. I like living my life elsewhere."

Alira's mouth fell open. She had always believed the pilots' off-world lives led to their oddities, not the other way 'round. "Nyros said he did it so others wouldn't have to leave home."

Ijydin shrugged. "I can't speak to that. But I've never been sorry. I miss you, and a few others. I miss our world. But the council? It's rules and restrictions?" She exhaled, a sharp puff of sound. "Not a bit."

"Do you think they would have mitigated you if you had stayed?"

"I don't know. Maybe," Ijydin said. "I think you're a strong candidate."

Alira shifted her weight and bounced the tuber in her hand. "Have you ever known someone who got mitigated?"

Ijydin grunted, her skin alight with purple and shot through with red veins. "Yes. Once. She had her sights set on the transport guild. The movers."

Teal patterns rose on Alira's arms. "That's an elite group. She was skilled, then?"

"In the beginning, yes. More than you would believe. Elders wondered if she might even herald a rebirth of the original Movers, the ones who brought us here in the before-time. But she never made her goal. We were maybe a season away from our Decisions. Something got crossed in her synaptic network. Simple instructions became too confusing for her to function in a rational way. She knew something was wrong with her but couldn't fix it. It ripped her apart, made her anxious and angry all the time."

Alira frowned. "Did you attend the mitigation rite?"

"I had to argue for permission, but yes."

"I've never seen one," Alira murmured.

"Then let me give you a preview," Ijydin said, her tone ragged. "They brought her to a cushion in the center of a small circle of witnesses and made sure she was comfortable. They explained that the treatment was a cellular adaptation, a re-routing of neural pathways to circumvent the brain's interpretation of certain chemical and electrical signals. They assured her that feelings and impulses would be subdued, easier for her to control. That it was an irreversible, lifelong modification to neurological processes. She would no longer be suited to the movers' guild she'd wanted so much and would be assigned to another, where she could perform simple tasks within the range of her skills."

She muttered a harsh expletive. "Then the healers surrounded her, laid hands on her—they said it was to comfort her, hah!—and the whole chamber went silent. While they worked, my friend's face faded to green. All her personality drained away and left behind a mask that no longer even resembled her."

She stopped, her fingers flicking at the rinds on the uneaten rufesh she still held.

Alira clenched her teeth with an indrawn hiss. "It must have been hard to watch."

"It was," Ijydin said, her gaze a slice of frigid ne'ani. "But she couldn't help herself. You can. Don't put me through that again." She stood, tossed the tubers back at the sack, and left, cursing the sticky door on her way out.

chapter 13

CUSHIONS RESTED IN A SEMI-CIRCLE, each one occupied by an eager student when Alira entered.

"Aes te nalya," she said.

"Nalena t'staani," they responded in unison.

"Let's get started," she said. "Who remembers their Firstrite?"

A chorus of affirmations rose around the room.

"What does it mark?" Alira called on a young female.

"Entry into the educators' house."

"And when does that happen?"

"Ten seasons."

Alira clapped. "Yes. Firstrite celebrates your move from the familial house, where you spend your earliest seasons, into the educators' house, where you live throughout your initial training. Who can tell me what the Firstrite has in common with every other ritual?"

The students looked at one another, no one apparently certain enough to speak. Alira shot a look at Trumo. He knew. She waited, but he wouldn't meet her eyes.

"Transition," she announced. "Every ritual marks movement from one role to another in society. Can someone give me an example?"

"Mourning Rites when someone dies."

"Yes. Who else?"

"Eldering, when frem are no longer fertile."

"Good! What about the beginning of that cycle?"

Nasim beat the others to the answer. "Potency!"

"And when does that happen?"

"Thirty seasons."

"Excellent." Alira loved teaching such bright younglings, helping to shape their expanding minds and prepare them for frem service, even limited as she was to classes in clerical studies. During all the seasons before her Decision, her scores in the subjects of teaching and training had rivaled those in spirituality and science. She had toyed with the idea of choosing the Educators Guild, but Lurien had changed Alira's mind. It hadn't been a difficult persuasion. Scientific discovery and the study of Musju excited her, yet teaching spiritual practices to younglings fulfilled her. Ironic. She, who argued against her people's customs, found satisfaction in teaching them to others.

Of course, it wasn't everything she wanted to change.

But maybe that wasn't true. If the council amended even one aspect of their society, wouldn't that carry wrinkles of transformation throughout the whole, as Nyros had said? As Sufamel had implied?

"All our rituals celebrate revision of status, but one in particular sets the pattern for the rest of your life. Who—"

"The Rite of Decision."

Gray rippled over everyone in the room, except Alira. Yellow twinkled down her arms and across her chest. Trumo had responded in class!

"That's right, Trumo. Can you tell us why?"

The youngling shrank back into his silence.

Alira neared him. "You know the answer. Won't you share it?"

He glanced aside at his classmates, then sat up straighter. "Because it consigns us to a single guild forever and we can never change our minds."

Amusement rippled across the other younglings. Trumo would surely hear about *that* later. At this point in their lives, with all their options open and the whole of their futures ahead of them, they could afford to belittle his misgivings.

Alira frowned. "Trumo is correct. When you leave the isolation that follows your Rite of Achievement, the council expects you to choose one guild for frem service. Once you announce your Decision, there is no going back."

An uneasy hush fell across the room. The younglings' colors flickered with unhappiness, uncertainty, and confusion.

"But isn't that how it's supposed to work?" one asked. "My ama says the council depends on us to make a commitment so they can plan for our futures."

"That is what they tell us, yes."

Another spoke up. "You disagree?"

Ah, so stupid. She needed to think before she spoke! Caution reared its head. Truth? Or doctrine?

"The council speaks with logic and reason. It's a valid argument. We need to know that all the service roles in our city are filled to capacity. Now, let's move on to—"

"But…." A timid voice again rose.

She turned back to Trumo.

"You've argued against the Decision," he said, his voice almost too low to hear. "I've heard you. Have you changed your mind?"

Where had he heard her say those things? How could she have been so careless? His trusting expression stabbed lavender streaks through her skin.

She couldn't deny her own statements, yet a suitable response eluded her. Guide them to the easier path with the council's approved rhetoric, and she'd lose Trumo as well as her own self-respect. Tell the truth, and salvage her own conscience, but set the younglings on a rocky road similar to her own. Every student followed her reactions as she struggled to find the right words.

She drew a calming breath. "For most of you, the choice won't be difficult. By the time you've completed your training, one or another of our guilds' work will call to you in a way you can't, and shouldn't, deny." Alira stopped, hoping that would do. "Let's—"

"What about the rest of us? What if no guild speaks to our hearts and we're not sure which way to go?"

"Yes, Na'ama, what then?"

"Such instances are rare." Alira's heart raced. She forced her breathing to remain calm, though veins of tension gave her away. "There are many guilds and different ways to serve in each. I don't expect any of you will have that problem."

"But if you do," one youngling said to the others, "then you pick one anyway or you get mitigated."

"I've seen a mitigant in the landing bay," Nasim said.

"When? You were never in the landing bay!"

"Was too. I snuck in to see one for myself."

"They're so creepy! Always the same color, hardly ever speaking…"

"Basu'tao!" Alira's hand sliced the air as she stared down each youngling. "All that is 'wrong' with mitigants is they didn't fit unammi standards of 'normal'. They deserve compassion. It shames you to denigrate them."

Shocked silence held the room until Trumo again found his voice.

"Does that mean even if I choose a guild and serve as frem with no doubt, I might still be mitigated because I'm different in some way? How does that serve society?"

How indeed. The others all waited for her response. Such bright younglings! Already they asked questions deep enough to rock the council's ease. How long would it take for unammi social pressure to bend them into expected patterns? Would any of them end up in the landing bay or mines or reclamation facility, out of sight and mind for compliant residents? Would Trumo?

Ijydin's description of the mitigation treatment echoed in Alira's mind while she teetered toward a choice.

Common sense objected. She shouldn't do it.

But what if she could save them from that fate?

Self-preservation tightened a band around her chest until it was hard to breathe.

She needed to end this discussion now.

She had no doubt the council tracked her every move. How much could she say before they stopped her?

Her heart pounding like drums at a rite, she blurted a response as fast as she could spit the words. "No social structure is perfect. Ours has its faults, and this is one of them. The process of changing it would be lengthy and difficult and might make things worse before they got better. *If* they got better. It's a risk to even try. But you should keep an open mind. Don't take for granted that what I or anyone else says is the whole truth. Listen to the elders' guidance but think for yourselves. When the council's generation is gone, it is you who—"

"Alira, *zhachi*!"

She whirled around. Lurien, bathed in red and white, glared at her from the door. Another cleric stood beside her.

"You will come with me at once."

Alira gestured. "But I'm—"

"At once!"

The other cleric stepped in front of the gathered students and began leading the discussion in another direction. Gray splotched most of the younglings, but Trumo had gone white, reflecting her own choking terror. In a daze, she followed her mother out of the classroom, past gawking others along the way, and out of the guildhouse, across the grounds and into the tunnels.

At last, with no one nearby to hear, Lurien stopped and twisted toward her daughter, fists clenched at her hips, skin pulsing in frantic patterns of white on red.

"What were you *thinking*?" she said, her voice a hissing whisper.

"I just—"

"Stop. Rakalesh was with me. We heard you." Lurien waved one red arm back the way they'd come. "You taught sedition to the younglings, Alira!"

"But they—"

"Enough!" Features puckered, Lurien closed her eyes and drew a slow breath to calm her display before she opened them again. "There is no excuse for what you did. The council is gathering as we speak to determine your fate."

So fast? Alira's heart thumped against the inside of her chest, no longer a tiny raneal like when the humans had come here. Now the fear stretched like the mighty beat of a niveym's wings threatening to burst free.

Lurien's shoulders slumped. "Go to your quarters. The council will send for you when they have reached their decision."

"They?" Alira managed to squeak. "Aren't you going to defend me?"

A jarring tangle of color rushed beneath Lurien's broad white blotches. She raised her hands in the space before her, fingers curled like claws as if to clasp her daughter to her, then dropped them to her sides to grip her wrap instead. Eyes wide, Lurien's jaw clenched, her white lips drawn back in a rictus of fear.

"No," she croaked. "I've been banned from the deliberation. Rakalesh says they're no longer interested in what I wish to say on this subject. I can't help you this time. You are sand in the wind."

chapter 14

ALIRA STOOD BESIDE THE MONUMENT, her mind racing like the wind on the plain. The council was going to mitigate her. They hadn't said as much, not yet, but she knew.

She'd tried to conform. For almost a hundred seasons, she had forced herself into the role the council designed, taught it to others who now served as frem based in part on her guidance, and backed down when councilors balked at her questions and suggestions. They expected her to teach accepted doctrine. The younglings expected her to tell them the truth. She had made her choice and had no regrets, even if her legs did tremble now.

She edged closer to the wind and rested a white hand against the sand-encrusted wall. Lurien had told Alira to stay in her quarters, to meditate on her future. And Alira had tried, but the shock of Musju's turbid brew proved too frightening. After a while, she'd given up and come here in search of something she thought she might never find again.

A sound at her back snapped her attention to the tunnel. There stood the messenger. A mitigant.

"The council is ready for you."

Alira heard his deadpan voice as if from a great distance. Her belly clenched into a knot. She clutched at the rockface and closed her eyes. Behind her lids, the shifting figure from her dreams appeared like a summoned Companion.

Change is, It whispered.

Her eyes flew open. Her Companion was visiting when she was awake now? Speaking to her? In the moments before her mitigation, of all times?

But the council was unlikely to grant her time to ponder that mystery. Numbness seeped in to dull the fear, calm the panicked heartbeat, and soothe the shrieking lungs. After a moment, she nodded and followed the messenger into the tunnel. She had told her students there was nothing wrong with mitigants. She believed that to her core, but oh, she did not want to be one of them! The winding course to the council chambers passed in a blur. Pity or scorn on every resident they passed told her word had spread through the joinedmind.

The corridor beyond the council chamber lay filled with unammi in a myriad of flashing, winking hues and she gaped. A few—more than a few—stood spotted with white. Did they share her longing for change? Were they teetering on the edge, waiting for a gust of strong wind to nudge them into action?

Would her mitigation at last kindle passion in their own hearts?

She looked past those in front to a solitary green witness at the back. Rashin.

Alira's knees almost gave way. He had good reason to revile this "treatment," to stay as far from this chamber and its horrors as possible. Yet he had come. He stood in the open, despite clear disapproval from others, so she would see him. Even if he could not stop this travesty, he had come to show his support for her. She had wondered why the council had seen fit to change him so, but she'd never asked. Now she never would.

She straightened her back and nodded once to Rashin. To the others. She couldn't hide her white skin, but she could maintain her dignity. She entered the chamber, and the drape closed behind her.

Inside, light globes hovered at the perimeter of the unadorned space. A small circle of witnesses surrounded a central cushion. Alira rejoiced that as an outcast, Ijydin could not be among them. Across from the door, the councilors sat waiting. Two, Cesar and Yoloron, wore conflicted expressions and a riot of colors. Cesar even toyed with the gold coin he always carried, the one he twisted between his fingers when he was disturbed or uncertain.

Alira forced her feet forward to the empty cushion before the council and knelt.

Rakalesh spoke. "Alira, daughter of Lurien, you have been judged and found guilty of teaching principles of discord to the younglings in your class. What have you to say?"

"With all due respect, Councilors, you cannot ask me to lie to them. The Rite of Decision came up in discussion during a scheduled part of their curriculum. They asked what would happen if they couldn't decide. I tried to lead them away from the topic. I explained that most of them would feel no conflict in choosing one guild over the others. They wouldn't let it go."

"You should have taught them to adhere to unammi social structures and expectations, not instructed them to voice their dissent."

"That isn't what I said, Na'ama."

Rakalesh grunted. "Semantics. We all know what you were trying to do. Our decision is final. The healers are ready." She waved frem forward from the chamber's periphery.

Another councilor leaned forward, elbows on his knees. "We know you're afraid. Don't be. It won't hurt—"

"Do you know that for certain, Councilor?" Alira asked.

He leaned back, veined in pink and red, and Rakalesh resumed.

"Alira, I will speak. You will listen. Is that clear?"

"Yes," Alira said, her voice pinched, her tongue thick in a mouth gone dry. She looked down at the cushion beneath her knees. Red and green threads wove through its silken gold cover and for a moment she wondered where the fabric had come from.

"The treatment is a process of—"

"I know what it involves. Please skip the description."

A moment of silence followed.

"Very well. Then you understand you will no longer be suited to spiritual or scientific work and will be shifted to another guild."

Alira shook her head. All it took to change guilds was mitigation and a complete loss of self.

Rakalesh went on. "Do you have any questions before we begin?"

"Which guild? Will I be stationed in the landing bay?"

A pause dragged out before Rakalesh answered. "No. Your friendships among the outcasts could prove problematic. You will work in the greenhouse dome."

"Will I know who I am?"

"Yes, but your memories will carry little emotional connection."

"Will I even care that I have been mutilated?"

"Zhachi! You are in enough trouble. Must you make it worse?"

Alira raised her gaze to meet the councilor's. "How could this possibly get worse for me?"

Rakalesh huffed. "Enough."

"One more thing," Alira said, her voice trembling. "We are taught that mitigation is an act of compassion, the council's last resort for a broken individual. I am a functional frem whose only offense was to speak out against your unrealistic standard, yet your solution is enforced compliance. Must all unammi keep silent or fear this fate?"

Rakalesh gestured to the healers. "Begin."

The healers knelt around her murmuring their prayers, then each touched her body and closed their eyes.

Alira kept hers open as wide as she could. Her white now edged with red, she faced the councilors on their dais. Let them see her fade to nothing. Let them live with that for the rest of their lives, knowing they had mitigated someone with no justifiable cause.

She could feel the healers in her head. In her mind. Smells arose to her awareness—unwashed bodies, moist loam, dry sand, muñise resin, and others unrecognizable and odd in this place. Something slid sideways in her thoughts, then snapped back into place. Again. And again. Then the sliding stopped. She felt them trying, their tugs and pushes distant as if she were experiencing them through another's mind.

The healer to her left shifted on his knees and started again.

Alira glanced at him, at all the healers. They were straining. She checked the other witnesses and found similar expressions there. On the dais, the councilors leaned forward, every brow furrowed, every eye locked on her.

The lead healer dropped her hands and sat back, studying Alira. She shook her head as if to clear it, then leaned forward and started again.

Gray speckled the councilors on the dais. Alira frowned. She didn't feel any different. How long—

Alira froze, along with everyone in the chamber, as the call for assistance rang through the joinedmind to unite all unammi with one cohesive thought.

Danger!

In that heartbeat, her fear took a different form. Alira joined with others in the no-space of the unammi's combined awareness and raced toward the source of the menace. A human ship, enormous in size, orbiting above their city. As one, the joinedmind reached out to evaluate the threat and heard the human's words as if all unammi stood in the trade guild's communications center.

"Iridosian city, I say again, this is Captain Beldra of the Consortium ship Frol de la Mar. We have come to trade for hematium. Admiral Skalar will not accept refusal. This is your last chance. Respond, or we will use force."

Well. A promise of harm changed everything. In the joinedmind, Alira and all unammi understood their logical choice: remove the threat. Dispatching the crew, who could only be eliminated one at a time, would take too long. Instead, the joinedmind focused on the ship. Enmeshed within that united perception, guided by their distance viewers, Alira flew with her people through the vessel's configuration, her/their unified efforts intent on defeating this enemy. Manipulation of inanimate matter posed more of a challenge than working with DNA, which had its own form of awareness. Still, any molecular structure could be adjusted, given enough time. Alira swarmed with the unammi consciousness through the vessel, seeking any weakness until....

There.

So small as to be invisible to the limited eyesight of human engineers or even the mechanical equipment of human safety inspections, one tiny fracture gleamed at the edge of an energy chamber, a beacon to combined unammi senses. Alira's awareness swept along with the rest of her people in a whoosh of resolve as they concentrated on widening that crack.

chapter 15

Iridosian Space
<u>Aboard the Leonid</u>

VISUALS FROM THE LEONID'S CLOAKED drones were still coming online. Crow scowled at the split-screen images on the tactical screen. What intelligent race would live underground for fuck's sake? Their bald, pale blue skin that lit up like those biting night-flies on Danua.… Stupid little pissant bugs. His lip wrinkled into a sneer.

Crow peered at the screen as Ling made final preparations to bring the Perseid out of hiding. He and eight other captains waited behind their ships' veils, five with an arsenal that could transform the puny settlement into a crater if the squibs refused, but it was already a done deal in Crow's opinion. He'd known the little shits wouldn't cooperate before his armada left New Canaan. It wouldn't matter much longer. Given a reason, any reason at all, he'd step on them.

"Commander Harley, ensure weapons ready," he called. "Eyes open for targets." Skalar had sent him here for an explicit purpose but for Crow, this trip meant so much more. Skalar's days were numbered, and some of those Crow had won to support his takeover bid rode with him today. What happened here might make or break their commitment to Crow's admiralty when the time came. Hopefully, that would be soon. A sly grin slithered its way onto his face. Maybe Skalar's idea on the hemi was a good one. Credits like those would finance the faction for a long time, and Crow could focus on other things, like making his mark in the Trader arena and bringing payback to the admirals who had betrayed his family so long ago. Not that his loser parents deserved it. Still.

Beldra moved back into view in the top right of his screen. "Iridosian city, I say again, this is Captain Beldra of the Consortium ship Frol de la Mar. We have come to trade for hematium. Admiral Skalar will not accept refusal. This is your last chance. Respond, or we will use force." Silence descended on the bridge of both ships as they waited for the squibs' answer.

Then something changed. Across the viewscreen, on every drone's feed, a shudder went through the squibs in the city as if they'd all heard the Frol's comm at the same time, and every last one had stopped moving. Crow squinted at the screen. What were they doing?

"Enlarge image sixteen," he said, and the screen obliged. Crow got to his feet, moving closer to the inflated visual of the squib who stood anchored to his spot, staring at something Crow could not see. "Bring that drone around. Let's see what he's looking at." The image shifted perspective. Still, Crow saw nothing. All of the other squibs were doing the same thing. What the hell—

Klaxons shrieked across the Leonid's bridge and Crow almost leaped out of his skin. He whirled. "Report!"

"It isn't us, sir, it's the Frol! They're in trouble!"

"What? Enlarge!"

Beldra replaced the squib at center screen, her commands punctuating the hauler's ship-wide containment alarm that bled through the vid.

"Beldra!" Tense seconds passed. The frantic actions on the bridge of the Frol de la Mar continued. "Is our comm functional?"

"I think so, sir," the comms officer said. "They—"

All sound from Beldra's bridge went dead. Eerie silence engulfed the Leonid bridge, and Crow spun back to the screen. Her feed was gone.

"Gimme visual," he ordered. "Exterior view."

There onscreen, the Frol de la Mar tilted sideways like it was navigating a hairpin curve in the atmosphere before a brief, brilliant sphere of light obscured the scene. Crow threw up a hand, shielding his eyes.

"Get us outta range!" he shouted. "*Go go go!*"

The flash dimmed. His crew scrambled. Beldra's ship, now in pieces of various sizes, sped away from the blast center in all directions. Several large chunks hurtled toward the Leonid, but Crow's ship was faster. The scene grew smaller on screen. "Enlarge image!" he shouted, and the visual jumped back to full. Across the debris field, Crow saw small dots of color spinning against the black.

"Enhance section nineteen."

Bodies and debris filled the center of the screen, following a trajectory different from the Frol. Beyond, remains of another ship flickered in and out of visibility. The light cruiser, Perseid.

Behind the expanded segment, Crow saw another brilliant flash of light fill the screen.

"Full image!" he growled.

Nineteen returned to its spot in time to see Frol debris take out another ship.

"Who was that?" Crow yelled.

"Solar Quest, sir," a voice said. "Captain Barr."

One of his frigates. Fuck!

"Are we in the clear?" Silence met his question, and he twisted around, almost snarling. "Are we *clear*?"

"Yes, sir. Calculations predict debris is past us."

Crow swung back to the screen and gawked at the devastation. Three ships from one explosion. Three fucking ships! He should have spread them out more like he would have in *any* other attack scenario. Around him, the Leonid's bridge crew watched the screen in open-mouthed, pin-drop silence.

"What the fuck just happened?" Crow shouted. Those crewmen in his line of sight jumped as if slapped. "I saw no weapons fire! It couldn't have been mechanical failure. Not that fast."

No one spoke.

chapter 16

<u>Iridos</u>

ALIRA AND THE OTHERS PREPARED to separate into individual awareness until a small movement caught the group's attention. In the temple cavern, a small hovering device descended into someone's view, its surface reflecting only high-end frequencies of the cavern's lights. Alira saw through another's eyes as he plucked it from the air, studied its mechanism, then smashed it on the ground. Immediately, its visual appearance dropped into the lower spectrum. Within seconds, others around the city found similar objects in the landing bay, the residential caverns, all the domes, even some of the buildings, and a frantic new summons recalled to the collective all those who had already disengaged. Alerted to the cloaking tech, the unammi joinedmind turned to the sky above their city.

Ships filled the space above their home. So many…*too* many! Shock sank into the joinedmind, precious seconds ticking away as the population tried to grasp the enormity of what they faced. Alira had one instant to recognize that her own personal drama paled in the shadow of this overwhelming peril. Hadn't she just asked how her fate could get worse?

Then calm rippled through the joinedmind. Alira knew it came from Lurien who was even now directing the whole of their combined efforts. Panic would solve nothing and would slow them down. One pragmatic response lay open to them, and with a united will, they set to it.

chapter 17

Iridosian Space
<u>Aboard the Leonid</u>

"HARLEY," CROW SAID, "SCAN THE debris. Get me a signature."

"Aye, Cap."

Onscreen, Sloane and Jos brought their frigates out of cloak, both captains moving into ready positions at safe distances from one another. Before anyone could speak, Sloane's ship exploded.

Crow's hands grasped the air before his torso, a guttural growl deep in his throat. *Fuck this.*

"Comms, bring us live."

"Go, Captain."

"Leonid to Ranger. Fire all LADRAS missiles. I say again, fire all LADRAS missiles." Over his shoulder, he called, "Mier, fire four of our six."

The weapons officer hesitated. "But sir, won't that irradiate the hemi?"

"Mier, you're relieved. Harley, take his place. Get us hot." Crow heard his second shove the other man aside to follow the captain's orders.

At the same time, Captain Surrey sent a mayday from the hauler Borealis, which was still concealed. It shuddered into view past the others, then blew apart with a blinding flash. The Ranger, his sole remaining shooter outside this battlecruiser, dropped like a stone to get clear of the blast.

Crow ground his teeth. "Hurry up, Harley."

Another second passed. "Disengaging cloak now. Missiles away, Cap."

"Roger that. Show me the target. Magnify." A minute passed. Another, before the first volley of tiny sparks lit the liminal space of the squibs' city, followed by flashes from the Leonid's ordnance. Around him, the crew waited in silence while excruciating minutes passed, but the fleet lost no more ships. Crow stomped his foot, grinding it into the floor. "Crows *eat* bugs, ya bastards."

He whirled and jabbed a finger at Walker. "Lieutenant Commander."

"Yes, sir."

"Explain to Lieutenant Mier why LADRAS missiles will not irradiate the hematium."

"Hemi doesn't undergo radioactive decay," she told Mier. "That's why it's so prevalent in interstel engine components."

"And?" Crow prompted.

"Our instruments show it's too far underground," Walker added, "and outside the limited dispersal of LADRAS to be affected, even if it didn't shed the tox."

Crow shot an appreciative glance at Harley, then reclaimed his seat. "Basic knowledge, Lieutenant Mier, which you *should* know. You are confined to quarters, where you will study the science behind interstel flight and LADRAS weapon systems. If you cannot answer my questions about the subject by the time we finish here, I will maroon you on this rock. Dismissed." He punched comm control. "Leonid to all ships, report."

One of the remaining vessels took damage with minimal casualties. Five ships left. Five. Out of ten. Fuck. What the hell sort of weapon could do that with no firing trace? Skalar was going to shit.

Screw Skalar. He wasn't here. He wouldn't be an issue much longer anyway.

"Somebody tell Jos to scan for survivors." Crow turned to his second. "What about us, Harley?"

"No damage, sir."

"What did you find in the Frol debris? What kind of weapon did the squibs use?"

"I got nothing, Cap. It looked like the Frol lost containment."

Lost— "That's impossible. What about the others?"

"Every single one read as mechanical failure, sir. No weapons signatures at all."

Which made no fucking sense. "Walker, what do you see on the surface?"

"I'm not getting much, sir."

"No life signs?"

"No nothing, Captain. Instruments can't latch onto anything."

"But they were working before."

"Yes, sir."

Crow grunted, frowning. "Figures. Comms." The officer gestured. "Leonid to all ships, we're going in closer. Hold your positions. Helm, take us down for a fly-by."

chapter 18

ATMOSPHERE MADE FOR A BUMPY ride even on a ship this size, after which surface images filled the screen. The city was flattened all right, but not much chance any of the ships could land there. Dark gaps marked buckled surface areas in at least half a dozen places. There must be tunnels zigging and zagging underneath the whole damn city, meaning the integrity of anything inside this valley was questionable. He'd have preferred to land to the north of the city, beyond the ridge where they had seen the metal in their scans. It would be easy to sit even a large boat on that open plain. But those mine entrances he could pinpoint had collapsed. He couldn't blast his way in without a significant risk of bringing the whole damn mountain down and burying the prize for all eternity. They'd have to access it through tunnels on the city side. Assuming there were any.

Shit.

"Walker, anything from the remains?"

"Not yet, sir. Instruments are all over the place."

"Very well. I give it about thirty hours before the surface radiation tapers off enough for it to be safe to go down in suits. We'll get the details then. Send word to medbay. As long as we're here, everyone is on radmeds whether they go down or not. Harley, see that canyon?" He pointed to the west of the city. "Open it up. We'll land outside the outer ridge and transport personnel, equipment, and cargo through there. It's far enough out that we don't risk collapsing the mines. Remind Talonn to check Ursa Major's radiation suits, and tell the haulers—"

"Hauler, sir," Harley said.

"What?"

"Only the Treasure Chest survived, Captain."

Crow blinked. "Of course. Tell Ronan to prep his holds and stage the mining equipment for deployment. The Chest will land. All other personnel and supplies will transport via shuttle."

"Yes, sir."

"Any questions?"

"Just one, sir. What do you want us to do if any squib ships approach?"

Crow had no idea when the little fuckers would come back. Skalar had mentioned wanting to keep squib ships to carry out parts of his plan down the road. Even if Skalar was no longer in charge of the Consortium by that time, Crow saw no flaw in the logic. The ships would come in handy, regardless. But they had no way of keeping the squib pilots from fleeing, once they'd grasped the current situation on their home front, no way to kill the pilot and keep the ship.

"We don't want any witnesses. If any appear, take them out." If they did come, at least it would give his crew a little more shooting practice, but the fucking squibs had cost him enough already. If he could avoid another confrontation, he might get out of here with the rest of his armada intact. "Anything else?"

"No, sir."

"Good," Crow said, his jaw clenched so tight it ached. He jerked to his feet. "When you're done shooting rocks, take us back to rejoin the convoy, and call me if anything comes up. I'm gonna get some sleep.

Part Two

chapter 19

<u>Iridos</u>

THE COMPANION SHIFTED BESIDE HER as she surveyed the utter destruction in the valley. Alira felt Its presence there. "Is this all that's left?"

"Change is."

"They wouldn't listen. I tried to tell them. We could have—"

What? What could the unammi have done against this? She moved into the wreckage on trembling legs, crunching glass and metal and stone underfoot. Ash whipped past in the wind, and she coughed.

"Change is."

She whirled. "That's what you said last time! Can't you offer something more helpful?"

Her Companion wavered, fluctuated, taking Its time.

"Wake up."

Alira awoke to shadows and pain. What....

Memory flooded back. The *humans!* Fear, hot and thick, jolted through her and she jerked her head off the floor, attempting to rise. Agony snatched a yelp from her throat, and she fell back, eyes closed against the dust, hands groping the debris that pinned her to the floor while she searched her body for injuries.

Nearby, other moans, shuffles, and scrapes pierced the ringing in her ears. The others still lived. Here, anyway. This chamber, far below the surface, had survived. As for those above, that remained to be seen. The surface...the *guildhouse!* Images of devastation from her dream flooded back and bile filled her throat.

"Ama...." Her voice quavered, and she swallowed past the thickness in her throat caused by more than dust. Two cycles ago she had promised to never forgive Lurien. Even this cycle, mother and daughter had fought. Now—

"Is anyone hurt?" someone called.

Other voices responded while Alira surveyed her own damage. She eased her head to one side and wiped some of the powder from her eyes and mouth with a trembling hand.

"I can't get up."

"Alira?"

"Yes." She raised her head as much as she could. Chunks of the ceiling had fallen from several spots, including one right above the center of the chamber. Onto her. Just big enough to knock her flat, break her ribs, and bruise her organs.

A face appeared above hers. Yoloron, a councilor and one of the elders. "Injuries?"

"Nothing life-threatening. What about the others?"

Yoloron looked around the room, then back at Alira. "A few serious. I've found no dead so far, but we haven't had much time to search." She gestured. "I'll need help to lift this."

"I can wait."

Yoloron nodded and withdrew.

Alira lay listening to the sounds around her in the surreal setting. Her body worked at healing while her fevered mind raced through all the times she had defended the humans. Argued with Nyros or Ijydin, or even Galen about beneficial human qualities. Suggested the unammi could learn from human diversity. But the elders had been correct about the aliens all along. Maybe everything else, too.

Except for her dream of an attack on the city. That's the one thing she'd gotten right.

In a room filled with choking dust and moans of the injured, the thought offered no comfort at all.

chapter 20

THE TREASURE CHEST'S STERN BLOCKED most of the entry to the blasted canyon. Crow landed his private shuttle as close as he could get to the rock. He would have to walk farther even to enter the canyon. Goddamn gravity and wind made for a rough trek. He reached the ruined city breathing hard, sweating inside his suit, and foul-tempered. He adjusted his suit's temp and spoke into his comm.

"Harley."

"In the tunnels, Cap."

"Come to the surface."

"On my way."

He squinted into the valley's gloom. Yesterday's flyby and his visor's visual augmentation array told him steep ridges rose to the north, south, and east of where he stood. There wasn't much else to see. Everything between lay flat, or near enough. Crow approached the edge of one blast radius and surveyed the damage. Damn, LADRAS did a beautiful job!

Breaching the western ridge might have been a mistake, though. Without that barrier, the relentless wind shot ash and grit through the valley at high velocity. It couldn't be good for the Chest's engines.

Crow crunched through rubble as he moved into the debris field. Scattered among the rest lay billions of shining melted fragments. He bent to examine the material. Glass—too much to be melted sand alone. They had to be building with it. Idiots. Nobody used that shit anymore. The colonies had shifted to plaz centuries ago and the shelters where he'd spent his juvie years used the most shatter-resistant varieties. Crow had broken a lotta windows in his day. Other kids in those government homes had, too, but at least broken plaz didn't make a mess like this.

He kicked at a section of collapsed wall and it crumbled, filling in the gap beneath. In between the chunks, something flickered. He bent to expose whatever it was but couldn't budge the blocks.

"Captain?" Harley's rasp sounded in his headset.

"Over here." When his second was near enough, Crow bent down again. "Help me with this."

Harley grabbed the other end of the stone and together they moved it aside. Beneath lay a body in colorful display, even covered in dust. It seemed intact.

Crow activated his external comm. "Get up."

The squib didn't move.

Crow kicked it. "Get up!"

Still, it didn't respond, and Crow pushed it over with the toe of his boot. Most of its face was gone, along with part of its middle. Crow's lip curled. Once, in his early teen years, he'd caught a cephalopod at the New Canaan wharf and slashed it to bits on the dock behind some crates. The whole time he was killing it, even long after it was dead, the thing twinkled in bizarre color patterns. His sycophants from the shelter had been impressed with his knife skill and the apparent lack of feeling that allowed him to kill with ease. They couldn't have been more wrong. If they'd known the depth of resentment hidden behind Crow's cool glare and beneath his skin, the rage which had guided his knife that day, they never would have come near him again. Even so, killing fish, animals, insects, or, later, other humans didn't assuage the vengeance he craved. Nothing but a long, uninterrupted showdown with the individuals who robbed him of his privileged life and landed him in the shelter would do.

Crow dismissed the corpse and raised his gaze to the rest of the ruined city. "Have any of your teams been through this yet?"

"No, sir. We've got every available crewmember working on the mining effort."

"Any trouble getting the equipment through?"

"Only a little. Once you get past the first huge cavern, the passage narrows. The Rolland processor wouldn't fit. We couldn't figure another way to get it to the other side, so we left it on the Chest. The rest is in place. They just got the equipment going to pull the first load."

"Good." Crow eyed the flashing, pear-shaped body. It was small, maybe 140 centimeters, but its feet were huge by comparison. The damn thing looked deformed. "Any survivors?"

"Not that we've found, sir. But we're still exploring."

"Still can't get life sign readings?"

"No sir, not even on our crew."

"Assume some of the squibs made it through this. Assign a team to check all tunnels in and out of our working area. Don't want them to take us out one at a time. Arm a few non-essential personnel with pulse rifles and station them in any open corridors and around the gaps on the surface. Bring any survivors to me. I've got questions."

"Got it. Do you want us to clear out the blocked tunnels so we can search farther down?"

"Negative. Let's fill our holds first. Confine your search to everything on this side of the obstructions. If we can't get to them, they can't get to us."

"Yes, sir." Harley switched to his team channel and started giving orders.

Crow moved farther out into the ruins, poking through what he could reach. Skalar wanted him to bring back anything that might prove valuable. So far, he saw no spoils worth taking. The farther he went, the more bodies he saw, most in pieces. Like the fish, all the bits still blinked. He wondered what evolutionary purpose *that* served.

Harley caught up. "Okay, sir. Security teams are setting up now."

Crow regarded the rest of the city. Even with his visaug, he couldn't identify the crap strewn about, not in this fucking murk. He could fly over on the way up, and check it out with the shuttle's lights, but that would have to wait.

"As soon as you get a team available, have them root around up here for any worthwhile salvage," Crow said. "Get a message to Ronan to move the Chest behind the ridge, out of the wind. And rotate your crew on the surface. Long-term exposure to this powder can't be good for the ship or the suits."

"Yes, sir."

"How do we get below?"

"That way's clear, Cap." Harley pointed. "The rest of the tunnels we found going down from the surface are blocked inside the passage."

"Figures."

"We hit 'em pretty hard. Can't say I'm surprised."

"You're objecting?"

"No, of course not, sir. You didn't have a choice. They sliced and diced us up there."

"I thought you said it was mechanical failure."

"That is what the scans said, Cap. Can't say I agree."

Crow grunted. Sooner or later, he'd have to go below. Skalar expected a report within the week, filled with firsthand information and yield estimates. Further, his leadership of this armada obliged him to see what they'd come for. He sighed.

He needed to suck it up.

"Lead on."

"Yes, sir," Harley nodded. "Be careful when we start down. The squib lights are all out, so we had to hang replacements along the walls. It isn't great, but we couldn't do much better in that tight space. Clearance in the tunnels is under two meters."

"Of course it is," Crow said through puckered lips.

Captain and commander picked their way back to the path cleared through the wreckage from the blasted ridge, Harley talking most of the way. Crow barely listened as they approached the pitch-black tunnel mouth.

The closet at the shelter had been dark, too, every fucking time the other kids had locked him in there.

Heart and respiration rates on his faceplate surpassed optimal numbers as he ducked and plunged into the blackness. Even though his visaug allowed him to "see," Crow cursed under his breath. Keep going, man. One foot in front of the other. The suit had plenty of air. He needn't panic.

On and on and on they went, the floor sloping down and down. Crew passed them going the other way, headlamps winking in the passage, but Crow looked neither right nor left. Harley claimed their destination was much bigger than this tight squeeze. At last, bright light from the chamber ahead shifted the transparency and visuals on their faceplates. Even so, Crow squinted as they rounded a curve in the passage and entered a cave. Eight hundred meters down, according to his readout. Holy hell.

Crow straightened, his eyes adjusting. This cavern was enormous, longer than it was wide, its walls and ceiling covered in some sort of shiny blue crystal save for the scattered chunks fallen during the attack. "These are rocks, Harley. I want metal."

"The hemi's that way, Cap," Harley said with a nod, "another five hundred meters down. You want we should take the crystals, too?"

Crow made his way to one of the rubble piles, booting aside the stones. Beneath lay chunks of the blue ore. He plucked one from the pile and held it up for a closer inspection. His visaug detected an unknown mineral with an unrecognizable energy signature, almost like ELF radiation. Consortium techs might be able to figure a use for it, but it also had plenty of visual appeal. Swirls and flaws deep inside the crystal caught the light, refracting it in a myriad of blue shades. Raw or set in jewelry, this ought to sell well in the markets. His mother might have worn something like it back in her heyday when she and his father spent much of their time among the elite in New Canaan. After his parents' arrest, of course, all his mother's baubles had been confiscated to pay for her child's expenses in the shelter. Besides, she'd had no need for such things in confinement, nor since she and dear old Dad had gotten out. They weren't the social phenomenon they had once been. No more dinner invitations. No more cocktail parties. No more business meetings. Not that Crow gave a shit.

"I presume the Rolland will fit in here?"

"Yes, sir."

"Very well. Divert a quarter of your mining efforts to this chamber." He stuck the shard in his suit pouch. Crewmen hustled through the space like a line of ants, flowing around the captain and commander as they carried necessities to and from the mine. Crow jerked his chin toward the other end of the cave. "That way?"

"Yes, sir."

Crow shoved away the crawling sensation at the back of his neck and set off in the indicated direction. The sooner he could get this inspection done, the sooner he could hand this off to Harley. He hadn't even seen it all, yet Crow hated this warren of worm holes and while he was at it, fuck this cave in particular. Parts of the ceiling had collapsed, even eight hundred meters down! And still they descended? Ahead, the maw of the next tunnel approached and the bio-readings on Crow's faceplate rose as he plunged into the tube with Harley right behind him. Lights strung along the wall made it easier to see crewmen passing each other in the confined space ahead, as well as fist-sized gaps in the ceiling here, too. Harley had said cave-ins choked most of the tunnels. Crow cast back in his memory of research on Iridos. Was it prone to quakes? Even if not, couldn't LADRAS hits trigger one? This far down, if the rock above collapsed, his crew might never dig him out.

He took a deep breath, adjusting the environmentals in his suit again. But the thought had rooted and wouldn't be dismissed. Every step farther down the passage snugged the walls and ceiling closer until they scraped Crow's comfort zone raw. He lurched toward the oncoming workers bellowing into their comm channel.

"Make a hole!"

Crewmen became one with the walls, features confused in the glow of their helmet readings as he hurtled past. Crow ignored them. The damn tube was getting smaller! How the hell did Harley get *any* of the mining equipment through this? A shiver chilled his nape, despite the sweat that still gathered there.

Crow pushed back against his fear of the tight space. If he could keep walking and power through this ordeal, he could get the hell out that much sooner.

Ahead, the passage curved downward—again—then leveled out toward a wider gap. At last! Crow burst through it, hyperventilating, and escaped into the mine to put some distance between himself and the burrow he'd just exited. Working crew stopped to gape at his bluster.

"Whadaya gawkin' at?" Crow bawled. "Get back to work!" He shot a glance at Harley, who looked away.

Crow ground his teeth. He needed to get himself under control. Crew talked. Losing it in front of 'em like that made him appear weak.

He squared his shoulders and took in his surroundings. The murky ceiling of this gallery, far larger than the crystal cave, would have been lost in total darkness without the visaug, not to mention the lights they'd brought. More-or-less horizontal shafts honeycombed the walls.

Hematium.

"How many shafts are working already?"

"Maybe a third, Cap. They're a tight squeeze for our people, but we're getting by. Shuttles from the Ranger and Ursa Major are still bringing teams down. We're at about half capacity now and are holding back relief teams so we can keep working around the clock."

"Good. Let's—"

"Commander Harley," a voice in their headsets interrupted, "Lieutenant Commander Walker."

"Go, Walker."

"Commander, we found a live one."

Crow pivoted, slow and clumsy, on his heel. "Where?"

"In the east tunnel off the crystal cave."

Another fucking crawlspace. "Bring it out so I can question it."

"I'm not sure it would survive being moved, Captain."

Figured. "Acknowledged. Stay put. Harley and I will be right there."

He should examine the rest of the mine in more detail, but fuck that. He had a crew. Let them do it. He passed Harley with a grunt, his testicles crawling as he pushed himself back into the tunnel. Darkness engulfed him, squeezing his lungs until every breath felt like sucking on a blocked tube.

Like the closet. Like his hands around that boy's throat, the one who laughed loudest when Crow'd pissed himself.

This time, word had spread and crewmen got out of his way without prompting. By the time he reached the crystal cave, Crow was sweating again, but he didn't slow down, and he didn't bother to readjust his suit's environment. One more unpleasant duty and he'd go back to the ship anyway. The bourbon in his quarters would taste mighty fine right about now.

The east tunnel, smaller and with fewer lights, felt even more cramped. Crow's breathing came ragged, uneven, and shallow. This was the squibs' fault. If they had cooperated, he wouldn't have had to come here in the first place, much less crawl through their damned nest. At the intersection of two blocked corridors, Walker and another officer stood over an injured squib that lay spread-eagle on the ground, its chest rising and falling in rapid, shallow movements. This bug was done. Part of its torso was squashed almost flat. One oversized foot lay useless, mangled at the end of its stumpy leg.

"Has it said anything?" Crow asked.

"No, sir."

Crow activated external comms and brushed past Walker. "Wake up."

No response.

"I said wake up!" Crow repeated, nudging it with the toe of his boot. Frenzied patterns raced across its skin, yet it didn't speak.

Crow squatted beside it. "I know you're still alive. Wake the fuck up and talk to me, or I'm going to gut every living squib I find on this dirtball."

The alien's eyes opened a slit, then wider until it gazed at Crow with that weird bug-like expression they always wore. Much better. "What kind of weapon did your people use on us?" Crow asked.

"Isja riba unammitu'lan."

Crow pulled a knife from his utility belt. "Speaka ze Eenglish."

"Ba'nostade puda ba'tujhoor."

Somewhere nearby, a hissing whisper registered in the back of Crow's mind as the squib's breathing grew erratic. Shit. He was losing it. "Where are your city's defensive weapons? How did you see my probes and destroy my ships?"

Flashing lids closed over the squib's eyes and Crow pulled them back so it would see him. "Hey!" He leaned closer and held up the dagger. "I ain't playin' here!"

The squib's breath rattled in response.

That odd rustling noise seemed to be coming from everywhere. Had it been there before? How long had he been down here? Felt like for-fucking-ever, and he was beyond ready to get back to his ship. He sneered at the dying squib. If it wouldn't answer his questions, Crow had no further use for it. Lip curled, he shoved the blade under the little fucker's chin, then wiped its blood on its clothes.

No one said a word.

Crow got to his feet, glaring at Walker and the junior officer. "What are you standing there for? Get me another one!"

He watched them go, pissed beyond all reckoning, then flicked his gaze back to the dead alien. The one survivor they'd found so far, and it wouldn't cooperate.

The sibilation grew louder and he raised his head, trying to locate the source.

"Harley, what is that noise?"

The commander squinted and cocked an ear as if he were listening. "I don't hear anything, Cap."

"Don't fuck with me, Harley. I know you can hear it."

"What does it sound like?"

How could he describe it? Crow turned, listening. It was coming from the rocks. Not the cave, but the cave-*in*. He frowned, walked toward the choking rubble. Was that…voices?

Zhachi!

Hair rose on the back of his neck, spreading gooseflesh down his arms and a chill down his spine. What the hell—

Ne'fasjtalen, sh'toi!

A hand landed on his shoulder.

Crow whirled, knife at the ready.

Harley reeled back. "Whoa, Captain! Take it easy! It's me!"

"Whadaya want?"

"You went all quiet, so I asked if you want us to clear this tunnel and check it for more survivors," Harley said. "You didn't answer. I was trying to make sure you're okay."

Crow panted. Readings in his faceplate redlined. What had just happened? Whispers fluttered at the edge of his thoughts, and he eyed the blockage once more, then pushed past his second. "I'm fine. Let's go."

"Did you want me to open up this tunnel?"

"Not yet."

"But we found no survivors anywhere else. It stands to reason there might be more behind—"

Crow flew at him with a roar. "Is there a *problem* with your hearing, Commander?"

Harley flinched. "No, sir."

"Then let's go!"

Crow stomped off toward the crystal cavern and the surface beyond. He couldn't *wait* to get off this rock. That bourbon sounded better by the minute.

chapter 21

Bel-Rhovan, Bejami
<u>Unit #N119-F42-39, Galen's Flat</u>

GALEN HUNCHED OVER THE FRAME loom while he selected a dozhan leaf and began to weave it through the warp. The gentle sound of rain with a flute's airy notes trilled and quavered their peaceful way through the flat. Galen hummed along off-key as he worked.

Alira didn't know it yet, but he intended this weaving for her: a mat of interwoven dozhan, painted with Bregainan dream patterns in unammi pigments. After all, she had provided the leaves and the paints for the project. She always had some such treasure to offer, items that often ended up in his artwork. Like the collection of framed pieces on his bedroom wall, woven from leaves, seed heads, feathers, and skins gathered on Alira's windwalks. Why her mother and others in the city found this so offensive about her he'd never know, but he admired the fact that she did it anyway. Every delivery came with stories of how she found the items, which made them all the more interesting. By the time he wove them into projects or painted them onto canvas, he sometimes lost the exact connection between prize and story. What remained was the clear recollection of every conversation her stories prompted between the two of them. She was the first person with whom he could meander through philosophic discourse without fearing censure.

The happy blush of affection and pleasure lit his body. What would Alira think of the dream symbols? Botha, a Bregainan elder and Galen's friend, had taught him their mystical meanings over the seasons of their friendship. Galen had shared a few with Alira, but this painting would depict them all. Then he could teach her their meanings so she could use them when interpreting her provocative dreams. She always seemed to welcome any opportunity to learn human oddities.

A chitter announced the arrival of a communique. "Answer, voice only," Galen said without taking his eyes off his work.

"Galen?"

His hands froze. "Nyros? Is that you?"

"Yes."

Galen straightened, his confusion tinting the light around him. "Where are you?"

"Downstairs."

"I didn't know you were coming."

"May I see you?"

"Is everything all right at home? Is Alira…."

"Please. It's important."

Nyros hadn't answered the implied question. Galen's heart thumped. "Allow entry to Rhys Bishop."

"Thank you. I'll be there in a few moments."

Galen furrowed his brow. Whatever the news, it must be bad. Even when they were friends, Nyros never came unannounced. Bejami was nowhere near the center of the colonial sector. Its closest neighbor, outside their nearby sister-colony, lay at least a full day away. In fact, if Galen wasn't mistaken, Nyros had just come from Iridos—a four-and-a-half-day trip—which meant he had come here before going home to Harajüd. Galen's breath grew shallow in the surreal moments of his wait, hands clutched before him as he considered and discarded every possible ill that might have brought his former ally back to his door.

The chime trilled. Galen went to the hallway and called out entry. The moment the door closed, the human form of Rhys morphed into Nyros' natural unammi shape, displeasure written in blue ripples across the canvas of his skin. Galen gestured, bringing his visitor into the great room, but Nyros didn't take a cushion. Instead, he walked to the frame table, eyeing Galen's project.

"Alira gave you these things?"

"You know she did."

"You can't see her anymore."

Galen sighed. "You came all this way to revive that old argument?"

Nyros turned with a hard look. "You won't have a choice. She was forbidden to spend time with any outcasts, even me. The council won't allow her to come to you when next you're home."

"Why?"

"Influence from outsiders makes her noncompliant."

"That's nothing new."

Nyros ignored him. "They must get her under control. She needs to establish normal relationships with acceptable members of society, and our interference is making that impossible. I'm her brother and even I agreed to this, for her sake. If you care, stop encouraging her."

"You speak of Alira as if she were a youngling. She's been frem a long time now. She can make up her own mind."

"And you act as if she can defy the council without consequence. Galen...." Nyros paused, the wrinkle in his forehead more pronounced than usual. "I believe they may mitigate her soon if she doesn't listen to them."

White shot through Galen's display. "She has argued with Lurien ever since I've known her. The council's threatened her almost as long. What makes you think they are serious this time?"

"You didn't see her. She raged at our mother's order to stay away from outcasts and mitigants."

Galen nodded. "That sounds about right."

"See?" Nyros waved a red arm. "This is what I'm talking about. You are almost as bad as she is, thinking such behavior's acceptable. If you weren't outcast, they would have mitigated you already."

Galen's fingers had gone numb from clutching them so hard. He took a deep breath, loosed his grip, and dropped his hands to his sides. Blood tingled back into his digits.

"When I took this role, I told myself I was like you. That I was doing it to save others from being banished to live among aliens. I didn't realize the truth until after I met Alira. I knew I wouldn't be able to avoid mitigation. You're right about me. I took this path of service because I'm a coward."

Nyros gaped at him.

"Your sister's audacity is one of her many remarkable traits," Galen said, pressing his advantage. "She is convinced mitigation is wrong. That we should be allowed to change and grow. The council will never permit such an evolution for our people, but Alira believes in her resistance."

"Conformity makes us who we are. It isn't wrong. She's screaming into the wind."

"That is your opinion. I agree with your sister. I would help if I could, but I'm not sure how except to believe in her, to listen and support her even when I fear for her future. I admire her courage. It's something we should all strive to emulate."

Nyros shook his head. "Then my trip to Bejami was for nothing." He pointed at the table frame. "You should make the best of these supplies. You aren't likely to receive more. I expect by the time either of us make it back home, Alira will be changed beyond recognition." He pushed past his host, changing to his human persona as he went, then walked out of the flat.

Galen let out a long sigh and shook his hands, which had gripped one another again without his notice. Was Nyros right?

As a youngling, Galen had seen a frem in the city whose behavior always seemed off-center. Once, a few cycles before his Rite of Decision, Galen saw that male make a scene over some argument in the dining hall. Soon after Galen joined the pilots, he had left to work with his mentor off-world for a time and had forgotten all about the odd frem. When next Galen saw him, the frem's former uniqueness had vanished behind a dutiful green facade. No facial expression beyond acceptance of his surroundings. Now, an image of Alira came unbidden to Galen's thoughts, her lustrous array of color suffused by green, no joy of reunion in her eyes when she saw him.

He shuddered, wringing his hands again. If the council was so close to judging her, there wasn't much he could do to stop it. Even should he be allowed to return ahead of schedule, what could he hope to accomplish? The council never would listen to an outcast's opinion on unammi social principle. Galen could hear them now. *You chose to leave. Your voice carries no weight here.*

He could ask Alira to yield, at least a little, to avoid the treatment, but he doubted it would work. The one time he'd tried to pull away from her was the sole instance of real contention they had ever shared. When he explained it was for her own good, she'd accused him of arrogance in presuming to know what was right for her. He listened with growing wonder as she explained how she alone was responsible for the difficulties she encountered, how she created them herself and must fix them herself, and how time spent with Galen was one of the few things that made sense in her life. He'd known then he would do whatever she asked.

No. Alira wasn't going to change without a fight. Nor did he believe he could convince her to leave Iridos and live as an outcast with him. She did her best to tread the precarious ridge between compliance and rebellion, but she'd always been fearless.

Galen grunted. The thought of Alira being mitigated consumed him, yet her stubborn persistence was the selfsame quality that made her unique. To forfeit her conviction for the comfort of those around her would obliterate her sense of self as much as mitigation would. Worse, in fact. Surrender was self-inflicted. Alira would never be able to live with the sure knowledge she had sacrificed her own principles for something that contradicted everything she held dear.

Speaking to her, regardless of how much he wanted to do so, was out of the question. Instead, he stretched his body from 146 centimeters to 168, fleshed his weight to a full seventy-seven kilos, and pushed strands of silky black hair from his scalp, forming it into a braid that hung down his back. Visual acuity diminished as he darkened his silver eyes to a rich golden hue, folding the skin above them to touch the lids. A final nudge lengthened his sweeping lashes as he approached the holorecorder.

"Comm, Botha," he said in his human persona's melodious voice.

A moment passed before his friend's leathery visage appeared in the holo. "Oho, Tenzin! You like to surprise me! What good news puts your face in my vid?"

Tenzin forced a smile. "I'd like to visit Bregaina for a while. Would that be permitted? Or is the guesthouse in use?"

"Tenzin is always welcome! If the guesthouse were full, we would take the others into our own homes to open it for you. Your timing is excellent. Bh'tati season starts in a few days. You can stay and help with the plucking and the eating! When should we expect you?"

"I'll be there tomorrow."

"Good! Good!" Botha paused, squinting. "I think there is something behind this visit, eh? A bad fish in your net?"

"I can't hide anything from you, can I, Baba?"

Botha shrugged. "Why would you want to? If I can help, I will. Now, put your things in a pack and come. Wait—I've thought it over. Don't bring anything. We will provide whatever you need. And don't worry. Between your knife and mine, we will cut that fish loose!"

Tenzin signed off and resumed his natural shape, along with the guilty struggle that always accompanied a trip to Bregaina. He wanted to confide all to Botha. What would it feel like to have a confidant in the outside world? Someone who knew who he was and trusted him anyway? He'd been tempted before but always resisted, not for his own sake but for Botha's, and the whole of Bregaina. If word got back to Iridos that he had let slip his mask, the council would send someone to fix his mistake. They pounded into the pilots' heads that the unammi mystique, once fractured, could never be restored. Galen might gain brief comfort in a sympathetic ear, but Botha would pay the penalty.

That was too high a price.

Galen rose and began preparation for his trip.

chapter 22

THE SOUND OF SHIFTING ROCK roused Alira and she raised her head. Her own injuries healed, or well on the way, she watched from her supine position while workers shifted debris to free others in the chamber. She lay back, waiting.

Dreams of the ruined domes and dead unammi drifted through her memory. Alira dived into the joinedmind and reached for her mother but sensed no response. Either Lurien was unconscious, or she was too distracted to feel Alira's call. Or—

No. Lurien was still alive. If she wasn't, Alira would know.

She pushed the thought away.

"Napping, are you?"

Alira's eyes snapped open at the familiar voice. "Ijydin! You're unhurt!"

Her friend shrugged. "Wish I could say the same about others. Let's free you so you can stop shirking." She nodded to Yoloron, then the two of them lifted the stone and added it to a growing pile at one side of the chamber.

Yoloron squatted beside Alira and leaned close. "How are you?"

"Better. How long since…."

"A cycle, maybe a little more," Ijydin said.

Alira winced. "How bad is it?"

"We're still digging out as many survivors as we can find. Tunnels leading past the echo chamber or south out of the dormitories are collapsed."

"Did…did everyone make it into the tunnels before it was too late?" Alira swallowed in a dry throat and searched Yoloron's face. "Did Lurien?"

"We haven't seen her yet," Yoloron said, her voice full of the compassion her features lacked. "She told me she'd wait in the guildhouse while the council decided your judgment. I assume she was still there when the attack came."

Purple and white painted Alira's limbs.

"Don't," Ijydin urged. "Grieving can wait. Even a tracker as good as Yoloron can't locate all of us at once. We're still uncovering survivors." She held out a waterskin. "Here. Small sips. Take your time, but don't drink it all. Our supply is limited."

Alira sipped, waiting a few heartbeats before sipping again. Water had never tasted so good. She forced herself to wait before drinking more.

"Have search teams made it as far as the guildhouse yet?"

"No," Yoloron said. "There aren't many of us to do the work."

Alira sipped again and gave the waterskin back to Ijydin. She needed to gather her wits, get back on her feet. If she could get some food in her belly, she would be strong enough to join the search. They needed every available frem.

"We still have lights. They didn't disable our wind turbines?"

Yoloron shook her head. "Not yet. Some of the light globes on upper levels are out, but most down here survived, along with filters and ventilation pumps. Those are powered by generators on the other side of the ridge. The attack must have destroyed the ones in the valley, and the humans haven't found the rest." The elder sighed. "Let's hope they don't."

"They're still here?"

"They aren't going anywhere." Ijydin jerked to her feet. "Not until they take all our hematium."

More of Alira's memory trickled back, a human voice echoing across the unammi joinedmind in the first few moments of the attack. Her eyes widened, skin pulsing white. "The miners!"

"They're in the fluorspar pits," Yoloron assured her, "too far south for the humans to detect them. They'll return once the danger is past."

"What are the chances the humans will find us?"

Ijydin shrugged. "Skalar's reputation says he wouldn't leave anyone to expose him later, but we're working on it."

Skalar. That's the third time she'd heard the name. "How?"

"When they came below ground," Ijydin said, "Dyson set up teams beside every tunnel blockage we could reach to help drive away the sh'toi. I helped as much as I could. Projection isn't my best talent, but I promise you the humans I reached will live in fear for their lives every second they spend under the surface here. Frem with more skill took their cue from history and planted seeds in the humans' minds for horrific dreams. Others made them more susceptible to the radiation from their own bombs."

"Radiation?" White speckles raced across Alira's skin.

Yoloron stood, brushing the dust from her hands, then helped Alira to her feet. "Nothing we can't handle. You'll see. Now, we should get back to work. Do you feel up to helping?"

"Oh yes. I'd like to serve on a rescue team."

"Come on, then. Dyson and Rakalesh are organizing the emergency efforts. After you eat, we'll ask them where you can be most helpful."

A chill ran through Alira at the thought of seeing the councilors again. If the attack had come even a short while later…although she hadn't felt any different. Still didn't. Yoloron and Ijydin spoke to her as they always did. In fact, the healers' behavior had seemed odd during the treatment, as if they were confused. Did her mitigation fail, as her Adjustment had? Her mind raced ahead. Would they try again right away? Or wait until this nightmare was over?

She reached again for Lurien. Still no trace of her presence. "Ama! Stay safe!" Alira said, her voice soft. "We're coming for you!"

chapter 23

TWO MEMBERS OF ALIRA'S TEAM carried away another injured survivor. It had taken a full cycle to convince Rakalesh and Dyson to assign her to a rescue team. Since, Alira and the others had worked their way up to the level beneath the surface buildings. Once there, progress slowed to a chauf beetle's pace. Humans patrolling breaks in the ceiling overhead presented an unquestionable danger. Unammi camouflage could blotch their skin to mimic surroundings, make them blend into the background so they all but vanished. Still, they couldn't rescue any survivors in those zones. Humans above might see rocks that appeared to move by themselves or debris that fell from piles, evidence to indicate the presence of survivors. Passing each collapse in the danger zones, they paused to feel for buried unammi, sending mental comfort and conceptual explanations to those they found, then moved on.

Her team had started half a cycle ago with six members. At the moment, it was down to Ijydin and Alira. The others would rejoin the effort as soon as they delivered the injured to the healers, but Alira didn't wait. Instead, she fluctuated her dermal pattern to mimic her surroundings, then loped in uneven, erratic steps along the ledge, staying in the shadows and avoiding obstacles. Above, she heard movement through the gash in the chamber's ceiling. She looked up. A human guard faced the ruined city.

Sh'toi. She should kill it where it stood. She stopped, focusing on its frail physique, deciding.

Ijydin squatted beside her.

Don't.

Ijydin was right. They had more important things to do. The humans could pay later. Alira continued down the gallery.

Ahead, out of sight of the gap, they resumed their normal skin patterns and moved to the first pile. A body, already past its deshtant. They left it and continued to the next collapse, liberating three survivors, two of whom were able-bodied. They helped the third toward the healers.

Yoloron rejoined their team and even Dyson came to help. Together they worked their way pile-by-pile across the level. Find and dig. Find and dig. Find and dig. Rescue and recruit or send back to the healers or see that it was too late and move on. Numbness crept into Alira. She stopped and glanced around, getting her bearings. Nothing was where it should be, but she thought they might be close to where the clerical guild had stood. She reached for Lurien again, calling to her across the collective. Still no response. Blue flickers joined Alira's display.

At a ledge blocked by wreckage, she slowed, straining her eyes and reaching with her other senses. In the limited ambient light from their bodies, she saw no safe path through the debris, nor could she sense any survivors inside. Ijydin came up beside her. Yoloron and Dyson weren't far behind.

Alira tipped her head back, then leaned out and searched the area in the gap below them. A whole building had come through the surface, then punched through this ledge and now rested precariously on the one below. The upper levels of it stood ruined, but not buckled. Her mother might be in there. "Is that the clerical guildhouse?" Alira asked, her voice low.

Ijydin scanned the area. "I can't tell. Everything looks different. But we're blocked here. We'll need to go around."

Alira whirled. "No! It took us so long to get here, we have to try!"

Ijydin flushed with lavender. "Alira—"

"Don't say it. There has to be a way inside." Alira eyed the line of debris from edge to edge on the side closest to them. No opening was apparent. Alira began pulling stones away from the base of the pile. Maybe there was an aperture behind some of the remains. If she could find it—

"Alira."

"What?"

Dyson's voice came closer. "What are you doing?"

"Checking for a way in." Alira's hands kept moving, fingers scrabbling against the wedged rocks, splitting and peeling her skin and nails as she worked.

"Do you think that is wise?"

"Wise?" she said. "What if there are survivors inside who are near death? We might not sense them! We need a visual search."

"How? It will be pitch black. We need lanterns."

She went back to digging. "I won't need lights to see an unammi in the dark."

Ijydin grasped her arm. "You *will* need light to see where you're going. You're putting yourself at risk. Come on. Let's go around."

Alira yanked herself free and pulled away another stone, revealing a dark gap. An opening. She set about widening it. "See? I knew it was here! Come with me! The more of us there are, the more light our bodies can provide...."

Hands gripped her arms on both sides, but she slid her feet into the crack and went limp, slipping out of their grasp. The drop into the dark pit felt like one of her dreams, like she might fall forever, until she landed. Rocky debris scraped both ankles and rasped up the side of one thigh. Sharp pain speared her leg. In her chest, another rib snapped. No matter. She'd deal with that later.

The sharp voices of unhappy elders echoed down through the hole. "Bring a rope," she called. Scuffling sounds filtered down from above. The others followed, no doubt to stop her. She hurried to move beyond their reach. Dust tickled her nose and throat and set her coughing despite the stabs of pain in her chest. Every step sent searing spikes down her leg—broken or sprained, she couldn't tell—and she slowed down to grope through darkness lit only by her body's display. Halfway through the second room, she spotted a fallen stone, part of its inscription intact. "…jha yetandu."

Alira had seen that stone in the main room of the clerical guildhouse all her life, its sacred passage a mantra for the guild. Estobael isja yetandu, Sintuna ba fojenas. *Where the mind finds a need, the heart opens a way.* A small, strangled sound escaped her, and she pressed forward, oblivious to pain or pursuers or human threats, delving deeper into the wreckage.

"Alira!" someone hissed behind her. "Come back here!"

She ignored the command. Lurien was here. Alira felt it.

"Ama!"

Quelling voices called to Alira as she felt her way through the next room, aiming for a spot across the way that seemed darker than the rest, another door perhaps. Something caught at her feet halfway across the tilted floor, and she fell with a yelp, ripping the flesh on both palms. She pushed herself back up and kept going. She'd been right. It *was* a door and beyond—

A victim, half-buried, flashed in its winking deshtant on the other side of the skewed space.

No. It was another cleric. It had to be. "I found someone!" She pushed forward on screaming legs, breathing in sharp gasps. "Come help me! I can't see who it is!"

Alira reached the body before they caught her. Fingers slick with blood found the silken cord around its neck, the bauble gone, broken in her fall perhaps. Whimpering, she threw aside pinning debris and rolled the victim over to see who it was.

A low keening moan welled up inside her. Alira fell to her knees among the jagged fragments and dragged her mother into her arms, rocking the corpse as if Lurien might awaken. The cry rose to a screeching wail that drowned the scuffles behind her. Alira ignored the elders' shushings and Ijydin's warning that her shrieks would alert the humans. Her mother was gone! She had returned to Musju, and no one had watched her passing, or even spoken her name!

"Ama, no no no! I didn't mean it, Ama, I'll do what you say, just *don't leave—"*

She drew a ragged breath and the dark world faded around her. Dyson and Yoloron groped in her mind, subduing her. Alira hugged Lurien closer, fought their attempts.

"Stop," she wailed. "Don't! I need to...."

chapter 24

<u>Bregaina, Bejami</u>

TENZIN FLEW HIS RENTED JUMPER out over Dairnen Bay and circled around to approach the village from the ocean side. Spread before him, Bregaina squatted above the delta, its white domed structures gleaming in the sun. He had heard of other tidal settlements, but this was the only one he had ever seen. Raised platforms lifted every structure above the islets and inland channels so that the tide could shift unimpeded. Even the landing dock stood on pylons far above the high-water marks. Anchored gardens bobbed about, buoyed by the tide while the villagers worked their crops.

The region's ever-changing landscape provided a constant reminder of forces at work on the river. There, between his position and the landing dock, gathered sediment peeked in ridges above the water's surface as the tide retreated. One day, those fragile sandbars would grow large enough to rise above the waterline even at high tide. Then they could be seeded with grasses and anchored to stabilize the entire delta. At some point in the distant future, the shoreline would creep far enough out that the villagers no longer would need to worry about the tide, or the Baisken would shift its course and find a new outlet, but not before Botha and many generations of his descendants had moved on.

Through the window, he saw the Baba's boat on its way to fetch him. Tenzin smiled. Visiting Bregaina was better than going to Iridos where even his own ama and siblings greeted him with reserve. Here, villagers welcomed him as if he belonged. He set the jumper down on the landing platform and secured its systems. Tenzin trusted the villagers, but younglings anywhere might be tempted to explore an accessible ship. He grabbed his pack and stepped out into a breeze thick with the tang of briny marsh. For Tenzin, like the residents, it smelled like home.

At the bottom of the ladder, the village elder's brown face crinkled. White teeth shone up at Tenzin.

"Hellooo up there! What are you waiting for? Come! My boat wants you." Botha's voice boomed across the water, echoing back from the pylons and moored craft.

Tenzin called a greeting as he climbed down into the dinghy and took a seat.

"I am glad to see you in the flesh! A holo-Tenzin is not so satisfying." Botha's laughter rumbled out of his chest while he poled the boat away from the dock.

"Thank you for your hospitality."

"Psht. You are welcome always. You should take a home here. We need new blood, and yours is honest. Not like what the Colony would send." Botha winked. "But that is not a topic for this day. The guest house is waiting. How long will you stay?"

Tenzin hesitated. He'd *like* to stay indefinitely. But he needed a guarantee of privacy. He could maintain Tenzin's mask for a day, two at the most, before he would require rest. He always worried someone would see him in his natural form and start asking questions. "I am uncertain."

Botha nodded. "Don't worry, my friend. I know you need seclusion. You will have it, on my word."

Tenzin gaped.

The elder lowered his head toward Tenzin. "You think I don't know there is a secret sunk in the banks of your soul? I don't know what it is. Unless you decide to dig it up with me, I respect that. But your eyes and your heart sing their own songs. You can't bury those." He poled the boat under a village structure. The shade cooled them both for a moment until they emerged on the other side. "Besides, whatever brought you here still needs deciding. Yes?"

A sigh escaped Tenzin's lips. "Yes."

"Hmm. This vexation. It involves your lover?"

"Yes."

Their boat reached the guesthouse, and Botha tied it to a cleat, then followed Tenzin up the ladder to the deck. "Put your things away later. Fill my ears."

Tenzin dropped his pack to the deck and took a seat. Now that he was here, he wasn't sure how to explain his fear without revealing too much.

"I'm torn, Botha."

"Yes. You have that look."

"Alira is unique. She doesn't conform to the expectations of her village elders, or her family. It's a constant source of contention between them."

"Does she wag her difference like bait in front of the others?"

"No. She isn't trying to start trouble, but she can't give them what they want without killing who she is. Her concessions to her own beliefs and needs are never enough. The elders want full conformity. They treat her uniqueness like a virus, like it might destroy the whole village."

Botha nodded, sunlight sparkling on the gold in his earlobe. "It will."

Tenzin frowned. "It—what?"

"It is a fact of evolution, my friend. If you plant a single red bh'tati in a patch of white bh'tati, soon blossoms will burst with all the shades of red you could want. Those who favor the white lilies will shake a fist and say they're ruined."

"That's change, not destruction."

"They are the same thing. To the larva, the moth is an assassin."

Botha's point lodged against Tenzin's convictions, poking him like a stone in his shoe. He gazed out over the sinking tide. Receding water hissed against the sand. Wading bala grawked their contentment as their long bills plucked crustaceans from the exposed banks.

"If Alira won't conform, they'll *take* who she is. *Make* her who they want. That would be like the moth becoming the caterpillar." Tenzin shook his head. "As a village elder, do you believe it would be a fair treatment?"

Botha seemed to consider the question. "I judge no elder until I know her village and no village until I know its elders. Your woman already has wings. Can she not fly to another village?"

"She chooses not to. She believes she isn't alone among her people. She wants to demonstrate that change can be beneficial and show how one voice can make a difference."

"Then fear for her. An infection must be removed or the whole will suffer."

"So, the good of the many outweighs the good of the one?"

Botha shrugged. "If the many are served well, yes."

Tenzin shot out of his seat and stalked to the railing, hands gripping the wood as if he would rip it loose. His sudden movement startled a bala that had crept near the guesthouse. Great green wings lifted the waterfowl in a squawking flutter of iridescence as it took flight. "You believe she is wrong to live her life by her own standards?"

"Those were not my words, Tenzin. I like your woman already. It takes courage to live your truth even when you know it might eat you whole."

Tenzin whirled. "They can't both be correct."

"Which has the greater right to freedom, predator or prey?" Green eyes peered out of Botha's brown countenance, a trace of smile on his mouth. "You cannot see the whole tree when your nose is against the bark."

A gust of wind pushed Tenzin's hair across his forehead and he brushed it aside. For a while, he listened to the bala, punctuated by rattling dune grass and chittering muil that swooped and dove for fish over the deeper water. Alira would love it here. If she managed to avoid mitigation until he returned, he might convince her to come here with him. They could make a life on their own. Couldn't they?

The whole argument would be moot if Nyros had been right. It didn't matter anyway. He'd never convince her to leave Iridos.

"What if the many aren't served well, Botha? What if the restrictions hold them back from a better life? What should the one do then?"

"The many must speak for themselves. If they feel tied back, your woman may be the knife to cut them free. Remember, my friend, a blade that severs bonds can also part flesh. Beware your woman does not cut off her own head. She can't prove her point from the next world."

A shout drew Tenzin's attention, but Botha grinned and got to his feet. "That would be *my* woman calling me home. When Bika speaks, all her partners listen. Tenzin," Botha began, then stopped, one hand on Tenzin's shoulder. "More talk can come later. Food waits in your house. Eat. Sleep. Think. We will hold space for you to dive deep."

Tenzin sat on the deck past the fall of twilight, caught between respecting Alira all the way to the treatment ritual or removing whatever influence he held to make her avoid such a fate. Somehow, that seemed a worse betrayal. So often they had discussed how far the unammi could grow given the chance, and every time he'd expressed his agreement with her opinions. How could he insinuate disapproval now by walking away? And anyway, his withdrawal would be a puny bluff against the threat of mitigation. If the one didn't stop her, neither would the other.

In the end it wouldn't matter. Alira would do what she thought best. He, and everyone else close to her, would have to live with the result.

chapter 25

<u>Iridos</u>

ALIRA'S BODY, WHITE AND STRUGGLING, jerked upright and was pressed back down.

"Calm yourself."

Reality mingled with nightmare. She stopped fighting and took in the faces hovering over her. Yoloron. Ijydin.

Behind them, healers observed from a distance, their bodies a physical barrier between their injured charges and the crazed misfit who might at any moment lose control. Again. Memory flooded back, saturating Alira's display with vivid purple.

Lurien.

"How do you feel?" Yoloron inquired.

What kind of question was that? She wasn't supposed to *feel* anything, was she? And, at the moment, she didn't. The deluge of grief and regret had washed over and through her leaving a yawning chasm in its wake. All she felt now was…empty. Alira regarded her newfound detachment with numb curiosity, holding it up like a lens through which she viewed those around her with greater clarity. Yoloron and her questions. Others nearby with physical injuries, who watched to see if she would break down again. Ijydin, who waited to see whether her rebellious friend would be mitigated after all.

If so, Alira hoped it would be soon. She didn't want to care when the pain and sorrow rushed back. She didn't want to feel different. She was tired of setting an example. None of it mattered anymore. Her mother was dead, the unammi shattered, their city in ruins. Humans waited to find and kill the rest of them. What use was there in being aware for that?

"I asked you a question."

"I'm fine," Alira replied.

"And you remember Lurien—"

"Is dead. I'm aware." The acknowledgement sliced into her calm. "You can tell the council I won't oppose them again."

"I'll tell them your words."

Alira focused on the elder. "Please ask them to put me back to work."

Yoloron exchanged a look with Ijydin. "You need to rest."

Alira turned away. "Whatever you think is best."

After a moment, Yoloron rose and left the chamber. Ijydin sat on the side of the cot, her hues fluttering with affection. "I didn't know who would come out the other side of this affair, whether there would be some stranger in your skin, wearing your face." Ijydin paused, considering. "I'm glad it's still you."

"How long did I sleep?"

"We pulled you out of the guildhouse ruins a full cycle ago."

"What did I miss?"

Ijydin hesitated, probably afraid of setting Alira off again. Alira sighed.

"Humans have overrun a portion of the city," Ijydin said. "Everyone not doing some essential task is sitting at the tunnel obstructions. We're few now, even with the injured we've freed from the wreckage. But...."

Alira waited.

"The sh'toi are taking our irolium."

The news slid off Alira's numbness. "It doesn't matter. What else?"

"Doesn't matter?" Ijydin wrinkled her nose at Alira as if she were some strange new reptile. "You aren't worried about the loss? What it might mean?"

"Younglings' tales."

"You don't know. That lore goes back a long way. If it's true, then without those stones, we won't be able to heal or morph or read each other or commune in muñara or the joinedmind. No more readers or truthseers or locators. We'll be dimmed, as ordinary as the humans!"

Alira waited for some feeling to swell in her. Nothing came.

Ijydin's frown deepened.

Alira could have said the humans would kill them all anyway and the irolium couldn't save them, but it would take too much effort. That didn't matter, either.

"I've been distracting myself by imagining what punishments the colonies would enforce if they learned what Skalar did here," Ijydin said.

"Why should we care? Our city will still lie in ruins. Our people will still be dead." Lurien would still be gone.

"I know." Lavender freckles fluttered across Ijydin's cheeks.

"Why would they punish him at all? His people call him 'admiral.' Isn't that like an elder?"

"He's the leader of a Trader faction."

"Rakalesh said they're privateers."

Ijydin seemed to consider this. "The term fits. They're holdouts from old human militias. When the colonials disbanded their militaries, some of the soldiers went mercenary. They didn't want to merge back into society, so they built their own ships and began running their own trade in the black market. Don't ask me what a black market is. I can't tell you all the things at one time."

Imagine that, humans not wanting to conform. Maybe she and this admiral had more in common than she'd like to admit. Was she a monster, too? "You once told me humans confined their rule-breakers."

"Not Traders. It's rare for one of them to be punished. Maybe half the human worlds contract with Traders. The factions can do whatever they want on their own land. They can't be prosecuted unless they break the law outside their own bases."

"Iridos isn't Trader land."

"It isn't in any colonial jurisdiction, either. Skalar shouldn't be able to get away with this, but I'm afraid he will."

Human societies would permit the perpetrator of this horrific attack to go free? "You think he won't be punished?"

"Who would know? Other humans never come here."

Skalar's people had. Others might, too. "They'll wonder what happened when we stop sending supplies or pilots for our regular trade." Alira's eyes widened. Pilots. Nyros! Galen! An abrupt flush warmed her neck and face.

Ijydin pressed Alira down onto the cot. "I already thought of the pilots, but there is nothing we can do about them. The humans would know if we sent a message from here. Even after they've gone, it won't be safe. I'd bet credits they'll leave behind relays to detect and report any signs of survivors, which means no long-range comms, no departures via our usual routes. But I doubt they have tech all the way around the planet. Our best bet is to fly low, away from their hardware, and leave Iridos space from the ne'ani side. Once I'm far enough away, I should be able to send a warning."

"Why can't we disable their devices?"

"If all their relays went offline at once," Ijydin said, her tone pitched as if Alira might have lost her mind, "that might reveal our presence. Don't you think?"

Alira's throat tightened. By the time the humans left, it might be too late for the pilots. There would be nothing left of the unammi. The stragglers of her people rode the current of Musju, guided by Na'Staani toward something they couldn't see. Indifference stilled the tiny worm of fear that sought to burrow past her apathy, but it wouldn't last. If she had been unconscious, unable to object for more than a full cycle, why hadn't they mitigated her like they had promised to do?

A hush moved through the room, and Ijydin's weight lifted away from the bed. Alira watched as councilor Rakalesh approached, her aged silver gaze riveted on Alira's. She dragged her leaden limbs into action and clambered from the bed, her gaze averted out of respect. By the time Rakalesh reached the end of the cot, every other sound had stilled.

"I didn't expect you to come, Na'ama."

"I shouldn't have. Far more pressing matters require my attention, but I wanted to see your reaction when I explained what you should have known. Your selfish outburst could have devastated what little we have left. What have you to say for yourself?"

Alira sighed. She just wanted to sleep. "I wasn't thinking clearly."

"You weren't thinking at all. Yoloron tells me you claim to be fine. She thinks we should give you another chance. I came to see for myself."

Another chance? No mitigation? Alira risked a peek at the councilor's expression. No clue to her thoughts rested there, nor in the swirls of green and blue and purple beneath her skin.

Rakalesh perched at the end of the cot and gestured. "Sit."

Alira lowered herself to the pallet. "I'm surprised to awaken intact."

"What do you mean?"

"Why didn't you mitigate me? Ijydin says I was unconscious for a whole cycle. It would have been a perfect opportunity."

"I thought you spurned the treatment. I believe you called it horrific, demeaning, unenlightened."

"That was before," Alira said to her lap. In her mind, she felt the elder's deft touch. Gifted with the ability to delve into another's awareness, Rakalesh could see behind the mask to the fears and doubts hidden from others. No matter. Alira had nothing left to hide.

"They tell me you've been dreaming."

"I was, Councilor."

"'Was'? The dreams are gone?"

Should she speak the truth? Or a lie? The councilor would know, either way. Alira hesitated a bit too long, and Rakalesh sighed.

"I see. Yet you say you are sound."

"Did you know my mother dreamed?" A flutter of gray in her peripheral vision told Alira the councilor hadn't known this about her friend Lurien. "It's true. She told me herself, even said my dreams bore similarity to hers."

"Lurien…never…mentioned—"

"Have your advisors revealed the content of my dreams?"

Rakalesh paused. "Some."

"In the cycles leading up to the attacks, I saw the destruction of our city, charred bodies raining down on the ground around me while unidentified blasts leveled the domes and every structure inside them." Alira dared to meet her eyes. "Do you still believe I should ignore my dreams?"

Silence met her confession. Everyone in the room seemed to hang on her words. Alira looked back to Rakalesh. "I'm better. My breakdown was unfortunate. I was tired, weakened, and in shock. It was too much, but I will honor my limits in the future and will comply with what you want of me. If you can't trust me to do this, then give me the treatment and be done with it. But allow me to go back to work. I need the distraction and you need every available pair of hands."

Rakalesh peered past Alira's purple facade and into her thoughts and intentions across their joinedmind. Alira again sensed the councilor's light mental touch before Rakalesh pulled them both ankle-deep into Musju's flow. Alira gasped. She'd never been taken into meditation by another before, didn't even know it could be done. Stunned, she waited while Rakalesh tested her resolve. Alira couldn't say how much time passed before she felt the cot beneath her again.

"I will allow it, daughter of Lurien," Rakalesh said, then turned to Ijydin. "You will stay with her every moment. Fetch immediate help if necessary."

Ijydin nodded, but Alira frowned.

"No treatment?"

"No. We need you."

"You need *me*?" Gray patterns flitted down Alira's arms. "Why?"

Rakalesh flashed a momentary gray before she shot to her feet. "We need every survivor."

Alira's mind swirled with confusion as Rakalesh left the room. The councilor hadn't meant to say that. Alira was sure of it.

Ijydin swooped down to thump the cot with an open hand. Alira jumped and drew back from her friend, who pointed at the bed.

"Hah! You can't keep her any longer. She is going back to work now!"

Alira shook her head.

Ijydin shrugged. "What are you waiting for? Let's go get an assignment."

chapter 26

New Canaan, Harajüd
<u>Admiral Skalar's Private Residence</u>

HANDS WRAPPED AROUND THE BAR, Skalar readied himself for one last rep in this set of deadlifts. One deep breath, blow out the last, tighten all the right muscles, and *lift*. His body straightened as he pushed his abs into the stiff leather belt, keeping his back flat as he pulled two hundred and seventy kilos off the floor. Hold, lock hips, knees. After a moment, he eased the bar back to the floor, exhaling all the way down. Not bad. Next time, he'd try to work up to two eighty-five.

He unbuckled his belt, his fingers marking the leather with chalk. After a quick wipe-down, he hung it on the wall and paused to catch his breath before the last phase of his workout. Almost done now. Like that agent he had captured, Dodger. He doubted she'd last another session. She had finally provided valuable intel, and confirmed Skalar's suspicions regarding which competitor he should…thank…for this intrusion into his territory.

Skalar shaved his calluses, then filled a cup with cool water and drank. "Incoming communique," the TICS said.

"Point of origin?"

"Consortium battlecruiser, designation Leonid, Iridos orbit. Message recorded twelve hours ago by Captain Crow."

About damn time! The armada had to have been at Iridos for at least eight days now. Skalar had expected a report much sooner. "Receive."

Crow's image appeared in midair across the gym, facing the treadmill. "Sorry for the wait, Admiral. I'll feed you the bad news first. I had to flatten the city. Sorry, but the squibs have some badass weapons. They took out half the fleet before we could launch our LADRAS load. A light cruiser, two frigates and two haulers, poof." Crow's holographic head shook in apparent frustration. "I've never seen anything like it. They saw *cloaked* ships. I haven't found their arsenal yet so I can't explain. The one living squib we found died before I got any answers. I'm waiting until the crew's finished digging to explore blocked tunnels.

"I sent teams to salvage a few survivors from one of the lost ships. Most were too injured to work. Some died soon after. Half my original crew means too few hands. It's gonna take longer than I thought, but I'll have the crew dig until we run out of room to stash the haul.

"The good news is I found some sort of blue crystal in two of the caves. I didn't see much else of value yet, but once the crew explores the rest of this bug-hole, we might find more."

"I'm late sending this because things have gotten weird." The holo-Crow paced. "Correction. They've been weird since we arrived. Whatever tech they're using, it's new to us. There is some sort of unusual radiation on the surface. It isn't LADRAS leavings, at least not that alone. It's messing with our scans on the surface and making my crew nuts. Some are physically sick despite meds, but others are losing their shit for no clear reason. Sometimes they can go back to the mines after a rest, but once they get loopy, it always happens again until they're worthless down there. Whatever is going on has the crew spooked. Even the captains are raising eyebrows.

"I ran some searches on TICS to see if there might be some precedent for this effect but couldn't find any records. Maybe it's a weird combination of LADRAS and some as-yet-unidentified planetary phenomenon. I don't know. If we can figure it out, you might want to look into weaponizing it. Might come in handy to affect large numbers of people without a clear cause.

"Also, a squib pilot came out of interstel a few days back. We couldn't save the ship, but we took it out before it could transmit. If you're still going to remove the others from play as you suggested earlier, you might want to do it soon. I'll keep you posted. Crow out."

Skalar snorted. Five ships! Between those and the lost crewmen, the Iridos job had already cost him more than he'd planned and that was before he considered revenues the lost hauler might have brought in. Didn't much matter. He was committed to this path now.

How had the Iridosians gotten past his people's defenses? Jarod's new hulls may have held up better. Once he had the haul from Crow's mission, he could set Jarod on a prototype. A small one. If it panned out, he would replace all the lost ships with the new design.

In the meantime, he needed to ready the drop site for the haul. "TICS, attend."

"Ready."

"Comm Mira Cohen on secure frequency. Override lockouts. Connect now."

"Stand by."

While he waited, Skalar washed chalk off his hands, wiped down the bar, unloaded the weights, and stored the equipment. Maybe the Iridosian weapons created the odd radiation, but what kind of systems would have such a result? He frowned. No human defensive network would do that. Still, what else it could be? If it proved to be an alien tech, Skalar would have it first. After he learned how it functioned, perhaps he would sell it to other factions or other corpgovs.

He changed his shoes and stepped onto the treadmill for his cooldown.

A chitter preceded the TICS voice. "Commander Cohen."

"Receive." Skalar waited. Mira Cohen's image materialized where Crow's had been moments ago.

"You called, sir?"

"Cohen, are you alone?"

"Yes, sir."

"Good. I've got a job for you." The treadmill speed picked up and Skalar's feet began a light jog which didn't further accelerate his breathing. "Handpick a minimal team, including your most trusted officers, and a few techs, and report to our outpost. Run a bio sweep on approach. If anything shows up that ought not be there, come home on the double. Understand?"

"Yes, sir. What is the assignment once we're on the ground?"

"It's been empty for quite a while, so run basic tests on the core systems. Ensure everything is functional, make necessary repairs, set us up for more regular use. Lock down long-distance comms, as usual."

"Got it. Anything else?"

"Yes. Upgrade those antique internal sensors. Tell no one but your two most trusteds. In fact, once the upgrade is complete, get rid of the techs. No one is to know, not even other Consortium crew. Also," he rubbed a towel over his face, "one of our cargo ships will bring our latest take in a few weeks. You should expect other pilots, too, with…acquired ships. Stash them dark outside the shield."

"Yes sir. How long will we be there?"

"Pack for a three-month stay. But you should know this is the first step in a big plan. You're going to be instrumental to startup on full-time operations there. I might want you onsite longer."

"Thank you, sir," Cohen said. "I'm honored."

"Can you be ready to go in a week?"

"Yes, sir. Six days is plenty of time."

"Good. That's all for now. Comm me with questions. I'll speak to you before you go."

Skalar wiped his brow with the towel as the treadmill pace picked up again. He ran in silence for a while, then slowed for a drink.

"TICS, attend."

"Ready."

"Send voice-only communique to Erin Flannegan, Saacharis."

"Ready."

"Erin, effective immediately, ground all Iridosian pilots registered through the Saacharis Organization. Every port. Every station. Falsify safety inspections, make up legislation, whatever it takes to keep them in port. Don't compromise the Consortium or expose yourself. If any manage to make it there from another colony, do the same for them. Run dark. Need-to-know. Inform me at once of any trouble. Skalar out." He waited until the recording concluded, then added, "Gold cypher encryption. Confirm."

"Cypher confirmed. Send message?"

"Affirmative. Request receipt notification."

"Confirmed," replied the TICS. "Message sent."

He sent similar messages to contacts in other colonial governments.

"TICS, record voice-only communique, destination to be designated."

"Ready."

"This is base. Contact high-end colonial resources and co-opt their silence on a wide run. Once they're on board, seek and eliminate Iridosian pilots in your assigned region. Follow usual expungement protocols. Leave no trace. Take possession of Iridosian ships, then deliver to outpost. Signal receipt of communique and completion of task. Base out." He concluded with cypher keys and coded addresses, then sent the messages, already salivating at the prospect of getting his hands on those boats. The entire Iridosian fleet, as far as he knew, came to life by way of the Syndicate, a rival Trader faction under the command of Admiral Rizzo, a lunatic with a brilliant mind who excelled at two things: torture and building specialized small ships. Finally, Skalar would get a chance to examine her designs and figure out what made them unique.

His response to Crow came last.

"Your report is acknowledged. Leave no native survivors, no trace of your presence. Since you had to use force, run this as a black op. Apparently, you'll get to use the Danua Clan shuttle in your bay after all." His lip curled. "Make the exercise required viewing for all crew as incentive to keep this job to themselves when they return."

He concluded and sent the message, then slowed the treadmill speed to an easy walk. The Clan shuttle had been a stroke of genius if he did say so himself. First, it would divert suspicion for the destroyed city away from the Consortium. Second, it would serve payback to that faction for sending slavers into his territory.

Of course, it wouldn't come into play unless the colonials found the ruins on Iridos. If that happened, the Consortium would no longer be able to pose as Iridosians and sell hematium as if nothing had happened. No matter. Slinging incriminating evidence around a crime scene was only the beginning of his intentions for the Clan, who should have known better than to screw with the Consortium. Skalar had mutilated its last admiral for the same damn thing. Before he'd drawn his last breath, the bastard had understood the price of enslaving Malcolm Skalar's little sister. The whole thing was a nuisance. Skalar didn't have time to teach this lesson twice, but since he was being forced to it, he would start by sending their agent back to her home base in a whole shipment of small, refrigerated crates.

For the first time all day, Skalar smiled.

chapter 27

Iridos Orbit
<u>Aboard the Leonid</u>

CROW SNAPPED TO AWARENESS AND strained to determine what had dragged him back from a priceless moment of slumber. His ears detected individual sounds from the normal white noise of shipboard life: the hiss of air processors, the engines' sub-bass rumble, an occasional blip from the TICS. Nothing out of the ordinary. He closed his eyes again, chasing sleep.

Then some idiot with a death wish touched his door chime.

"Who is it?"

"Harley, sir."

Crow rolled out of bed with a groan and padded into the public area of his quarters.

"Come." The door slid aside to admit his second. "The ship is on fire, right? Or the squibs are shooting our ships down again? There are few valid reasons to wake me, Commander, so make it good."

"Sorry, Cap. I thought you'd want to know the crew situation has gotten worse on the surface and in the tunnels."

Harley stopped.

"And?"

"Crewmen are fighting in the tunnels, especially in the side shafts near the cave-ins. Commander Jarrett stopped three. I waded into at least two myself."

"You woke me to report that you broke up a fight?"

"It isn't just fights. Each crewman involved swears she or he heard voices, or that crewmembers plotted against them. Others are hallucinating, too, but at least they aren't fighting over it. I've reassigned three dozen workers in the last shift alone. Here," he reached into his pocket and pulled out a TICS pad, "check out the vid."

Crow glared at his second. "You recorded evidence of the surface op?"

Harley raised a hand. "Not me, sir. I confiscated this from one of the crew, and threatened the rest within an inch of their life if they did the same. But you might wanna see what she caught." He threw the vid to hover between them.

"TICS," Crow said, "play vid." The holo was small, grainy, but clear enough. In the first images, miners working away at the rock dropped their tools and controls for no apparent reason and began backing away from the walls as if they heard or saw something that scared the shit out of them. Behind them, in another clump of workers, two miners turned from their equipment and lunged into another crewman, beating and kicking him as he fell.

Hair on Crow's nape rose to attention. Chillbumps raced down his arms and across his back. This came too close to his own tunnel experience for comfort. "How much hemi is left?"

"We're nowhere near done."

"How much longer do you need?"

Harley shrugged. "A week, ten days maybe, *if* we maintain a full working crew. If we lose too many to the heebie-jeebies, we'll never finish." He shifted from one foot to the other. "Permission to speak freely, Cap?"

"You always do."

"It seems to me you know more about what's going on than you're admitting. I can't be an effective second or run the show down there without you if I don't know the whole story. What gives?"

Crow sighed and wiped one hand down his face. "I'm guessing this is due to a combination of the LADRAS radiation with some oddity specific to Iridos. Never seen this kind of thing happen before, but if I'm right, it won't get better until this stinking rock is eating our wake. We need to suck it up and finish the job, the faster the better. Tighten the screws on diggers who can't keep it under control. Make an example of one if necessary. Anyone who can't mine, send 'em up in shuttles to secure all orbital debris from our lost ships, anything that could identify the Consortium. We can't leave that shit behind."

"Okay." Harley sighed.

Frowning, Crow looked closer at his second. Harley's color seemed off. "What's wrong with you? Are you sick?"

"Just losing sleep."

Not Harley too. Ever since they started surface ops, sleep disturbances grew commonplace and showed up in minor injuries, irritability, and bug-shit craziness. At first, Crow had given the chief medical officer a strict rule that no one received equilinus or sedolyn or any soporific without his personal approval. He couldn't afford to run out. But after more than fifty requests in two days, he had approved one dose per thirty-hour day to anyone who wanted it. Hell, Crow hadn't been back to the surface since his first trip, and even he had trouble sleeping. But why? He juggled the chicken-and-egg question again. Did the bad dreams and delusions cause the sleep loss? Or was it the other way around? Medical couldn't tell and didn't have the means to do in-depth testing on such a widespread issue. For the time being, med staff had been treating the symptoms, but it wasn't enough. Surface crew still dropped too fast. He might end up doing this whole job himself.

"How is Walker holding up?"

His second offered a limp shrug. "She doesn't seem to be affected."

Oh? Interesting. "Have her pull a double shift. You get some rest. Take two sedolyn with your hooch of choice and sleep it off. That's an order. Dismissed." When Harley was gone, Crow commed medical with permission for his second to receive a double dose.

He poured himself a drink and sank into his favorite chair where he gulped down half the liquor with a grimace. Might as well sit up a while, try to get some work done. He wouldn't sleep again anytime soon without pharmaceutical assistance. Every time he shut his eyes he was back in that damned tunnel, hearing those voices, feeling a creeping sensation up the back of his neck. At the time, Crow had been certain he'd caught some sort of virus from the squibs, but doc found nothing wrong.

It didn't make any fucking sense. He couldn't remember the last time he had let a job get under his skin, unless maybe it was the first one he had worked on as a full-fledged Trader. Hell, that's the job where he earned the name he now bore. Before then, he'd been Rupert Farley, the escapee from the shelter who had hovered at the faction's fringe, taking odd jobs for the faction for five whole years until Skalar's predecessor had admitted Rupert and sent him with a boatload of others to raid Danuan territory. He had almost shit himself when the commander dispatched them each on lone raids, but at the end of the day Rupert claimed the biggest haul of all the crewmen. Twenty-nine years later, he didn't even remember what the take had been. What he did recall with crystal clarity was the feeling of power that victory had bestowed, and the hunger it instilled in him for *more*. Not once since then had fear ever been a problem.

So why now?

It wasn't fear, exactly. He didn't like being closed in.

As opposed to the vast open spaces of shipboard life?

But that was different. He could breathe on the ship. The air was recycled, fresh. The light was different. It was easier to get around.

He ran a hand over his braids with a sigh. The Leonid was a good ship, a great one, in fact, with quiet quarters. Other than the inescapable noise of surrounding equipment and processors, no sound intruded and after a moment, he sat the bourbon on the table beside him, kicked his feet up, and leaned back. Pleasant emptiness filled the space behind his lids, warm, comforting, carrying him farther toward sleep. Crow relaxed, drifted deeper into the swirling mist that thickened with every passing second, closing in until it solidified into dark, dank walls amid stifling air.

Before him on the floor lay the squib they'd found, Crow's knife still buried under its chin. Whispers edged into his awareness, grew in intensity. Crow's shallow breaths came faster, and he stepped forward to retrieve his knife. As he leaned over the flickering body, it sat up, its huge buggy eyes wide and peering into his own.

Zhachi!

The shock yanked him back to wakefulness and he fell thrashing to the floor, upsetting the chair and his bourbon. In a wink, he sprang to his feet, glancing around as if he stood in the tunnel. Reality eased away the nightmare and he forced himself to take a few deep breaths.

A dream…just a dream.

Crow righted the chair and picked up his glass. It took him almost half a minute to pour the refill. Even then, a third of it spilled on the way to his lips. The rest of it went down in one gulp and he poured again at once, then took two sedolyn from his personal stash—captain's privilege—and went back to bed. In the darkness, memory of the tunnel haunted him until he growled a command to increase lumens, low. Better, he thought. Still, he tossed abed in the dim room while he chewed over the dilemma of his mission and tried to ignore the whispers at the edges of his mind.

Sleep was a long time coming.

chapter 28

<u>Iridos</u>

ALIRA EYED THE GROUP AHEAD, its members clustered in the joinedmind, their determination bent on the humans outside the tunnel's blockage. Even here, a good distance away, their combined power tingled against her skin.

"Who's directing our intent?" she whispered.

Ijydin shook her head. "No one could be spared for that. Join my effort or someone else's, or do it on your own. I told you what some of the others are doing."

"Yes." Drive the humans off our world, Counselor Dyson had said, while the unammi still survived. So why weren't the sh'toi gone already? Either the humans were less vulnerable than the unammi thought, or Alira's people needed to push harder. "How do we know if we're having any effect?"

"Well, they haven't tried to get past the collapses yet. Besides, almost every team has a reader or an empath or a viewer. They say it is working."

"Are you sure they're right?"

Ijydin squinted. "Did you just ask a truthseer if she was sure?"

"What if they think it's working? That would feel genuine to you, wouldn't it?"

"In some cases, yes, but not here. Not now. I know."

She hadn't recognized Alira's truth about the failed Adjustment, though. Now would probably not be a good time to bring that up. "I believe you. Let's go."

Together, they crept to the edge of the group and settled down onto the floor. In an instant, Ijydin was engrossed, intent on her work. Alira took a bit longer to adjust. She trusted Ijydin. But a visual on what was happening outside their confinement would help Alira direct her efforts. Projection had never been her strength. Cellular manipulation, however, was a whole different matter. If she had a line-of-sight on the selfish, greedy aliens, she would give them a host of good reasons to leave Iridos and never look back. Monstrous as they had been, the sh'toi deserved no compassion, no consideration.

She dropped into the joinedmind and focused on the invaders, reaching…reaching…. Yes, she sensed them and their incongruous natures, each one unique even though they were alike in so many ways, and yet she felt no bonds between them, no connection from one to the others, no shared awareness. Each stood isolated, even surrounded by its fellows, every individual intent on its own part of the process. Nyros, Galen, and Ijydin had all told her humans couldn't share a collective mind whenever they wanted or needed to do so, but she had never believed it until now. So strange…no ability to blend their thoughts so that they operated with a single mind, no way to send and receive instant instructions or status updates to those within range so each one knew how to adjust her actions to benefit the goal. Where was the failure? Had evolution passed them by, or did they have the ability and choose to ignore it? How could they work together as a whole with such a weakness? They would have to stop and verbalize every single instruction or adjustment to the task. How did they accomplish anything at all?

Nyros and Lurien were right. Unity through conformity worked better.

Tendrils of her awareness stretched forth from the collective, passing through the stones to project fear. These sh'toi, perhaps even the one she now reached, had destroyed the city's domes. New wisps branched from her projections to touch another invader with seeds of unending nightmares for collapsing the guildhouse. In the dim recesses of her individual thought, it occurred to Alira maybe she hadn't given this skill enough attention before. This was quite stimulating. She pressed forward with more verve. Whispers to remind that human what it did here. Horrific visions to drive that one mad. Yes. Let fear be their constant new companion.

Ire smoldered as she worked, here bolstering a preexisting phobia, there injecting resentment in one sh'toi against its neighbor. Why, if they compelled the humans to turn on one another—

"Alira!"

Snapped out of the collective, she opened her eyes. Ijydin stared at her.

"What?"

"You're going too far."

"But…." Alira drew back, teal speckles peppering her arms. "Dyson said to get rid of them."

"He didn't say kill them."

"I'm not."

Ijydin got to her feet and pulled Alira away from the others. "No, but you'd have them killing each other."

"So? How is that different from killing them aboard their ships?"

"That was a defensive effort to dissuade them from landing at all. It didn't work. Sh'toi don't think like we do." Ijydin's voice distracted two of those in the group, and they hissed at her to be quiet. She dropped her volume. "If you get them angry enough, they may bomb the rest of us into oblivion for spite."

"But making them fearful isn't working. It's taking too long!"

Ijydin pushed her face closer to Alira's. "According to your timetable. This is Dyson's plan. The council's. Trust me. We don't want to rush this. If you can't pace yourself here, we'll go get another assignment."

Her words sank into Alira's newfound appreciation for cohesion. Maybe it was time she started listening to and respecting the experience of others. The fire drained away, taking with it the vigor that had begun to revive inside her. She sighed, the numbness creeping back into her limbs as she nodded.

"You're right. You know more about the sh'toi than I do."

"Good. Let's get back to it."

chapter 29

Iridosian Space
<u>Aboard the Leonid</u>

THE HAGGARD, GAUNT FACE REFLECTED back at him couldn't be his own—hollow eyes, grayish-brown skin, braids drooping. "Gods, man," Crow said to his reflection. "Get your shit together." In response, the man in the mirror raised a hand to his stubbled jaw. "And shave, while you're at it." Crow activated the sonic, peeled off his clothes, and stepped under the light mist, vibrating away the stink. He took a moment to collect his thoughts.

Two weeks since they had flattened the city. Four days since Harley first told him about the altercations. Two days since the crew finished mining the blue crystals—should have chucked the crystals and put his whole team on the metal, but that would have meant admitting his mistake—and began to die either from the fights or from radiation. At least a tenth of their hazmat suits had been damaged, some beyond repair. Rad techs scanned the mines every shift, but readings always fell within acceptable levels. This shouldn't be happening. Between the suits and the meds, it was impossible for such low-level radiation to kill them this soon. So what the actual fuck was going on?

The comm sounded while he shaved. "Voice only. Yes?"

"Sir, the other captains are waiting in the conference room to see you."

Crow paused the razor mid-stroke. Walker? "What do they want?"

"Sorry sir, they wouldn't talk to me. Said it was urgent."

No doubt they had questions similar to his own. "Acknowledged. Send Harley in here."

Pause. "Commander Harley is in medical."

"What's wrong with him?"

"Radiation, sir."

Shit. "Very well. Come to my quarters, Lieutenant Commander. Crow out." He finished shaving, squeezed excess moisture from his hair, and shoved his feet into socks, then pants and boots.

A chime sounded from the door.

Walker.

"Wait one." Crow pulled a shirt over his head on the way to the door, which slid open at his approach. He pushed past her. "You're with me. Report."

She fell into step beside him. "Crew reloaded the Rolland onto the Chest, sir. Most surface teams have been rerouted to the hemi mines."

"How is Harley?"

"Medics say it's acute radiation syndrome, sir, hematopoietic variety."

Crow stopped. "How bad?"

"He's at stage three, sir." Her features showed no emotion. She might make a good officer, at that. "Medics gave him potassium iodide and protein meds, but it's too late to be much help. We don't have enough supplies to do transfusions."

Shit. Harley was his leading supporter in any takeover bid for the faction. Crow resumed his trek. "Understood. Have medical cease treatment and switch Harley to comfort care."

She hesitated. "Yes, sir."

"How many dead so far?"

"Twenty-two, sir. And more are sickening. We're at about two-thirds workforce capacity now, and about a quarter of those can't go back to the surface because, as Commander Harley put it, 'they go bat-shit down there.'"

Crow muttered a curse as they stepped into the lift. Fuck of a time for a confrontation, especially since he had no good news to give his captains. Keeping them in line without killing anyone would take finesse. These weren't green crewmen serving their first terms on a Consortium mission. Between them, the four remaining captains had logged thirty-plus years in Consortium command. The convoy might be under his command, but their ranks equaled his own. He couldn't make one of them an example unless they committed a serious breach of protocol.

Shame, that. This dance would cost them all valuable time and effort which could be used in more productive ways.

Damn it. Trader command structure should make it an unequivocal fact that no one questioned an order from any officer in authority. Take Skalar, for example. The admiral tolerated no debate. He gave an order and people jumped to while he moved on to the next thing. Hell, that leadership model had even served Rupert's parents well for years. People had all but bowed to his security chief mother, begged favors from his father in intercolonial relations. Young Rupert had himself dreamed of a position of such power in the colonial hierarchy until dear old mom and dad had fucked up in a major way and got themselves shipped off to confinement. That was the day all Rupert's plans changed.

He snorted. No problem. The day would come when his command was the last word.

The lift stopped and he stomped through the corridors, then entered the conference room where an animated discussion fell silent. Crow sat at the head of the table.

"What is this about?"

The other captains exchanged a glance before Moyra spoke.

"We need to get the hell out of here."

"Job's not done," Crow said.

"This job ain't worth what it's costin' us," Ronan said, staring at the table.

Crow regarded the others. "You all share this opinion?"

Talonn leaned forward, hands flat on the table. "It isn't an opinion, Crow. Whatever the reason, LADRAS residuals are too strong. People are dying. Half the personnel I brought for this job are either in makeshift medicals or working other duties because they're useless on the surface. We've had to pull in crewmembers from other duties on all five ships to fill in the gaps. That's not an opinion. It is a fact."

"This isn't LADRAS. Or if it is, then it's augmented by something else. Radiation doesn't stir up fights or give people bad dreams and hallucinations." Crow's green gaze found them all one at a time. "Oh, I'm with you. I know something is wrong here, but it isn't as simple as residuals. I've shared my theories with Skalar. If he wants to share them with you, that'll be his call. In any event, I'm not leaving until we've sucked this planet dry or run out of onboard storage room. Clear?"

Pandemonium erupted among the other captains, and Crow let it run for a few seconds. "I asked you a question," he shouted over the din. "Are we clear?"

"How are we supposed to comply," Jos asked, "when our crews are dropping by the hour? How long before there aren't enough of us to get these ships home, much less finish the job?"

"Come on, Jos." Crow grinned. "That's a bit of a stretch, isn't it? My officer tells me there are only twenty-two dead."

"They don't have to be dead to be unfit to fly," Talonn said.

"Lieutenant Commander," Crow said, "since all workers are now focused on mining the hematium, how much longer will it take the crews to finish the job?"

"At least a week, sir, maybe ten days."

Fuck. Crow frowned. Harley had said that four days ago. "There, you see?" Crow forced a calm tone. "We can manage six more days."

Talonn threw up his hands, but Ronan leaned forward. "Ain't gonna be no week. The way crew's fallin', work's slower with every shift. Longer we're here, longer it's gonna take."

"There is no logic in your statement," Crow said.

"Ain't no logic to any o' this."

Crow pointed at them. "Which one of you wants to explain to Skalar why we came back with empty holds because a few people got sick?"

Everyone shifted in their seats.

"That's what I thought," Crow said. He slapped his palm to the table with a thump. "Look, I'll make you a deal. Speed up the process. Boost your numbers on the surface so we can work harder and faster. If we aren't full by the end of a week, we'll leave regardless. If we fill our holds before then, we'll leave sooner. Is that a compromise you can live with?"

"*We* ain't the ones on the surface," Ronan muttered.

"Since when do you bargain with your crew?" Crow shouted. "I'm talking to captains of Consortium ships in *my* fleet." The subtle emphasis wouldn't be lost on them. "Your options are clear. Stay under the terms I've laid out, or go back without us and explain to Skalar why you did so."

Ronan leaned back with a grunt.

"A week," Crow said, taking advantage of the hesitation. "No more. That's the deal. Are you in?"

Jos sighed, then nodded. The others dragged their feet all the way to an agreement.

"Good," Crow said. "Once we finish, Ronan, you'll take the haul to the outpost for unloading."

Ronan shook his head. "Don't like that place."

"Why not?"

Ronan dropped his gaze. Talonn's lips puckered. "He has a valid concern."

"Ronan, you've been there before. Why is this time any different?"

"Step in front of a weapon enough times, luck runs out," Ronan drawled.

Crow waved away his concern. "Skalar says that base was never infected."

Moyra sighed. "Missions there were aborted, it's true. I read about it. The unions sent personnel to outer colonies when the diseases got bad. They abandoned the site before it could be contaminated."

"That doesn't mean it was never infected," Jos said.

"If there was any contamination, we would have known it years ago. Skalar's people have been there off and on since he found it. They've never gotten sick." No one replied and after a moment, Crow leaned forward. "Okay, so another week, tops. Ronan will deliver the haul, then meet us in New Canaan. Any questions?"

No one spoke up.

"Then let's get back to work." Crow acknowledged the knot in his stomach after they'd gone. That went better than he'd expected.

But his parents had gotten greedy too, and see where it got them? If this was a bad decision, he'd get to say goodbye to his comfortable lifestyle all over again.

Crow hesitated to court the admiral's displeasure. He couldn't take over as admiral if he was dead. This was the correct course of action. Even so, anxiety climbed his spine and blew a chill breath on the back of his neck at the choice before him: Skalar's rage or the mysterious Iridos syndrome. At this point, which did he fear more?

chapter 30

<u>**Iridos**</u>

"ALIRA, WAIT!"

Alira walked on. She didn't need a keeper, but after nineteen cycles trapped in the tunnels with no way to escape her own people, she *did* need a moment alone. If the council didn't trust her by now, they never would.

Ijydin caught up and shot her a sideways glare. "Wow, thanks. Nice of you to slow down."

Alira closed her eyes and stopped. Others brushed past her in the corridor, and she stepped to one side. "Sorry. I'm tired. And hungry."

"We all are," Ijydin said. "Personally, after that last work period, I wanted to punch a wall. I might have, except I was afraid of bringing the ceiling down. Again." She pressed a hand to her lower back. "Right now I want to sit down almost as much as I want to bathe. If I can't have both, I'll at least get off my feet while we eat."

They resumed their progress, passing other corridors where work continued in one or another of the countless tasks facing the people. Ijydin seemed to pay the other projects no mind, but Alira scanned each as they went, comparing how far they had come since the city's fall to the journey that still lay ahead of them. Reconstruction weighed heavy on their shoulders, a monumental task which threatened to overwhelm them all. The more survivors they recovered—

Alira's feet halted and she wheeled, mid-step, reversing direction.

Ijydin stopped. "Where are you going?"

"I thought I saw…." Alira paused at the junction of the last corridor, watching a small team at work. A frown pulled down her brows and tugged at the weary ache in her head. "What are you digging for?" she asked them.

One glanced at her. "We're trying to clear a channel down to the springs. The others are clogged." He took stones from the worker at the rock face and set them aside.

"Has anyone examined the blockage?" Alira asked. "Checked it for stability?"

The pair digging grunted in response. "No builders available," said the same male. "But we have to try."

She stepped closer. "Be careful," she cautioned. "You—

As she spoke, the shallow hole they had dug collapsed, spilling stones, gravel and dirt out onto the diggers and into the corridor. Alira rushed to them.

"Are you hurt?"

All three spat out dirt and brushed it off their faces, but shook their heads. No. Not hurt.

Her heart raced, and she blew out a breath. "Good. That's good." She squatted next to them to help brush away the dirt as Ijydin came around the corner and stood, hands on hips.

"Go ahead if you want," Alira told her. "They're trying to break through this blockage. I'm going to help, if I can."

"Uh huh," Ijydin said. Pink flashed through the dirt on her skin. "You, the skilled and experienced digger."

"I know a few tricks."

One of the others looked up as if seeing Alira for the first time. "You do?"

"I'm no builder," Alira admitted. "But I know how to stabilize the top and sides of the channel. It will slow you down a bit, but it will hold."

Ijydin exhaled in a show of exasperation and joined them. "At least I can sit for this job."

They cleared the debris and Alira showed them how to dig one shallow layer at a time, then place and stack stones up the sides just so, turning and adjusting each to interlock their planes one with another. Each supported the next, their layers curving up and moving inward as they neared the top. The other workers helped hold the stones in place as she set each one. At the peak of the arch, she placed a single rock, braced tight between those to either side. Tension held them all together and stabilized the entire support. The more pressure came at them from above, the stronger their lock would be.

"I thought you were a cleric," one of the diggers said, his eyes wide, his display speckled with gray.

Alira nodded. "I am."

"How did you know to do that?" another asked.

"Because I didn't listen only to clerics." She stood and brushed the dirt off her knees and rear end. "Do you think you can do it now?"

The others murmured assent.

"I'll leave you to it then." She stepped over the rocks, still brushing her hands together, and set off again.

Ijydin caught up and squinted sideways at Alira as they walked.

"Go ahead," Alira said. "Speak your mind."

"Nothing on my mind," Ijydin said, swinging her gaze forward. "Nope. Nothing at all."

chapter 31

IN THE MEAL HALL, THEY claimed two seats. Others nearby moved to a different spot. Ijydin called out a thank-you, but Alira sat quiet. Long narrow tables ran the length of a space much smaller than their old dining hall. There, even with the larger space, dozens or hundreds of conversations rang off the stone walls. Here, silent diners sat atop mismatched stools and benches salvaged from dorm quarters whose residents no longer needed them. Those who spoke at all did so in hushed tones. It felt sad. Empty. Blue and purple swirled through Alira's skin.

"Don't think about it," Ijydin said.

"How can you not?"

"We can do nothing for the dead." Ijydin leaned back to give space to the workers who brought their food. At the first taste of unheated rations, Ijydin tapped her spoon against the bowl. "Have I mentioned that I prefer my soup cold?"

Alira speckled with amusement, then darkened again to blue. She dipped a spoonful of soup and held it above her bowl. "There are so few of us left."

"Even fewer now. There was another rockfall last cycle."

"Another one?" Alira leaned forward, soup forgotten.

Ijydin nodded. "Killed three frem. Not counting the miners, three hundred sixty-nine frem remain. Maybe sixty or so younglings. That isn't even the worst of it. Some of the guilds have no survivors."

"Not even younglings in training?" Alira's shifting Companion stirred in her thoughts.

"Don't know," Ijydin shrugged, "but even if there are, it isn't much comfort."

Alira shook her head, red speckling her arms and hands. Generations of guild knowledge, all gone, and for what? A load of metal and all the unammi's irolium. For a moment she didn't know which was worse—stupid, greedy sh'toi or obstinate, inflexible councilors. "This is my worst fear come to life. I warned the elders or tried to. How are they going to fill gaps in our knowledge base?"

Ijydin didn't respond.

"Who told you about this?" Alira asked.

"Nobody." Ijydin slurped a spoonful of soup. "I overheard Yoloron and Dyson talking. Caught news of the latest collapse and comments about having the miners check the ceilings in all the main chambers and corridors for stability. That's when they saw me and changed the subject. Probably shouldn't have told you, come to think of it."

Alira, still smoldering, stirred her cold soup. "I understand we've always done things a certain way. I see the logic in that, but I wonder if we aren't racing against time here. None of us even remember a time before the guilds. Who knows how long it took our ancestors to gather such a reservoir of expertise and knowledge? Generations, at least. How long do you think it will take us to rebuild them?"

"I expect the council has a plan."

"I'm sure they're working on it, but think about how much we'll have to rediscover, how long it will take to be functional, much less masterful at any of the lost skills. Meanwhile, we sit here helpless, the hands of our enemy at our throats, and we can't even build a tunnel. That lost knowledge is crucial, especially now."

"What do you expect us to do?"

Alira put her spoon back in the bowl, no longer hungry. "I'm processing all of it. I mean, can we survive this kind of lack? I don't know.

It seems reckless to keep going through the motions as if nothing has changed."

"You said you'd comply." Ijydin regarded her across the table. "You gave Rakalesh your word."

Alira's colorful array reflected confusion on the table in front of her and she dropped her gaze.

"You aren't going to be able to keep it, are you?"

"I'm trying. I am."

She picked her spoon up again, pushed it around in the bowl. Rakalesh had said they needed Alira. Rakalesh had also said they needed everyone. If Alira broke her promise, maybe they really would mitigate her this time. If they could. She searched Ijydin's face.

"But we never planned a strategy for the total destruction of our civilization. Our old paradigm is inadequate to address it, not in time to save us. I hear what you're telling me, and you make good points. Yet every instinct I have screams this is a legitimate concern."

Ijydin muttered under her breath, lavender patterns running beneath the other colors in her display. "You're going to make me regret opening my mouth, aren't you?"

"I'm calm," Alira said. "I just don't understand how no one else can see this truth. I've said it before, but it's even more true now, after this tragedy. Our survival as a species, much less a civilization, needs a broader foundation, more sustainable traditions. If we had been training outside our own guilds even for the last fifty cycles, much less fifty seasons, we'd be better off right now."

Ijydin didn't offer an immediate response, and Alira at last tasted her soup. For a while they sat surrounded by the subdued sounds of the chamber, Alira lost in her own thoughts until Ijydin choked on her soup. Alira looked up to see her friend grimacing at the rear of the room, and turned in time to see Rakalesh and Dyson sit at one of the smaller tables near the door.

"I'll see you later." Alira stood.

Ijydin jerked to her feet and grabbed Alira's arm. "Don't. Leave it alone."

Alira glanced down at her arm, then back at Ijydin. "I'm not going to make trouble."

Ijydin released her and sat back down.

Alira took a deep breath and made her way between the tables toward the corridor. At the last moment, she veered toward the councilors' table and stood until they noticed her. Their expressions and colors betrayed apprehension, either from their people's predicament or her appearance beside their table in this moment.

"Maybe," she said, her tone pitched to their ears alone, "now is a good time to diversify our social structure. We're rebuilding everything else. Why not that, too?"

She left the room without waiting for their response.

chapter 32

Iridosian Space
<u>**Aboard the Leonid**</u>

"Report," Crow said.

"Equipment's loaded. Crew's lockin' it down now. We're full up."

"You had enough room then?"

Ronan shook his head. "Had to shift some personnel to Talonn's carrier. Used their bunks for the last o' the haul since bay three's got that special cargo."

Crow grunted. The last week had piled them up. "You checked with the doc one last time? Might be more by now."

"Yep. I got 'em all, stored in the bay under medical seal like you said, twenty bodies to a bundle. Good idea. Make it easier to chuck 'em toward this system's star on the way out. Won't leave no trace."

Bundles of bodies. Surprising, how few they'd found in the orbital debris. Far greater numbers died in the tunnels. Or in the fights. Or in the sickbays. Crow's stomach clenched, pushing a guttural grunt from his throat, and he rubbed his eyes. Fuck if even he wasn't on the verge of losing it. He no longer cared about Skalar's anger or lost profits. Nothing was worth this torture. Crow couldn't wait to get the hell away from this rock so he could sleep.

"Once you've jettisoned the cadavers, deliver the rest of the haul to the outpost. Remember to keep that leg of the trip dark. No outside viewscreens, no one but your navigators peeking at location. Nobody leaves the ship but cleared crew." Ronan's moue drew a smirk from Crow. "Fine. Keep them all on the ship if it will make you feel better. Use drones to unload the stash. It will take longer, but you won't have to go to the surface. When you're done, you can go back to New Canaan."

Ronan muttered something.

"What was that? I didn't hear you."

"Nothin'."

"Then finish your checks and get off the ground. I wanna say goodbye to the squibs." Crow leaned back. "Your crew knows about their percentage of the take?"

"'Course they do."

"Good. Don't forget to make damn sure they also understand if they discuss this job at all with anyone, even each other, everyone loses their share. They won't be given a second opportunity to fuck up. Clear?"

Ronan shot him a skeptical look. "Did that. Won't matter. Ain't gonna be easy to keep this quiet."

"Which is why you should ensure they know the consequences if they blab. This trip already cost the Consortium plenty. A few more pissant recruits or junior officers won't make much difference. I'm setting up a little reminder right now to help drive the point home. Make sure Leonid's transmissions are live on every deck of your ship for the next half hour."

"What kind o' reminder?"

"A combination of motivation and CYA. There is too much at stake to take chances. Jos and the others understood this. Nobody else whined about the gag order."

"Ain't whinin'." Ronan's expression hardened. "Tellin' a fact. Can't help you don't like it."

"'Like' isn't part of this equation," Crow grumbled. "Just do it." He signed off without waiting for a response and reached for a stim capsule as the door chime sounded. "Come."

"You called me, sir?" Walker asked.

"Yes. Front and center."

Frowning, the officer came to stand at attention before Crow's desk.

"Lieutenant Commander Vandana Walker, pending Admiral Skalar's approval, you are hereby promoted to the rank of commander with all the attendant responsibilities, rights, and privileges afforded a Consortium officer of that rank."

Walker's eyes widened above the "O" of her mouth.

"Further, as Harley's second-in-command," Crow continued with a resigned sigh, "you are hereby assigned to the temporary position of my second."

"Wha—"

"Don't interrupt. Whether or not the position becomes permanent will depend on you. I expect you to give this position your all, Commander. I will not accept mediocrity and if you cannot perform to my expectations, you can be replaced. Am I clear?"

Shock gave the officer pause. Her features twisted as his words sank in.

"Commander, am I clear?"

"Yes, Captain. But if I may ask—"

"Harley's dead. Congratulations on your promotion." Crow dragged himself to his feet. "Did you follow my orders?"

"Yes, sir. I pulled the crewmen you specified and had them take fifteen bodies onto that unknown shuttle. They're waiting aboard, ready to launch at your command."

"And the last two LADRAS missiles?"

"Loaded and ready, sir."

"Fine. You're with me." Crow swept past her through the door and onto the bridge, his feet working of their own accord.

Behind him, Walker called out an order of her own. "Captain on deck."

"As you were. Tell the shuttle to launch. Gimme visual."

Minutes passed as the command was sent, and they waited for it to appear.

"TICS, put me live to all ships. Transmit visuals to the Treasure Chest at the surface."

"Ready," replied the TICS.

"All hands, this is Captain Crow. You have been informed of the consequences for any discussion of this operation, even among yourselves. I regret to inform you that several crew members disobeyed this order. I'm forced to take punitive action. Weapons," he barked. "Ready conventional missiles. Target the shuttle."

The TICS began to ping with incoming comms, one from the doomed craft. Crow ignored them, and after a moment the shuttle came about, goosing its engines in a frantic attempt to escape.

"Ready, Captain."

"Fire."

"Firing now, sir."

The Leonid's bridge crew watched in utter silence. Moments later, wreckage and bodies splayed out before the shocked armada, detritus that would orbit this rock for a long, long time. Crow spoke to the other ships once more.

"Behold the Consortium's punishment for traitors. Learn from their mistake or share their fate. Leonid out." Turning, he grunted another order. "Weapons, ready LADRAS missiles, aim for the low center of the ruins. We don't want to blast the mines. Comms, run a check. Let me know the second the Treasure Chest is off the ground."

Brief pause. Then, "All Consortium assets are clear, sir."

Crow whirled. "Surface view. I wanna see this."

At once, a distant image of the valley region filled the screen.

"Fire."

"Missiles away, Captain."

Seconds ticked by. As far as Crow was concerned, they couldn't finish this piece of work fast enough. Oh, he'd waited out the week he had demanded from the other captains. Couldn't let them know he thought they'd been right, but he had paid a staggering price. Twenty percent of the remaining crew and one hundred percent of his peace of mind. He would feel a lot better when this damnable rock was a grave still settling somewhere far behind him. What a fucking nightmare!

Tiny flashes of light sparked in the image of the valley. Crow grinned so wide his face ached.

"Fuckers." He settled into his seat. "Send the cleanup team. Leave the ship debris and the bodies but snag that crew's idents. And make it snappy. I want to get the hell outta here."

chapter 33

<u>Iridos</u>

EXPLOSIONS REVERBERATED THROUGH THE ROCK above, raining pebbles on Alira's head and dropping a heavy chunk of ceiling behind her. Shouts rang out in the surrounding chambers, alarm racing among the survivors in white pulses that lit the corridor and sparkled on the falling dust even as Alira lurched into the joinedmind. No clarity to be found there, though, only confusion and dismay. Whirling, she climbed over the rockfall and ran back the way she'd come.

More dust and small stones fell along the way, but no further collapses blocked her path. Others joined the race to assist as she passed. The closer she got to the upper levels, the more damage she saw. By the time she reached the first collapse, she joined a crowd. Even Ijydin had beaten her here. Yoloron had taken lead, directing those among them freshest from their beds to begin clearing the debris.

Alira saw in Ijydin's face the same question that came to her own mind. How many would they dig out this time?

Together they approached the murmuring crowd surrounding Yoloron and waited for an assignment, but the elder raised a hand.

"Basu'tao," she called. "If you have been awake for nearly a cycle," she said once they quieted, "you're no good to us here. Go and rest."

Mutters of protest rose, and Yoloron shook her head. "There is limited space, and dust in the air makes me think the vent is blocked in this chamber. That's our first priority. I've sent a team to check and clear it, but until we assess the stability of the chamber, no more than ten workers. Go back to your tasks or get some sleep. This mess will still be here after."

Alira moved back into the corridor, pushing scattered stones to the side as she did so. No need for a trip hazard in an already chaotic environment.

Ijydin appeared beside her, squinting at the ceiling with apparent suspicion. A pebble fell a few steps ahead, and Ijydin pointed at the spot where it originated. "Don't you do it! You stay right where you are."

Alira continued walking, and Ijydin matched her steps. "I told you if we made the sh'toi mad they would strike out of spite."

The words stoked Alira's embers again. "Yes," she snapped. "You're right. I'm wrong." She felt Ijydin's reproach and chided herself for taking her frustrations out on her best friend. She wasn't the sole victim here.

"You need to think about something else," Ijydin said. "For example, we still need to get beyond reach of any tech the sh'toi left behind so we can warn the pilots."

A small huff escaped Alira's throat. Galen and Nyros had been close to her thoughts throughout this whole miserable affair.

"You know," Ijydin said, leaning near as if imparting a secret, "my ship has room for two."

Alira stopped cold. "The people need us here."

Ijydin waited a short distance ahead. "And the pilots need to know what they're up against. Someone needs to go." She shrugged. "It wouldn't take long. We'd be back before they missed us."

She wasn't wrong about the need. The survivors needed every last unammi for the extra workers, yes, but also for their genetics. With their numbers so low, even a few additional frem might make a difference in their population's viability.

"You'd finally get a chance to see what it's like to be off-world." Ijydin tilted her head at a jaunty angle.

Alira tried to imagine how it would feel to get on Ijydin's ship and fly away. But to leave her people, now of all times—even for a short while—she couldn't do it.

"Just think about it." Yawning, Ijydin resumed her way toward her bed. Alira followed.

Sometime later, in a chamber filled with sleepers recharging before another shift of hard work, Ijydin snored beside her while Alira lay awake. Eyes closed, she tapped into the running collective to follow its focus. Most prevalent was the knowledge that now they could begin to dig out. Already, the miners were on their way with tools to hasten the process. Once freed, the people could assess the damage, calculate their remaining resources, and decide where to begin. Remote viewers told the collective the damage was colossal, that they would have to start over. The thought sucked at what little hope Alira had managed to retain.

It was doubtful that they would build above ground again. Cleared of debris, their underground space would serve their reduced numbers, at least for a while. But many seasons of nurturance and education stood between her people and a restoration of balance. In the meantime, every available frem worked every waking hour to get the people to a starting point. Even here in the collective, a pall settled over the foreseeable future, shading all possibilities as if she saw them through a haze of windblown sand. Alira withdrew from the group mind and sat up, feet dangling over the side of the cot.

What about the loss of their irolium? Younglings' tales spoke of what would happen to the unammi without it. No one even knew where those had originated but, if true, her people may have survived one disaster in time to confront another. Could they call that living? Perhaps, if Musju proved merciful, the unammi would die out first. Except…would they still be able to rejoin Na'Staani after death?

Her arms and legs blanched. From birth, every youngling suckled at the connection to Na'Staani as much as at the breast of its mother. The relationship between the people and the Source of All meant as much to them as the air they breathed. As a cleric, she taught younglings to see the energy of Na'Staani as the Flow of Musju, to tap into it by stepping into the water in meditation, to feel its touch and interpret its urgings as messages from the Source. Every cleric taught that life and death were part of the cycle that began with and ended in Na'Staani. Na'Staani incorporated All That Was. To imagine that there might not be a reunion with that Source at the end of this life stippled her flesh and shortened her breath.

Her studies and experiences in the clerical guild never addressed such a philosophical quandary, but reason scoffed at the possibility. If the unammi were *of* Na'Staani, then of course they would be reabsorbed when their physical bodies no longer separated their pithasia from the Source. She put that fear aside for the moment to consider another concern.

If the irolium grew once it would grow again, given time and exposure to the symbiosis between Iri and unammi. But would her people last long enough to learn whether the tales were true? They were about to find out, though even the clerical guild's scientists had no data on what to expect. Without projected figures for the extent of individual variance or factors of susceptibility, without answers to even the most basic questions—would the dimming happen all at once or in a progression of decay?—they couldn't even begin to prepare for such a horror.

Alira's thoughts knotted into a tangle from which a single question and all its ramifications emerged. How long? How long would it take to regrow their stones? How long before the shining unammi began to dim? How long could they last in a dimmed state before the species would be unsalvageable?

At last, she lay on her side, the seed of worry in her heart knotted into an urgency she couldn't shake until she drifted off to restless dreams where her enigmatic Companion offered only silence and a shimmering presence in her mind.

chapter 34

Bel-Rhovan, Bejami
<u>**Land Port Station**</u>

TENZIN'S SLIGHT, ANDROGYNOUS FORM SLIPPED through the crowds. As Galen, he had flown in and out of this port so many times over the years he could almost navigate it in his sleep. But after more than two standard weeks in Bregaina, the bustle overpowered Tenzin's senses. Even outside on the lots, travelers jostled past in their rush to wherever. His fear for Alira still troubled him. He tried to stay near the fringe as he surrendered his jumper and worked his way through the rental concourse.

Inside the port proper he moved with the throngs toward the first intersection. Security seemed heavy today. He'd seen three peace officers outside on the landing flats, two more toward the south gates, and another two here. Tenzin thought he knew all those assigned to this port, but many of these humans were unfamiliar. New inductees? Doubtful. Not that many new constables all at once and all in the same place.

Something smelled wrong.

He veered from his original course toward the main exit and wound his way through the corridors and down into the narrower passages near the private ships. Even more officers roamed here, far more than was usual and most of them unfamiliar. Worry wormed through him, even though he couldn't fathom how this oddity would be connected to him. He had renewed his licenses and permits when they came due, paid his fees without complaint. The humans had no reason to come for him. Even if they did, it wouldn't have required so many of them.

Still....

Tenzin rounded the corner and came within sight of his own berth. Three unfamiliar peace officers waited outside his ship's companionway and two others exited, as if they had been aboard. He darted a glance down the concourse. Ships to either side sat unmolested.

His heartbeat thundered in his ears. He *was* the target. Tenzin continued past the dock, toward the far end of the concourse. Every instinct screamed *run,* but first he needed to know what he was running *from.*

His feet carried him, at a pace that felt as slow as the creep of ice on ne'ani's frozen tundra, to the next set of docks where he ducked into a public lavatory. Some of the colonial worlds surveilled everything except a personal flat, especially Harajüd and Zebalu. But most, like the Bejami Trust, gave public toilets a pass. He'd find privacy here, but he would need to invent a disposable persona. If stopped, he'd have no background to back it up, not to mention that a lack of ident card would set off alarms in certain areas of the port. Risky. Still, it seemed a better option than portraying a peace officer he knew, someone he might encounter in the corridors.

Minutes later, he emerged wearing a uniform, a made-up face, and a badge with the name Donato Boyd, and roamed back the way he had come, alert for anything out of the ordinary. Nearby, another unfamiliar peace officer leaned against the wall, her eyes on the guards outside the Iridosian ship. He made his casual way toward her until he was within arm's reach, then put his empathic skills to work.

"No sign of him yet, eh?" he asked.

She turned. "And you are?"

"You're not from around here, I take it." Donato smiled. "Bejami Trust, special security Donato Boyd, at your service."

"Why haven't I met you in the two weeks I've been here?"

"I only now dragged myself back from holiday." He felt her size him up and decide to believe him. Donato forced his smile to remain.

"Luccyn Stoorman. And no, we haven't seen him yet, Officer Boyd."

"Donato, please. My da' was Officer Boyd." Donato's attention shifted to the guarded berth. "Your boss ain't gonna like this delay, Luccyn."

She grunted, shifting her own gaze back to the guards. "No one ever accused Skalar of being a patient man, but I'm even past my own tolerance at this point."

So Harajüd's Traders held ties to governments on other worlds, or at least here on Bejami. Skalar's people wouldn't be able to run a search like this otherwise. Worry blossomed into full-blown anxiety.

"How long did your team wait before going in?"

She raised a brow. "Why don't you know that?"

"I know what the records say. I wanted a firsthand account." Donato winked but withheld a smile. "You know how it is."

"Let's say it has been long enough." She squinted at him. "I told the other Trust people. Now I'll tell you. These are *my* crew. They aren't on your payroll, so don't try to order us around."

Donato held his hands up in mock surrender. "No argument from me." He stood with her for a moment. "I didn't see a reason for this drama in the report."

Luccyn scowled. "What?"

Donato shrugged, gesturing toward the guarded companionway. "Why this squib? He's docile enough, never got into trouble. As far as I know, he's never even been to Harajüd. What is the Consortium's complaint against him?"

"I don't ask questions." Luccyn's flat tone spoke volumes. "If I did, I'd wanna know why he wants 'em *all*."

Donato's breath hitched. "He wants all unammi dead?"

Luccyn squinted at him. "What did you say?"

He shook it off. "Sorry. Local slang. Skalar told you to kill them all?"

"All the pilots. And who said 'kill'?"

"Please." Donato smirked. "I'm not a fool. Skalar doesn't launch an operation of this scale just to ask questions." Bile rose in his throat. "How many are left?"

"I can't say." She looked back at the dock. "My team's responsible for Rubene and Bejami. We've caught one out of three. Still looking for the other one on Rubene. And *this* one's taking his sweet time, ain't he? We thought maybe he was already dead on the ship, and nobody knew. Would'a made my job easier, but no such luck. Maybe he got wind of our orders and took off." She shrugged. "Won't matter. We'll find him. Not many places a squib can hide for long. They stand out, don't they?"

She laughed and Donato joined in. "Indeed." He paused. "I suppose I'd best get back to work. Maybe I'll see you later."

"Not if we find him first," she countered.

Donato veered back toward the next dock set and kept going past his earlier changing spot. Skalar, eliminating unammi pilots…the why didn't yet matter as much as warning the others, but a comm sent to the pilots using Tenzin's ident, or sent from his flat, would link his primary alias to the unammi. Better to use a public comm. Plenty of kiosks lined the corridors, though Donato had no way to access them.

He chewed the inside of his lip. Earlier, Tenzin had walked past a number of officers without attracting attention, but Luccyn and her people were already twitchy about their evasive prey. How long before they began to screen the surveillance vids and do the math? Maybe it was time for a clean break, a persona so removed from Galen's they wouldn't connect to him at all, even with the vids.

In the next public toilet, Donato shifted from 183 centimeters of bronze, male security guard to 180 centimeters of curvy human female, deepened the skin tone to a rich brown, and pushed out a scalp full of shiny black hair chopped at uneven angles. She envisioned her gray eyes in a face designed to discourage confrontation as she reached into her rear pocket, pulled out a slim black case, and thumbed it open. Inside lay two cards: Galen's and one other he kept for emergencies such as this one. Long slender fingers pulled it from its slot, replaced it with Tenzin's, and slid the case into her pocket. Prying tech in the concourse scanners would now skim past the two cards in the case and see Thrace Baldric. Her identity, with a full stash of credits and linked to a flat on nearby Rubene, would provide all necessities until she could set course for Iridos.

Back in the concourse, Thrace made for the kiosks, her mind racing faster than her feet. Everyone spoke colonial English, but all the human worlds still babbled in a wide array of languages. Chances are no one would even notice if she spoke in Galen's native tongue. She didn't know which of his Rubene colleagues survived, but she'd leave a message with both, then go to Rubene and wait. Bejami felt too hot right now.

She approached the first stall, entered the requisite comm addresses and selected "audio only," then spoke in soft, rapid Unameze.

Skalar's killing unammi pilots. Stay away from the ports! Send this warning on to the others as fast as possible. Look for me on Ynysbedd in seven cycles.

The brief time lag in communiqués between Rubene and Bejami meant quick receipt. If the sh'toi who had killed one of the Rubene pilots received the message, they wouldn't understand it. With luck, the other pilot still lived and controlled a ship. It might mean the difference between life and death for them both, as well as the other surviving pilots. Ironic, she thought. This was the very reason many pilots argued in favor of living aboard their ships, that doing so would make escape faster and easier should the need arise. Yet they'd been trapped, easy prey, while Galen's choice to live disguised among the humans had saved his life, even if escape did now appear problematic.

Thrace had no idea how to reach most of the other pilots living disguised on the colonies, nor did she think it wise to try and contact all of them even if she did. No. Let the pilot from Rubene warn the others from the safety of space. The best thing Thrace could do was to get out of sight and lie low. Thank Na'Staani for Botha's training in focus, which had helped Galen maintain his Tenzin persona for longer periods without a rest.

Botha! Ah, no! He had never met Thrace and would never know why Tenzin had dropped out of his life. It felt like a betrayal, painful enough to twist Thrace's features and pluck at her concentration, something she couldn't afford right now. With an effort, she pushed aside her grief. No distractions. Get out first. Mourn later.

Still frowning, Thrace moved on to the next step in her plan. No one paid her any mind as she joined the throngs of tourists swarming toward the main lobby, not even the Consortium guards who still clustered around the Iridosian ship's berth. Thrace ignored them. That resource was lost to her, as were the other established identities whose cards would be found aboard, the flat registered to Tenzin Dawa, and Bejami as a whole. She hoped the human ident cards would engender, at worst, vague suspicion that the unammi sold forged identities. More accurate assumptions about the cards bordered a new paradigm of fear for the unammi, one Thrace didn't want to consider.

In the foyer of the port building, she passed Luccyn—who prowled, restless in her pursuit—and joined the line awaiting a ticket vendor. Rubene and Bejami shared a star, but their differing orbits made for irregular travel between the two ports. By her calculations, the two colonies were in opposition now, which meant a delay. When her chance came, Thrace stepped to the machine and entered her destination. She'd been right. The next shuttle ran in two days, but ticketing closed four hours ago due to a full load. Thrace booked the last seat on the shuttle after that, paid her passage and loaded the confirmation onto her ident, then lined up a small flat in the port's short-term housing. When she turned away, Thrace almost ran into Luccyn, who growled a warning.

"Watch where you're going!"

Thrace stepped aside, then continued on her way.

chapter 35

Iridos

THE SOUND OF SCATTERING ROCK and calling voices echoed off the walls of the wide tunnel in an odd, disjointed pattern as if the noises originated within the pile before her, instead of around the other side. Alira's numb mind toyed with the audial illusion to distract her from despair. Even the arrival of the miners, who still dug toward the tunnels with their excavation equipment, offered little hope of arriving in time. Rescuers like Alira's team kept searching, but anyone trapped in this last attack would be dead before they were found.

Her burning conviction of last cycle, doused by fitful sleep and restless dreams, moped in pale shadow among the towering obstacles that beset them. When had she ever been this tired? Torpor sapped the last dregs of her frustration and cast her people's reactions in a new light. Given this terrifying predicament and their uncertain future, of course people would cling to what they knew. Despite what she had said to Ijydin at their shared meal, Alira no longer had faith in her own instincts. She had no idea what they should do next. Whatever the council decided, Alira would obey.

She pulled away rockfall, clearing a space, then crawled forward to brush aside more gravel and extricate smaller stones. Fingers groped around the edge of the next large slab, working between it and the surrounding rubble in search of a solid grip, then heaved it up and rolled it out of the way. Dust and grit fell in a choking haze. She sat back and waited for it to settle.

After a moment, she crawled forward again, swiping at the detritus when her fingers touched warm flesh. The heavy coating of sand and rubble fell away, revealing the weak colors of a survivor. Her instant excitement reflected off the surrounding walls.

"I found someone!" she cried, then leaned over the victim. "Be still. Let me help you."

She uncovered the face, brushed away the dust.

"Are you conscious?"

The barest whisper came in response.

Alira's thoughts dipped into Musju, scanning the trapped body to assess its physical damage—too massive for one person to heal. This required combined efforts. She dove into the joinedmind to call for aid.

"Alira!" This time the voice was stronger.

She dropped out of the collective.

The victim's eyes fluttered open.

Those features beneath the dust…was that—

She bent closer. "Na'apa Cesar?"

A coughing fit seized him, spraying droplets of fresh blood onto his lips where they gleamed against the chalky powder.

"Somebody help!" Alira shouted. Her hands, white beneath the layer of grime she wore, yanked rocks off the elder's upper torso and both his arms.

"You should have been there," he croaked.

Alira paused, peering at him. "Been where?"

White raced through his colorful pain. "When she died."

"Hurry!" she shouted again. Where were the healers? Twisting, she moved another stone off his broken form and reached down to touch him. "Who, Na'apa? When who died?"

"Lurien...." His eyes squeezed shut, then flew open to lock on hers. "You're next—"

His hand twitched toward hers, pushing something into her grasp, and Alira pulled back a coin. Cesar's gold coin. "Next for what?" she blurted, her heart's rhythm leaping like drums at a rite. "What are you talking about?"

Words rasped out as fast as he could speak. "You aren't ready, but you're strong. It might be enough. She—"

Another spasm of coughing from the dying elder spat blood onto Alira's face and she winced, blinking. When she looked again, he lay still.

"She *what*?" she yelled. "Na'apa, what did you mean?"

For a moment, she thought he might speak. Surrounding sounds seemed muted, distant, as she waited.

The impact, almost physical, struck her dumb. Images slammed into her, one atop another atop another, layer upon layer of rich, full memories.

...riding on someone's shoulders to the temple cavern....

...celebrating Founder's Day with a family she didn't recognize....

...lovers who were now aged or long since dead....

...details of historical accounts and events she herself had struggled to learn, now clear and concise in her mind....

...the view from a council seat over the heads of gathered unammi at a hearing....

...fingering the treasured gold coin shaped and gifted by a first offspring....

Alira gasped, her body quaking with shock as the deluge continued, this time more relevant to her own concerns.

...a conversation with Lurien about her dead sister, taken by the harvesting malady....

> *harvesting what?*

...talk of Lurien's daughter, born of the Founder, following the line of his seed as Lurien had done, and her sister and mother before her, and *her* mother before that....

...a conversation in which Lurien worried about how much longer she could keep the council from mitigating Alira....

When it ended, Alira reeled forward onto the rubble beside Cesar. In the far reaches of her awareness, she knew others approached, spoke to her, retreated. Their concerns brushed against her as wisps of smoke, drifting over and past while her mind careened into the bewildering truth. *Cesar's* memories…*Cesar's* knowledge. How….

Other memories—her own?—darted through her mind, images of Lurien at dozens, hundreds of deathbeds. *Thank you for your knowledge*, Lurien always said. Is this what she had meant?

The answer was there, in Cesar's cache. Only the Founder's line birthed soul harvesters.

soul what?

Alira's fingers, gray from more than the chalky dust that coated her skin, scrabbled at the debris beside Cesar, gripping and releasing as she struggled to understand what just happened. What was still happening. Did this mean the Founder was her apa? Is this why Lurien wouldn't speak his name? All ama's comments on inheritances and blood, and her desire for Alira to lead the council one day—

Threads of understanding began to weave together. No wonder the council had deliberated over her status for so long! Half, ignorant of her heritage, pressed for treatment while the rest, including three wise to the truth, rallied against it. *You're not ready*, Cesar had said, even as he laid this at Alira's feet content in the belief that this was the way of things. She wanted no part of it, but if Cesar was right, she had no choice and neither did the council. Their threat no longer held any power. They *couldn't* mitigate her now.

Cesar's body flickered in its deshtant a hand's breadth from her face. Perhaps his pithasia was even now blending with the Flow, or…would it wait until the deshtant concluded? A gentle touch on her shoulder brought her head around to see Rakalesh beside her, waiting. Watching.

"Are you injured?"

She knew. She'd known all along. "You should have told me. "

Rakalesh's mouth tightened as she glanced around. "Not here. Can you walk?"

"Of course." Alira shifted, then leaned close to Cesar's ear. "Thank you, Cesar, for your knowledge."

chapter 36

ALIRA FOLLOWED RAKALESH INTO THE council chamber, where the elders had so recently passed sentence.

"Sit," Rakalesh said. She cast a silent glance at Alira's fingers, which twiddled Cesar's coin over and over.

Alira looked down at her own hand as if unaware of its actions.

Cesar used to do the same thing.

Rakalesh sat beside her. "I assume you discovered your gift. That you're a Founder's Daughter. A soul harvester, like Lurien. It must have come as a shock."

"Shock." Alira's flat tone clashed with the frenzy of her confused color reflected on the cushion and floor beside her. Cesar's memories, a lifetime of them, threatened to overwhelm her own thoughts. "How long have you known about this? Wait," she said, finding the answer in Cesar's recollections. "I already know. Since Lurien decided to conceive me. Why didn't anyone ever tell me? No," she continued. "I see that one too. Because I was too unstable to entrust with such a responsibility."

"Yes. Your mother's sister couldn't take the stress. She—"

"She died," Alira said in a monotone. "The harvesting sickness."

"Yes. Lurien struggled to avoid it most of her life," Rakalesh said. "It is horrific. The harvester stumbles into madness, wastes away. Our healers could never touch it. Once its manifestation is complete, the harvester always dies. Lurien came close. She didn't want that torment for you, so she waited. In her defense, you never showed her or anyone else you had the equilibrium to manage even one harvest, much less season after season of them."

"But this ability is inherent in me. Wouldn't it have appeared whether I was ready or not?"

Rakalesh sighed and closed her eyes for a moment. She nodded. "Yes."

"Then why not start training me earlier?"

"In retrospect, perhaps we should have. Lurien kept hoping you would change."

Alira spread her hands. "This makes no sense. People have been dying ever since the attacks. Why did this harvest happen now? Cesar wasn't the first—"

"He's the first to die *in your presence*. In the beginning, you'll only reap those who are within range to alert your physical senses. Later, with more experience, your skill will improve. Lurien could reap the dying even while she slept."

Alira thought back to Lurien's vigil by the bedside of countless others. "Cesar's harvest came into me at the moment of his death. Why did Lurien always wait for the deshtant to finish before thanking the departed pithasia?"

"She never discussed it with me. Maybe because she never lost her fear of the mania. Perhaps she always waited to be sure her own mind and memories would still be intact at the end of the deshtant."

"Do you know how many harvests she managed?"

"No. She didn't talk much about it. The things she absorbed were private. Lurien always respected that."

"She would have harvested her mother, though."

"Yes."

And if Lurien harvested her own mother, who had harvested her mother, who had harvested *her* mother.... Alira touched her wrinkled forehead. The skin there felt hot. "She must have had memories going back to the beginning."

"Near enough."

"Then…." Alira swayed at the implications. "If harvesting is isolated to the Founder's line…with Lurien dead, we have to start fresh."

"Yes." Rakalesh sounded weary, too.

Alira's heart constricted under the staggering weight of responsibility, the loss of such a vast reservoir of knowledge, so many memories encapsulated in one being. She wanted to stand, to move, but wasn't certain her legs would support her. *Ah, Ama! You should have told me sooner!*

"Why is this ability confined to the Founder's line?" she asked, her voice pinched. "Was that deliberate?"

"Lurien believed the Iri manipulated the Founder's DNA in the vault so his progeny possessed unique gene markers specific to this trait. I always assumed this was the reason behind keeping the high cleric's position in that same line, but something else has occurred to me of late."

"What?" Such a generic question that could lead to so many specifics. What occurred to you? What were you thinking to keep this from me? What will I do next?

The elder hesitated, as if sorry she'd mentioned it. "I didn't know Lurien dreamed like you do until you told me. Perhaps it's another attribute of the Founder's genes. Maybe the high cleric is always of the Founder's ancestry because the Iri find it easier to speak to those descendants."

"Speak? Did…the Iri *speak* to Lurien?"

"No," Rakalesh shook her head. "Not like I'm speaking to you. I don't know if they've ever done that with anyone. But Lurien did feel their presence more than anyone else, even more so in meditation. They might not have used words, but she knew what they wanted."

A whisper rustled in Alira's thoughts. Her Companion spoke with words. "You're saying that's why my ama dreamed? Why I dream? The figure in my dreams is the Iri?"

"I don't know," Rakalesh said. "Maybe."

"Then why the accusations against me, Councilor? If you knew or even suspected the Iri were behind all this, why make me believe that my dreams meant I was out of control?"

"I told you I didn't know before about your mother's dreams. And yes, I suspected the Iri guided our hands, but I singled you out because you *were* out of control. Lurien feared—"

"Don't blame her. It wasn't Lurien who was afraid, was it?" Alira heard the edge in her tone. "*You* wanted to keep me from my council seat because *you* worried that in Lurien's place, I would bring change to the people."

Red colored Rakalesh's sharp defensive gesture. "Lurien was part of the council. We *all* feared you would be a danger to our community unless you learned greater self-control. If you had, Lurien would have trained you long ago. Once you taught your bizarre notions to the younglings, we realized you could never manage it."

"You said the harvesting would manifest regardless. What if the gift had awakened after I was mitigated?"

"We believed mitigation would halt the reapings."

"But you didn't know. If it is difficult enough to manage with my faculties intact, how much more horrific would it be for a mitigant?" Alira said, her voice trembling. "How could you even consider it?"

Rakalesh sliced the air between them. "Enough. What's done is done. I—We did what we thought best at the time. I'm not going to defend those choices to you."

alira, stop. you don't know the path that led rakalesh to this place. show some respect.

Alira's planned retort froze in her throat. Gray patterns skittered down her arms.

cesar?

Rakalesh still shimmered with red veins. "You hear him, don't you?"

Alira blinked.

"I wondered how long it would take. It isn't just the memories and knowledge you harvest. It's the essence of the personality. Lurien told me she heard the voices of everyone she ever harvested. They're part of what sometimes leads to the sickness. You can't let those you harvest take control. You have to dominate them."

The words fell from Rakalesh's mouth as if she had experience in this. Would it be as easy as she made it sound?

"How am I supposed to do that?"

"Learn more about those you harvest, about their impact on the people around them during their lives. Speak to their families and friends. Use discretion, of course. They know nothing of the harvester's gift, nor should they. Ever." She squinted at Alira. "Do you understand what I'm telling you?"

"No. I mean," Alira touched her head, "yes, but if I can't tell anyone about these memories I've absorbed, then what's the point of the harvest?"

"Lurien never knew," Rakalesh said. "Nor did her ama, or her ama's ama. As far as she could tell, none of the harvesters in her line ever knew what purpose their gift served, beyond speculation."

"Which was?"

Rakalesh sighed. "They believed their purpose was to capture and hold safe the knowledge of all those they harvested."

"Like a mental history of our people?"

"Yes," Rakalesh said. "A record that could be accessed if there were ever a need."

"And has there ever been such a need?"

"Not to my knowledge," Rakalesh said. Her voice sounded weary.

"Then why keep the gift alive?" Alira's skin still prickled with the shock of the harvest. "What use is it to us?"

A tinge of annoyance touched Rakalesh's display. "Because every Founder's Daughter has been convinced harvesting is a gift from the Iri, something we shouldn't take lightly. Lurien told me they all believed there must be a reason, a purpose to their trials. They all hoped to be the one to discover what it was." She gave a tiny shake of her head, an almost unnoticeable movement. "It would seem the Iri haven't yet seen fit to share this with us. But you mustn't tell anyone. Trust me. You will live to regret it, not through any action I might take, but because if you do, you will never have another moment's peace. The others will drive you to distraction, pester you for information, demand that you speak for their lost ones."

Alira nodded. "I hear you."

"Good. Make time after each reaping, if you can, to incorporate the new details and memories into your own experiences, but keep in mind that having knowledge doesn't infer automatic comprehension or the wisdom to act on it. I'm certain every harvester found her own way of coping. You'll learn through trial and error what works best for you. The crux is if you can't manage them, the absorbed personalities will take your sanity and then your life. That sort of discipline comes hard, more so perhaps for you."

Alira squinted at her. "You don't like me much, do you, Councilor?"

"No, I don't. I resent your selfishness, what you put Lurien through, but my opinion of you is irrelevant. Lurien was my friend. She wanted you to succeed, so I will do what I can to help you. I will still speak my mind."

"It isn't as though you have a choice, though. You couldn't mitigate me now no matter what I do. That's what you meant before when you said you needed me."

alira!

Remorse, hot and stinging, twisted Alira's features, but Rakalesh heaved to her feet and jabbed a red finger in Alira's direction.

"That is precisely why you're a disgrace! Why would you say such a thing? How can it possibly be helpful? Your arrogance tempts me to withdraw my support and leave you to fall apart on your own. You're so quick to judge my animosity. You might first measure your own."

Alira dropped her gaze to the floor. "Apologies, Councilor. I don't know why I said that. It's just—I feel trapped by this. It's a lot to absorb. I know it's my duty. I'll do what is required, but it's going to take time to acclimate. If I had known this was coming, if Lurien had trained me...." The words shriveled on her lips, and she sighed. "That's water around the bend, isn't it?"

Rakalesh didn't state the obvious.

Alira's fingers intertwined in her lap, Cesar's gold coin among them. "Without her guidance, I'll need all of you if I am to help our people get through what lies ahead."

"Don't expect to step into that council seat yet. Wait to see how you manage Cesar's reaping, and the ones that follow, first. I have little faith in you, but I won't stand in your way."

Her words stung, but Rakalesh had been right earlier. Alira hadn't given them reason to believe she could endure any of this. "I understand." She raised her gaze to the Councilor's. "So, it now falls to me to produce the next harvester."

"A Founder's Daughter, yes. But not until we've stabilized the city."

An image of the locked chamber buried deep in the bowels of the monument flashed through her mind. "I see a special vault in Cesar's memories. The Founder's genetic material is stored there in the monument? Along with our own frem samples?"

Rakalesh hesitated. "Yes."

"But…." Alira's words faltered, her features contorting as a new and repugnant realization slammed into her. "Wait. Wait." Her jaw went slack. She squinted, tilted her head. "No. No, this can't be right. Because if all the harvesters are from the same stock, then that means…." Her body dry heaved before she could stop it. She brought a hand to her mouth to stop the rising bile. "My mother was my *sister*? This is…."

Rakalesh tried to interrupt, but Alira ignored her.

"And you speak to *me* of violating taboos. How—" Alira began, breathless, then stopped, swallowing hard. She closed her eyes and inhaled, long and slow.

"It isn't—" Rakalesh began.

"How is my entire lineage not a string of genetic mutations, each generation worse than the last?"

"Because Founder's Daughters are products of more than a simple pairing," Rakalesh blurted, her display flickering with a bizarre mix of color. "The section of the vault you saw is encrusted with irolium, and used exclusively for the Founder's genetic material, which undergoes constant symbiotic evolution. It has since the beginning, when the irolium began to form. Each generation's Daughter is a seed, sired by DNA that differs in significant ways from the previous pairing, enough so you may as well be the product of a different lineage. Lurien was your mother, not your sister. The DNA that sired her was as different from that which sired you as Cesar's would have been."

Alira's mind spun. "Why would we do something so aberrant and convoluted rather than relying on simple copulation to produce offspring?"

Rakalesh scowled. "Because regardless of the changes it undergoes, there is something consistent in the Founder's DNA that produces a soul harvester. We don't know what it is, and believe me, our ancestors searched. Lurien said earlier generations tried numerous alternative methods. Some were disastrous. None worked. This is the only way."

Alira sat in stunned silence, lavender mixed with gray and green and blue rippling across her limbs. No wonder she had felt so different. As a product of such strange stock, how could she ever be like anyone else?

"Listen to me, for once in your life," Rakalesh said, leaning close. "Forget about your sire until it is your time to bear a Daughter. Then you will see for yourself how it works. Let this go. You've enough to consider without adding that."

Alira heaved a ragged breath. "The Founder died generations ago. How many more Daughters can he spawn?"

"The vault is a subject for another time, but pay attention, Alira, because this is important. Few of us shared this secret—Lurien, Cesar, me, and a few trusted healers. Now there are two, you and me. The rest of our people don't know the Founder's DNA sits in the vault nor that the Iri prefer the Founder's descendants to speak for them on the council. You mustn't reveal any of this. It isn't news they're prepared to hear. Understand?"

"No, but I'll comply."

"Good. Comprehension will come, I assure you. Now, you've a great deal to absorb, I think. Stay here a while. I'll see to it you have some privacy. Take time to process what has happened. Integrate Cesar's harvest. Find your balance. Meditate, stand in Musju's flow. When next you sleep, ask your dream companion for guidance."

"I will."

After Rakalesh had gone, details and complications chased each other through her befuddled brain. Of course, it wasn't only *her* mind any longer. Or was it? Now that Cesar resided within her, were her thoughts her own? How would she know the difference?

you'll know.

Ah. Well, then. If Cesar's thoughts were all this plain, it wouldn't be so difficult. Would she also reap his gifts? He had been a reader, which would be most—

no.

Oh. She sighed. If Lurien had trained her, if she'd been there to harvest Lurien's memories, this would all make much more sense. Without context, she would have to decipher these new mysteries on her own.

Rakalesh said Lurien feared losing herself, her own memories, with successive reapings. Was that the reason why some harvesters went mad? If she knew what to look for, how to compare one harvest to another and what the danger signs might be, it wouldn't be so worrisome. But if the sickness was inevitable once it matured, by the time she recognized it her own sanity would be forfeit. How could Lurien have made such an irresponsible decision? She'd known this lay in her daughter's future. Now, without the necessary training, Alira would have to fumble through the harvests on her own, like making her way through a pitch black, obstacle-strewn cavern with no map, no strategy, no aide.

How many more troves of knowledge would they lose? With the sh'toi gone, the number of dying should diminish, but as the unammi's harvester, she would need to be present at every one. Already they were the poorer. Complete loss of Lurien's ancestral memories, population at a fraction of what it had been, guilds destroyed that might never be rebuilt, the loss of their irolium and the looming threat that implied....

She froze. The irolium! If she dimmed, would she still be able to harvest memories? White rippled through her confusion. She felt as vulnerable as a wingless niveym on the wind-swept plain. The humans had the crystals. Even if she knew where they were or could bring them back, shards detached from the cavern walls and thus from the Iri may not provide renewal. What did the stories say of that?

Urgency ran hot through her blood. Ijydin said she would bring the pilots home. Wouldn't greater exposure and more unammi bodies expedite the stones' regrowth?

Yes. Yes! Bring back the pilots as soon as possible. The more the better. A slim hope was better than none at all.

Alira shot to her feet and left the sanctuary of the council chamber. To her surprise, workers had dug through from the landing bay to the rest of the tunnels. How long had it taken to harvest Cesar? How long had she conferred with Rakalesh? Everything seemed changed now. Ghosts of memories from before her time shadowed the familiar passage as if two sets of eyes peered out from inside her head. She dragged her fingers along the wall, steadying herself.

In the bay, Ijydin emerged from the hatch of her ship when Alira approached.

"Ijydin, I need to speak with you!"

"Not now." Ijydin charged under the belly of the ship, checking panels and connections.

"It's important." Alira touched Ijydin's arm. "Please."

Ijydin stopped with an exasperated grunt. "What?"

"Is your ship functional?"

"More or less."

"What do you mean?" Alira frowned.

Ijydin sighed. "One of the cargo bays is compromised. I'll have to seal it off from the rest of the ship to preserve life support. Lighting in some of the compartments is glitchy—"

"Glitchy?"

"It doesn't work right. Winks in and out. Auto-nav is down. Food storage is gone. Screens—"

"What about comms?" Alira interrupted. "Can we send word to the pilots yet?"

"Nope. Short range is fixable, but long range is down hard. I don't have the materials here for repairs. That needs a shipyard."

Alira's legs went weak. "You mean we can't warn Nyros and the others?"

"Not from here." Ijydin resumed working.

"What, then?"

"Harajüd has comms aplenty. Better yet, Nyros lives in the capital. From his flat—"

"So," Alira said, hope coloring her display, "the ship will fly?"

Ijydin's head wobbled left and right before she shrugged. "Maybe. Probably. We'll have to go as soon as—"

"We?" Alira stepped back. "No, I can't leave. You have to do it."

Ijydin gaped at Alira. "Come on. I saw the way you reacted when I brought it up before. The mere mention of getting off Iridos flushed your whole body yellow."

"I can't." How could she explain? Rakalesh's warning wasn't even cold in Alira's ears.

"Why not? What's stopping you? It isn't like you fit in here anyway. You know it. I know it. The council knows it."

"I made Rakalesh a promise," Alira said, her words sounding weak even to herself, "one you reminded me of. Besides, she's going to train me to take Lurien's place. If I leave, I'll lose that opportunity."

"You. Take Lurien's place. You aren't serious."

Her friend's words rang too close to those of the councilor, moments ago. Deep heat seeped into Alira's cheeks. Did no one believe in her? "Oh, but I am."

Ijydin raised both hands to her head and glared at the belly of her ship. "She is going to make me insane." She waved toward Alira and stomped out from under the ship, moving toward the tunnels. "Fine. Stay here with the people who intended to mitigate you. But I don't want to hear your complaints when they—"

A cracking sound reverberated through the cavern and they both looked up in time to see a section of the ceiling tumbling toward them. Ijydin shoved Alira, who landed hard on her side beneath the ship. Her teeth slammed down on her tongue and the taste of blood filled her mouth. Ears ringing, she sat up and looked back.

A heap of stones lay settling where her friend had stood.

"Ijydin?" she cried. "*Ijydin!*"

Alira staggered to her feet and ran to the rocks at the same time as several bay crew. Together, they clawed away the stones, peeling back skin on knuckles and knees. Revealed at last beneath the crushing weight, Ijydin lay on her back, her neck bent at a grotesque angle.

"No! Ijydin!" Alira brushed away the pebbles and dust as she had done for Cesar, her voice rising. "Ijydin, speak to me!"

Ijydin smiled, an odd human expression, and cut her gaze toward Alira's voice. "I guess—" her voice hitched, "I won't be going after—after all."

Alira dropped into the muñara, reaching into Ijydin's broken body to begin the healing. But this…Alira knew at once it was no use. A team of healers couldn't fix this, not in time. She touched her forehead to her friend's temple.

"No…oh, no…."

The harvest crashed into Alira, thick, fast, and strange. Wracking tremors shook her. Human experiences jumbled into typical unammi rituals and traditions in a confusing mishmash

mishmash?

of images and sensations and feelings. Alira held fast to Ijydin's bloody head as the memories gushed through

lovers with Nyros?

and in those moments/cycles/seasons, she lived every breath of her friend's life. When it stopped, she lay gasping and spent on the rubble pile.

"Alira?"

She couldn't move.

"Alira. Speak to me."

"Ijydin is dead," she managed.

A sigh. "Yes. I know. Are you whole?"

Alira rolled to see Rakalesh squatting beside her. Was she whole? Two harvests in less than half a cycle. Whole? She was whole times three. *Three is me.*

"Alira, answer me."

She drew a shuddering breath and stretched over to whisper something in Ijydin's ear.

"Alira!"

"Hold your horses, Rakalesh."

Gray dotted the councilor as she drew back. "My what?"

Alira sat up in a groggy fog, wiping dusty, bloody hands down her face. "I'm fine."

"You are certain?"

"Yes," Alira nodded with finality. "In fact, I'm going after Nyros."

Part Three

chapter 37

<u>**Iridos**</u>

"NO. IT IS OUT OF the question."

"The council still won't allow them to return?" Alira asked. "Those pilots are our kin."

"That isn't the issue, and you know it." A confusion of purple and red colored Rakalesh as she walked away, then spun back. "You confound me. After our earlier conversation, I can't believe you would even suggest such a thing. You *know* we can't spare you."

"Of course you can. I'll go to New Canaan, alert Nyros, and be back in six cycles. He can warn the other pilots without my help and bring them all home." Alira took a breath. Who was speaking through her lips? Oh, for some private time to sort through the jumbled memories! But she'd have plenty of that on Ijydin's ship. *Her* ship. "Besides, you have genetic samples for my whole family tree. If I don't come back, you can make another harvester."

"No," Rakalesh said through her teeth. "We can't."

Alira frowned. "Why not?"

Rakalesh drew herself up straight, her breathing erratic. "Because the vault has been damaged. Many of the genetic pods were tossed about in the attacks."

White splashed across Alira's display. "We lost them?"

"We don't know yet." Rakalesh began to pace. "Some seem fine. Others, we can't tell. As long as the internal containment is intact, the pods will preserve the samples with integrity for some time even outside the vault, but to be certain of their status we would have to break the seals. If we do, and the external shells are damaged in any way, we may not be able to reseal them." She looked at Alira. "And with the vault already compromised…."

"Degradation would be unstoppable."

They stared at each other.

"The Founder?"

Rakalesh shook her head. "His samples are safe. That section of the vault is twice protected."

"What about the others? We have to open them sometime."

"After we repair the vault, restore its sterility. Then we can check the samples, transfer those from compromised pods to intact, clean ones."

"How long will repairs take?"

"I don't know. Many cycles."

Alira threw her hands up. "We can't wait that damn long, Councilor!"

"Ugh." Rakalesh flushed gray. "Do you hear yourself? You sound like a human."

Alira stopped. "Ijydin? Did you make me say that?"

"Don't," Rakalesh said with a grimace. "Don't talk to your harvests. Not in front of anyone else."

Another addition to the list of things she shouldn't do. Great. "Ijydin knew the pilots were in danger from Skalar's people cycles ago. If they aren't already dead, they soon will be. Even if they managed to escape the Traders, they may not be able to get to their ships. They would have no way to get home. You can't abandon them to that fate!"

"We have to."

"No. We don't. Take an ovum sample from me now. You can use genetic material from that if you need to."

"Haven't you heard me?" Rakalesh huffed. "There is no way to preserve a fresh specimen! Even if we could, it would take many seasons to raise a new harvester. Too much would be lost in the meantime. We need you here. Now. Ijydin's passing is a prime example. If you hadn't been nearby, her memories would have been lost."

"Good point. I *was* here. I *did* harvest her knowledge, which means I can fly her ship. I'm the only one who can."

Rakalesh sighed. "I explained this. Knowing isn't the same as doing. You won't be able to operate her craft without a season of practice."

"Watch me." Ijydin knew every seam in that ship. Ijydin now lived in her head. Alira could fly her boat. "We need those pilots. They may still have invaluable supplies in their possessions, maybe even materials to help repair the vault. Besides, the more of us there are, the faster the irolium will regrow."

Rakalesh rolled her eyes. "You don't know that."

"It makes sense, doesn't it? We've always known the temple held no irolium when the Founders first settled here. That the crystals result from symbiosis."

"Yes, but—"

"Then it's a logical assumption."

Rakalesh seemed uncertain. "According to the samples in the vault, there were more than five hundred among the original Founders. We are far fewer now."

"All the more reason to gather as many as we can."

"We don't know that we'll dim without the crystals."

"Granted," said Alira. "But isn't it typical unammi to err on the side of caution?"

"Suppose you're right. What makes you think we won't dim before the irolium grows back? We have no way of knowing how long it'll take."

"For all we know new crystals will grow faster, especially after so many generations of symbiosis." Alira peered at the councilor. "I mean no disrespect, but your reasons don't support your objection. Think about what I'm saying. Yes, there are unknowns. How is that different from anything else we face now?

"Say for the sake of argument," she continued, "I'm wrong. I bring the pilots back and the irolium grows no faster. They would still be additional able bodies to assist in rebuilding, and a wider variety of genetics to grow our population. Where's the harm?"

Rakalesh opened her mouth to speak, and Alira stepped forward, one finger raised.

"But what if I'm right? If the younglings' tales are true, we could lose my capacity for harvesting along with so much else! Can we afford to take that chance?"

The air in the chamber thickened with silence, and Alira held her breath.

"You sound like Cesar," Rakalesh said, her voice rough. "How will you know how to act on human worlds?"

"Ijydin can guide me. Besides, I used to be pretty good at a human disguise, remember?"

The councilor flickered with amusement. "It has been a while. You'll need to practice."

Not as long as she thought. Alira's recent classroom demonstration flashed through her mind. "I will. You might want to warn people. I need to repair the ship before I can leave, so there will be time. Maybe when I come back, the vault will be well on its way to repair, and our worries will have been needless."

Somber colors rushed through Rakalesh's skin as she regarded Alira. "Six cycles."

Alira nodded. "At most."

chapter 38

ALIRA SAT STRAPPED INTO A safety harness atop her ship—hers *now*—and struggled with knotty repairs. Beneath the panel, a fine mesh of wires resisted her attempts to reconfigure necessary connections. It looked similar to the wiring configurations Rashin and the others had taught her, but this was comms, not lighting or mechanicals. All her attempts to apply the knowledge of one to fix the other proved fruitless. Oh, how she wished Rashin could help her now! But his body lay with the others, awaiting the mass rite.

Purple surged through the pink in her display. Alira slapped the curved surface beside her and shouted at the confused tangle.

"Stop fighting me!"

Her voice echoed around the bay, drawing the confused curiosity of workers still clearing the exit so she could leave once the ship was ready. Alira ignored them, listening instead to Ijydin's guidance in her head.

calm down. getting frustrated won't help.

Maybe not, but it made her feel a little better. Alira didn't want to admit Rakalesh might have been right, that knowing every detail about the ship didn't impart the understanding she would require to fly the damn thing. Didn't matter. Circumstances dictated by the Flow demanded she learn by doing.

She shifted her attention to her surroundings. The rock fall that killed Ijydin had been cleared away after the accident, but Alira thought the sharp smell of her friend's blood would linger in her nostrils for the rest of her life. The hull plates before Alira reflected the purple and blue of her own grief.

Presence fluttered at the edge of her awareness like downy odasen seeds caught against the glass of the domes. Her Companion. Alira bent back to her task and fought the urge to pivot her head. The first time It appeared beside her, just after Ijydin's death, she had been as startled as if someone had snuck up behind. No one else could see It, which didn't surprise her, and from that moment forward her meditations had transformed. In each, the Companion observed from the shore while Alira stood waist-deep in a seething current, but now the water seemed to urge, not fight, her efforts to move. Eddies formed and vanished in the taut surface of the water, transitions in What Would Be, though she couldn't even guess at Musju's message. Even now, she felt the swirling, surging Flow pressing her to....

To what?

"I don't understand," she murmured to her nebulous Companion. "You'll have to speak Unameze."

both unammi and humans will think you odd if you talk to yourself.

"I wasn't talking to myself, Ijydin. I was talking to—"

i know what you were doing.

"Then keep your comments relevant. Like how to fix these wires."

A mitigant working beneath her ship stepped out to frown up at her in confusion. She'd already shocked him earlier by emerging from the ship's hatch as a human. Maybe she should back off for a while. Mitigants didn't cope well with such things.

Alira lifted a hand. "I'm fine. Back to work."

Her next efforts met with success, though Ijydin's voice tsked in her mind at the untidy mess Alira had made of the connections.

"It'll work, right?"

i hope so. you can't enter harajüd airspace without short-range comms. go to the internal comm controls and test it before you close the hull.

She lowered the hoist and unsnapped her harness, unable to shake the oddness of her situation. Three cycles ago, her attitude toward the cargo vessel was one of distant respect, a curiosity she had understood in the most basic sense. Now its dichotomy of strange and familiar, daunting and comfortable, distorted her perception.

Inside, closed doors off the passage on the main deck hid kitchens and nonfunctional food storage, lavatory, and bunks. Decks above housed cargo and storage bays while those below held water reclamation and purification, engines, interstel drives, and a host of technical compartments. Alira turned in at control—she had fixed the sticky door last cycle after she ran into it twice—and sat before a wall of devices and panels. Behind her, a floor-to-ceiling screen allowed external view when desired, but for now she repeated the commands Ijydin barked in her head. To her relief, the short-range array worked. She slumped in the seat, wiping her face. Three repairs down, five to go.

She'd lied to Rakalesh. A lie of omission, yes, but if the councilor knew how dangerous this flight to Harajüd really was, she would have had Alira confined, monitored every moment. New Canaan was Skalar's home base. The minute she landed at the city's port, he would know. How much time would she have to escape the land port before he sent other sh'toi after her?

Ijydin offered the option of landing outside the city, but that would delay Alira's reaching Nyros. And if a comm was sent from an unammi ship to a human flat, they could pinpoint her brother too. No, she had to go to Nyros in person. It was the only way to be sure. Hard as that would be, escaping Harajüd afterward was the real challenge. The unknown factor chafed.

you get us to new canaan, and i'll get us to nyros. together, we'll get back home.

"Right," Alira muttered.

too bad you won't get the chance to sample human food, or some of their perverse entertainments.

"You did?"

what do you think?

"I think you're a strange creature, friend-in-my-head." She rose with a sigh and went back to search the undercarriage of the ship. Here, several mitigants worked nearby, and Alira made a mental note to keep her running commentary silent.

yeah, you should make that a habit.

hush, you. aren't any of my thoughts private?

nope. you'll never be rid of me now.

"That explains the threat of madness," Alira muttered under her breath.

chapter 39

New Canaan, Harajüd
<u>Consortium Trader Base</u>

SKALAR POURED A BRANDY AND turned toward his second. "You shredded the armada."

"No, the squibs did. We never figured out how." Crow cleared his throat. "You told me to ask first. Otherwise, I'd have come in shooting, and dug the mines out later."

"Did you leave any survivors?" Skalar sat behind his desk and leaned back.

"No, sir."

"You're certain?"

"As much as I can be." Crow shifted in his seat. "The little shits nest underground like ants. Unless we dug out every cavern and tracked every passage, we would have no confirmation of their status. However," he held up a placating hand, "we did collapse their entire freshwater basin with the last two LADRAS missiles on the way out. It won't keep us from getting to the hemi later, but I'm sure it squashed the majority of those left. I don't see how any stragglers could survive for long after that."

"You understand if Iridosian survivors make trouble for me later," Skalar said, "I'll be expecting you to either resolve the matter or take the blame."

Crow's jaw tightened, but he said nothing.

"So, you didn't get all the hematium, then."

"No. We got all we could. Between sickness and lost crew and having a single hauler…." Crow shrugged.

Skalar picked up the blue crystal from the desk. "Yet you took all of these?"

The audible grinding of Crow's teeth belied the controlled expression on his face. "I had teams working both at the beginning of the op. Thought I'd have plenty of time, even after the weirdness began to show up. It didn't get bad until we'd gotten the last of the crystals but by then the longer we stayed, the worse it got. All due respect, Admiral, you weren't there."

Skalar squinted at the dark hollows under Crow's eyes. "Very well. What do you suggest?"

"We go back later with a fresh crew and dig a while. If they start acting weird, then come back and send out replacements."

"That is an expensive mining operation."

Crow shrugged. "Less than if you bought it from HHU."

Skalar dragged his gaze back to the crystal in his hand. He would pass a few pieces to his techs, see what they could learn about it. Meanwhile, it did have a sellable look to it. Maybe one of his metalsmiths could use it in jewelry for the market. As the sole source of such rare gems, Skalar could dictate prices as high as he wished. "Granted. You sent the majority to the outpost?"

"Yep. Told Ronan to drop it off and head back."

"Excellent. Anything else?"

"One thing. Harley didn't make it."

"Who replaced him?"

"Vandana Walker. Commander now. She's the one you sent to Iridos in the first place."

Skalar's lips puckered. No imagination, that one. Not stupid, but not officer material. She would never make a viable second for Crow. "You are sure you want her?"

"Pending your approval. It wasn't intentional. Harley pressed for her on the team. I made her his second so I wouldn't need to babysit. After he kicked it, and with things going so wrong on the job, I thought it would be bad for morale if I reneged on an implied promise." He shrugged. "I must admit she surprised me out there."

Skalar sipped his brandy, considering. "You have a certain amount of leeway to choose your own teams. However, as second to my second she now sits far too close to a leadership role for someone with so little experience. Commander Walker has one month to prove herself to me, or…." He shrugged. "How did your demonstration with the Clan ship go?"

"As shocking as expected. I think it's safe to say everyone understands the consequences of violating your gag order."

"Good."

"Are the squib pilots out of play yet?"

"Some."

Crow leaned forward in his seat. "Any chance I could go after the ones on Danua or Rubene, or both?"

"I'm afraid not. You'll have to put off your vendetta a little longer." Skalar rose and refilled his drink, already thinking ahead. Several of his assets were on their way to the outpost with Iridosian ships. He wanted to meet them there, examine his new resources. "I want you to take care of the ones here, on Harajüd. Get started today. Save the New Canaan one for last. I want you in town later this week so you can take charge of the base while I'm away."

"You're going somewhere?"

Indeed, he was. His second had been right about one thing. Running the hematium, and now these blue crystals, from the outpost meant full-time staffing. It also opened up another venture potential—exploration of a whole new region of space for additional income resources. At least seven planets in the same system, six of them viable, four with moons. Other systems within reasonable reach. With the quarantine so close by, he would bet no other corporate foragers even thought of taking steps in that direction.

His second awaited a response. Skalar raised his glass, allowing the pause to drag on before he spoke. "Dismissed." Crow left in an apparent huff, probably annoyed at being kept out of the loop. Too bad. The captain needed an occasional reminder that he didn't run this faction. Not yet, anyway.

chapter 40

Iridosian Ship IR528
<u>En Route to New Canaan</u>

ONE CYCLE TO GO. LESS than a standard day before she would take her first step onto a human world, even though she had memories of doing so numerous times before. Alira faced a holographic image of herself two meters away, took a deep breath, and let it out, stretching her squat body up and out. Her skin color changed from luminescent pale blue to light brown. Fine hair in black and gray tones sprouted from her head until it covered her scalp with a few centimeters' length. Wide silver eyes shrank and darkened to deep brown. Woven fabric stretched over her flat chest and wrapped around her legs, male genitalia bulging at the groin beneath the drab human-style coverings. Lips plumped, muscles pulling them into a smile as the reflection smiled back.

"Hello. I'm Amadi Patel."

The hardest part of holding a morphed persona was thinking about herself,

himself. stay in character.

as the actual person she

he!

he portrayed at any given moment.

He considered his reflection, checking for accuracy. Weren't those ankles too frail to even walk on? Amadi took a step toward his projection, stumbling once—such tiny feet, and those clumsy things

shoes.

making them worse!—before he recovered. He'd already set the ship's gravity to mimic the lighter pull of his destination, which made this even more challenging. He examined his disguise in detail, rotating it to be sure he built the back as well as the front. Ijydin didn't voice any complaints. It must be satisfactory. He nodded to himself, practicing his greeting once again.

"Hello. How do you do?"

The voice still sounded a little forced, the words stilted. Ijydin waved that aside with a thought.

don't worry about it. they'll think it's an accent.

Cesar's whisper joined in.

remember, morphing will make you vulnerable.

Amadi's likeness melted with ease into Alira's natural form. "I've been morphing my whole life."

cesar's right. prolonged focus is difficult in a dangerous situation.

Amadi appeared again, inspecting his reflection, pacing several steps to get accustomed to those dainty appendages. "I'll be there less than a full cycle, just long enough to get Nyros and find a way out. I can stay alert that long." He practiced sitting and rising from the pilot's chair which sat too close to the floor for this human body. It felt like his knees were beside his ears.

really? even through this?

Sudden sensory overload engulfed him. Amadi cringed as Ijydin's encounters in human cities cascaded through his memory. Bright lights gleaming off lurid colors. Constant, blaring noise and intrusive strangers. A fetid miasma so strong he could taste it. Amadi's holographic projection swerved as he did to avoid the imagined crush of humans in all shapes and sizes bumping into and pushing past him. Caught up in the memories, he saw his holo image slip, melt, flicker between Amadi and Alira

see?

and Alira concentrated harder to hold Amadi's guise, hanging on by a slender thread.

don't forget about public transport and polite social customs and avoiding security and—

"I can do it."

be certain. humans can't be allowed to know.

"I understand, Cesar."

no, you don't. if anyone catches you morphing or sees your disguise slip—

"I know, Ijydin. I'll need to kill them." Like Nyros had done, Amadi thought.

Skalar was doing the same thing, killing unammi to cover up his crimes. The sh'toi had already demonstrated his belief that the unammi were disposable. Using them in laboratory experiments as Nyros feared would be no different. Still....

When the invaders were destroying the unammi city, Alira had felt no qualms. In New Canaan, though, Amadi would be the intruder. He clung to the belief that not all the aliens were like those who attacked his people, but even a compassionate human could bring ruin down on the unammi. Only a reader like Cesar or an empath like Galen could distinguish between the cruel and the kind. Either way, the act of taking a life over an accident of timing versus doing so for self-preservation was as different as ha'ani and ne'ani.

Damn it. He paced alongside his holo twin, each of them fiddling with Cesar's gold coin. Could he kill a human? An image of the ravaged city raked the coals of Alira's enmity, dragging behind it the pain of Lurien's death. Cesar's. Ijydin's. All the rest.

At least if Amadi got into any dangerous encounters, Ijydin could take over. She already knew the Amadi disguise, had idents for two others, and a special sheath to hide them from the scanners at the port.

Amadi's figure melted back into Alira's and she rested. It felt odd, portraying a male, but Ijydin said it would be safer, since humans interacted differently with males. Ijydin's primary human persona, Zachary Moss, had also been male. Other false idents she had held waited back in Zachary's flat on Saacharis, along with the rest of Ijydin's belongings, items the survivors could use. Too bad that would add at least eight additional cycles to Alira's trip. She'd promised to return home in six. Rakalesh would need to send someone back later.

For now, those items were out of reach.

Maybe Nyros would have some supplies he could contribute, though how they might manage to get them offworld, she wasn't sure. She ran through her planned route once on the ground in New Canaan—public transport

not the metro, remember. too easy to get trapped there. use the hoverbus.

from the land port to the Mari Bay water docks. Street children had built a warren there among the forgotten shipping containers in long-term storage. Other citizens also had a vested interest in keeping the space hidden. Surveillance cams there never worked for long. Changing to Amadi or one of the other disguises would take a bare moment, then she could take the next bus to the northside housing district and Nyros' flat. That's where her imagination fell short.

She drew a ragged breath and got back to her feet, her reflection stretching into the new physique. Walking, sitting, speaking, Amadi put his reflection through its paces, searching for any slip and starting over when he found one, until his fingers fumbled. The coin *tinked* on the floor and rolled under a panel. Amadi dropped to his knees to retrieve it.

don't lose my coin.

would you put that damn thing somewhere safe? alira, you—

"Amadi," he said, his voice muffled by the panels.

what?

Coin in hand, he stood and faced his reflection. "The name's Amadi."

chapter 41

<u>Ynysbedd, Rubene</u>

THRACE ADJUSTED HER CORE TEMPERATURE in the frigid gale that whipped down off the glaciers across the channel and swept this tiny scrap of rock. Her rented jumper's limited scans showed no other life forms on the islet. Still, best to be sure. Not that there was much to investigate beyond a narrow skerry whose every edge dropped in sheer cliffs straight down to the churning sea. No trees, no animals, no shrubs, no grass, no moss, no algae. Why the humans had named it at all remained a mystery to her. Nothing grew here. Even snow didn't linger on the surface with nothing to hold it against the constant wind. Strange. In that, at least, it seemed reminiscent of Iridos. All it lacked was sand.

It was summer here in the southern hemisphere. Situated as it was in Rubene's polar region, Ynysbedd bathed in unrelieved daylight for months at a time—good for Thrace because she could see approaching problems while still far away, but bad for her because her jumper would be as conspicuous as a human at a Telling, with nowhere to hide if trouble knocked.

It isn't like this patch of sky saw much traffic. Except, of course, from people like Thrace who flew the long way around to thwart satellite detection.

She walked the entire perimeter, glancing over each edge. On one side stood the polar mainland across a wide strait. In winter, when months of darkness loomed over the region, ice connected Ynysbedd to the larger hunk of land. Now, the water flowed unimpeded. Off the other side of the rock at about the same distance sat a larger, lumpier island of permafrost, its top layer boggy in the relative warmth. Even now a mist hung above it, wisping into the winds.

And there, beyond the brume, a small black dot hung in the sky. *A ship.*

Thrace jogged back to her jumper and fell into the flight seat. "Comm, approaching ship, audio only. Aes te nalya. Galen asal."

The comm blipped to life. "Nalena t'staani, Galen. Tiral asal. May I be of assistance?"

Thrace released the breath she'd been holding. "Yes, please!"

"Are you safe?" Tiral asked.

"I am now. It's good to hear your voice. I was afraid my message would come too late."

"Your timing was perfect. But you could have left me a little more room to land."

Thrace lifted the small jumper off the rock, thrusting it aside to hover over the channel until Tiral's ship had settled onto the islet, then set back down in the hauler's shadow. Within minutes, she'd shut down the jumper's systems, grabbed her essentials, and left the craft behind. At the hauler's hatch, Tiral waited.

"Welcome aboard," he said, closing the hatch behind her. "I don't believe I've seen that persona before."

"It's a spare," Galen said as his own features appeared.

"Good thing," Tiral said on the way to control. "If you were right about Skalar, then we have a problem."

chapter 42

New Canaan, Harajüd
Land Port Station

CROW STOPPED HIS JUMPER NEAR the admin wing of the port, where his contact waited. "Well?"

"Another squib ship landed. Docking just cleared. Squib should be coming out soon."

Crow's green eyes narrowed. Why? Visiting the one who hid somewhere in the city?

"Where was its ship registered?"

"Don't know, but I can find out if you want."

Wouldn't be from Harajüd. He had removed most of those from play. "Later. Anything new on the ship that was already here?"

"Not yet. It's been landlocked for a couple'a weeks now, ever since Skalar's people got the order. Nobody has even gone near it. I finally got to the security vids, but they were no help. I wasn't able to track the ship's pilot."

He grunted his thanks, dismissed her, and focused on the main exit nearby. Ever since he had returned from Iridos, fear had snatched Crow from sleep with that same old dream where he'd left evidence behind, like his parents had done. Or the one where his parents promised adult Crow that he had covered all his bases, but the authorities said his parents missed something and now boy Crow had to live in the shelter. One new dream even featured squibs crawling out of the grave he'd made of their city, then finding him in New Canaan and dragging him back into their holes with them.

So instead of sleeping, he'd spent his off-hours rehashing the Iridos job. It was imperative that he'd left nothing behind to point to himself or the Consortium. He had tormented himself over what decision he might have altered to change the outcome. He would give his left nut if he could go back and keep this ugly little drama from ever starting.

Maybe this new squib would lead them to the other one they hadn't been able to find. If so, he could net two of the fuckers at once. Chattering passengers and tourists formed a steady stream of traffic through the main access, but no squib. Minutes ticked by in the hot jumper until Crow began to wonder if he'd missed his target.

He couldn't go after it in public like this, even if it paraded in front of him right now. Too many witnesses, and not enough corporate big shots in the admiral's pocket. Skalar couldn't buy them all, though he'd tried, and the ones who stood up to him wouldn't take it well if faction crew started killing "innocent" visitors. Despite his need of the moment, Crow could understand their reasoning. Imagine the travel promos: "Visit New Canaan, Harajüd colony's largest, most exotic city! Try your luck at the gaming houses…Visit the bustling markets…Take a Consortium knife in the ribs…."

Yeah. Bad for business, that. Besides, a public approach would link the Consortium to the dead squib if anyone got to asking questions later. He'd have to wait until his contacts could help him get quality private time with the squib in exchange for the right number of credits. If he could find it.

He swiped a trickle of sweat off the side of his face. What if the pilot from the other ship had been with this new one, and now they were both inside the port or, worse, had escaped out another access and traveled away from the city? His temples throbbed. Crow rubbed a hand over his clenched jaw, debating whether to abandon this post in favor of a more dynamic search inside the port building when a squib emerged and boarded the public transit with the others. He frowned. Was it going to ride the hoverbus through town as if it hadn't a care in the world?

What had he expected? That it would walk or fly across town?

Crow pulled out to follow the whining transport. This new squib would lead him to the one in hiding. It *had* to. Then he could strike one item off his to-do list and get a bonus squib for his trouble. Only one other Harajüd pilot remained, but it had slipped through his fingers. Its ship hadn't been in port for weeks, and port contacts had no idea when to expect it. If the damn squib was holed up on another colony world, someone else would take it down. Skalar's orders. The whole thing was so irksome. If another agent fucked it up, it would be Crow's ass in the sling. Boy, why did *that* sound familiar?

Skalar should have let Crow handle them all. Simpler. Easier. More peace of mind for Crow, but the admiral wouldn't budge on the topic. He *would* pick now to leave town. Crow had made one last attempt to learn the admiral's destination an hour ago, but Skalar remained tight-lipped on his way out. Why? What was he up to?

Ahead, the hoverbus stopped to pick up passengers, then resumed its trek. Crow lingered long enough to ensure the squib didn't hop off, then followed again.

Well, Skalar could go fuck himself. It had been his idea to wipe the squibs off their rock over hemi he could have gotten another way. Then the fucker promised to trample his second if the job came to light. Any loyalty he still might have felt for the man—small though it was—had died the moment those words left Skalar's mouth.

This was all Jarod's fault. That little shit needed to have an up-close meeting with Crow's blade in a dark alley, away from the cams. Ever since the tech brought his stinking hull plates to the base, Skalar had been acting out of character, keeping secrets, locking his second out of the loop on essential details. On top of the rest, Skalar had thrown down a threat Crow couldn't ignore. The showdown between admiral and captain screamed toward them and truth be told, Crow was over the whole fucking situation.

He slammed his fist on the console beside him, jarring a momentary error message on the array, which he ignored.

Maybe he should make his move now. He would rather wait a few more months, but most of his people had been in place for over a year. Government contacts both here and on other colonies backed him. Yeah, the Iridos job went bad, but the colonials wouldn't know about it. Yet. He'd lost a few supporters on that fuck-job of a mission, and Harley's death had been a blow, but not crippling. Walker could even make a good second, given the right training from the start. If she didn't join the program, plenty of others would kill to take her place. And with Skalar out of the way for a while....

The hoverbus stopped again, this time to let passengers off before it continued.

On second thought, maybe he shouldn't gut Jarod yet. With all the hemi at the outpost, his talents could help Crow generate an ongoing profit for the faction, a detail which wouldn't go unnoticed by the crew. He could even win over Skalar's rank-and-file supporters by promising a share of the wealth.

The single crimp in moving up his timetable was not knowing where Skalar had gone. Hacking the admiral's TICS back at the base might net some info. One of Crow's data whizzes could do it. If they left tracks, Crow could claim ignorance.

Why'd he need to know where Skalar was now? Crow could set him up here in New Canaan when he came back. Get him outside that fucking house he was so proud of. Even better, take him down when he reentered the base, so HHU couldn't come after Crow.

Yeah. That could work.

Ahead, the bus slowed again outside the Mari Bay port. Of *course* it would stop at every fucking station all the way across town. But if he could get two squibs, it would be worth his time investment. Crow started after the departing transport when he realized the squib had gotten off. Shit. Here? What the fuck could it want at the wharf? He took quick stock—passengers and workers all over the place, heavy equipment loading and unloading cargo to the shrieking tune of metal on metal, and generalized chaos amid the overarching fishy reek. But there went the little blue shit, cruising on through the pandemonium like it had been coming here all its life.

He threw the jumper into lockdown and leapt out to follow. The squib had a good head start and moved at a snappy pace, winding its way through the crowd. Crow shoved people out of his way as the squib passed the docks and moved into shipping storage. Here the crowd was thinner, the noise less deafening, and he took more care to stay out of sight. When it kept going toward the ghost-town of long-term storage, Crow frowned. Stowed or forgotten crates and equipment parts littered the alleys. Concealment proved easier, but who the hell came back here? Nobody, that's who, except street brats and second-rate black-market dealers. Where was it going?

Ahead, the squib slowed.

Crow dodged behind a pile of antiquated and forgotten rigging assemblies.

The winking blue head glanced around before it ducked past a ragged pile of shipping bins.

Crow slunk from his cover and crept closer, peeping through gaps in the pile, except the fucking crannies weren't big enough to see squat. He relocated from hole to hole until he saw…he wasn't sure *what* the actual fuck that was. It was like plaz being melted and pulled into some predetermined form, except it also changed color and size, and what the living hell—

Sudden movement in the…blob…sent Crow scurrying under cover to view through larger peepholes as a man walked by. The moment the coast was clear, Crow shot out of his hiding place and around to where the squib had stood a moment before. Empty, and not another visible soul nearby. He craned his neck, searching. A man walked back the way they'd just come. He looked like any other guy one might see in the port, average height, average weight, graying hair, light brown skin. That was the squib. It had to be.

Well, fuck. No wonder the other squib got past them. The little shits could appear human! No telling where it was hiding. It could walk right under their noses, like this one was doing now, and his people would never know. He darted after his target and raised his wristcom to spread the word, then stopped. What if there were squibs hiding among his own crew? Then they'd know he knew, and his advantage would be wasted.

Besides, this juicy tidbit of intel was worth more than all the Consortium's hemi right now. Better to keep it for himself. Such details might come in handy during a takeover bid. The squib's direction took it back into the more populated areas of the port and Crow got closer amid the cacophony and crush, blending in with others when the squib checked behind it. His gaze went to the crowds along the docks. What if some of those people were squibs? How many others were out there walking around the city in their cozy disguises with none of the human residents any wiser?

Had they been here all along?

Crow followed the squib to the station and waited for the bus to pick it up. Once it was gone, he jogged to his jumper and set out after it again feeling better than he had in weeks.

chapter 43

THE TRANSPORT TRIP TO THE wharf had felt endless, and the thought of morphing in a vulnerable public space had sent Alira's heart racing. In the end it had proven easier than expected. When Amadi walked out, no one even looked twice at him. Now, near the back of the opensided hoverbus behind most of the human jabber, that bewildering double-perception of awe and boredom colored everything. Ijydin advised he not talk to himself, though she needn't have bothered. Amadi remained far too absorbed in his surroundings to speak. Shipboard practice paled in comparison to full-blown immersion in a human environment.

The closer they got to the city center, the more crowded the bus grew until humans were as thick as unammi at a rite, their cloying scents saturating the air and tickling the back of Amadi's throat. He coughed, choked back nausea, slid as close as possible to the fresh air, and drank in the passing scenery. Such a difference from Iridos! No ha'ani or ne'ani,

faster rotational period. all the colony worlds are like that.

but alternating cycles of light and darkness. Plants and animals thrived almost everywhere. Pedestrians seemed to have dominion, although vehicles like the bus and smaller craft like the one behind them now dotted the streets, their passing *brrrrr* adding to the transport's hum in an almost hypnotic way. This, then, is where Nyros chose to live his life.

not nyros. rhys bishop.

Amadi blinked. The name evoked a remembered image: pale skin, yellow hair that hung over his brown eyes, slender limbs, small knots of metal dotting his ears. "What is the purpose of those?" Amadi muttered to himself, drawing a few raised brows before the other passengers ignored him once more. He tried to imagine Rhys Bishop riding a public transport, walking down the city's streets with the humans, buying his food in the market, and preparing it himself.

Thoughts of Nyros brought Amadi's sobering purpose here crashing back into the forefront of his mind. How would Nyros react to the news of the city? of Lurien? Amadi couldn't remember ever seeing Nyros project any facade other than solid, dutiful service. Would he wail as Alira had done? What a shock that would be.

The transport plodded into the north side of town, leaving the city center behind. Around them on the streets, larger transports began to thrum past, hauling what seemed to be tree trunks,

logs.

loads of silica, other necessities for a city of this size. Amadi observed it all while beneath the mask Alira wanted more than anything to stretch into this newfound freedom and explore all its mysteries. Except now she didn't dare. Now it wouldn't be her mother or the council tracking her every move. Human reactions posed a far greater threat than mitigation if she slipped even once. She didn't dare relax for a heartbeat. She—He! He was Amadi Patel—felt his mask tighten.

Scenery around the transport changed in a constant flow. Underneath Amadi's curiosity, apprehension returned. Something in his belly twisted, demanded he move, until he fidgeted on the bench in search of a more comfortable position. It didn't help. Now that he was here, he was no longer convinced it was a good idea to come. New Canaan felt like a trap. Getting in had been the easy part. Getting away would be far more difficult. Ijydin had no doubt Skalar would be surveilling the land port, so escape via either Ijydin's or Nyros' ship would be out of the question.

should have thought of that before you left iridos.

Amadi plumbed Ijydin's knowledge for anything to spark an idea. The Trader admiral on Saacharis might help. Perhaps Amadi and Rhys Bishop could take a passenger carrier to that world? Maybe. It would take longer to get home than she had promised, but at least they'd be able to collect Ijydin's supplies while they were there.

The thumping of his heart echoed in his ears, blood pumping faster while fingers found each other in his lap and twined there, tangling and untangling as if they had lives of their own. He looked down at them, the scenery forgotten.

"Be still," he murmured.

Again, passengers nearby scrutinized him. One got up and moved to the last empty seat. Amadi ignored them. His attention locked on the buildings ahead, row after row of identical structures so tall they seemed to touch the sky. Northside Housing, location of Nyros' flat. How did the residents tell them apart? Dread rolled into him like a boulder broken from the ridge.

Sooner than he would have liked, the transport plunged into the district, winding through the streets and around the indistinguishable blocks until Amadi had lost all orientation. The complex extended outward in every direction, oppressive and stinking of gloom. His throat tightened, constricting until his breath came in short wheezing wisps when the bus stopped between two of the structures. A number of passengers shuffled toward the open sides to step off.

this is it. he's in the building on your left. ring the flat of rhys bishop.

"Wait."

Amadi sat, head cocked to one side as if listening to a sound only he could hear, while passengers loaded and unloaded.

"Something is wrong here."

The remaining passengers near Amadi moved as far away as they could.

Before he could respond, the bus began to move. Amadi lurched to his feet and the automated craft stopped.

"Please remain seated," droned a disembodied voice, "while the vehicle is in motion."

But Amadi hovered in indecision. He clung to the grip beside him until another passenger yelled at him to make up his mind.

Amadi stepped down to the ground. When the transport had gone, he surveyed the area. Humans came and went. Ground cars and jumpers and hovercraft whizzed past or stopped or pulled away. What weakened his knees? Alira's Companion loomed ominous and silent in his mind and all at once Amadi wanted to be anywhere else. A mesmerizing sensation wriggled through his awareness. Bold outlines of objects nearest him began to shimmer, waver. Cesar and Ijydin howled in his mind, an icy shriek of warning that raced down his spine and snapped his focus back into sharp acuity.

Amadi blinked, horrified at what he'd almost done. No slipping! No failed masks! Not here. Not in front of so many people. He shot a furtive glance at nearby passersby. No one ran. No one saw. He'd caught himself in time.

He drew a slow breath and turned back to the waiting flat house, feeling as heavy as if he'd swallowed cold stones. One hand shoved itself into his pocket and grasped his coin. He needed to see Nyros, but Amadi did not want to go into that building.

what's the problem? it's a residential flat like all the others, ubiquitous surveillance.

Surveillance at the wharf was nonfunctional.

that's different. colonials maintain these cams. no one except security can enter unless a resident buzzes the door. i promise you, it's safe.

Flinching at every sound, Amadi crept on trembling legs across the green to the door and its resident panel. Ijydin directed him how to operate it, and soon Rhys Bishop materialized in the comm screen. Amadi took in the flat brown eyes, the faint scar on his left cheek. Even in a human guise, Alira's brother had a little wrinkle between his brows.

"Yes?"

Amadi checked his surroundings. No one stood near enough to hear. "Nyros," he said, his tone low.

Rhys hesitated. "Who—"

"Alira asal."

Rhys' face blanched, went slack.

"We don't have much time." Breathe, Amadi told himself. Concentrate. "Something has happened. I need to see you.

"Of course. Come up. I'm in—"

"I know where you are. I'll be right there." Amadi signed off as the outer door clicked. Once inside, he followed Ijydin's direction up the lift and through the corridors, his mind racing. He wondered again if this had been a mistake, but it was too late to back out now.

At the door to the flat, Rhys stood waiting and ushered in his guest without comment. Amadi stepped into the corridor and had enough time to register the lingering fragrance of muñise resin before the door was closed and secured. Still morphing, Nyros whirled, gray and red competing for space in his display.

"What are you *doing* here?"

Amadi shifted to Alira. "Humans attacked our city."

All his red flashed into white. "How bad?"

"There isn't much left. They flattened the domes and most of the central plain. We managed to dig through to the landing bay to access Ijydin's ship. That's how I got here, but we'll be rebuilding for a long time. Few of us survived."

"Ama?" Nyros' voice, so small, carried the weight of his abrupt purple flush.

Alira shook her head. A struggle played itself out across her brother's countenance, and she waited for him to react, to wail or weep. Instead, he passed her, disappearing into a room down the hall. Ijydin and Cesar were silent for a change. Good. This was difficult enough without the additional input. She followed Nyros into the flat's great room where he knelt before his altar, placing the cover back on his thurible. Fresh smoke rose white and fragrant from its vents.

Nyros spoke to the altar. "Who was it? Do you know?"

"Consortium Traders. Skalar's people."

Now the red rushed back, and Nyros' mouth tightened. "What were they after?"

"Hematium. But they took all our irolium, too."

TICS-generated wind sounds filled the silence. For one fleeting moment, Alira was back in the lee of the monument on Iridos.

She grabbed a pillow from the nearby pile, dropped it near his, and knelt, touching his arm. "I know this is a lot to take in, but right now we need to get out of here. Skalar'll go for the pilots next. You know this. We have to warn the others, find a way to get ourselves and them back home."

"Pilots," he murmured. White flashed through his skin. "Ijydin! She isn't waiting on the ship, is she? They'll trap her there, they—"

"Ijydin's dead."

More purple. "Then how did you...."

"It's a long story. I'll tell you on the way back to Iridos. Right now, we need to get moving." She started to rise, but he did not move.

"You shouldn't have come. You could have commed your warning. It would have been faster."

He must be in shock. "We didn't dare," she said, "not at first. What if Skalar's ships left behind relays or some other tech that would report signs of our survival? We intended to fly Ijydin's ship beyond Iridos space, send a warning from there, but her long-range comms were too damaged."

"How long ago did this happen?"

"Thirty cycles. Maybe more."

Nyros took this in. "Skalar has probably gotten to most of the pilots by now. If I'd gone back to my ship...."

She blinked. "I'm glad you didn't, but it's possible you're not alone in that. We have to find out, find a way to tell them."

"If he catches you, you're dead," Nyros pointed out, his voice shaking. "Pilots were always expendable, Alira. You should have saved yourself, played your role."

She sat back, her hand slipping from Nyros's arm where she had rested it as a comfort, for him or for herself, she wasn't sure. So...no wailing. Only more reprimands. "I'm following the guidance of the Flow. Educators and clerics and elders taught me all my life to listen to Musju's whispers. You told me time and again to heed their wisdom. But that isn't what you meant, is it? What you all wanted was for my behavior to fit your expectations, regardless of what Musju or Na'Staani might say to the contrary."

Nyros reached toward her. "Alira—"

She rose, and paced away, her limbs a riot of confused color. Murmurs roused in her mind, Cesar and Ijydin joining in Nyros' censure, and she shushed them both, pushing them behind a brittle wall of emerging control. She was right about this, though it didn't change anything. Her people still needed her, and she would do what she must, but right now she was going to speak the damn truth.

"Even when I do what you've told me to, you say I'm wrong. My attempts to conform never satisfy anyone, least of all me." She turned back toward him. "No matter what I do, someone finds fault."

"That's life, sister!" He lurched to his feet. "Frem accept that they can never please everyone, yet do what is necessary anyway. Individual opinions are irrelevant. What matters is what's best for the unammi as a whole."

"Who sets those parameters, Nyros?"

"The council! Alira, you *know* these things! How have you come this far in your life and not yet accepted this truth?"

Red flashes streaked down her arms. "I'll tell you what I see, brother—"

A chime sliced through her retort, freezing her words in her throat.

"What was that?"

Nyros frowned. "Someone's at my door. It must be a neighbor. No one commed from the entry. Wait here."

As he stalked through the living space, Nyros morphed into Rhys, then entered the hallway and everything slowed down and

the flat's sliding door swished open, and

Rhys blanched, gasped, shied back, and

she leaped toward him and

a knife found its mark in Rhys' eye and

Nyros fell back with a grunt and

a brown human male with a bright green gaze stepped into view

and

and….

and….

And the world slammed into high speed and everything ran together and Alira's feet skidded on the floor, white limbs backpedaling away from the booted intruder while her brother's body began its deshtant. His terror tore through her with frenzied awareness of what had happened, memories from a lifetime inundating her own senses. Cesar and Ijydin roared in her mind

kill that sh'toi! KILL HIM!

as the grinning human stepped over Nyros

"Goin' somewhere, squib?"

and the sh'toi draw back an arm with yet another blade and Nyros' voice joined the others in her thoughts and

alira! don't—

now her brother *and* her mother were gone and she wouldn't be able to warn the others and it had all been for *nothing*, and

alira! you have to—

shut up! shut UP! SHUT UP!

the onslaught shattered her fragile wall of control around fresh harvests and overwhelming loss and a lifetime of suppressed expression. The breath she'd drawn exploded from her in a wail of grief, fear, and rage as she brushed aside the sh'toi's killing throw and lashed out, heaved all her fury toward the human threat…reached *into* him and squeezed his organs to pulp, saturated his loathsome body with toxins and hormones and blood…arteries and veins burst in his brain and electrical pathways tore themselves one from another and blood flowed from every orifice and all the while his awareness watched from within the battered shell as she ripped him apart from the inside until at last he fell, too shocked to utter a sound, and the harvest took a perverse, sickening kink when the dead sh'toi crowded her mind with images and sensations she couldn't—didn't *want* to—recognize, and all the while her trembling body convulsed in white and purple and red.

Her wail faded and she sucked in a ragged, wheezing gasp, staring at the loathsome human. There lay the antithesis of everything she had ever been taught, of the self-control she had tried to cultivate, her perfect opposite, and she'd killed him, swallowed her own shadow, harvested all his filth. All the foibles she'd hoped to squelch in herself now tainted her to the core, damaged her beyond any healer's grasp and she fell to her knees, her stomach hurling its contents onto the floor

> *stop, alira! take time to—*

and she swiped the back of her hand across her mouth

> *alira, get out of here! someone will have heard.*

then heaved again, sickened by the shredded human emotion—raw, ugly, unrefined—swelling inside her

> *sister, LISTEN to me.*

and Alira rasped a laugh as if she had been doing it all her life and

> *what the actual FUCK.*

images of Nyros and Galen in friendly debate tumbled over snatches of young Crow in a spacious household with

> *hey, that's not your business, why don't you—*

servants and private tutors and expensive clothes, and Nyros and Ijydin tangled in coitus while

> *you fucking killed me you dirty little squib.*

Cesar sat in the familial house with his firstborn, its tiny fingers wrapping around his and

> *alira the harvest is sacred, you must—*

his i'shin looking on, and Ijydin taking human lovers out of curiosity because they

> *sister, stop, you have to get control of—*

were so similar in form to unammi and she wanted to know if it would feel the same

> *alira, get OUT!*

but now it was all mixed into a gale like the winds on the northern plain where the lines blurred and the memories ran together into a chaotic frenzy as if

> *shut up squibs, I'm the one with relevant information here.*

the TICS had run multiple holovids all at the same time in the same space and she couldn't

> *alira, calm down.*

make out one from another. She sat upright, her stomach still churning, the metallic smell of blood thick in her nostrils, the enormity of the harvest still bloating inside. Manic laughter burst from her lips. The unammi abjured even their own civilized feelings. *Her* pathetic efforts to emote weren't even in the same ballpark as these.

> *ballpark?*

Alira tried to stand but the room spun and she crashed hard to the floor

> *push them back, you can control—*

her palm already healing from the blade's slice when she

> *find the flow!*

dropped into choppy meditation and stood waist-deep in the raging water. Her Companion stood on the shore. Shifting. Waiting.

> *what now?*

But It offered no reply. She hadn't expected one. Instead

> *the fuck? what—*

a vile voice raked across all the others and the human was there on the shore with the rest of her passengers and they argued, shouting over one another, shoved into one another's faces with vivid reds even on the sh'toi and Alira drew a shuddering breath and blew it out with as much control as she could muster.

> *i can't listen to you all at once you're going to get us all killed shut UP SHUT UP the LOT OF YOU SHUT THE FUCK UP!*

Blessed silence filled her head, broken by the roar of the rushing water in the Flow. Eddies raged around her in a frightening gush. There was no fighting that torrent. Why had she ever tried? It was all she could do to even stand still. Ahead, just downstream, the water's course careened around a sharp curve and flowed out of sight.

She glanced behind her, upstream where all this trouble started, and maybe it was her fault, maybe if she had followed her own instincts none of this would have happened and she stared at the roiling water, dwelled for a moment on her struggles to buck the pull of her intuition

> *regardless of what i do, someone will find fault.*
> *what matters is what's best for the unammi.*

then she turned forward and, with Musju pushing at her back, took a step.

She opened her eyes in Nyros' flat and sat panting, heartbeat and wind sounds pounding in her ears. Her brother's flashing body lay across the room, his blood soaking into the floor. The sh'toi's putrid shell lay even closer, his blood a wider pool that spread to almost touch her leg. Alira scrambled back and away from his gore as if its touch would defile her even further.

wouldn't be the first time i've been bled by an enemy.

She considered the ruined sh'toi, appalled at the damage she'd wrought. She had killed him. Killed an intelligent being

kill doesn't begin to describe what you did, squib.

but he'd killed Nyros and she was next and—

—and it had been Crow who flattened the unammi city, Crow who desecrated the bodies of her people, Crow who killed a wounded and helpless unammi with his own hands and given the order to take their irolium, Crow who sent two final weapons against the buried survivors. She saw the fall of her city through his eyes, felt his disgust and contempt for her kind, knew that if he could, he would kill them all, leave no unammi breathing. It wouldn't matter whether someone else ordered him to do it. He *wanted* to kill her people, despised anything or anyone who differed from himself.

Maybe Lurien had been right. Maybe humans weren't intelligent. Not like the unammi. But humans were part of Na'Staani. Like the unammi. Like all life. To destroy even one of them went against all her people's beliefs.

Alira pushed back against the guilt. She'd had no choice. It had been him or her. Now she must live with the decision.

She tried again to rise, this time with quivering success, and hopped across the mess that had been Crow. She knelt next to her brother and pulled the blade free, then stroked Nyros' bloody temple while his first memory of her replayed in her mind. He was a youngling himself, twenty-two seasons old when she was birthed, and had come to the familial house to visit his ama and see his new sister. Ama had explained that this babe was special, and he would need to protect her, and he had given his word. Even though he grew to resent the attention Ama showed his sister and even though he chided Alira along with everyone else, he had always admired her courage.

"Why didn't you tell me?" she whispered.

alira, you need to move.

"I know," she said aloud, her voice still shaking. She sat back on her heels to think. *What matters is how best to serve the unammi.* Right. So…what did her people need more than anything else right now?

they need you, dumbass.

Alira rooted through Cesar's and Nyros' and Ijydin's memories, but it was Crow who provided the answer—an image of Skalar on the other side of a desk, holding a piece of irolium while Crow reported taking it all.

Think what more we stand to lose, she'd said to Rakalesh.

Her people most needed irolium. And Crow knew where it was. Crow could get it back for them. He was disgusting, yes. Cruel, too. But he was a human, with a wealth of information to contribute. She mined his knowledge.

tell me crow, how long before someone comes to investigate my shout?

Not an unlimited period, but he had been unconcerned about discovery, had paid his HHU security contact well to cover him. Eventually, someone would find Crow, but no time soon. Not for many days, if Alira could help it. She still had a use for him.

you can't be serious.

you have a better idea?

She set the flat's temperature and humidity as low as it would go. Back in the great room, she programmed Nyros' TICS to reflect her movements as she had done on the ship. Crow's torso was a mess, but his face and head was almost intact, so she wiped away the blood and started there. Slowly at first, her features stretched and exaggerated into an aging brown mask with follicle growth

mustache.

on the lip, black-with-gray hair in dangling strands

braids.

and green eyes. Lean human musculature rounded out the wider shoulders and chest, and extended the height to almost 178 centimeters, its clothes matching those the sh'toi wore. He looked from the holoprojection to the corpse, back and forth, adjusting his own image to match every visible detail. Crow's memories filled in most non-visible bits, pushing scars onto the skin with images from their acquisition and a twinge of remembered pain. He should strip the body to be sure of his mimicry, but he had no intention of getting that intimate with it. He wouldn't need those details to fool passing visual and concourse scanning identification.

Crow grinned at his reflection,

this is some fucked up shit right here.

then frowned, then laughed in the sh'toi's deep, resonant tone at the plasticity of human features. *Again,* Ijydin said, and Alira's own shape emerged before it returned to Crow's. After the first two times, the Crow in her harvests began to coach her and together they went back and forth until shaping the new disguise came easily. When he was satisfied, he took the sh'toi's ident card. A corpse wouldn't need it again.

don't forget the wristcom, squib.

i won't be wearing you long enough to need that. besides, it can be tracked, right?

huh. squib's got a brain.

He added Amadi's and Rhys' idents to the special case in his pocket. Cesar's coin. The case was there, but not the coin. Where was it?

"Okay, where the hell did you go?"

Crow scanned the floor, searching the gore and the scattered cushions. There, next to the wall. He retrieved the treasure, flipping it over and over in his fingers as he surveyed the room and the few things Nyros had treasured enough to exhibit for his own enjoyment. That's when he noticed the shrine to Nyros' deviant sister—a small shimmering stone, a white niveym feather, a cured atlish skin and a small gourd rattle made from a muñise husk. He had thought it one of the oddest things she'd ever made, but he had kept it for almost a hundred seasons. Crow went to the low table, touching the items. After a moment, he plucked the skin from the collection and tucked it into his pocket along with Cesar's coin.

At last, Crow crouched to touch Nyros' hand.

"I can't sit with you for your deshtant, beloved," he rumbled. "But I'll host your Telling among the surviving unammi. Thank you for your knowledge. Ba'riba asatu'lan, Nyros. Pidai'ba livitu, ba'riba t'ujhendun."

aww. ain't that a fucking tear-jerker.

shut up, sh'toi.

Crow swept out of the flat, rode the lift to the ground floor, and stalked across the grounds toward "his" jumper. Ijydin had been more right than she'd known. Alira's study of humans and their culture fell far short of what the aliens *felt*, who they *were* inside. Sitting a moment in the jumper's seat, Crow's fingers at last touched the controls and he set out in the direction of the land port, and Nyros' ship.

chapter 44

<u>En Route to Land Port Station</u>

THREE OF HIS FOUR HARVESTED dead knew how to drive a jumper. Crow had expected an easy cross-town trip. It might have been fine if he could get the voices in his head to SHUT UP.

But no. They dogged him without end until he pulled the craft to one side of the lane, got out and walked in circles under the trees behind the zoo. He commanded all his passengers—aloud—to speak one at a time while he was operating a heavy moving vehicle at high speed through populated areas. The sh'toi could get them off Harajüd. Therefore, he would lead. For now. Crow tried not to think about Galen. Get out first. Worry later.

skalar told me not to leave.

"Skalar isn't here."

Pedestrians passing nearby glanced at him with concern. He invited them to fuck off, then went back to pacing. Of course, the fact that he didn't know Skalar's whereabouts was concerning. But by the time Skalar got back, Crow would be long gone.

already am.

So, the crystals now sat in an outpost that was, what, eight days' flight from here one way, sixteen total, plus the time it took to find and load the crystals once he got there. He'd be late getting back to Iridos, but when he came with a full load of irolium, Rakalesh wouldn't stay angry. Besides, this would be a now-or-never opportunity. Once Crow's body was found, this mask would make a poor disguise at the outpost.

His internal voices objected.

"Enough!" he growled. "Crow leads until we're off this rock. Understood?" Other pedestrians watched him as they passed, but he ignored them.

why should i help you? you killed me.

because as long as i draw breath you live through me.

Silence reigned. Satisfied, Crow resumed his trek. The irolium was stored at the outpost. Thus, he needed to go there. Except Crow wasn't sure where on the base he might find it. He'd have to search and hope the skeleton crew didn't trip over him, which was the only way they would know he was there. He was surprised those ancient scanners worked at all, but until now it had never been an issue. No one went to the outpost except Skalar's hand-picked few, at least until this latest job. A whole crap-ton of people now knew there was a secret base, even though Ronan had been ordered to obscure its exact location.

The rest of the trip passed in blessed peace. Crow arrived at the port building and sat outside. He knew more or less what to do, but he hesitated to give over full control to the sh'toi. Could that voice take over? Possibly. He didn't want to find out the hard way. For the millionth time, he chewed his lip at Lurien's irresponsible failure to train her daughter. Not that Lurien would have known how to contend with *this*.

Crow took a deep breath and got out of the craft, making for the main access. Time to deviate from his norm, take a new approach. His regular contact may not notice, but this harvest had yet to stabilize. Crow didn't want to set off any alarms.

That meant he would need to rely on his winning personality to make Skalar's lackey see reason.

A security officer hailed him. "You can't leave a jumper there!"

Crow waved a hand and kept walking. "Consortium business. Be right back."

Inside, he made his way to the port authority office and stalked to the counter, ignoring protests by those already in the queue.

"Sir, you'll need to wait like everyone else."

"Who's in control here?" Crow demanded, then raised his voice to shout over the desk cells behind the main counter. "Where's the supervisor?"

Colonial employees leaned out or stood at their stations, gawking at all the fuss. Some of them recognized him. He saw their concern as they passed the whisper. Within seconds, a scrawny, balding man with a hooked nose came forward.

"What is the trouble?"

Crow grinned. "You and me. Right now."

The pasty-skinned manager glanced around, then gestured. Crow followed through the maze to a private office in the back and, when offered a seat, dropped into the chair and swung his booted feet up onto the desk.

"You risked my neck coming here," the manager said. "How will I explain to my bosses why the Consortium's second-in-command cornered me in my office?"

"That's your problem." Crow shrugged. "Make something up. Just give me the squib ship."

The man's brows rose. "Admiral Skalar didn't say you'd be coming."

"Plans change. A new squib ship landed today. Skalar wants me to take the old one elsewhere."

The supervisor shook his head. "I can't. I have my orders."

"So do I, and mine trump yours."

The other man hesitated. He leaned back, tapping his fingers on the desk. "I'll need Admiral Skalar's personal countermand."

push back...like this.

Crow dropped both his feet to the floor and rose, leaning across the desk, and squinting at the scrawny, pale obstacle standing between him and his goal. "Either you remove that land-lock right now," he said, "or I'll pry it from the ship with your bones."

"You can't touch me. I'm a colonial port authority, and Skalar—"

"Skalar himself will roast your flesh if you refuse again, Mr. Colonial Port Authority. It would be a shame if the surveillance cams along your route home failed at an inopportune moment."

The supervisor's face went even whiter.

Crow projected fear into the man's quaking thoughts. "Don't…fuck…with me."

Crow saw the man's resolve crumble as he touched his TICS array and gave the command to release the ship. "If the admiral has a problem with this—"

"He won't." Crow pushed off the desk and stalked out of the office. Stupid waste of time. He needed to get to Nyros' ship—never mind the humans at the dock. They could report on him all they wanted—then get the hell off Harajüd before anyone discovered the carnage in Nyros' flat. He could send a warning to the other pilots, to Galen, once he was away from this shithole.

   okay, back off a bit.

  fuck that. you owe me.

    i don't owe you a damn thing. you owe me. you owe all unammi.

   you fucking slaughtered me. i should bake you cookies?

Crow winced, still trying to absorb the fact that in a critical moment of choice, he had reacted with such violence. But the sh'toi had earned it. Besides, he'd seen them morph. He had to die.

Still, maybe pulverizing the sh'toi's organs and causing him to bleed out had taken things a bit too far. The familiar weight of shame, alien to the sh'toi memories, settled in Crow's gut while unfamiliar human sensations rioted in his mind, clashed with the unammi voices, and threatened to sicken him. Again.

He rounded the corner and came within sight of the dock where Nyros' ship was berthed. No wonder the unammi had renounced emotional expression. Right now, he would give credits to be free of it, but something told him this twisted harvest made that impossible. Irrelevant. The deed was done. Guilt would get in the way.

Crow choked back the conflict and entered the ship almost without thinking about the latch override. Nyros directed his steps through the ship to the control room where he found panels identical to those on Ijydin's. Wearing Crow had been a good idea. The captain's face would buy a bit more time.

"TICS, record communique to Commander Vandana Walker."

A chitter sounded.

"Commander," he said, "I'm going off-world on an unexpected assignment. I'll be back as soon as I can. You're in charge until then.

what? no! you can't leave her in charge!

Don't fuck up. Crow out."

Then he squeezed his ass into the bitty chair and began his prep.

"Comm, traffic control. Audio only." A brief pause.

"HHU Land Port Station. Traffic control."

"IR749 requesting permission to depart from dock slip 965124," Crow said.

"Destination?"

"Aberville, Levyron."

"Wait one." The controller's voice blanked out, and Crow waited, tapping a foot until the woman's voice returned. "Your vid isn't working. Check with maintenance first."

"Negative, Control," Crow said. "It's only the vid signal. The rest of the comm is fine. I'll get it checked at the other end. I'm already running late. Probability of ship failure due to vid loss between here and Levyron is practically nil. It will be repaired before I come back."

"Okay, but I'm noting your file, 749. You are cleared to depart. Uploading flight vectors now."

"Thanks, Control. 749 out."

Crow maneuvered the hauler away from the dock and onto the pad, then took it up and away from the port, his body shrinking, hair retreating into his scalp until Alira sat in the pilot's seat. She couldn't engage the interstel drive for another ten minutes, plenty of time to plot a course change to the sh'toi's outpost and record a vidcom for the rest of the pilots. For Galen. Between Nyros' memories and Ijydin's, she could reach more than half their ships within hours. They could warn the rest.

If it wasn't too late.

chapter 45

**On Approach to Consortium Outpost
<u>Aboard the Nebula</u>**

SKALAR'S COMMAND CRAFT DROPPED INTO normal space and slowed on approach, while he reviewed his notes on which systems needed complete overhauls. Full-time operation with a larger on-site contingent needed upgrades across the board, but crew concerns alone had occupied the last two days of this trip. This detail made him most nervous. He couldn't pull just anyone to man this base. Whoever he chose needed to be discreet, loyal, tight-lipped. If anyone talked, and the colonies learned that the Consortium operated a base here with personnel traveling back and forth between a quarantined region and the rest of colonial space, his plans to maneuver a seat on Harajüd House's board of directors would be moot. It was doubtful the board would let him cast votes from Bejami's prison continent.

"TICS, comm Mira Cohen."

Moments later, a small holo of Mira's head and shoulders appeared before him. "Glad you made it, sir! We caught your ship's signature on approach."

"I'm beyond ready to put ground beneath my feet, Commander. Meet me at the main access. Skalar out."

He neared the surface, swung the craft around, and set down outside the cargo bay. Already suited, he donned a helmet in the airlock, muscled the interior door shut and opened the outer valve. The hiss of cycling air joined the shrill alarm. Skalar gritted his teeth and waited for the chamber to cycle and the irritating noise to abate. Flashes of red light from the depressurization alert sprayed crimson blotches across the screen of his closed lids.

At last, the cacophony fell silent. Skalar breathed a sigh of relief. The external port looked out onto black sky pricked with clear specks of light. He undogged the door, heaved it open and stepped through the hatch, securing it behind him. The pedestrian access wasn't far. He step-hopped across the distance in a fraction of the time it took him to drive home on Harajüd.

Inside the base airlock, Skalar dogged the door shut behind him and waited while the chamber pressurized, then removed his helmet and stepped out of his suit. He ran a quick hand through his hair, brushed his dark, loose pants and shirt back into perfection, and turned the scuttle to open the internal hatch. Mira and three other crewmen waited.

"Report," he said to the commander.

"Everything is on point, sir. I set it up like you said. Most equipment checks came back normal. The few under par were easy fixes."

"Good. How many Iridosian ships have come in?"

"Fifteen so far," she said.

Skalar's mind slid forward to future months. A new fleet meant repairing that damaged landing bay, getting it ready for regular use. It also meant pilots, mechanics, medics, loading and docking crew, not to mention staff to feed and clean up after them, and security to patrol the grounds. Round-the-clock viral detection would soon be a necessity, along with a lock-down mechanism in case there was an outbreak.

"How many crew on site now?"

"Thirteen, counting you, sir."

"Any of them pilots?"

"Two in the barracks, sir. My remaining crewman flew the rest of your specialists to New Canaan. He should be back in about ten days."

"Very well. As you were. Cohen, you're with me."

Mira fell into step beside him.

"Now," he said when they were away from the others, "tell me the rest."

"The techs oversaw installation of the new internal sensors first thing. I already ran tests. They tagged every life sign inside the base with ident signatures."

"What about the pilots, and the hauler crew?"

"The pilots, yes. Didn't get the chance to run the Treasure Chest's personnel, sir. Drones moved their whole shipment to the surface."

Ah. Yes, Ronan always was squeamish about this place. "You told no one about the sensor upgrade?"

"Not beyond my two operators, sir, as you ordered."

"What of the installation techs?"

"I took care of them myself, sir, dumped 'em in a distant ruin. The rest of the crew thinks they went back with the pilots."

"Good. Keep it that way. No one else knows. If word gets out, I'll come to you."

"Understood, sir."

"Where is the haul?"

"Interior vaults around the perimeter of the occupied sector," she said. "Heating for the surface bay and the pyramid is still set on need-based activation so we can spare our generators until they can be upgraded. No sense using the juice unless we need to."

"Good thinking, Commander."

They walked past the mess hall where energetic camaraderie and the aroma of some sort of stew wafted out into the corridor. Inside, four officers hunkered at one of the tables, meal packs set out in dishes while the crew played some unknown hologame.

"How is the crew coping with the assignment?"

"They're a good lot, sir, selected for their ability to take whatever I throw at them. We fired up the entertainment system in the rec room for games or holos or music. We bunk together in a contained segment of the dorms, eat and sleep and play in shifts. Since I insist on strength training, I set up a loop in the corridors for daily runs. They're on a tight schedule, including time on the surface for every crewmember when our rotation is right, so they can get a change of scenery. They're dealing."

"No complaints? No fights?"

Mira shrugged. "Nothing I can't handle. I told them before we came, no booze, no recreationals. They can do that when they get back, but not here." She gave him a little smile. "I'm sure they'd love to wrap their mouths around some different food for a change. After four weeks, meal packs get a little monotonous."

"Indeed."

"Sir, there were food items on some of the squib ships. Dried goods and such. We moved them into the surface storage vault. Maybe we could dip into those?"

"Maybe. I'll let you know. You ran the bio checks first thing before landing?" He didn't mention the biohazard check he had run on his own approach to the base.

"Of course, sir, and every thirty hours since."

"Set the system for continuous sweeps effective immediately."

"Yes, sir. By the way, I warmed up a separate room for you at the opposite end of the dorm. There isn't much luxury, sir, but I think it will be sufficient."

"I'm sure you're right."

They continued in silence. Skalar had performed extensive scans on this base before landing here the first time. Once convinced it was safe, he'd sent a team into the dome to search the entire complex, building by building, file by file, for info on the diseases that had killed off Earth's remaining population so long ago. The team found half a dozen decon chambers, but no mention about rampant viruses or quarantines. Incredulous, he'd ordered a second, and then a third search and still his people found nothing stranger than journal entries from a group of religious researchers who had edged into radical zealotry. But those seemed unconnected to the plagues.

Skalar always suspected biological warfare gone awry, though he couldn't prove it. Even if the research and genetic modification for the initial virus hadn't been done here, in isolation, there should have been some mention. He never found a single word. Someone must have purged any datafiles or holos during the early colonial era, maybe after the settlement of Harajüd. Not surprising if one of the twelve remaining colonial entities had played any part in the plague's creation to begin with. No one wanted to take the blame for having destroyed their own homeworld as well as one of the first extrasolar colonies.

Ronan wasn't the sole member of the Consortium nervous about using this facility. Crow had expressed concern too and had been assured that there was no chance of infection. Skalar believed it or he never would have sent a team, let alone come himself. Profit would be irrelevant if billions died and the colonies collapsed because infected members of the Consortium brought an epidemic back to the settled worlds.

A larger crew would be harder to control, making it more difficult to maintain silence about the base and its location. But this close to the biohazard, his bigger concern was hotheads determined to portray a show of fearlessness. One dip into Earth's lower atmospheric layers and it wouldn't be only the Consortium who paid a price.

"I know I said to pack for a three-month stay," Skalar said, "but I need you here longer. I'll send additional supplies and crew in a few weeks. You're in charge here for the foreseeable future, answerable to me alone."

"Thank you, sir."

"Run checks on the dormant systems, beginning with most essential. I'll start replacing the rest of the old equipment soon. And get a team started on assessments for repairs in the landing bay. I want to know what it needs to get up and running."

"Yes, sir."

"That's all for now, Cohen. I'm going to finish my walk-through before I tour my new ships. Dismissed." Mira went back the way they'd come and Skalar continued a short distance, then hitched right, skirting the sealed sections. Those weren't yet back in use. Lights and heat ran on auto-sensors. Gravity and pressure, base-wide systems, were ever-present. They would grow into these sectors soon enough, but for now he left them alone. Nothing in them anyway besides trash, old holo equipment, broken-down furniture, paper files that had decayed to dust ages ago, or would at a touch. Maybe one of those chambers would make a good brig. He would need one when activity here heated up. Surveillance, too. He didn't trust any of these people to tell the truth about anything if their own necks were on the line. He made a mental note to add cameras and audio equipment to his list of essential upgrades, then moved into the next section of the base to complete his rounds.

chapter 46

<u>Iridos</u>

GALEN CROUCHED IN THE LEE of the monument. Six pilots had returned. Six out of thirty. Nyros and Alira weren't among them. She'd been foolish to leave in the first place but nobody, not even Galen, could have convinced her otherwise. It was so like her to risk her own safety to warn the outcasts. He told himself again that she and her brother escaped Skalar's grasp but hadn't yet found a way home. Anything else was unacceptable. So much had changed. Now they could be together. At least that one good thing had come from this tragedy.

The call to council surfaced through the collective, and Galen groaned. The last thing he wanted was to be surrounded by others who could still somehow manage to make him feel alone. Pilots were used to it, but…well, he'd hoped for more from his kin after all that had happened. Besides, he was angry at the council. They had come so close to mitigating Alira! If the sh'toi hadn't attacked the city, she'd now be working in a guild mismatched to her extensive skill, her hands busy with tedium but her questions silenced, her sparkling mind forever dulled.

At least he knew she had been safe a few cycles ago. Two pilots received her warning, which saved them, but he suspected that hadn't been her sole intent for the trip. She had a plan of her own, one she'd not shared with anyone else.

He pointed his reluctant feet toward the council's summons, plodding past the wind-song through the cleared tunnels to the temple. Such a pitiful gathering. The last time he'd attended a council session—many seasons ago—the chamber squirmed with vibrant unammi, all talking at once as they awaited the call to order. Now the survivors stood almost silent, their numbers covering a tiny fraction of the cavern's floor space, not even enough of them to set the irolium alight.

Of course, the crystals were gone now. Somehow the changed space felt hollow, stripped of its sanctity.

At the front of the group, Rakalesh rose and stepped forward.

"My people, too many issues beset us. We've chosen the two most pressing, the first of which seems uppermost in your minds."

Galen peered at the lines of weariness on her face. How old was she now? Hundreds of seasons, at least. She was one of their eldest. She probably hadn't planned to take on a leading council role this late in her life, yet Rakalesh never would shy from her duty.

"Many of you expressed fear that the presence of outcasts in our community will upset the balance we've begun to reestablish, subvert our younglings, or corrupt our teachings. You feel we've encountered enough shock to our society that we won't endure if we invite havoc into our midst. You believe they should leave or, if they must remain among us, you wish to segregate them from the main population. Have I stated it right?"

A murmur of assent rippled in excited array through those assembled. Galen's hands, clutched before him, flashed gray, then red. Isolate the pilots within the community of survivors? He cringed at the depth of his people's antipathy. Perhaps it was just as well Alira wasn't present for this gathering. He could imagine how she'd respond. He glanced farther afield, searching for the dull, monotonous green of mitigants and found a small group of them standing apart from the rest of those gathered. They, too, were spurned. How many more enclaves could the larger population afford before the whole species was doomed?

Rakalesh's voice rose again, this time directed at the outcasts. "Do any of you wish to respond?"

Tiral stood, veins of red a hint at what was coming. "I'll speak, if the council and the rest of my people will hear me."

Galen waited for someone to object. No one did.

Rakalesh gestured. "The council will allow it."

"I'm Tiral," he said, "son of Rakalesh, and I want to state outright what you can't admit, even to yourselves. Your desire to see us exiled has nothing to do with fear of contamination."

He studied those around him, nodding. "The humans' actions here have proven some of them can be cruel, so I understand how that would lead you to distrust their species even though most are caring and kind. But you scorned these beings long before now, even as you craved the foods, textiles, and curiosities from their worlds."

Galen saw more than one gaze drop. How many here wore clothing made from colonial fibers?

"You knew those things carried a price," Tiral said, "one you could afford to ignore because we paid it for you. We sacrificed so you didn't have to. We are your providers, your protectors. We serve every one of you. Yet now, when our people stand on the brink of extinction, you avert your eyes and call us outcasts. Why? Because we are constant reminders of your hypocrisy. That is the real reason you don't want us here."

Ouch. Discomfort from those around Galen roiled in his own belly. The others shifted on their feet.

Tiral waved an arm to encompass their circumstances. "Look around you. Our city is fallen, our population devastated, our civilization shattered. Even we six might tip the balance and save our species. And what if our fearful new ideas could save you? This enemy already bested you once. You need our knowledge of them! You are fools to rebuff us because we unsettle you."

Confusion and uncertainty snaked through the clustered people, the colors stirring Galen to his core.

"The council will decide our fate based on what is best for the whole of our people, as they've always done. But don't lie to yourselves about your role in the outcome. If you refuse us sanctuary, we are doomed. Be sure you can live with that."

Tiral resumed his seat. Galen felt the mood around him shift. Yellow excitement skittered across his skin. Tiral's words may have swayed the minds of many gathered here. Did the outcasts dare hope?

Dyson stood, his movements slow, ponderous.

"We'll allow time for all to consider the ramifications of any decision in this regard. For the moment, treat our pilots as unammi survivors, a rare breed."

His gaze swept across those assembled before he sighed. "There is one other matter we must address. You already know of the radiation spread across our city and into our underground spaces, including this chamber where the Iri have thrived since before the Founders first arrived. At first, we paid it no mind since we could negate the effects. We all had other things to worry about."

Galen frowned, his confusion mirrored in all those around him. Even from here, he could feel Dyson's angst.

"Unfortunately, surviving this poison will require long-term modification of our own cellular structure, which may alter our capacity for symbiosis with the Iri."

Galen blinked. A surge of white across those nearby and an abrupt onslaught of their fear and confusion added to his own, overwhelmed his senses, and shortened his breath. There must be some mistake.

"Can't the Iri help us?" a female called out.

Dyson sighed. "Their communication has been sporadic since the attacks. It is possible they're affected as well. Haven't you noticed their song has become intermittent?"

Galen had wondered about that. Others nodded, too.

"We believe," Dyson added, "if this plight is allowed to run its course, our races may soon be isolated one from the other."

"Can't we ask them what to do?" another frem asked.

"Oh, please," Galen shouted. "It doesn't work that way."

"He's right," Dyson said. "Unless we can solve the puzzle for ourselves, this may mean an evolutionary divergence for our two races."

"Can we move?" Galen asked.

Gray surprise splashed the crowd, but another pilot spoke up in support.

"It is a valid question. If neither we nor the Iri can continue in our present forms or relationship in this location, can we find another, uncontaminated site here on Iridos?"

"Not that we know of," Dyson said. "We're running scans of the habitable zone with the equipment we have left. So far, we've found nothing suitable."

"Then what about another world?" Tiral said.

A nearby frem whirled toward him, her entire body pulsing red. "Another *world?* Easy for *you* to say." She jerked her attention back to the councilors. "Haven't we endured enough turmoil? Can't we try to—"

"Try to what?" a pilot shouted, crimson hues suffusing his display. "Allow the unthinkable to happen because circumvention feels too awkward? You are unprepared even to live in different surroundings. How will you adjust to a new existence? A new body? New functional needs for yourself and your younglings?"

"We would have to leave the Iri behind," another frem said. "How would that be any better than where we are now? At least here, we know what we're facing!"

"Besides, for all we know," the first female added, "the Iri will adapt *with* us, and all our worry will be for nothing."

Galen, patterned with his own fear and anger, glared at her. "Your argument ignores Dyson's facts and informed opinions. Listen to what you're saying. Think what we could lose by staying here." He turned to Dyson. "I affirm Tiral's question. What about the unammi homeworld? Can we go back there?"

Rakalesh shook her head. "We don't know where it is."

"Then we find another one," Galen insisted. "I understand the stress of such a drastic change, believe me. But we can't afford to dismiss this option outright. Humans have explored countless worlds. Maybe we can find one in our ships' databases that will suit both us *and* the Iri."

Loud retorts spread through the survivors, growing in volume.

Rakalesh stood again. "Basu'tao!" she shouted over the clamor.

Little by little, the crowd quieted. Her weary silver gaze passed over them all. "Ae'staani te Musjuva. Choice was stolen from us along with our irolium. Unammi do what is best for the whole."

Galen could feel her willing them toward calm, but fear still skittered in white blotches across many bodies.

"The council can't decide this matter yet. We need more information. Tiral was right about one thing in particular. Our outcasts—" Rakalesh cleared her throat. "Our *pilots* know more about the surrounding space than we do. I charge them with scouting potential new locations in case we need to leave Iridos, and with consulting the miners to configure a plan by which we can move the Iri with us. Dyson will provide you with whatever you need. The rest of you've been assigned tasks and schedules. Plenty of work still stands between now and any decision we might make, so for the time being we shall continue as we have. Once more detailed data is available, we'll reconvene. This council session is ended."

Galen waited until the gathering had begun to disperse, then drew closer to the other outcasts. "There are plenty of places on the colonial worlds where a small group of us might go, somewhere outside the cities."

"You mean the pilots," Tiral said.

Blue washed over Galen's features. Here he was, thinking only of himself. Alira would be ashamed. "Yes."

"Human satellites would detect our presence," one of the pilots said.

"I know, but—" Galen began.

"Their immigration people would send someone to investigate," another added. "They would never allow us to live independent of the planetary government."

"We'd have to stay ahead of them all the time," Galen said. That fear was at least familiar.

"If the tales are true about the irolium, without it we won't be able to hide," Tiral said. "You're talking about a life on the run."

Galen shrugged. "It beats the alternative. We don't know what long-term cellular modification will do to us either." Galen regarded each of the pilots. "I can't speak for the rest of you, but if the council decides to stay, I'll take my chances among the humans."

chapter 47

<u>Unammi Ship IR749</u>
<u>Farside Orbit, Earth</u>

STARS SLURRED THROUGH THE TRANSITION into distant points of light on the screen as the craft slowed. Ahead, brilliant against the inky backdrop hung a blue jewel. The birthplace of humans. Alira caught her breath at its loveliness. Harajüd, too, shone beautiful against its surrounding space even with traces of brown in its atmosphere, but it held none of the ethereal allure of this much smaller world.

don't even think about getting closer. the whole place is fucked.

A wrinkle appeared between her brows. Why was it fucked? How did it get that way? She plumbed Crow's memories but found little historical knowledge of this world beyond a vague yet acute fear of infection.

"Don't worry, Crow. I've got other priorities." She aimed her ship at the planet's satellite, her maneuvers much smoother now than they'd been when she set out from Iridos. Rakalesh had advised Alira she would need time to incorporate the knowledge, but what the elder hadn't said—couldn't have known—was that compounded knowledge and memories increased the rate of adaptation. The more knowledge Alira harvested, especially where experiences overlapped, the faster her proficiency grew. Between Ijydin's, Nyros', and Crow's piloting expertise and her intensive and frequent use of those skills over the last few cycles, flying felt almost natural.

She thought again about the other pilots. Nyros and Ijydin had known how to contact eight of them. So far, two had acknowledged her comm, neither of them Galen.

Alira chewed her lip. Everything had changed for the unammi. At last, all the outcasts would be welcomed home. She and Galen could finally share a life. She didn't want to lose that chance now. He had to come through this. He must.

The planet's satellite loomed larger in her viewscreen. This base, normally unmanned, now held a small crew complement. Their equipment was old, but it did the job. No reason for a fly-by. She wouldn't see them, but they'd see her. She would have to land out of sight under their horizon and walk the rest of the way, easy work outside the base with this moon's lighter pull

yeah, because you have so much experience in low-grav environments.

but even inside the dome and the connected tunnels with their artificial gravity she would be more dexterous than the sh'toi. Still, fear crawled along her skin in white streaks.

Just above the lunar surface, she fired thrusters, pushing the ship's nose up. The ship continued on, hugging the curve of the ground and following Crow's memories toward the base. Such a bleak place! Abandoned domes, their surfaces dulled by dust or damage, sat among other scattered ruins. The surrounding area, much flatter than the cratered ground outside those vestiges of habitation, must have been leveled for convenience much as the Founders had done on Iridos. It made sense for above-ground construction such as had been erected in both locations. And these complexes had to go down, as well as up. Surface structures were too small to be of much use otherwise. Apparently, not all humans held the same distaste for underground habitation as Crow had.

Thrusters reduced the craft's forward motion and Alira edged as close as possible to visibility before she set it down and cut power. The hum beneath her feet died away, and she sat in the quiet, reviewing her plan.

Ijydin had advised her to use camouflage and blend into the background rather than wearing a sh'toi body. But maintaining that sort of dermal pattern meant she would need to move slower, with more deliberation. Crow thought she should move fast. She distrusted her alien passenger, but his input carried more weight in this circumstance. He'd been inside this place. He knew how to act in this environment. If the Consortium sent more crew here before she could find the irolium and get out, they might see her ship. Faster seemed better.

Alira grabbed Crow's ident card in case she ran into other humans and thought about what lay ahead. So far, flight had been her most pressing need and the voices in her head had proven useful, if cacophonous. Now that she was here, she had but one source of guidance for the skills she would need, which meant this would be more of a challenge.

you're confusing a challenge with suicide.

not as long as i have you, sh'toi. i die, you die.

If she kept to the perimeter vaults in the uninhabited segments of the base

they'd keep it closer.

she was less likely to be seen. If the irolium wasn't in those, she could drop back and regroup. Timing would never be perfect on this little joy ride.

the sh'toi's not your only guide. he's never used our nanopod. listen up....

Following Ijydin's direction, Alira stepped inside the small airlock and heaved the inner door closed, then stepped into the nanopod, feet apart and arms outstretched. "Fit and apply standard environment suit. Omit communications. Focus on flexibility, maneuverability, and multiple-use." Sensors hummed to life, sweeping over her with optical measurements and calculations. The pod's tight quarters had been configured for unammi bodies. Crow's much larger form would never fit inside. She'd navigate the surface as herself, then hide her suit inside the dome

stupid squib, i told you, not the dome.

or wherever she entered to keep it safe for later retrieval. She had no plan to get the stones onto her ship. Even a small crew presented a huge obstacle to her goal. Subpar scanners on the base made things easier, but she would have to be quick. They wouldn't know Crow was there unless he spent enough time

you'll have five minutes.

in any one compartment to kick in the thermal systems. If that happened, his little game of hide-and-seek would be over.

Alira played back Crow's hazy memories of chambers inside the base. Some of those rooms were so crammed with obsolete equipment and crates of who knew what, it would be impossible to check every cranny. A quick sweep would have to suffice to determine if there was a vault and, if so, whether it was occupied. Once she found the stones, five minutes wouldn't be long enough to retrieve them. She would need to disable the thermals or distract the crew in some major way for that part.

Measurements completed, the pod gave its ready signal and began to weave the suit around her. Light, supple fabric started at her feet and worked its way up.

Crow's memories told her where the crew would hole up. But she'd have no way to know their locations if they moved around inside the structure. If they stumbled across "Crow," he could tell them Skalar had sent him on some errand, a test perhaps, or maybe even to bring back the irolium, anything to get him away from the base and off this fucking rock. Alira couldn't afford to let them detain her or, worse, figure out who and what she was. If she didn't make it out of here, the irolium would be lost to the unammi forever. No one else knew where it was or what she was doing. Now, she wished she'd told someone where to find it. Just in case.

what could they do against a consortium base, squib? you couldn't keep me from flattening your city.

and you couldn't keep us from killing half your fleet.

Crow's voice fell silent, and Alira grinned as the pod completed the base layer of the suit and began constructing the insulation.

stay with me crow. show me what I'm walking into.

His normal procedure took him through the pedestrian access by the loading bay, which was out for her. In fact, most of the surface access hatches would set off alerts in Control when they were opened. The one that didn't sound an immediate klaxon accessed the enormous surface vault.

no, they wouldn't store your precious rocks there.

Since the crew had been using it to bring in their hauls so often, they'd installed a one-minute delay on the alarm years earlier. The vault would be pressurized, but equalizing the airlock would take a few seconds. If she timed her entry right, the crew would never notice.

The pod finished the insulation layer of her suit and started on the jointed outer shell and headgear.

Once the airlock finished its cycle, she could stow her gear and don her disguise, then work her—no, *his*. Damn, this was confusing—way through the storage vault. No one was expected to come this far into the sealed sectors of the base, so Crow would have a bit of freedom to explore. As long as he didn't exceed the time limit in any one room, all should go well.

until you see i was right about this whole fucking thing.

Unless she saw facts to the contrary, Alira chose to believe this was a workable idea and would act on it. If Crow was right, and the stones were stored under the human's noses, she'd have to come up with a bolder plan.

At last, the pod signaled its completion. Alira swallowed the lump in her throat, stepped out of the pod and opened the airlock's outer valve. The hiss of cycling air, whine of the alarm, and flashing lights overwhelmed her senses until the cycle completed. Ears still ringing, she passed through the outer hatch, and left the ship behind.

Earth's star now shone on the opposite side of this moon, casting thick gloom like a blanket over her head. Even her sensitive eyes relied on the suit's faceplate array to avoid pits and rocks as she stumbled, fell over her own feet, bounced, and learned to walk all over again

told you.

shut up. it's the suit.

if you say so.

through the murk toward the base complex. Progress was slower than she'd hoped, due to rough, uneven terrain. Twice along the way she saw more ruins—not domes or habitation, but enormous dish-like devices embedded in the pits along the surface. Her faceplate marked them inactive. Even so, she gave them a wide berth. By the time she reached the periphery of her destination, her legs and back trembled, and she hunkered down for a rest while she observed the base from a distance.

Ahead lay a flat plain bounded in a perfect circle of raised ground. An impact crater. One ridge segment to her right rose to a respectable height and near its feet lay the domed enclosure of Skalar's base. Like the relics she'd seen on the way in, a few structures squatted at the foot of the mountain, but in this case she already knew most of the facility hid inside the rock. On the far side of the dome and connected by a short tube lay a rectangular outbuilding.

the cargo bay. stay away from that.

In the distance beyond that, her faceplate showed dormant ships, some human and some unammi. She couldn't tell whether Galen's sat among them. A pang stabbed through her at the thought of the unammi who had flown those craft and who would never again see home, but she couldn't help them now.

do what you came to do, squib, and get the hell out.

She ripped her gaze away and searched farther afield, then turned her attention back to the dome and began to scour the base closer to her position under the edge of the rim until—she stopped, holding her breath.

Silhouetted against the rock and attached to the dome by another squat tube stood a replica of the Founder's monument.

the surface storage vault. that's where you go in.

Except…Nyros's small wrinkle rose between her brows. It wasn't quite the same, was it? This one was much smaller. Not like the one on Iridos, though its outline seemed similar.

there's a pyramid on iridos? where?

Her weariness forgotten, she searched the area, saw no movement, picked her way down the crater's interior slope, and crept close enough to examine the vault's surface. Its exterior felt much smoother than the one on Iridos. Maybe not as old. She leaned back, peering up at its apex. The slanted side of the Founder's monument at home hinted at the presence of a similar peak, though the ridge had long ago hidden that part of the edifice. Even so, this one's shape wasn't quite the same. It was smaller, too. Why would the humans build such a thing here?

chop chop, squib. get moving.

Right. Crow guided her around the edge of the vault to the hatch and she rested a moment with her hand on the access panel.

last chance to change your mind.

No one would fault her for abandoning a hopeless task. In fact, the council would forbid this. She tried to imagine walking away without the stones. Going back to Iridos to wait with the rest of her people for their end. Her shifting Companion joined the party in her head and hovered behind her eyes.

well?

Its image fluctuated, flowing one into another—sometimes familiar like the form she'd first seen before Nyros' last trip home, other times alien and indescribable—but it offered no word of advice. A moment longer she waited. Then she opened the hatch and stepped inside.

chapter 48

<u>**Consortium Outpost**</u>

SKALAR POKED AROUND IN THE belly of the last Iridosian ship. All the boats had been relieved of their haul upon arrival. Some of it, like basic foodstuffs, could be used for the onsite crew, as Mira had requested. The rest would go to his colonial market booths in small batches. Unless a particular world's government owed him for some past service, he would be obligated to pay negligible import taxes, but no matter. He could make it back in smuggling or counterfeiting anyway.

He climbed the ladders, investigating one level at a time. So far as he could tell, this ship was identical to the others. Outside seating and other crew-sized appurtenances, they were large craft, barely small enough to dock at the colonial land ports. Each held six cargo bays, as well as sleeping quarters for a crew of four, even though every boat looked as if it could be run by a single pilot. Skalar wandered through, uncertain how to identify some of the devices and controls. Government standards required Colonial English as the primary verbal command structure on any ship built on colonial worlds, but the buyer could have secondary languages installed as well. The written language on these wasn't Standard. Good thing the craft would fly on voice commands until Skalar's people could decipher the markings.

In the control room, he gave an appreciative nod. The Consortium was no stranger to shipbuilding, but they focused on larger craft. Skalar had always wondered why most orders for smaller boats went to the Syndicate. He had even tried to buy one through his own contacts. But the admiral of that faction, Rizzo, was no fool. She'd seen through him and his people, rejected every attempt. He hated to admit it, but now that he saw her designs up-close he understood why. She'd incorporated tech he wouldn't expect to find in a ship and used it in unorthodox ways. Half of what he was seeing he couldn't yet place. Once he got a chance to experiment, fly one, take it apart bit by bit for analysis, he could be more competitive, take away some of her business. He laughed. Rizzo would never know how he did it.

Akimbo, Skalar basked in the pride of this enormous win. A hauler full of hematium and a unique crystal. Free access to the rest of the metal. And fifteen ships. Fourteen, rather, since he'd lose one to research. Their use would be limited in the beginning. For the moment, Harajüd and Saacharis held exclusive agreements with Iridos for the hematium, but that wouldn't last long. Once "Iridos" opened up the market, other worlds with shipyards would jump at the chance to buy direct. Contracted colonial governments wouldn't dare to sanction Iridos for the crime of breaking a contract. As reliant as they had become on their sole source of hematium, they'd have no choice but to continue to buy.

As for other raw materials the Iridosians had traded, he could send an audio message to declare Iridos no longer wanted any direct contact with humans, that they were suspending all trade except hematium, and future transactions would take place via drone. It might raise a few eyebrows at first, but Iridosians had always been odd. No one would think twice about it.

His suit comm chirped, loud in ears grown accustomed to the sound of his own breath. "Skalar."

"Sorry to bother you, Admiral," Mira's voice said, "but I wanted to get my people started setting up quarters for Captain Crow. Do you want him near your room?"

Skalar paused. "What did you say, Commander?"

"I asked if you'd like Captain Crow's quarters set up near yours, sir."

"Why would you need to set up quarters for Crow?"

Long pause. "I assumed he would be staying long enough to need sleeping space, sir."

Staying? Skalar frowned. "What are you talking about? Crow is on Harajüd."

Longer pause. "Then we have a glitch in our sensors, because he popped up on them a couple of minutes ago."

Crow? Here? Skalar started toward the ladder chutes on his way out of the ship. "He didn't comm on his way in?"

"No sir."

"Is his ship outside the airlock near mine?"

"No sir. Not that I can see."

"And he hasn't shown up in Control?"

"No sir. He's moving through the surface storage vault."

"Did you comm him?"

"Twice. He hasn't responded."

Then it wasn't Crow. But who was it? Could he hear this exchange?

"Scramble communications at once. Switch to our secure code. Confirm."

"Scramble and switch confirmed, sir. One moment."

He switched his own suit's code.

"Done, sir."

"Good. Do not engage, Commander. Keep your people clear of the intruder but set up a watch around your sector. Lock down the outer hatches. No one gets in or out except me. Confirm."

"Stay clear. Set a watch. Lock down all exits. Confirmed, sir."

"I'm on my way. Skalar out." He caromed through the narrow corridors in his haste. At the hatch, he jumped out and down to the surface, then buttoned the ship back up and loped to the rover. A minute later he was jouncing across the plain toward the base. The sensors said it was Crow. Since that was impossible, then someone had gotten their hands on a forged ident. A good one. It wasn't easy or cheap, but it could be done. Hell, his own people produced and sold quality forgeries all the time. But why bring it here? How the hell had anyone outside the Consortium even known about this base?

Only one possibility.

Skalar's rapid breathing rasped in his ears. This facility had been all but abandoned for years, used to store occasional hot merchandise until it could be sold. A mere smattering of people even knew about it until the Iridos job. So it had to be someone in that fleet. Someone from Ronan's crew. Once back in colonial space, a comm could travel to any of the factions in less than a day. Plenty of time since then to prep and send a scout. It could have been someone staffing the site right now. Not Mira or her two trusteds, else the intruder would have known about the sensor upgrade and been smarter about their entry.

Regardless, this hobbled his plan. If another faction had discovered the site, he'd be forced to collaborate with the intruding admiral or move operations to a new locale, neither a viable option. Shifting the haul would be easy but pointless since he couldn't run Iridosian ships out of his bases. Nor did he trust his competitors enough to collaborate on something this huge. They were just as inclined to steal from him as he was from them. They might even turn him in.

He'd gotten complacent. Made a mistake. Most of the other factions would hesitate to oppose him in such a way, so this netzyl must have thought he had a foolproof in and out, or an ironclad bluff to carry them through a crew encounter.

So who? Rizzo?

Maybe. She had the capability and more than enough nerve. It was a sure bet whoever was sneaking through his base right now didn't walk here, and a faction's ship always bore telltale signs of origin. If the snoop didn't talk, his ship would.

What if he wasn't alone?

If the rival ship was manned, it too might be monitoring comm chatter. All the more reason for Skalar to attend to this by himself.

Damn, he hated surprises. Getting caught off-guard meant he wasn't in control. If he wasn't in control, he might make additional mistakes, which could cost him everything and send him back to the gutter.

No. He wasn't going back there. Not ever.

The dome loomed ahead. It would take him a few minutes to pressurize the airlock, get out of his suit and make his way across the base to Control. He'd go there first, get an update. Then he could seek a proper, isolated interrogation away from all witnesses. Until he knew who was behind this betrayal, he trusted no one.

chapter 49

CROW CURSED UNDER HIS BREATH at the inadequacy of human vision in this darkness. How the hell did they see anything? The third time he tripped over something, he shifted his eyes to their natural silver

ugh. squib eyes on MY face.

i should let them hear us instead?

and at once his vision cleared. Around him lay an empty corridor littered with small debris, the first intersection straight ahead. He tried to calm his breathing, but a niveym was loose in his chest, its panicked wings pounding a rhythm in his ears. He'd never hear anyone coming over that noise. He needed to stick to the goal and focus.

He veered left at the corner, toward the first door, which swished open at his approach. Crow glanced back—had anyone heard?—then tiptoed inside and dropped to a crouch when the lights came on.

don't panic. it isn't full power, they won't see you yet.

Precious seconds ticked away while he tried to subdue the thrashing bird inside his ribcage, then scuttled across the littered floor, dodging furniture and crates to check the vault in the back. No good.

next!

The neighboring vault also was empty.

And the one after that.

And the one after that.

After the sixth, Crow started to think the sh'toi had been right. His mind cast about for alternative plans while he searched. Three sectors of the base lay empty of crew. This was the first. If this one was a dead end, he could either repeat the process for the others or…go straight to the human crew and tell them Skalar sent him. A wrinkle folded his brows. It was a bold plan, but he might have no choice. On the upside, if he took that route, he could grab a human environment suit on his way back, fly Nyros' ship right up to the base, and walk in the front door like he belonged there. Once inside, maybe he could convince the crew, even get them to do his loading for him.

maybe?

At the next intersection, he checked both ways, then sprinted down the last accessible corridor in this direction, already glad he'd skipped his last meal. He'd forgotten what a fucking maze this place was. Another room gave him nothing, and another.

Maybe he should have made the direct approach his first choice. It would have been easier. Crow was good at bluster, bullying crewmembers into doing what he wanted even when it wasn't in their best interest. Yeah. Skalar sent me. Wants the rest of that blue shit Ronan brought. Load it for me while I eat. Sorry, can't stay. Gotta get right back. Skalar wants this cargo yesterday. You know how it is.

He trotted across the hall toward the last door. When the mechanism hesitated, his feet skidded on the floor and stopped him just as the panel slid open—and jammed.

fuck.

that's what i was going to say.

The crew would know this door hadn't been open before, but he couldn't stop now. He plunged into the room, no longer noticing the low-end lights. This room's layout was different, larger, with tiled pillars at regular intervals down its length. A workroom, maybe. Tables stood scattered around the floor, piles of debris clogging the open space, dusty equipment and crates at odd angles, some jutting out into what passed for aisles between the working surfaces as if whoever vacated the space had done so in a hurry. Crow wound his way through the obstacle course, walking the length of the room

less than four minutes, squib.

and found the vault behind a bank of shelving and storage space in the center of the room.

Its door was closed.

His heart thumped in his ears. Could it be? If it was locked, he might be in luck. He sprinted the last few meters, hop-stepping over a pile of crates rather than going around, and tugged on the door. Nothing happened. Crow's heart leapt into his throat

three minutes.

as he touched the old-fashioned keypad and pulled the door again, hard. This time the heavy door budged, creaking with such a racket someone surely would hear. Centimeter by centimeter it opened.

Nothing.

fuck. FUCK!

Enraged, Crow whirled and kicked the pile of crates. The top one crashed to the floor, its contents spilling out, blocking the walkway.

good job, squib.

Hands balled into fists, he eyed other routes around the room's confusing layout but the fastest was the same way he'd come in. He gauged the distance to a clear space on the floor, then jumped over the mess he'd made. Long legs, powered by underlying unammi strength, carried him farther than he'd intended. Crow landed wrong, stumbling into a table which skidded away. Feet, legs, and arms fought to right his careening body, but it was a dusty piece of equipment that caught him. Flailing hands triggered its mechanism to resume an old holovid, its speaker already mid-sentence at what sounded like the vid's top volume. Backpedaling as hard as he could, Crow scrambled away from the machine until a heavy metal desk stopped him cold, his heart threatening to leap from his chest. He stared at the shouting, faded image, shook his head and looked again, his mind struggling to understand what he saw.

There before him stood a projection of Alira's ever-shifting Companion, or at least its human form.

Crow pushed himself forward beneath the room's bright lights and approached the image. Same coppery hair. Same green eyes. Same pale skin. Crow reached toward those familiar features, his fingers distorting the projection. "What is this?" he whispered. "Who are you?"

One by one, the recorded words began to sink in.

"—realize I have no choice," the holoimage said, "but to follow the Spirit's guidance. Earth no longer feels like home. I—*we*—all feel as though we're caught in a raging current, swept along in a ship no longer under our control, and it feels glorious! My Guide gave me the coordinates long ago and assured me that it was uninhabited and would sustain us well if we take along seeds and crops and the means to set up a greenhouse. We can be self-sustaining from the start. Now I've *seen* our new world, and been given its name. By the end of this year, our ship and our people will be ready to leave for Iridos—"

A chill sank into Crow's body despite the warming air around him. Iridos? The projection continued speaking, but Crow heard nothing over the ringing in his ears. What the actual fuck—when did humans go to Iridos? He fumbled at the controls

> *move, squib! get us out*
> *alira!*

until he managed to start the recording over. The vid's image leapt anew into the air before him and the human voice filled the room.

"Elias Sullivan, journal entry for February 19, 2131. They've started calling me the Founder."

Crow didn't recognize the strangled sound emanating from his own throat.

The Founder? A *human?*

Elias Sullivan's holoimage sighed. "I've tried to dissuade them, explained I'm no different than they, but it doesn't help. The visions brought them to me, they say. Their dreams revealed that I would lead them to a new and better life. They've made me into some sort of religious leader, but even though I'm the only one who sees the Spirit Guide, we all came to this decision because of our individual visions. Gods know I've had them all my life, but they didn't crystallize for me until my nebulous Guide began to appear."

The human paused, brow furrowed, searching for words. "I wish I could give an adequate description of this Guide. It shifts from form to form, some humanoid and some not. Its most intriguing shape is that of a shorter, squatter human-like being. Same number of limbs, one head, translucent skin, pale blue and bioluminescent, demonstrating an astounding array of colors and patterns. I wish the Spirit would hold this aspect longer so I could see more detail, but it never does. I get the clear impression it is a conglomeration of diverse Beings all working together to project an image I can begin to accept, and that it is doing its best to convince me to create this promised new world.

"It isn't like we have much reason to stay here. Earth's society is falling apart. I had hopes for a turnaround with talks of a Triad and uniting into one cooperative global community, but that was twenty years ago and they are no closer to their goal. These last two years have been worse than ever. Skirmishes increased between nations, as well as between ethnic and economic groups in the North American Union. It's a simple matter of time before the Unions declare all-out war. I don't want to be here for that. None of us do."

Crow's head shook back and forth

hello? stupid fucking squib you gotta—

as if it sat on a swivel. He was misunderstanding this human. He *had* to be. It sounded as if this Elias Sullivan

elisul?

was saying....

No. That's not possible. There had to be more and he wanted

alira! ALIRA!

no, needed to hear the rest.

The human ran his fingers through that long red hair, pacing in the space before Crow. "I can't say I'm surprised by any of what has happened. I've predicted for years that humanity's greed and violence and selfishness would be the death of this world one day. Now I fear I'll be proven right. Citizens of Earth have forgotten they are part of a larger whole, and I can't see a way to change their direction. I think they've gone too far to be saved. That's why I listened to my dream Guide and why, when it started sending others like me, I began to gather them together, especially the movers. They're the most essential part of this plan. We can't go anywhere without them."

Crow blinked. The mythical Movers were real? Were *human*?

"My Guide urged me even then to relocate, to found a new society where we could build in whatever way we saw fit. I must admit I was skeptical…until I started to see it in my dreams, to imagine its potential, a new world separate from the rest of humanity where we could abjure greed and exclusion and entitlement and center our efforts on acceptance and compassion in a unified society whose members all support one another…that was when I began to realize I have no choice but to follow the Spirit's guidance. Earth no longer feels like home. I—*we*—all feel as though we're caught in a raging current, swept along in a ship no longer under our control, and it feels glorious!"

Crow watched, unable to stop. The voices in his mind faded to an indiscriminate buzz.

"My Guide gave me the coordinates long ago and assured me it was uninhabited and would sustain us well if we take along seeds and crops and the means to set up a greenhouse. We can be self-sustaining from the start. Now I've *seen* our new world and been given its name. By the end of this year, our ship and our people will be ready to leave for Iridos. Our first vessel showed us where we needed improvements, and the final design is well underway. The movers still practice with the prototype so that when the time comes, they can maneuver the pyramid ship to our new home…."

The holoimage continued, listing the stores and supplies they planned to take, knowing they'd never return to Earth, but the audio flowed over and around Crow as he chewed on this new kernel of truth.

Humans founded Iridos. Humans begat unammi. But how? They were two different species, weren't they? or….

The wrinkle between Crow's brows deepened, voices of teachers speaking in memories from Cesar, Nyros, Ijydin, evolutionary equations and how physical traits adapted to fit environmental factors. Iridos' higher gravitational pull lingered in Crow's memories. That alone would account for the shorter unammi stature, thicker build in the feet and legs, any number of other details. Bioluminescence would have evolved to aid survival in a dark environment. Most creatures on Iridos used it thus. A different planet didn't account for all the differences, yet if it served to feed Na'Staani's purposes, then symbiosis between the unammi and the Iri could have boosted divergent evolution on its way at an even faster rate, right?

Right?

Implications of this discovery buried the buzz of voices in Crow's thoughts. If unammi evolved from these ancestors, then diversity was an unavoidable part of who they were as intelligent, compassionate beings, and squashing it harmed them all. Both species demonstrated emotion. The main difference lay in how. Humans utilized facial expression, body language, verbal clues while unammi relied on dermal displays, the only means left to them after unammi society took the Founder's plan to the extreme and made taboo any other type of manifestation. Elisul—that *had* to be who this was—said humans had forgotten their place in the larger picture. Had the unammi, in trying to rise so far above their origins, forgotten too?

Ah, Na'Staani! If this was true, the traditional unammi greeting held an even deeper significance. It meant Alira's violent, horrific execution of Crow profaned everything the Founder had set out to establish. If the humans gave rise to the unammi, then both races were of the same blood. Alira had killed her kin.

great. fan-fucking-tastic. we're related. now, cousin, GET YOUR ASS MOVING!

Crow flinched as if hearing the shout in his head for the first time, then moved through the holoprojection toward the door as if in a daze. Had Lurien known? Of course she had. If Lurien had harvested the memories of her predecessor, and so on back to the dawn of the gift as Cesar and Rakalesh had indicated, would those memories about the Founder be there? Did the harvesting go back that far? It made sense, given Lurien's past references to Alira's heritage and bloodlines. Crow twined the new data into the growing picture in his mind. He—

His feet stopped again, ears roaring. Bloodlines. Lurien had meant more than just distant ancestors, hadn't she? Memories both reaped and experienced through Alira flooded back. Conversations of Lurien's planned daughter, conceived with genetic material, evolved or not, donated in the beginning by the Founder.

By Elias Sullivan.

Lurien's daughter was half human.

Crow's stomach flipped and his head reeled until he staggered against a pillar. How could Lurien have kept this from her daughter? Pieces of the larger puzzle began to fall into place but so many others, essential to full understanding, lay blank and now…now that unammi survival hung in the balance, how could he put it back together without all the facts? So much knowledge lost, not only in the guilds whose members lay beneath the rubble on Iridos, but all those generations of vital memories in the mind of one individual, lost beyond his reach!

A groan ripped from his throat, frustration welling up until he spun and swept an arm across the littered surface beside him, brushing everything within reach to the floor.

"Lurien!" he growled. "Yetandu unammi bale! Bejhur asane!" Your people need you! I'm not ready!

He braced against the table, his whole body shaking with sobs. "I'm not ready, Ama…."

An unexpected voice—one *not* inside his head—startled him from a few meters away. "*What* did you say?"

Alarms clanged in his mind. Without thinking, Crow started to run.

chapter 50

FROM THE DOOR, SKALAR FIRED his stunner.

Crow wavered, collapsed, and shrank into a small, squat body flashing erratic white patterns.

Skalar blinked and looked again. An Iridosian? The scanners had said it was Crow. Skalar had known better, and yet he'd questioned his own judgment the moment he spotted his second in this room. If he hadn't seen the figure change, he wouldn't have believed it.

The Iridosians were shapeshifters. How had he never known this? Further, how had the Iridosian known to come to this base? It couldn't have followed Ronan's ship through interstel space. And if the city was as flattened as Crow said, Skalar doubted the Iridosians had any functioning comm systems to monitor chat between the armada boats, even if his captains had been stupid enough to discuss such a thing on an open frequency.

Then how? And why?

He stepped closer and crouched down, turning it over and lifting its limbs, examining it. Apparently female…burn mark on the upper back, which shouldn't have happened. His weapon was set for a low energy burst, enough to stop a man Crow's size, but not enough to cause this kind of damage. A dry, spicy tang filled his nostrils, odd, but not unpleasant. Was that the burn? or did it always smell like that? At least it was still breathing. He'd get a chance to ask it some questions, find out if Iridosians reacted the same way as humans to his special skills.

On the floor beside it, he found a crude coin-like metal disc, which he kept, and some sort of disgusting animal skin, which he tossed aside. He also found the ident—which explained why the system tagged it as Crow—and the special case, which he didn't open. If it was a blocker, opening it would reveal additional idents on the scanners. The Consortium had its own version of these little black-market beauties, but this one had a few improvements. More of Rizzo's work? She was becoming a regular thorn in Skalar's side, but now his techs could disassemble it, and use it to map upgrades for their own design. Maybe he could even sell its secrets to the Saacharis Organization, throw a few twists into Rizzo's operations, get her out of his face for a while.

Behind him, the yammering holoimage fell silent, and Skalar glanced around at the debris on the floor where Crow, or rather this alien, had shoved it off the table. Something had pissed off the Iridosian. Rising to his feet, Skalar stepped over the unconscious alien and set the holovid to replay, then viewed it with a frown. He'd seen this before, some religious extremist prattling on about how he and his followers would found a brave new world. What about any of that had set off the Iridosian?

Playback reached the point where Skalar had stopped this holo the last time he'd seen it—zealots grew tiresome after a while—but this time he let it continue to rehear the rest. Oh yes…now it was coming back. He remembered thinking the first time he'd seen this recording how odd it was to learn humans had gone to Iridos long before the colonies were established. Hell, before interstel flight had even been possible. He'd wondered at the time how they had managed it, or why colonial history never mentioned prior contact with the aliens. Since it hadn't connected to the diseases he was investigating, he'd not given it any further thought.

Until now.

Had the religious settlers fought with the Iridosians over territory? Had the Iridosians killed the humans before they could even land, the same way they'd destroyed half the Consortium squadron? Where was the link?

Skalar restarted the vid, paying closer attention this time, but a second viewing didn't clarify the connection, nor did a third. He scowled at the flashing body on the floor. Was it alone? If not, he might have a problem on his hands, given that the aliens could take on human likeness and he would never know the difference. But if it thought its disguise was foolproof, why had it run? Had it killed Crow to impersonate him? Skalar found it difficult to believe a being this size could overpower Crow, but before his second's reports of the attack on Iridos, Skalar had believed the Consortium's unrivaled cloaking technology made his ships safe from detection. And until a few minutes ago, he hadn't known the aliens could change their appearance. As of now, he wasn't making bets on anything.

"Control."

"Yes, sir?"

"Continue scrambled comms and the lockdown on the inhabited sector. Do not leave for any reason. No one comes in or out but me. Notify me at once if any additional life-signs show up that shouldn't be here."

"Then…." Mira paused. "It wasn't Captain Crow, sir?"

Skalar squinted at the unconscious Iridosian. If this one's partners had already infiltrated his crew, how would they react if they learned Skalar knew their secret? "Yes, it was Crow. Set up quarters for him next to mine, as you suggested earlier."

"Of course, sir, but…."

"But?"

"Just to clarify, sir, the intruder *is* Captain Crow, but you want me to keep an eye out for other unexpected life signs?"

"Yes, Commander. We may have a situation. The captain is updating me now. I don't know how long we'll be. Skalar out."

As soon as this meddler was either dead or no longer a threat, Skalar's next order of business was to comm the real Crow and demand a report. That is, if Crow still drew breath. Skalar considered this possibility. No, if the Consortium needed a new second, Sa'abah would have contacted him. He needed to return to Harajüd ASAP, straighten out this nuisance, and ensure his leadership remained uncontested. But first, he needed answers.

How should he proceed? He had no way of knowing how long it would remain unconscious, or how long he'd have to persuade it to talk once it awoke. This room, with its stuck door, didn't offer the privacy he required. Nor did he have restraints or any of the tools of his specialized trade. He dared not leave the Iridosian alone to go back to Control for supplies, nor would he risk having any crew member bring them here. He'd have to make do with the resources available.

Skalar nudged the alien with his toe, but it was still out cold. A quick survey of the room identified items that might serve to keep his guest confined to a chair. With sharp, quick movements, he grabbed them, then seized the alien by one huge foot and dragged it through the debris and out the door in search of a better interrogation space.

At least there was a bright side to this. A nosey Iridosian didn't present nearly as big a problem as a faction competitor.

Part Four

chapter 51

<u>Consortium Outpost</u>

THE FAMILIAR THUNDEROUS CURRENT CAME first, layered beneath the tinkling splash of water on the stones along the shore. Sounds from the rocks, the trees, the nearby meadow filled her with a sense of belonging she seldom felt outside this space. Then came the sweet smell of damp ground, so different from the spicy dry fragrance of home. Warmth seeped into her flesh, surging to her waist, the soothing water a comfort.

Alira knew this place. Sensations from immersion in the Flow bore no rival. She paused, as at the apex of an indrawn breath, head tilted to one side, listening to a distant voice. Outside, electrical signals raced in a frenzy through her physical body, confused by the energetic blast of the stunner and fighting to heal. But that was a whole world away. Here she felt no pain, no struggle, only communion. She spoke without opening her eyes.

"I know you are there."

Silence met her challenge, and she looked to the side. There, on the riverbank, stood her Companion wearing Elisul's face. Long coppery hair fell in waves down his back, a few strands caught in the breeze. He was tall for a human, his skin paler than most she had seen.

"What do you want?" he asked, his voice rich with the same lilt as Elias Sullivan's holovid.

Alira turned toward him. "Now you speak to me?"

He thought about this. "Communication takes many forms."

"Lurien said something similar," Alira said, almost to herself. "That you convey information by a sudden sense of knowing or symbolic dreams. But you speak to me. With words."

"Lurien's modification muted our voice." He tilted his head. "Unmodified, you hear us."

"Unmodified?" She frowned. "What—"

The Adjustment. He was talking about the Adjustment! For the first time in her life, Alira was grateful for that rite's failure in her. She tried to remember where else her Companion might have interacted with her since she'd left Iridos, but her mind had been so full of voices she'd been hard pressed to hear herself, much less her Companion. On the heels of that thought came another.

There were no voices in her head now. She was alone here, with Elisul.

"Where are the others? How did you silence them?"

He ambled to the river's edge and sat on a large stone, feet dangling over the water. "They are overwhelming you. If you cannot achieve balance, you will not survive."

The harvesting madness. "Yes. I did come into this gift unprepared, didn't I?"

"Lurien should have trained you."

Her arms flushed gray. "My ama never thought I was ready."

"She was wrong. Without a connection, we will need to start over."

"What kind of connection?" Alira peered at him. "You mean the unammi?"

He sat, silent, on the shore.

"Who are you?" she pressed.

"The Founder."

"No, I mean who is behind the Founder's countenance? Are you Iri?"

Again, he considered her question. "We have many names. Iri is one."

"You have many faces, too. Why? Who are those other beings you've shown me?"

"Connections."

Clarity flickered, a tiny glimmering light in the vast Iri shadow. "Like the unammi?" she asked. "Like me?"

Elisul shifted through his repertoire once, twice, thrice before settling again into the red-haired human.

Many guises. Many names. Many connections. "How can you assume the forms of all those entities? You aren't like us, one intelligence per body, are you?" Her own questions echoed back at her. *She* could wear many guises. *She* had more than one intelligence in her body.

"We are Many. We are One."

Yellow rippled across her display. "Then you're of Na'Staani!"

"Nalena t'staani."

Alira's eyes widened at his use of Unameze. She'd always been taught the Iri were simple organisms living in the surface of a cavern wall. This encounter told her they were far more than that.

"Then why haven't you helped me? You could have told me how to avoid Skalar. Why do you let him hurt me?"

Elisul sat, his expression bland, but she sensed turmoil beneath the surface. The Iri were more concerned than the Founder's image would demonstrate. Otherwise, he wouldn't have come at all.

"Your reticence isn't constructive," she pressed. "I'm in real trouble and not at all sure how to get free of it. If you haven't come to offer advice, then why are you here?"

"To ask what you want."

"I don't know!" She slapped her red palms against Musju's surface. "I used to think I wanted the freedom to be myself, to live by my truth, to feel without shame. Since I reaped a human, I want some distance from his rage. I wanted Ama and my brother to approve of my choices at least once, but they never did. It's too late for that now, isn't it? They're gone, along with most of the unammi and our city. Now I want to help my people, take back our irolium." She gestured toward Elisul. "This should concern you, too. Will we dim without it?"

His lack of response felt like an answer. Alira nodded.

"I was afraid of that," she said. She huffed a sigh. "At least now I know our stake in this. But I don't understand how this benefits you. What do the Iri get from our partnership?"

Her Companion shifted through its panoply, stopping again on Elisul. "Presence."

The word filtered through her awareness, settling into her growing impression of these beings who were so disparate from either unammi or human, yet could resemble them both. Elisul had said all the species reflected in her Companion's forms offered connections. The Iri's relationship with the unammi, at least, provided presence. Were those two things related?

"What do you want?"

She borrowed a scowl from Crow. Why did he keep asking that? As much time as he spent in her head, he might know the answer better than she. She opened her mouth to reply, then stretched her lips back with a hiss of indrawn breath. Somewhere in physical space her body suffered. Skalar had grown impatient while she tarried, inflicted pain to bring her back to awareness. Here she felt no discomfort, just the distant link between her pithasia, which stood in Musju's Flow, and her physical shell, which endured Skalar's attentions. So strange to feel that attachment in such a remote way! She glanced down at where the water now swelled almost to her breast, and still it rose as if to swallow her, sweep her away. Alira looked back to Elisul, her eyes wide.

"Am I dying?"

His gaze held her fast. "What do you want?"

A small wrinkle formed between her brows. With Lurien and Nyros both dead, the respect she'd so craved no longer felt important. What she would give to go back to the moment the sh'toi first appeared on Iridos! No, even earlier, to a time prior to that awful watershed. It hadn't been perfect, but even mitigation would have been preferable to all that had happened since. Now she would never get another chance to feel Galen's touch or windwalk to the grove or attend another Telling. Even if she could escape, the humans knew her secret. How could she hope to get past so many of them to accomplish what she'd come here to do? Skalar would have questions and no moral qualms about using whatever means of persuasion the situation required. She had the answers, and would probably tell him everything before it was over, unless—

She had a choice. No one would blame her for succumbing at this point. She'd done everything she could, even harvested and portrayed a human, to help her people. But Cesar had been wrong about her. She wasn't strong enough. And she was exhausted. It would be easier to surrender to the Flow before Skalar could question her, let the current carry her to see what lay beyond the next curve. Unammi tales of death and what came after promised reunion with Na'Staani. She believed it, every word, though her people had no way to describe what to expect from the experience. How could they? Such a homecoming would involve sensory profusion on a scale incomparable to anything she or any living unammi ever knew. Lurien wouldn't be there, nor Nyros, not as they'd been here. There, all really were One. Would there be pain or joy at last? Would she even be aware of the transition?

"There is no return from that," Elisul whispered.

The curve ahead hid the future from her sight. Such a mystery, this! Standing in Musju's Flow granted an awareness of things beyond the physical, a recognition of continuation beyond this life, yes, but underneath lay complexities to this experience the unammi had yet to grasp. Such a truth as vast as Na'Staani held layers beyond what simple corporeal entities could ever hope to understand. Clerics and elders and councilors thought they knew so much. Compared to the rest of their people, they did. But in light of everything the unammi still had to learn, they were as babes in the birthing house.

The water rushed away, following its own purpose downstream. Where was it going? What lay around the bend? No way to know whether the unammi would pull through, but if she bowed out, it wouldn't matter. The unammi connection would belong to the next Founder Daughter. If there was one.

No return.

His words echoed in her mind, rebounding and building in intensity, sparking a thrill in her, excitement compressing her breath into a short, rapid rhythm. Elisul was right. Even if she endured this, too much had happened. She could never resume her old role. Once around the bend, a new vista spread out to offer fresh ideas, opportunities, and hopes. Everything was changed. That was the whole function of a turning point, wasn't it? You couldn't go back. You could never go back.

"What do you want?"

Alira gazed across the water at Elisul, her heart full of wonder, and smiled.

chapter 52

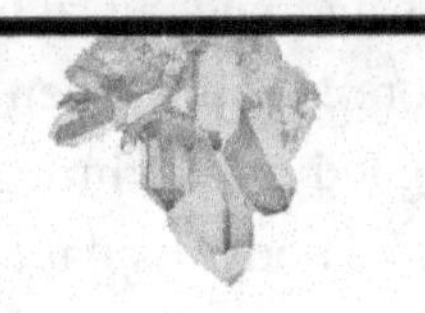

SKALAR GRIPPED ANOTHER OF THE Iridosian's stubby fingers and bent it back. "Wake up, netzyl. You are running out of digits."

A dull snap sent frantic white freckles dancing over the prisoner's naked skin. Skalar had never been this close to an Iridosian before and, after dragging it here, had spent the first few minutes examining it, checking for weak spots. Its skeletal structure looked similar to a human's, so most of its vital organs would probably lay inside the ribcage. If fingers and toes didn't do the job, he could progress to shallow cuts, just enough to hurt. Small bones in the extremities could follow, then the limbs, one joint at a time. Other bones could be crushed without killing the victim, but by that time he'd be dealing with a consciousness issue. If not, he would peel away the layers of its dermis to find where its luminescence came from and, lastly, dig in to see whether its soft belly held the same sort of viscera as a human's.

Skalar's lip curled. Wetwork always struck him as so banal. Any idiot could wield a knife or bludgeon, with often unreliable results. Given different circumstances, he would have taken his time, stretched this out with more proven psychological tactics, but this situation denied him that luxury. For the moment, he had bound it to a small, makeshift chair. Crude.

Old school. Devoid of elegance, but he wasn't going for style points. He wanted answers, and the faster the better. Already it had kept him waiting too long.

He wrapped one hand around the back of its head and the other around its nose and mouth. One-one-thousand, two-one-thousand, three-one-thousand, four-one-thousand....

The Iridosian began to squirm.

...five-one-thousand, six-one-thousand, seven-one-thousand....

Its movements grew more frenzied, pushing a stifled scream from its throat.

...eight-one-thousand, nine-one-thousand, ten-one-thousand....

It was strong for its size and bucked so hard it almost freed itself. His grip tightened for a few more seconds, then Skalar let it go and stepped back. Its breath came in ragged gasps through lips gone blue. Or maybe they were blue to start with. Its body displayed a confusing array of erratic color blotched with white.

"Welcome back. I was beginning to think you were a lost cause." He leaned against the secured door, crossing his arms. "You already know where you are. Since you tried to run when you heard my voice, it's a safe bet you know who I am, so we can skip the introductions. Here's how this is going to work. I will ask questions. You will provide answers. Failure to follow this procedure will cost you. Are we clear?"

It regarded him in silence. Skalar was no expert on reading Iridosian body language or whatever those colors in its skin meant, but it didn't appear angry, or even afraid.

"I asked you a question. Do you understand?"

Still it sat silent. Skalar sighed, stepped forward and slapped it. "Answer me, netzyl. Who are you?"

It glared up at his towering form, its eyes huge and silver, its tongue sneaking out to lick blood from its lip. So, they bled in red. Good to know. When it didn't respond, he slapped it again, this time in the other direction, knocking its chair over and bouncing its head on the floor as it fell. Skalar righted the prisoner and slapped it again. Its face shot back around, flickering with red spots and glaring at him through pupils dilated and uneven. Damn. Probably concussed.

"Unammi asal," it murmured.

"Speak English. Who are you?"

"Ba'nostade puda ba'tujhur."

Skalar bent and snapped its last unbroken finger. White freckles peppered its red skin. A brief flicker of pain skittered over its features. "How did you know about this base?"

No answer. Skalar drew his blade along its inner thigh, leaving behind a trail of red droplets. "Why did you come here?"

The Iridosian retched to one side, heaving even though its stomach was apparently empty. Definitely concussed. Irrelevant, as long as it could talk. He needed to keep it focused. Skalar sliced again, this time along the bony part of its upper chest. "Where are your friends? I doubt you came here by yourself."

He pinched a bit of skin on the Iridosian's arm with a slow twist.

"Where is your ship?"

No response.

Another slice. "How many of your people survived my armada?"

No response.

He flipped the knife in his hand and brought the metal grip down hard across the top of its foot. "How did you make yourself look like Crow? And by the way, where *is* Crow? The real one, I mean?"

Still no reply. Another strike, this time on the other foot. "Speak, netzyl."

Numerous cuts and blows later, he stepped back, glaring at the prisoner. Its pain threshold lay far above that of most humans he had questioned in the past. Discomfort registered on its face along with something like defiance, its skin mottled white and red. By now, droplets of blood from almost a dozen shallow cuts lay silhouetted across the Iridosian's freakish glowing body. Skalar dropped his knife tip-first into the floor and wrapped his hands around its head, nose, and mouth. "If you won't speak, then you don't need to breathe."

The Iridosian's immediate struggle tightened Skalar's grip as he counted off the seconds. At about seven-one-thousand, he noticed something odd. Wasn't there a long slash on its thigh moments ago? He released it and stepped back as it gasped and heaved for air. Yes…yes, and another on its chest, which closed as he watched. His frown deepened and he shoved it forward against its bonds to better see the wound on its back where his stunner had scorched its skin.

What burn? Where?

Skalar retrieved his knife and sliced into the muscle at the side of its leg. A groan tore out of the prisoner's throat as it renewed its struggle against the bonds. Blood flowed from the wound for almost thirty seconds before it began to congeal around the slash. In less than a minute, it stopped, and thirty seconds later, the wound closed.

A new expression wiped away Skalar's frown. Shapeshifter *and* speed-healer. What else could this netzyl do? More to the point, how could he use this to his advantage?

He gripped its chin in his fist and tilted its head back. "That's some talent you have there," he said, grinning. "It comes in handy, I'll bet. Perhaps shallow cuts aren't much of an incentive for someone like you, so let's try something else. I'll ask my questions again and if you don't answer, we'll find out if you can regrow a whole limb."

chapter 53

THE CUTS WERE NOTHING, NOR were the broken fingers or toes. The head trauma concerned her more. The room blurred, and Alira retreated from the interrogation, diving into her own body to examine the brain injury. There, electrical impulses and chemical exchanges carried out regular functions everywhere except the site of the impact and a point opposite. Both flickered with electrical interruptions and chemical confusion where signals came to the end of healthy neurons and stopped short, no way to continue. Healing was automatic, but she added her own efforts to the process to speed things along.

Crow beckoned her toward a dark, narrow anger

he's the one who killed your people, squib. i pulled the trigger, but on his order.

whispering his plans to take Skalar down over the years and

why is everything spinning so?

with her help he would succeed. A vicarious reward was better than nothing. Still—

The room tilted around her, churning her gut until her empty stomach spasmed and heaved. He cut her again and she winced, straining to focus through her confusion. She needed to manipulate him, convince him to do what she wanted, but that had never been her forte.

oh yeah, you specialize in graphic mutilation. gut him and be done.

shut up, crow. little busy right now.

Skalar's interminable questions continued. He pinched her arm, etching a grimace into her features

elisul, where are you?

then broke the bones in both feet and stepped back. Pain speckled her legs with white, drew a hiss from her lips, gritted her teeth. Alira peered at this despicable human whose orders had sent Crow to Iridos. Yet he came from Na'Staani, as she did, as all life did. She and he were One. The thought disgusted her. Crow and Skalar were nothing like the Founder. How could Na'Staani have brought forth such putrid excuses for sentience? How could these beings stand in Musju's Flow and not contaminate the whole?

The urge to let her anger take control ran fierce in her blood, even hotter in those drops still falling outside her skin, but she couldn't kill him

what the fuck! you killed me but not this bastard?

yet. The base crew must have seen her when she came inside

no way. sensors aren't keen enough.

you're sure about that, crow?

and if she killed him now, they might know. She couldn't allow him to leave this base alive. He'd seen her morph. But what about the others? did he tell them?

doubtful. he would worry about other squibs hiding among the crew.

If that were true, she'd be able to save the rest. Maybe. Assuming she could find a way out of this mess. The cells in all her hurts worked to bond skin to skin, clear the neural pathways, straighten and mend bones. Alira took a ragged breath and studied her enemy. His cold eyes regarded her as if she were some sort of lower life form

lab rat.

while he spat questions and called her by a strange name. Elisul's figure, on the rock above Musju, filled her mind

what do you want?

and Alira felt the Flow surge inside and around her as she had never experienced outside meditation. Its energy moved with instead of against her, invigorating her efforts while she reached into the molecular bonds in her restraints, searched for their weak point, and began to sever their connections. She—

Without warning, the sh'toi's fingers wrapped around her face and Alira's lungs heaved

fish out of water.

craving the next breath as they had the last time

what the fuck, squib? feed him lies, buy us some—

before Skalar released her and she sucked in great gasps of air. He pulled her forward, shoved her back, sliced her leg, then gripped her chin. Tilting her head back to a painful degree, he threatened to cut off a limb, and she believed he meant every word. Flashbacks of Crow's gruesome death overlaid her view of Skalar. Torn between the hatred she couldn't deny and the new knowledge that she was—all unammi were—part human, she wavered. Voices clamored in her thoughts, all debating the apt fate of her captor.

Alira drew in another ragged breath and wheezed through lips puckered by his grip. "You want answers, sh'toi? What will you give me in return?" She concentrated again on the straps at her wrists.

Skalar released her and stepped back, a small smile curling the corners of his mouth. "So now we're negotiating price. Very well. You demonstrate some very interesting abilities. Maybe my scientists can find a way to instill them in humans somewhere down the line. It would be a lucrative addition to our Iridosian mining operation."

She worked her jaw to dislodge the ache he'd put there. "That isn't helpful in the way of incentive."

"If you cooperate, I'll let the other Iridosians you brought along go free."

He hadn't found the ship, then. Good. "I came alone." She felt the restraints at her hands go slack and gripped them with freed fingers so they wouldn't fall to the floor.

"How did you find this place?"

"Crow told me where it was."

"Oh? When?"

"When I killed him in New Canaan."

perfect answer, squib! make him sweat.

The smile vanished. Skalar's voice dropped to a whisper. "So, my second is dead."

"Without question."

"And you speak of incentive."

Alira shrugged, her mind working at the restraints around her feet.

"I know who *didn't* come with you. My people already eliminated most of your Iridosian merchants and brought me their ships."

Her heart skipped a beat. Galen! Colorful ripples raced across her display, a reaction the sh'toi couldn't miss.

"So, if you came alone, all the remaining Iridosians must still be on Iridos." His fingers stroked the hair at his chin

beard.

as he considered this. "Crow was mistaken, then, when he thought no one could live through his attack there. I'll have to go back with another armada and rectify that little oversight myself."

Waves of white rushed over her belly and legs. She forced a calm note into her voice. "There is no one left. I'm the last one. I came here to kill you."

Skalar advanced on her again.

She recoiled. "Fine. You win."

He took a step back.

Alira sighed. Drawing on Crow's memories, she stalled. "Everyone who is left came with me. They're all on the other side of this moon, in the tunnels under one of the abandoned domes."

"Sure they are."

do better, squib.

i will, if i can just....

Alira flushed red again. "Why would I lie when you can confirm or refute my veracity in less than an hour?"

Skalar regarded her through narrowed eyes.

"Can you release my hands while we talk, at least?" She jerked her head to one side as Crow might do. "These restraints are uncomfortable."

"That's the intent."

She sighed and sank farther into the chair. "I'm half your size. I'm unarmed. You still think me a threat?"

"Not especially, no. But since you're in a more talkative mood, tell me about these special talents of yours. Can all Iridosians do that?"

"No, only me. I'm considered a freak among my own people."

"Of course you are," Skalar nodded. He leaned against the wall. "How do you change your appearance?"

The bonds around Alira's ankles came loose to lay across the tops of her feet and she turned her full attention to the human.

"Is it a gland in your brain?" he asked.

"Yes," she said, "it is something about the brain." Riveted on a spot behind his brows, she envisioned synapses and electrical signals rushing through the construct inside his skull and searched for the most efficient and vulnerable point.

Skalar leaned against the wall. "Is it a strict visual transformation? or a full physiological shift?"

"It's a complete transmutation," she said, finding the sweet spot and

> *sister, have you done this before?*
>
> *oh yeah. she's got experience.*

pulling apart the connections there.

"In-in-interesting," he stuttered. "Where are the limita-ations?" A slight frown furrowed his brow, and his arms slackened at his chest.

"There are none," she answered. "We can look like anything or anyone and can hold a shape forever if we wish."

"We," he said, his voice flat, toneless. His arms fell to his sides. "You s-sa-aid you were th-the o-only-ly one."

Alira stood up, watching fear fill his eyes as he tried to move toward her and found he was no longer in control. "I lied."

"Wh-what's hap-hap—" Skalar slid down the wall, still observing every detail. His mouth twitched as if he were trying to speak.

She squatted beside him and stripped his body as naked as her own. What irony. After Crow's reaping, she'd hoped never to harvest another human, yet without killing Skalar, she couldn't know how to portray him. She needed to see the physical aspects. She rolled Skalar over to survey his form, then shifted her own to match. He ran through a mental check: body hair, scars, clothing, shoes, eyes, everything seemed in order, though he had no TICS holo to confirm the appearance. He would have to take a chance.

okay, crow, talk to me about skalar.

Memories flooded in, complete with emotional attachments. The morphed admiral steadied himself against the wall as his awareness filled with images of avarice, egoism, ruthlessness. Crow's feeling toward the man comprised a confusing tangle of admiration, fear, and hatred. Skalar's vision and demand for absolute excellence made him a despicable taskmaster. Yet those traits Crow both loathed and admired also granted success in Trader business. The other five factions all emulated Skalar's tactics now, but none even came close to his success rate. He had controlled the largest faction more than twenty years and for good reason. No one crossed him and lived. Portraying that vile sh'toi would prove a challenge, and he set his mind to accomplish it.

Crow's knowledge didn't tell Skalar how many crew were on base now, though they were sure to be located in the sector surrounding Control. He doubted they knew unammi secrets. If they were clear, he could send them back to New Canaan. In the meantime, he needed a plan to evacuate the base.

The most probable reason for Skalar's visit was to inspect his haul, check out the ships. Maybe the sensors were upgraded. If he'd planned to run a larger operation from here, Skalar would have seen to heightened security. Crow hadn't expected it to happen so fast, but it was possible. If so, then the crew would have known "Crow" was on site, which would explain how he had been caught. Maybe Skalar could use that.

why would you have come here, crow?

i wouldn't. skalar told me to stay put.

then what sort of emergency would have made you defy his order?

maybe a plausible threat from another faction.

What if another faction had discovered this base, and planned to seize control?

that might work.

Yes…Crow would never have commed such info, because a leak like that would have come from inside the Consortium, maybe even from someone here, on site now. He would have come himself, landed unseen to avoid alerting any possible mole, and delivered the message in person. That story would also give Skalar good reason to evacuate and abandon the facility. As far as Crow knew, there were no weapons here beyond what the human ships carried. It was as good a plan as any, and vague enough he could modify it as he went. Time was not his friend. Already he found it difficult to believe the others hadn't come to see what was taking the admiral so long.

Skalar looked down at his incapacitated twin.

"I hate you. You understand why, don't you?" he whispered to the defenseless admiral. Skalar could almost pity the man. Unless unammi healing techniques were brought to bear, his brain would never again operate his limbs. "Regardless, I'm not going to leave you like this any longer than necessary. Even with Crow in my head

hey!

I'm not that much of a bastard."

He strapped on the admiral's wristcom, exchanged Crow's ident for Skalar's, retrieved Cesar's coin and left, securing the door with one of Crow's private codes.

Memory led his steps back toward Control, where the others waited.

"Admiral on deck!" called Commander Cohen.

"As you were," Skalar said. "Cohen, you're with me." He walked out, the commander two steps behind him. When they were alone, he stopped.

"Report."

"We're still on lockdown, per your orders, sir. Nothing new to report. If I might ask, what did Captain Crow have to say?"

keep it short, squib.

"We have a leak."

Cohen paled. "How bad, sir?"

"This base is compromised. Another faction is on their way right now."

"Which faction, sir?"

cohen is not your friend, she's your crew, she's a cog! an insect!

Skalar's cheek twitched. "You don't need to know."

Cohen drew back.

"I'm shutting the base down until we seal the leak and deal with this threat."

"But," Cohen said, her expression confused, "couldn't we use this as a way to test and tighten our security? We have three ships with weapons. We can defend ourselves. Besides, all our hemi is here now and—"

Skalar gripped her upper arms and shoved her hard against the wall, leaning close to her face while she gawked.

"'Our' hemi?" he growled, his nose centimeters from hers. "Make no mistake, Cohen. Everything on this and every other Consortium base is mine. Not yours. Not ours. *Mine.* You use it by my grace. Got it?"

"Yes, sir," she wheezed, eyes wide. "Apologies, sir."

"Good." He backed off. "The hematium is locked down?"

"Yes, sir."

"Then you have two assignments. First, send half your crew to stow those blue rocks, as many as possible, onto one of the Iridosian ships, whichever one is closest. And second, send the rest to pack all your shit onto the boats that brought you and prepare for your trip to New Canaan. You have two hours to remove any trace of Consortium presence here."

"We'll leave behind all your hemi, sir," Cohen said, her voice mechanical, "and all the squib ships. Won't—"

"Let me worry about that."

Cohen nodded, her skin pale and uncommunicative. "What of my crewman, sir, the one who's on his way back? Should I comm him and tell him to go back home?"

"Yes. Send him home. The rest of you will follow as soon as you're packed and ready."

"Yes, sir."

Cohen spun on her heel and retreated into Control, where Skalar followed to ensure Cohen carried out his orders. Numerous questioning looks came his way, but no one challenged him and soon he stood alone in the compartment while crewmen loaded the ships. He checked the panels, seeing them through Crow's memory. The scanners *had* been updated. That's how they'd found him so fast.

told you, crow.

piss off, squib.

Skalar ached to oversee the irolium transfer, but what if exposure to so many of the stones provoked a reaction beyond his control? He had no way of knowing whether the irolium would provoke a visible response in Alira's body after she had been so long away from its influence. If it did, his secret would be out. He wasn't confident he could overcome so many of the crew at once. Better to keep his distance.

Restless, he left Control to stalk the corridors. It wouldn't hurt to keep the humans under observation to stop them going after "Crow," who still showed up on sensors. Skalar would be relieved when the crew was gone and he could finish what he'd started back in the other room.

chapter 54

"MALCOLM, COME SEE WHAT I made!"

"In a minute," he called from the fence. Beyond lay exciting rides in the amusement park. He never got to go there. His mother couldn't afford the admission and Harajüd House stood fast, unsympathetic even to basic needs like larger quarters or an increased food allowance for four children. They weren't about to cover a frivolous afternoon's entertainment, so whenever it was Malcolm's turn to mind the youngest, he always brought her here. At least he could see the other kids inside the fence and try to imagine what it felt like to swoop and roll and be shot into the air only to fall back toward the ground at hair-raising speed before the safeties kicked in.

Somewhere behind him, a group of kids laughed and jeered, but Malcolm was glued to the spectacle before him. Every time the riders swooped past, their eyes lit with the thrill of fear, he could almost feel the wind rushing past his own flushed face, his own voice squealing in exhilaration. A warm summer breeze completed the illusion and later, Malcolm was never sure how long she'd been screaming before he realized it was his sister's voice he heard. Whirling, he saw the bigger kids around her, dwarfing her, pushing her back and forth between them. In an instant, his feet pounded against the ground. He shoved his way past the bullies to snatch his sister from their grasp and thrust her behind him.

Now, they had a new target.

"Oh look, boys," the largest said. The girl who stood head and shoulders above him. "Mal-cum to the rescue! What'sa matter, Mal-cum? We dain't treat yore pore little baby sister awright?"

"Leave us alone!" Malcolm shifted his feet, readying himself for what he knew was about to happen.

"Or whut?" taunted one of the boys. "Whut'chu gon' do, Mal-cum? Call yore mama? Oh, wait, you cain't do that, can you? Yore mama workin' two shifts to feed you. Ain't nobody comin' to hep you, Mal-cum."

Malcolm's rage led his fists, and he landed a single blow. The bullies dealt the rest while his sister screamed. A couple of adults sent the bullies running and one man offered to take Malcolm to the medfac, but he waved away the concern. His family had no privileges there. He would be fine. It was just a cut lip and a few bruises. Angry, bitter, he'd left the nonplussed grownups standing in the blood-spattered grass while he dragged his sister toward their flat in the East side.

"Malcolm stop!" she said, finally planting her feet against the ground and refusing to go another step.

"What, dammit?"

She glanced around, shocked. "Ooh, you better watch your mouth! Mama would be mad! Let me see." Her small hands came up to his cheeks, drawing his head down closer so she could see the split lip and the cut above his eye, his cheekbone already bruising. "That's gonna be a purty color, Malcolm." She touched it with pudgy fingers, then met his gaze and smiled. "Thanks for saving me."

Her gentle spirit calmed him when no one else could and he grinned, even though it hurt. "I'll always save you, Rugrat. What were you gonna show me?"

"It's nothin'. I made a bird house outta twigs."

"You did?" Malcolm spun back the way they'd come. "Well, let's go and get it!" He had already taken three steps before she could stop him.

"No, don't. It was a dumb little thing."

She smiled, despite something else behind her eyes.

"That bitch stomped it. Didn't she?"

Rugrat shrugged. "It was stupid anyway. Come on, let's go home. Mama would say you should put something cold on your bruise."

Skalar came to on the floor, his body shivering despite the thermal system's continuous operation. From the angle of his head, he saw through dry, blurry eyes a half-meter of tiled floor in need of sweeping. He still drew breath. Still felt his thumping heart, the puddle of saliva beneath his face on the floor. An itch between his shoulder blades. The warm wetness at his groin. He tried to sit up. To raise his head. To lift a hand. To move a finger. To shift his eyes. Nothing worked like it should.

What—

Oh yes. The Iridosian. It hadn't even touched him until he was already on the floor. How did it do that?

Maybe this…whatever it was…would get better. Maybe it would wear off so he could get up and go after it. The thought of confronting it again filled him with fear before rage erupted to storm his every thought.

No! He was done with fear. Admiral Malcolm Skalar of the Harajüd Consortium was a man to fear. He held the power. He dictated the rules. No one pushed him around. Not anymore.

Except this netzyl. And he hadn't even seen it coming.

A nugget of cold logic pushed revenge to the back of his mind. He'd deal with that later. Right now, survival took priority. He needed to get up. Get out of here before it got back. Because if it could put him down this hard and never break a sweat, who knew what else it could do. Is this how the Iridosians had killed the armada ships? If so, he hoped this one was alone. Otherwise, he and the crew were dead.

It didn't come all this way for nothing. But what did it want? And how could he stop it? He had a stunner somewhere and its body hadn't liked the effects of that. If he could get on his feet, he could take back his base. His eyes burned with the need to blink. How long had he been lying here? Cohen or one of the others would come searching for him soon. Unless….

The image of Crow sweeping the tabletop clear of its debris in the lab flashed back to Skalar's mind. He had known for sure his second was on Harajüd, yet he'd almost fallen for the Iridosian's disguise. Maybe it could look like him, too. Perhaps it already did, which was why his crew hadn't come. They didn't know he was missing.

Oh, he did not like that thought at all.

The door swished open, and Skalar strained to shift his gaze, to see who was there, what was coming. Seconds later, feet came into view—those were his shoes—and seconds after that a man squatted and rolled him over, propping him up so he could see the blurry image above him. His "twin" hunkered there for what seemed an eternity before it shifted into its natural form, its silver eyes staring into Skalar's own.

If he could negotiate—wait, netzyl, I can—

"I really want to make you suffer," it said.

A chill raced down Skalar's spine.

chapter 55

A TRICKLE OF SALIVA ESCAPED the sh'toi's slack lips. Crow hated this man. Animosity rose like bile in Alira's throat, threatening to choke her control until a vision of Crow's violated body danced its now-familiar tango across her mind.

do it! do it, squib!

no. not again.

Confusion and reluctance and anger vied for space on her mottled limbs as she frowned toward Skalar. "You're such a bastard, so eaten up with greed and arrogance and scorn. How can you live with that much sickness inside you?"

he was a mama's boy.

more so than you, crow?

Her unammi passengers argued with each other. Kill him. Don't kill him. The council would say—

But the council wasn't here. She was. She tilted her head. What was the catalyst behind this human's despicable nature? Maybe he couldn't help himself. Maybe he was broken, like Crow. The unammi believed every pithasia came into this existence shining, that its corporeal personality resulted from a combination of parentage and environment and, sometimes, the inescapable anomalies that occurred in the genome of an otherwise healthy fetus. Unammi mothers monitored development of their embryos, often tweaking and adjusting the fetal DNA as necessary during gestation, but on rare occasions their efforts met with limited success. What about humans? Could they adjust the fetus if something went wrong in the womb? Or was that one of the Iri's gifts to the unammi?

She laid her arms across her knees. "Is that what happened to you?" she whispered. "Your mother couldn't fix you in her womb?"

These were answers he probably couldn't give even if he wanted to. Alira dropped into the Flow. Water streamed past while her dream Companion shifted on the shore, but all her other reaped cohorts followed and before they could speak she held up a hand.

don't.

Her eyes went to her Companion. "Should I end him?"

Its form slid from one shape to another.

"I chose to stay," Alira pressed. "Have you no further guidance?"

For a moment, it settled into Elisul

no coming back from that.

then resumed its changing phases and fell silent.

Another turning point. Every harvest changed her, the human ones most of all. How many would it take before she lost the person who lay beneath? Already the lines between herself and "them" grew fuzzy. Maybe that was part of the process, or maybe it was part of the madness. She didn't know the difference, but did it matter? Her path was laid. If she didn't take it, others would pay the price.

She didn't want another sh'toi in her mind. Shared ancestry or no, their differences disgusted her, sickened her. She couldn't leave Skalar here in this cruel state, despite what she knew Crow would want. She could heal the admiral, but that would mean another confrontation between them at some future date and time, when he'd be forewarned and better prepared for her tricks.

Besides, he knew enough unammi secrets to doom her people if he were allowed to go free, and she couldn't wipe his memory or change who he was at a fundamental level. No unammi gift granted that ability.

"Na'Staani," she whispered aloud, "which is the right thing? I don't know what to do."

The water flowed past, its musical sound offering peace, but no answers.

Cesar stepped before her in the Flow, one hand extended, and she touched her fingers to his.

what would you advise, na'apa?

He nodded, seeming to acknowledge her turmoil even as blue and purple swirled in ripples across his own form.

you know what you must do.

The elder's words sunk in, weighing her down in the water, and the wrinkle appeared between her brows. Yes. She knew.

Alira took a deep breath and returned to the cluttered room. Skalar's vacant gaze still regarded her from where she had propped him up.

"Don't worry. It won't hurt." She closed his eyes, then gripped his hand in hers and finished the job.

Memories poured into her…years of crimes against his own people, many done in collusion with those in positions of colonial control…the moue of disgust on his mother's face when she learned he'd joined the Consortium…Rugrat's ruined body on the docks…torturing the slaver who damaged her…names of crewmen caught working behind the admiral's back, the price each had paid…seeing his brothers evade him in the market…the insatiable hunger for recognition an average life could never grant and his determination to acquire it at any cost.…

Crow's harvest may have sickened her, but it had prepared her for this darker reaping. Revulsion and compassion and shared pain contorted her features and a bone-deep groan ripped past her lips. These humans were alike in so many ways, different facets of the same stone, one born to privilege to have it later ripped away, the other birthed into a common home and always reaching for more, more, more…both intent on the prize, both broken and horrific by unammi standards, yet heroes in their own minds. Their sense of morality seemed counter to the good of their species.

Is this what it felt like to be human? It couldn't be…Elias Sullivan had held higher ideals. Perhaps he and his companions comprised a minority. Why else would he want to escape his home world? Hadn't he said as much in his journal entry? If humans came from Na'Staani as did all of life, then Crow's and Skalar's hatred must be something acquired in this lifetime, perhaps as a result of their brokenness, the sh'toi nature that set them apart from others of their race. She chose to believe this. The alternative was to accept that hatred and its ilk came from Na'Staani, which couldn't be possible.

now what, squib?

Good question. Without a deshtant, Alira had no way to know when the detachment of Skalar's pithasia would be complete. Even if she did, she couldn't return Skalar's shell to the elements inside the base, nor could she do it alone. She couldn't leave him lying on the floor. At home, they could expose him on the surface and let the wind do the work, but that wasn't an option here. She searched Skalar's memories and found cold storage pods

cadaver racks.

in the northeast sector of the facility. Were they still functional? Alira dragged Skalar through the base to the proper section and tried the controls. They worked, sort of. But for how long? It was amazing they functioned at all. Alira hoisted him to the lowest rack and slid him into the unit, then closed the door. She would decide later how best to respect his pithasia. Her immediate concerns lay in another direction.

Back in the lab where she'd found Elisul's holojournal, Alira experimented with visuals on the equipment until she was able to play back the few remaining viable journal entries. If there had been others, they were gone now, corrupted over the intervening years since their recordings. Most of the equipment lay broken or far beyond a functional age. The pieces she could manage to operate served no useful purpose for her needs, and after a short while she moved on, stalking the base as she rooted through Crow's memories.

In Control, he told her how to bring up a holoimage of the rocky moon on which she stood. When Skalar had viewed this image, he'd sought other usable construction left behind by humans in the early days of Earth's expansion. She examined it now in search of underground fissures and found dozens of them, except none stretched more than a few kilometers. Why had the Founder come here? Why not leave for Iridos from his own home world? She adjusted settings on the equipment to show nearby Earth and ran the same search. Hundreds of cave systems lined the image, some reaching far into the planet's depths and stretching for hundreds of kilometers in both directions. Then why had Elisul gone to Iridos at all? True, his own dream Companion called him there, but why? If the Iri wanted nothing more than to bond with him and the others, why draw them away to a whole new planet to begin with? Why not isolate them from the rest of their race in one of these underground chambers?

The human memories among her harvests told of disease. Alira found nothing in a computer search of Earth's history beyond what those memories recognized as normal human ailments, but Skalar whispered to her of the horrific latter days of human-era Earth, ecosystem destruction that released and exacerbated persistent and lethal microbes. The Founder's ship and population must have left before the pestilence took hold. It should have been safe, though perhaps Earth's cavern sites had already been inhabited.

She shrank the Earth image and called up a projection of this star system in its place. She enlarged it until the vid closed in to show the planets closest to the star, then set it in motion and stood back. Earth's rotation rate exceeded its orbital rate, as did the other worlds humans had colonized. So different from Iridos!

When she had flown past on her way to this base, she'd glimpsed Earth from too great a distance to get a feel for its character. Alira again enlarged the holodisplay of Earth with its multicolored surface of green and brown, as well as enormous swaths of blue. But her human memories had no clear idea of how long it had been since this image was made. The standard year of contemporary human worlds differed from seasonal time measurements in the era of the Founders. Even with updated equipment here in Control, this image would be out of date. No planetary surveys would have been completed since the humans quarantined Earth. What would it look like now? Did humans still live there?

> *no no no no...you can't go there, squib, i told you—*
> *it's contaminated, netzyl...we can't—*
> *alira what are you doing? our people need—*
> *sister, these are inanities.*

Except they weren't. Earth spawned the unammi! Here, within reach, lay the home of all unammi ancestry. Could she even consider going back to Iridos, more than seven cycles away, without at least visiting this world? The news of their origins would unsettle her people, no doubt

yeah, especially when you bring back a lethal PLAGUE.

but once they came to accept this truth, they may want to know about the world of the Founders. Wasn't it her duty to gather as much information as she could before going home? She shushed the arguments in her mind. A single cycle wouldn't make that much difference in the larger scheme of things.

Alira donned her nanosuit and headgear, picked up the crate of supplies she'd gathered for the trip back, and glanced around Control. Nothing else here she needed just now. She made her way through the center, shutting down everything except the cadaver racks as she went, and pointed her feet toward the loaded unammi ship. No one spoke. She had told her harvests she was going. What more could they say? In the blissful silence, she felt the Flow around her, *in* her…the same Flow that had carried the Founders from these alien roots to their evolved symbiotic existence, the Flow that now carried their race toward some unknown and unknowable future. She, too, was caught in its course, going back to the beginning of her people's evolution to complete the circle. Riding its current felt almost effortless now. When had that happened?

Outside the loading bay, she boarded the closest unammi ship, double-checked the irolium in the cargo bay—grateful for the renewed vigor the crystals granted her even now, detached as they were—and stowed the supplies in the galley. Then Alira settled into the pilot seat, lifted off the lunar surface and headed toward Earth.

chapter 56

<u>Iridos</u>

"HOW DO WE KNOW THEY'RE in this piece of rock?" Galen asked.

"Look." One of the miners indicated thin veins of irolium on one side, then flipped it over to show the plain, unmarked surface where the stone had broken away from the ceiling. "If they're at the root of the irolium, then they are in this chunk."

"Explain this plan again," Dyson said.

Galen pointed at the temple walls. "If the Iri could spread through the rock here, then they should do it elsewhere. We take these as seedstones, attach them to crevasses in the caverns of our new home, then leave the Iri to do what they do."

Understanding dawned in the elder. "Then," he said, "when the irolium begins to form, it should link the old stones to the new and stabilize the whole thing."

"Yes." Galen turned to the miners for verification.

"It should work," the second miner agreed. "We'll need to bring as many seedstones as possible to have a better chance at success."

"That is in progress." The first miner gestured across the cavern at a team working on a lifted platform, chiseling away layers of the walls where once the vivid blue stones had grown.

"Very good," Dyson said on his way out. "Keep me informed."

"Thank you for backing my plan," Galen said to the first miner. "I'm sorry I didn't come to you sooner. We've been friends since we were younglings, and—"

"I didn't do it for you," the miner said. "I don't care what Rakalesh said. Outcasts don't belong here." Without another word, he rejoined his team at the platform.

The second miner lingered. "It's hard for him," he said. "When you left the first time, he mourned as if you had died. He told me once of nightmares where humans kept you as an amusement. He never understood why you would abandon our people."

Galen's hands grasped each other in front of him. "But I—"

"Don't," he said, his palm facing Galen. "I tell you because he's my i'shin, and I know he is hurting. Please don't come to him without need. I don't want him to suffer more than he already does." He nodded at Galen, then went back to his guildmates.

The feeling of isolation from last cycle's council gathering swelled within Galen, tightening his throat.

Tiral stepped up beside him. "Let it go," he said, his voice quiet. "If he doesn't see, if *they* don't understand even after my words in the gathering, they never will. Your explanations are sand in the wind."

"I'll try," Galen said, voice thick.

"We'll go ahead, start the search for a new home. Join us when you feel ready," Tiral said.

Galen heard them leave, his gaze still locked on the miners. It boggled his mind how the other unammi could be so cold, so uninterested in all the ways pilots could contribute. Before he had become an outcast, he'd seen pilots as exotic, strange. Somehow, he had thought then, they had a different bearing, as if their lives in the human colonies had altered them in some way. He'd wondered what stories they would tell, given the chance, but his ama had forbidden him to approach them. Everyone saw basic vids from the trade guild during their time in the educator's house, but unless you were an initiate in the trade guild, you weren't allowed to learn anything about that specific role.

Why should it be thus? No matter what a person chose at their rite of decision, their guild became part of who they were. Their work within it colored how they saw things, how they formed opinions, how they interacted with others. Yet only the pilots were ostracized in this way. He shook his head and followed Tiral and the others.

Lost in thought, he wound his way through the busy tunnels until traffic slowed almost to a stop. A knot of individuals awaited care in the passage outside the temporary healing room. Workers speckled with gray tossed curious glances at the unusual congestion before they pressed through to continue on their way, but Galen stopped. He approached a frem outside the chamber door.

"Has something happened?"

"Some of the younglings are sick," she replied.

"What kind of sickness?"

"Ask the healers, outcast."

Yoloron appeared beside Galen. "I believe Councilor Dyson asked us to treat the pilots as we would our own."

"But they aren't. They're outsiders, foreigners. I'll work beside them and act civil if I must, but I don't have to converse with them beyond that."

"I suppose not." Red tinges colored Yoloron's response. She gestured toward the chamber. "You can go in. They've cleared a pallet."

The worker ducked inside without another word. Galen nodded to Yoloron. "Thank you for the effort. It's appreciated, but I doubt it will do much good."

Yoloron touched his arm, drew him aside from the crowd. "You've always been so sensitive, Galen. Even as a babe in the birthing house, you latched onto others' pain as if it were your own." She waved toward the now departed worker. "Don't take misguided words to heart. She'll come around. They all will."

"I hope so. But what is this about the younglings? They're sick?"

"Yes, from the radiation," Yoloron said, weariness and frustration swirling through her skin, her gaze fixed on the filled cots.

"Why don't they regenerate?"

"Some have. These are too young."

"Can't the healers manage their symptoms, help them move past the reaction?"

"They're trying."

"How many are sick?"

"About a dozen, so far." Yoloron paused, her mouth twisted to one side. "We think they're dimming."

What? But that wasn't….

Galen peeped inside the sickroom where several of Alira's students lay. The one she favored most, Trumo, stirred in one of the beds.

Ah no! Alira told Galen she felt akin to Trumo because he didn't fit in with his peers. She would be devastated if he died or, worse, if he were dimmed beyond all hope. Right now, his chances didn't seem good. The youngling's eyes were tarnished, not their usual bright silver. Weak facial patterns shone through his muddy display. Sores from the radiation, which should have healed by now, still oozed on his chest and arms.

The tales were true.

Yoloron's voice filtered through Galen's shock. "We don't know how to stop it. Without the irolium…." Her words trailed off. She didn't need to complete her sentence.

"Will this happen to all of us?" he whispered.

She hesitated. "It is a credible concern."

"Why weren't we told this earlier?"

"I argued against it." Yoloron wiped her face. "No one could do anything to prevent it, and everyone already carries such a heavy burden. I didn't want to lay this at their feet, too. Not until we know for sure there is no hope. It would only frustrate them more."

Galen's fingers tangled together. A sick chill churned his colors. What kind of future would that be for the unammi?

"Have the pilots found a potential new home for us?" she asked.

He fixed on her words and her display, where prickles of white winked beneath her dominant colors. "Not yet, but we were under the impression that leaving was a contingency."

"They will soon see we have no choice. But please don't share that yet. The announcement will be wrenching for us all." She looked around.

"I can't imagine living anywhere else. No other world could be so beautiful, so comfortable, so perfect for an unammi city. I don't *want* to leave, but we don't have the luxury of time to consider our options at length. The longer our transition, the worse our repercussions."

Galen flushed white. "Is it that bad?"

"It will be, if we don't escape this poison."

"So, we find a new world, or we die."

"Not physically, perhaps. Not right away."

Galen didn't miss the insinuation. "But we've just begun to list viable worlds. We've not yet considered preferable candidates or lists of supplies we might need. This can't be rushed."

"Then we may need another option," Yoloron said with a sigh. "We've all made physical changes to our bodies over a longer period than usual to avoid the sickness. We didn't consider all the ramifications, like how it would affect fertility rates going forward or whether the adaptations would linger over the long-term."

She might as well have kicked him in the stomach. "Are you saying we're now sterile?"

"Please keep your voice down," Yoloron cautioned. "Long-term effects remain to be seen. Right now, I can tell you the unammi's future is uncertain."

"I don't accept that," Galen said. "We'll find a solution. We need to get away from here, right? If we can't find another world before it's too late, we can live aboard our four ships until we do.

She frowned. "Hundreds of survivors living in four cargo vessels?"

"You have another idea?"

"I might." She stepped closer to him. "What about human worlds?" she whispered. "You pilots already do this. You could teach the rest of us. Aren't there remote areas on any of those colonies where we might hide until you can locate a new home for the unammi?"

He had suggested the same thing to the other pilots less than a cycle ago. But they were a small group of individuals already adept at living behind masks, and at dodging detection among humans on their own worlds. Teaching and taking everyone else—that raised matters to a whole different scale. "Councilor, you can't know what you're saying."

"I know it is a rash suggestion. But perhaps we could consider it as a last resort."

"How long do we have before it's too late?" he asked. "Ten cycles? Twenty?"

"Just don't dally." Yoloron sighed. "And please don't discuss this with anyone."

Long after she'd left him, Galen stood in the corridor, shaking his head as if disavowal would make this nightmare go away. No more younglings equaled no more unammi. No, Na'Staani, please. That couldn't become their fate.

<h1 style="text-align:center">chapter 57</h1>

<u>Earth</u>

ALERTS LIT UP HER COMM panel when she was still eight hundred kilometers from the surface. At Skalar's urging, Alira activated the audio and a voice shouted loud enough to make her ears ring.

"Warning. This is a one-hundred percent lethal biohazard zone. Do not approach Earth. Advertencia. Esta es una zona de riesgo biológico cien por ciento letal. No te acerques a la Tierra. Avertissement. Il s'agit d'une zone de—"

She slapped off the blaring audio and blessed silence filled the space once more. What in the—

it's saying in multiple languages that this is a stupid move.

She pulled up short at her present altitude and continued without slowing, witnessing the scene that unfolded in the space ahead. The gloom of ne'ani lay across the human homeworld. Beyond Earth's comfortable spot in orbit, its star shone in bright ha'ani on the planet's opposite side. Alira followed the curve of the planet, her own ship deep in the shadow cast by the abandoned world. But was it? Had humans survived here despite Crow's and Skalar's fears for their ancestors?

She ignored her passengers' arguments and regarded the viewscreen. What lay down there? Her sh'toi passengers shrieked incessant warnings of disease. A tiny thrill of fear curled her toes. The plague might have overcome the remaining humans, but she had no doubt plenty of life remained on the surface. Most viruses and bacteria were specialized, attacking one species or jumping to similar ones, while ignoring others.

stupid squib, you're half-human.

Below, all lay in darkness, save a few scattered patches of pallor and a swirl of vivid green which shimmered and danced in the upper reaches of the planet's northern hemisphere, drawing her closer to investigate its beauty. What was *that*?

aurora.

colonies have 'em too.

so does iridos…can't see it from the city, though.

Ship warning systems alerted her to a threat

too risky for your nav and holo systems, alira.

back the fuck up, squib.

so she lingered at a distance, watching the gossamer strands of light ripple across the sky below before resuming her previous course. Such a large world. Not so enormous as Harajüd, but far wider than Iridos with its narrow band of habitable space. With no true ne'ani or ha'ani, every piece of Earth's surface must be livable

was. WAS livable. BEFORE the plague.

but with its rotation, temperatures would vary in lesser extremes from warmth in periods of light to cold when the darkness came.

Onscreen, a glowing crescent appeared before the ship. Ha'ani approached. The slim sliver of light broadened to reveal colors below. Within moments, Alira emerged squinting into the star's light and gasped. Earth's glory stretched out, resplendent in blue and blue and more blue

water. humans call it an ocean.

far below whorls and puffs of irregular white that gleamed in bright contrast.

"Oh!" she breathed, her own brilliant hues swirling at the sight. Harvested memories compared colony worlds to this vista and came back wanting. None of the voices marred the moment while she reveled in discovery. Before long, the horizon ahead shifted to blankets of vivid greens and swaths of rich, varied browns, still broken by random shreds and blobs of white.

clouds.

On the colony worlds, her passengers claimed, clouds sometimes heralded rain or snow or, on occasion, horrific storms that swept away everything not tied down.

She drank in the bands of colors creeping past. Clouds came and went as the land below varied in its texture. Ripples and folds in green and brown and white spread wide and narrow, while dark veins branched across the ground. Time seemed to slow. With Ijydin's help, she set the ship to a wide-ranging orbit for maximum collective survey and flew with simple enjoyment of the marvels evidenced on the planet below, until at last she heeded the unammi voices in her head to do what she'd come for and go home.

Despite the sh'toi warnings, she sliced deeper into the atmosphere, going in for a closer survey. Shades and tones in the landscape grew more subtle, more complex as she neared, blending into an indescribable palette no Iridos-bound unammi would ever see, so striking it almost hurt her eyes. Now she could see the dark fingers were water. One flowed over the edge of a precipice to plunge through a roiling cloud into a pool far below. She had never imagined green could have so many different shades! Here and there, spots of blue, yellow, pink, or red grew wings and passed beneath her. Like the niveym on Iridos, but all the colors of the spectrum. More than plants had flourished here. If there were birds, other wildlife must have thrived as well.

She tore her gaze away from the screen and scanned for tunnel systems. A holoimage took shape in the air before her. Alira slowed and set the system to automatic. Underground systems wound in irregular distribution around the globe, but followed erratic paths or held whole sections filled with water or broke the surface through steep shafts that shot straight up from their depths. Most were unsuitable to long-term habitation without a lot of preparation.

So maybe the Iri hadn't had a choice. Maybe there had been no tunnel system here conducive to building an isolated colony, and the Founders saw no other way to segregate themselves. Humans tended to ignore rules, sometimes at the most inconvenient times. She knew all about that. Understood it, even, which pointed to a strong human tendency in her. Maybe that's what Ama had meant about her "weakness."

She pinched the holo at either side, turned its image bit by bit, checking out the fissures and caverns. Perhaps Elisul's flight from Earth wasn't so mysterious after all.

With a sigh, she allowed the screen to draw her focus again. Yet as she released the holo and it swung into position, an anomaly caught her eye and yanked her attention back. Fingers expanded the image to better view the striking detail. There…underground construction. Not a natural cavern system. Its passages were too regular, too level, and widened out at intervals into larger cavities.

It had to be made by human hands.

The niveym in her chest stretched its wings. She checked the coordinates on the holo against the ship's physical location, adjusted her heading, and entered the destination. Sooner or later, she intended to step foot on the ground. It might as well be there.

She next checked for bio-organisms in the atmosphere

now you do that? after it's too late?

which might bring her harm or infect the unammi or human populations. The system took seconds to show the result.

what the actual—

logan himself told me earth was—

She ran a second, then a third biocheck, to confirm. All three found microbes with similar constructs to the one the sh'toi feared—close cousins? evolution at work?—but nothing harmful, no apocalyptic plague. Then why had the humans declared Earth off-limits? Weren't they checking its status

why? sister, they have twelve other worlds now.

maybe it's taboo.

they wouldn't have risked it. too dangerous.

as their homeworld? Wouldn't they want to go back, once it was safe?

not sure i would call it safe, netzyl. all the colonies would squabble over control of these resources. they'd see only profit.

"Why do humans insist on hoarding resources that should belong to all of you?" she muttered, not expecting or receiving an answer beyond the certain knowledge that if Skalar had known this sooner, he would have claimed Earth himself without telling a soul other than those crew he sent to plunder it. He would have done the same to this planet's moon. To Iridos. This pristine world's stable biome would hold no value for him beyond what it could contribute to his power and prestige.

you disgust me, sh'toi.

just business, netzyl.

Alira slowed to examine the terrain that rose and rose, a rolling landscape far above the ocean. Dotted across the horizon lay mountains that dwarfed even this high plain. Closer ridges, lined with colorful striations, abutted a wide range of towering pillars, implausible stone shafts in all shapes and sizes. Most amazing was that many of the columns, as well as the cliff face, were dotted with contrived openings made by some living thing. Animals? Humans?

The ship chittered its arrival at the designated coordinates, and she set down on a wide flat spot. An atmospheric check found no toxic gases, and oxygen levels were well within an acceptable range. She would need no suit, then. As the hatch opened, Alira caught her breath. Before her lay a vast open space far greater than anything she'd ever seen on Iridos, where unammi seldom looked up. Why would they? There was nothing to see beyond stone ceilings, the curving glass dome or sand-filled firmament. By contrast, Earth's sky, much bluer than any colony world's, seemed to have no end. She stepped out, gripping the handholds as if she might fall *up* into that blue expanse. Vegetation and pebbled sand dimpled the callused soles of her feet. Blown grit on Iridos formed a much finer grain, so light that it could find its way into your mouth and nose on a windwalk. Here, on a world that showed all its faces to its star, the wind lacked any desperate push to reach ha'ani. As if to emphasize her thought, a warm gentle breeze caressed her, tickled her nostrils with potent, exotic fragrance. Nearby, an unseen creature called from the foliage of a small tree. Another answered from a distant hiding place.

Alira released her hold on the ship and stepped away from its safety, pulse pounding in her ears. The ground beneath her feet crunched at each step like walking the ice pack in ne'ani at home. The sound of her movement startled a small animal—a larger cousin to the raneal?— basking in the light of ha'ani.

At a distance from her ship, she pivoted in a slow sweep of her surroundings. One segment of the panorama showed an open vista reaching all the way to the feet of distant mountains, broken by occasional foliage. Another held scrub and brush scattered around more of those stone spires, each capped by cones or rocks with odd shapes. Behind her rose the cliff face, the roots of this particular ridge and her destination.

It didn't take long to find an access, though she had to clear away some rockfall to clamber inside. Smooth floors and walls met her gaze, but even her eyes would need a light source. She jogged to the ship for a lantern and a handheld mapper, then reentered the passage, her whole body trembling. What if animals lived here now? Predators probably held sway on this world, but she had no weapon other than her own gifts.

should have taken my stunner, netzyl

Her steps faltered for a moment before she decided to continue and deal with encounters as they happened. Wonder soon replaced worry. Echoes of this place's ancient past whispered to her imagination as passage after passage, chamber after chamber appeared. Scans had shown an enormous complex spanning many kilometers and linked to similar compounds in surrounding areas via long tunnels. She'd never have time to explore it all in one visit, but she couldn't make herself stop yet.

There must be ventilation shafts. Though the air smelled dusty, it was fresh, not stale. Many compartments could be suitable to any number of uses, while others seemed made for quite specific purposes. Each level was marked by large circular stones at its entries, and each section held numerous wells, most still filled with water. Whoever created this haven had dug and shaped its chambers with the purpose of sheltering an enormous community. It had to be the work of many hands over many seasons, maybe even uncounted lifetimes. But why? Surely humans of Earth hadn't all lived below ground. So what made these particular humans dig down instead of building up, the way they did on the colony worlds?

Alira tried to imagine what their lives were like. One spacious hall made her think of the temple cavern at home. Carved supports punctuated this room, yet it would hold many humans. Had it been a ritual arena? Filled with cheers and music and joy like the temple on Iridos?

She continued to explore the underground city until the reaped voices grew loud enough to convince her to stop. By the time she left the tunnels, ne'ani had found her again and the light had gone. She emerged onto the plain under a dark sky alight with glittering jewels. The pale albedo of Earth's satellite, home to Skalar's base, shed plenty of light, much brighter than the surface at home.

Alira paused outside the cavern entrance, gazing up at the sight. One day she would come here when there was no hurry, when she could explore every cavern, every alcove, follow the connecting tunnels to the other cities and know them all, one by one. The humans who had lived here must have prized this as a safe place, protected from outside dangers by all those layers of rock above them. Since the sh'toi had ransacked Iridos, would the unammi ever again feel the same sense of sanctuary?

The wrinkle popped up between her brows. Iridos would always be home, but it felt tainted, marred by a blemish that would take many seasons to disappear, if it ever could. She glanced over her shoulder into the darkness of the tunnels and envied the humans for what they'd had here, then put the cavern at her back and headed toward her ship.

<h1 align="center">chapter 58</h1>

<u>Iridos</u>

HOME! ALIRA GAZED AT THE sight of Iridos, growing larger in her viewscreen by the moment. More than seven cycles of flight time since she'd left Earth behind gave her plenty of time to assimilate the conglomeration of new knowledge packed into her mind. Time and enforced collaboration had compacted her passengers' voices so she sometimes had trouble telling which one was her own. Unammi and human memories still mixed into a confusing array of nostalgia and fear, devotion and loathing, loyalty and greed, an emotional chimera yammering in her thoughts from every direction. For the moment, however, her passengers were mute. She tried to envision her reception.

She would be outcast now, tainted by her exposure to the humans. For a moment, Crow coiled a smirk onto her lips. Odd, but after so many seasons of arguing against that sentiment among her people, she had come to appreciate the reasons behind it. Unammi cultural foundations ran like narrow bridges, ripe to collapse, over strange and unusual ideas. Time spent among humans widened the pilots' worldview, broadened their understanding of the universe and their interrelationships within that larger setting. Even the brief time she herself had planned to spend in human society would have been enough to change her. But her encounters had gone far beyond simple contact and veered into full immersive experience with a different culture, as well as ordeals inconceivable to the rest of her people. She tried to imagine explaining it in detail to Rakalesh or Yoloron or any of the rest, but words fell short.

She set the ship's course and dropped into meditation, reached for the joinedmind. There, just on the edges of her perception, she could feel her people and, more importantly, they felt her, knew she posed no threat. Only then did she enter the atmosphere and close on the city.

The northern plain near the landing cavern, speckled with other pilots' ships, pumped spots of yellow into her skin. She landed as close as she could, but by the time she got to the protected cavern, Dyson awaited. Alira waved at the activity near the other ships as they passed on their way into the tunnels.

"What has happened?"

"Quite a lot," he said, his voice weary and grim. He explained the sick younglings, and the potential for mutation among the survivors. "We are loading the ships in order to be ready when we find a new home or so we can live aboard them away from here until we do."

Gray sparkled across Alira's arms. The roar of a raging Flow echoed in her ears. A new home.

"Then I bring good news for all of us." When he walked on in silence, she snuck a glance in his direction. "You look tired, Na'apa."

He grunted. "And you seem more content than I've ever seen you. The life of an outcast agreed with you then?"

Alira almost laughed. A season, even twenty cycles ago, his comment would have sent her spiraling into guilt, shame, and self-doubt. Now…he had no idea. "I met the challenge."

It felt strange to be back. Comfortable. Familiar. Smaller than she remembered. As they hurried through the passages, Alira couldn't help imagining the surrounding flurry of activity in the tunnels on Earth, unammi feet treading the floors worn smooth by so many others. She could see a life for her people there. The council wouldn't like her suggestion, but she was accustomed to that.

Dyson ushered her into the chamber where the other elders waited.

"Aes te nalya," she greeted.

"Nalena t'staani." Rakalesh waved toward a cushion. "Please join us."

Alira dug Cesar's coin from her pocket and settled on the proffered seat, still waiting for the usual anxiety to settle around her heart.

"Where is Nyros?" Yoloron asked.

"He's dead, Na'ama, killed by the same human who attacked our city. I killed that human, *and* the one who sent him here in the first place."

Conflicting colors bloomed in the elders.

"I know the council doesn't take such a thing lightly," she said, her fingers flipping Cesar's coin. "But the first one killed Nyros and was about to kill me. The other saw me morph—"

White streaked the councilors' displays.

"—and he saw me heal. I didn't feel I had a choice."

Dyson regarded her through narrowed eyes. "We agree."

"You made me a promise, Alira," Rakalesh accused. "Six cycles, no more."

"I apologize, Na'ama. An unexpected side trip delayed me. But I brought back our irolium."

Every councilor's face flashed gray before significant patterns of relief fluttered through their displays as they took in her revelation.

"Where did you find it?" Rakalesh said.

"On one of Skalar's bases. A good thing if, as we now suspect, the tales were true." Her own re-exposure to the stones back on the outpost had been a strong, tingling surge of energy that lingered long after she'd started the trip home. How much more intense would it be for those who were sick, or on the verge of dimming? "The stones still grant renewal, but constant use will drain an individual crystal. I brought as many as would fit in my ship. Let's hope I've come in time. Councilor Dyson also tells me we need a new home," she said.

Rakalesh squinted at her. "Why? Did you find one of those too?"

They'd never accept the idea, not by choice, but what else could they do?

"Maybe."

"Tell us," Rakalesh said.

Alira's gaze touched each of the councilors before looking again to Rakalesh. "We could go to Earth."

Sparkles of pink and red suffused their displays as Alira had expected.

"Earth?" Dyson growled. "Home of the sh'toi who destroyed us?"

Rakalesh glared at Alira, but another councilor shook her head. "No, thank you. I'd rather live crammed aboard one of those ships."

"You say that because you don't know." Alira's soft, flat tone seemed to seep into their ire, settling them into an uneasy quiet.

"Don't know what?" Yoloron asked.

"You aren't going to like what I have to say, but please hear me out." Alira toyed with the coin until they agreed.

"First, the planet boasts a wide diversity of plants, animals, and environments, as well as a few reminders of past human presence. No humans now crawl Earth's surface nor its underground chambers as far as I could tell. I ran numerous scans to be certain. Nor are they likely to ever come near that world again. Apparently, the ancient humans set loose a disease there which killed everyone still present within the atmosphere. Contemporary humans fear the threat enough to keep their distance." She left out the outpost, for now.

"Reason enough to dismiss Earth as a candidate," Rakalesh reasoned. "We are already dealing with—"

Alira held up a hand. "With all due respect, Councilor, a disease on Earth would be a different matter from radiation sickness. In any event, whatever pathogen the humans loosed all those lifetimes ago, it isn't there now. There are microbes aplenty, but none that threaten us or humans." She saw acceptance take root in Rakalesh, though the elder refused to acknowledge it. Yet.

"Continue."

"Second," Alira went on, "Earth holds underground spaces where we could set up and reestablish our colony. Most read as natural cavern systems that would require a great deal of work for habitation, but several are of human construction, seemingly designed as a sub-surface city like this one, complete with rooms adaptable for living quarters, gathering spaces, even storage chambers. The one network I explored sinks deep into the planet and goes on at great length. It is dusty, and at least a few chambers are damaged, but the ventilation shafts are mostly functional. With a bit of repair and cleaning, we could live there for generations.

"I didn't take the time to explore more than a tiny fraction of the area. I wanted to get back to you with the irolium. But what I managed to see had much to offer. Fresh water abounds both on the surface and in the tunnels, as do fertile areas where we might tend gardens above-ground. Earth's orbital period is much faster than Iridos. There is no constant ha'ani or ne'ani because their star's light touches the entire world by cycles. We would need no domes."

No one volunteered a word of resistance. Every councilor sat as if hanging on her words, their skins a riot of color. She hesitated, assessing the best way to tell them the rest.

"Go on," Yoloron said.

Alira took a deep breath. "Before I went to Earth, I visited its satellite where Skalar's Trader faction has reclaimed an old human research station. That is where I found the irolium."

"I thought you said humans wouldn't even go near this planet," Rakalesh blurted.

"Earth's satellite is far from the planet. Closer than we'd like, perhaps, but few humans go there. Most won't even enter the star system. They'll never know the lethal microbes are gone, because they don't dare get close enough to sample the atmosphere." She paused, but no one else objected.

"While at the station I found an ancient holorecorder and accessed a small number of journal entries recorded long ago by one of the researchers there. I played them all several times, disbelieving at first what I saw, but there is no mistake." She hesitated, choosing her words with care.

"The human in the holoimage is the same one that has appeared over and over in my dreams. He said his followers had begun to call him 'the Founder' and that he and his people would soon be leaving Earth behind to set up a new society on Iridos."

Silence draped the room. Alira waited for the anxiety to consume her as it would have before she'd left. Before she'd awakened.

"What are you saying, Alira?" Dyson said.

"The Founders were human."

"And, by association, so are we?" he asked, a tide of red inundating his dermal patterns.

"No. But we're related."

"That's the most ridiculous thing I've ever heard," he spat. "We have nothing in common with those aliens."

"Yes, we do, Na'apa. From my…dealings…with Crow and Skalar, I know their blood is as red as ours, and their anatomies and internal organs and body functions resemble our own."

"Biological similarities needn't mean we're of the same stock," Rakalesh said. "Anatomy and physical construction is a shallow comparison. Councilor Dyson is right. Evolution of the deviations between human and unammi would require hundreds of millions or even billions of seasons. You've made a mistake."

"Under normal circumstances this would be true, Councilors, but we all know there has been outside intervention in our case. We've taught our younglings for generations that the unammi evolved with assistance from the Iri," Alira said. "That our constant exposure to their presence and the irolium gave us our many gifts. Our present circumstances support my theory."

Slight signs of doubt touched the elders. "Even if it proved our symbiotic gifts," Yoloron said, "your theory doesn't explain the difference between human diversity and fervor, and unammi conformity and restraint."

"Those are learned behaviors, not genetic attributes. The Founder stated in his journals their intention to weed out aggression, selfishness, greed—the elements of their societies that held them back, turned them against one another. He never intended for his people to eschew all emotion, only those that set them against one another and tore their civilization apart." She saw again the image of Elisul in the cluttered room, heard again his words about how his species had forgotten their part in the larger whole. "After all these generations, we've lost sight of his original goal. We've forgotten who we are."

"Careful, Alira," Dyson said, in a warning tone.

"Why would you reject an analysis based on extrapolation of events and probable outcomes from known facts? If we descended from humans—and I now believe we did—then emotions and unique characteristics that set us apart from one another are natural. Suppressing them harms us." She squinted at them. "You know I'm right, too, don't you?"

Rakalesh leaned forward. "You walk a fine line. We—"

Alira barked a humorless laugh, spraying gray across the councilors. "You do. I can see it. Maybe you didn't know about the human connection, but you are fully aware that it's unnatural for us to suppress our emotions. If we were instinctive conformists with innate restraint, our younglings would conform fresh out of the womb without needing to be taught. There would be no reason to isolate the pilots, or pressure initiates, or mitigate anyone. Ever."

Dyson lurched to his feet. "You are using our tragedy as a platform to support your own arguments. I won't hear it."

shut the fuck up, old man.

calm down, crow. i've got this.

"I didn't design our natures," Alira said. "I'm just pointing out the obvious."

"Basu'tao," Rakalesh interjected, her sharp gaze on Alira. "This is not a forum for argument."

"I intend no offense, Na'ama. But use that unammi restraint you're all so proud of. Put aside your aversion to the humans for a moment. Consider what I'm saying without the taint of prejudice."

Rakalesh threw her hands into the air, her shoulders and neck flashing pink. "To suggest we leave Iridos and go to Earth strains our patience, Alira."

"From what Councilor Dyson said, and from your own words moments ago," Alira replied in an even tone, "the decision to leave was a foregone conclusion. All you lack is a destination."

The councilors exchanged an uneasy glance before Rakalesh focused again on Alira. "You've given us much to consider. You may go, for now."

"Fine. Will you tell the others of their heritage?"

"We have yet to confirm this information," Dyson said.

"Of course," she said with a nod, her jaw tight. This was getting more personal than she had expected. "You're right. Let's pull the Founder's DNA from the vault and test it. See for ourselves."

Rakalesh flushed red from her head to her feet. She gestured in Alira's direction. "You know we can't do that now, not until we can verify the integrity of the vault and its samples."

"Then how will you 'confirm' what I've told you? Unless you come to Earth's satellite and see the recording for yourself, what is there to discuss?" She regarded each of them. "Do you plan to risk the survival of our species because you dislike my findings?"

"Zhachi!" Rakalesh shot to her feet and pointed toward the door. "Go. Now. Don't discuss this with anyone else."

Rising, Alira left the chamber without another word.

chapter 59

"WAIT!"

The shout from behind halted the pilots just inside the passage. All six of them turned as Kobe approached.

"Excuse the interruption," he said. "I thought you'd want to know. Alira is home. I would have told you sooner, but she has been with the council."

Galen straightened. "Where is she now?"

"The healer's chamber."

"Is she…."

Kobe nodded. "She's well."

Knots of worry in Galen's shoulders and neck loosened all at once. "Thank you, Kobe." He whirled toward the other pilots. "Will you wait for us?"

Tiral glanced at the others, then nodded. "Perhaps she can lead our rite."

"I'll ask," Galen called as he darted away. Alira was safe! She was home! Whatever else happened, he would be better equipped to cope as long as she was nearby. His pace quickened as he raced through the passages. Others stepped aside to let him pass. Word always traveled fast here, and his feelings for Alira were no secret.

A moment's worry brushed his heart and slowed his feet. She'd been through so much since he saw her last. He could guess at what she had faced among the humans. New experiences and challenges changed a person in unpredictable ways. Alira wouldn't be the same as when they last touched. His throat tightened.

Would she still want him?

He came around the corner to the sick room and stopped. Though Alira knew many of those lying inside, she was there to visit Trumo. Galen didn't wish to intrude. He peered through the door. There she was. There she was! Yellow waves of excitement rippled through his confusion.

Yoloron joined him.

"I thought you were with the council, Na'ama," he said.

A small sound escaped her throat. "I was," she said, her words slow, considered. "Now I'm not." She nodded toward Trumo's visitor. "Has she seen you yet?"

"No. I can wait." Galen nodded at Alira. "Is she well?"

Yoloron nodded. "Better than, and still acting both hero and villain, same as always."

He frowned.

"Didn't you hear? She brought back our irolium."

Gray flushed out Galen's confusion. "How did she manage that?"

"It's her tale to share, not mine. She was right, you know. About everything." Yoloron held his gaze far longer than the norm, then entered the room to tend her patients. Most of the frem were improving. The younglings, too, seemed brighter, livelier. Could they dare to hope?

Inside the room, Alira sat on Trumo's bed while dull yellow ripples plodded across the youngling's skin. How did she get their irolium? She hadn't marched into the Consortium base and demanded its return…had she? He shook his head. Alira was many things, but never stupid. His experience in the Bejami land port raced through his mind, accompanied by the fear that had throttled him from the moment he'd sensed the trouble until the moment his feet had touched Iridosian soil. The thought of trying to find the stones, much less work against the Consortium to retrieve them, made his knees weak. Such an idea never even occurred to him, nor to anyone else among their people. She not only thought of it. She did it.

Yoloron had said Alira was right about everything. Alira would have a Telling all her own, and Galen couldn't wait to hear it. *If* she still wanted to share it with him. He drew a deep breath and let it out, content for the first time in many cycles. She was everything he wanted to be, and more besides. How could anyone see and experience the honesty of her actions, the authenticity of her example and not be moved? Galen wanted no one else as his mate. If Alira still wanted him, he'd do whatever it took to stay with her.

<h1 style="text-align:center">chapter 60</h1>

TRUMO STIRRED AND WOKE, HIS skin brightening to dull yellow.

"Na'ama Alira!"

"Shhh." She patted his arm, speckles of white touching her own display. His eyes had turned gray! "I brought you something." Alira held up a closed fist, opening her fingers with slow deliberation, revealing the blue stone inside.

"Irolium!"

His excited whisper threaded golden highlights through her own skin. "Yes. Take it. It's your own special piece."

Trumo's small fingers plucked the stone from her hand, his body already reacting. "But what about the others?"

"They each got one. I wanted to deliver yours myself."

He touched her fingers. "I didn't think you'd come back. I'm glad I was wrong."

"As am I. Go back to sleep. The healers will scold me if they see you awake."

"No, they won't. They'll see you make me feel better. Where did you go?"

She sighed. How could she explain to him all that had happened in a way he might understand? She watched his expectant face, so trusting and sincere, and knew she could not brush aside his questions. "You know the humans who attacked us?"

He nodded.

"Their leader was a resentful, greedy man who would have gotten into trouble with his people if they learned what he did to us. I was afraid he would kill our pilots to stop that from happening."

"Did he kill them?" Trumo asked in a hushed whisper.

Alira hesitated, then nodded. "Yes, some of them. I went to Harajüd to warn Nyros, and to use his ship's comm system to alert the others. But I wasn't fast enough. The human killed most of them before my warning could reach them."

"He's a sh'toi," Trumo said.

"Trumo! Such a foul word!"

"A lot of frem have used it since the attack. Did I use it wrong?"

"Well, no, not in this case. But not all humans are like that."

He dropped his gaze to the irolium in his fingers, staring at the glimmers of light on its facets. "Where is Na'apa Nyros?"

Her purple blush answered before she could. "He died, chithe."

"I'm sorry," Trumo said.

"So am I. But his pithasia is in the Flow now, reunited with the others and with Na'Staani. I'm sad for myself, but I'm happy for him."

"Did you see him die?"

The wrinkle appeared between her brows. Quiet little Trumo, so reserved and withdrawn that his teachers thought him slow, had finally found his tongue.

"Yes."

"What was it like?"

Ripples of surprise disrupted her purple. "It happened in a flash, chithe."

"Was it the sh'toi? Did he do it?"

Alira's frown deepened, not because Trumo was angry. He'd lost his ama and his apa, most of the frem and younglings he'd ever known. Their city was in ruins and he lay in the healers' hands, dimming and sick. She would have been more bewildered if he *weren't* angry. So where were the red or pink hues in his skin?

"Yes. It was the human who destroyed our city."

"Did you kill him back?"

yeah, squib, tell him about that one.

Alira sighed. "Yes, I did. But listen to me, Trumo, because this is important. Ending someone's life is almost never the right thing. Sometimes, though, circumstances present nothing but bad options. I did what I did because he would have killed me, and then I couldn't have warned the other pilots. I had to choose between his life and the lives of others. I hope I never have to make such a choice again." She paused. "Do you understand?"

He nodded, his countenance filled with an emotion she couldn't identify. "I'm glad he didn't kill you."

"Me, too." She tried to gauge his thoughts. He was covering. But what? and *how*? "You can tell me anything. You know that, right?"

He fiddled with the stone. "Na'ama, I'm…." He took a deep breath. "I'm afraid."

Gray flitted across her skin. "Of the humans?"

He mumbled a response so low she missed it. "Speak up, Trumo."

He looked up at her. "Of everything, Na'ama, of the humans, of sickness, of dimming."

"Dimming?"

"I'm even afraid of being afraid," he whispered, his eyes darting around the area near his bed to ensure no one would hear. "What if they find out?"

Alira had no doubt who "they" were. She brushed soothing fingers over his brow. "If they find out you emote?"

He rolled away toward the wall.

She flashed back on Trumo in class the day the humans came. The day she was almost mitigated. Now his questions made more sense.

"Oh, chithe," she breathed past the lump in her throat.

"Don't tell anyone," he whispered at the wall, dim white speckles dotting his flesh.

"Shhhh," she soothed, stroking his cheek. "It isn't wrong to feel things. All of us do. We just aren't supposed to act out those feelings. You'll get better at hiding them, but in the meantime, don't worry. I'll keep your secret and tell you one of my own." She leaned close to his ear. "It's hard for me, too," she whispered.

He turned toward her, his skin flushed with dull gray.

She nodded. "It's true. Sometimes I feel happy or sad or worried or angry or even afraid, and I express it more than I should. You're not alone."

Trumo hesitated, then sat up and embraced her, startling a brief gray flush over her arms that mellowed to golden hues. For a moment, she patted his back, then extricated herself and pressed him back onto the pallet, fighting the urge to scan the room. Who had seen?

"I know you're afraid, but you can't do that again. I understand it, but others won't. You know this."

there's irony for you, sister. remember that time i stepped on your fingers and you wept like a human?

at least now we know why.

His little head nodded. "Yes. But why is it wrong?"

"That's a good question." She pinched her lips together, searching for the right words. "Do you ever feel angry?"

"Yes, sometimes."

"So angry you want to hurt someone?"

His expression thrust a pang through her heart. "No!" he hissed, then wavered. "Well, I might if I had to, like you did. But I don't want to!"

She'd said the same thing once. "I know. I know you don't. But a long time ago, our ancestors did."

alira you aren't supposed to tell.

"They allowed their anger and their pain and their greed to take control. It almost destroyed them, so they decided it was better not to express their feelings at all."

"But…." He studied her. "Didn't they ever feel happy? Happy wouldn't hurt anyone. Happy feels good. Why couldn't they feel only the happy and not the other things?"

Alira gazed at his sweet face. "Because happy is one tiny piece of feeling. Other emotions come with it. You can't have just the one. And sometimes, they get so mixed up they're hard to control."

"So, we hide them all?"

"That's right, chithe."

"Even our happy?"

"Even our happy." She took a deep breath. "That may change one day. I hope it does, but for now you should try to remember the council has our best interests at heart. They made those expressions taboo because they believed it was for the good of the unammi and would help us keep our feelings in check. You understand, right?"

He nodded, not speaking. He didn't understand yet, but he would. And maybe one day, his younglings wouldn't need to hide their happy.

"Good. Then we will keep each other's secret for now. I know you're angry and sad and confused about all that's happened. But the council and the frem will figure out a way to make things better."

"I know." He looked up at her. "Are you going away again?"

She opened her mouth to say no but changed her mind. "I don't know. I must do what our people need of me. That's what being frem is all about. If it means going back to the human worlds, then that's what I'll do. But I hope it won't be soon. I'd like to see you get better, first."

Yellow sparkles raced across his cheeks, then something near the door caught his attention. Alira followed his gaze.

Galen! How long had he been standing there?

Trumo's fingers stroked the back of her hand. "Your i'shin's waiting. You should go say hello."

"Who told you he's my mate?"

"I heard it," he said, eying his fingers, "somewhere."

"I see," she said, amusement mingling with her concern. "You're right, you know."

"I like him."

"You approve, then?"

"Yes. If you still come to see me."

Alira nodded. "I promise. But for now, you should rest. And you," she said, addressing the stone in his small grip, "make him better, faster!"

"I'm glad you're back," Trumo said, yawning. "I missed you."

She stroked his shoulder. "I missed you, too." She sat with him until his breathing deepened, then made her way to the corridor where Galen waited.

"Relax, Galen. I'm fine." She held out a hand. "I'm ecstatic, now that I've seen you!"

He touched his fingers to hers, yellow and lavender and coppery desire all mingled in tangled webs across his display.

She waited for him to speak, waited so long she grasped his hand, squeezed it in her own. "Say something."

"I'm trying," he said. "I can't find the words."

She bent toward him, and he touched her forehead with his own. They stood a moment before he pulled back.

"Yoloron said you brought back irolium."

"Yes."

"I have so many questions!" Emotions twisted on his skin, switching so fast she had trouble keeping up. "I want to keep you to myself, hear your Telling, show you how much I've missed you."

"But?"

"The pilots missed the Mourning Rite. We were about to do our own when Kobe said you were home. I—we—wondered if you'd like to join us, maybe lead the rite."

Remembrance snatched at her breath. Lurien would lead no more rites. As far as she knew, the council hadn't yet selected another to take the role. Alira could perform all the motions, say all the words, but a cleric's job went beyond that and into the realm of guide. Could she escort others through mourning when her own heart still ached with loss?

Uncertainty colored his display. "If you don't—Is it too soon?"

"No," she said through tight lips, "it's fine. You're going now?"

He nodded. "Yes, unless you need to rest."

A bit more time to walk the corridors of home, to revisit favorite spots, would be nice. But that could wait. The pilots were as much her people as anyone else here, maybe more so now. If they needed her, she would provide. Besides, calling the names of her dead would feel right, a closing of those doors so the departed and the living could both move on. Alira sighed and nodded. "Let's go."

FALLEN: The Founder's Seed, Book 1

chapter 61

IT SEEMED SO LONG AGO that she'd stood at the monument for a Mourning Rite and called Sufamel's name. Now a list of dead, friend and foe, paraded through her mind. Each had taught her valuable lessons. Each deserved anamnesis. No one else would call Skalar's name, or Crow's. Neither of them had friends, and both had spurned what family they had. How sad that she, the person who had ended them, would be the only one to remember them.

But what if they appeared on the shores of Musju, as they had before? Explaining their presence, especially the humans, to the other outcasts would be difficult. At least this was a small group, and not the throng that had attended Sufamel's rite. She sent a silent thought

be still, all of you. stay out of our rite.

before turning to the task at hand.

She glanced at the pilots, their names and details drifting in from the archive of her reapings. She knew them all, loved them all, though some of them had yet to know her. Each offered a greeting, but Galen spoke for the rest in the end.

"Thank you, Alira, for leading our rite."

"Frem asal. I serve the unammi."

All her life she'd trained for this. Season after season, she had assisted Lurien at the altar, seen her ama drive the reactions of their people in ceremony, and hoped to wield the same mastery in ritual when the job became her responsibility. For the first time, she stood alone at the center. Where was her longing now?

"I'll make a few modifications. Wherever I deviate, follow my lead."

The pilots nodded, and Alira began.

"We come here today to mark the passage of our loved ones through our lives. We mourn their loss even as we celebrate their reunion with Na'Staani. We cut our ties to their pithasias so we can learn to live without them."

She held her arms out to her sides, closing her eyes, picturing the visages of their lost ones.

"Aes te nalya, Livit Dutahni! Livuce'ba wenaes bujhul!" We are One, Beloved Dead! Your loss diminishes us!

Hands reaching up and out, she stretched higher onto her toes as if to embrace the winds above them.

"Na'Staani bu bale, Livit Dutahni! Ba riba te'lan!" Na'Staani receive you, Beloved Dead! We will speak your names!

She lowered her arms to her sides with slow, fluid grace.

Then, Alira began to sing.

Not a song with words, but vocalizing a long, clear musical tone. When her exhalation ended, she took in another deep breath and did it again, louder this time. One by one, the outcasts joined her, adding their rich voices to the sound that blended and harmonized as they breathed in rounds and maintained the notes. Louder and louder they sang, competing with the winds, and energy rose in Alira until, at the moment she felt sure it would spout from her head in a shower of light, she grasped the hand of the pilots on either side of her. They followed her example to form an unbroken circle and step into meditation.

In her hundred plus frem seasons, she had attended plenty of mournings. This rite seemed more portentous than all the others put together, though she couldn't say why. A mere seven outcasts stood vigil in the current, voices raised in wordless chant. No lost friends or family lay at the center of their circle, yet the act of standing in Musju's waters comforted, united. The connection of the Flow maintained the tie beyond this world and now, after her encounter with Elisul in this space, she sensed it stronger than ever. She had personal reason to believe in a link that transcended death. Those she'd reaped still lived on in her thoughts. Had it been like that for Lurien and her predecessors?

After a time, she led the mourners back to the shore, back to normal consciousness. Their song reached a natural end when she released their hands and stepped into the center of their circle.

"No bodies lay before us," she said, voice raised against the keening wind. "But it doesn't matter. *Those* aren't our beloved dead. Our amas and apas, our brothers and sisters, our i'shin and friends and guildmates are reunited with Na'Staani and have no further need of their shells."

The outcasts shouted in unison. "Ae'staani te Musjuva!" We are in the Flow.

She looked from face to face, taking in their colors, their expressions, their grief. "We honor the elements to which their bodies have returned."

"Ae'staani te Musjuva!"

Alira thrust her hands toward the dusky sky, head back to shout.

"Pidaies'ba livitu, ba'ribaes t'ujendun!" she shouted. Your bodies are dead, but your names live on!

The pilots cried out in response. "We remember you!"

Alira lowered her arms, and regarded her fellow mourners, hesitant. The bodies of their dead had already gone. With no materials to dismantle, no complex forms to separate into their component elements, this part of the rite felt empty, pointless.

"Pidaies'ba livitu," she chanted out of habit.

The others moved closer to Alira, encircling her in a tight embrace. "We complete the task."

well isn't this cozy, all you little fuckers huddled together, chanting some bogus mumbo jumbo.

Her thoughts fastened on her human passengers, grateful that they had stayed out of the shared meditation. Yet she had brought about their deaths in isolation. They would get no rites or public Tellings. Now was as good time as any to fulfill her responsibility to them, and she called their names in silent remembrance, and honored the memories from their lives.

Her voices fell still. She stood in the flood of impressions from all her reapings, their torrents swirling thick, hot, and swift around her, eddies of emotion the sole clue to their existence beneath the surface of her calm. Their strength filled her with sensations as real as if they were her own until she trembled with reaction. She might have fallen, were it not for the pilots' embrace. It felt right to trust herself to their care and accept responsibility for theirs in exchange. After her off-world experiences, she'd become one of them.

If she'd thought it difficult to conform to expectations before, it would be impossible now. She hadn't only spent time among humans. She had harvested two of them. She never would fit here, and her people never would understand why. She could provide them with a Founder's heir, but she couldn't be their next high cleric. Even if they could accept her as she was, leading rituals and offering spiritual guidance and harvesting the dead would feed her spirit no longer. Musju had carried her beyond that life to a different shore. As Elisul had said, there was no going back.

The others remained silent around her, each of them caught in their own memories and honorings as they clustered, comforting one another in such an uncharacteristic way.

"Enuji, Ama!" Galen said at last. "I remember you!"

chapter 62

AFTER THE RITE, THEIR SMALL group returned to the relative quiet of the temple to assemble in one corner for their Telling. Even with such a small group of mourners, stories of their many dead took time. Alira listened with relish to her new friends' tales, all of which made her own feel inane by comparison, though Lurien's story of Sufamel and the bashito blossom amused everyone who heard it. As accustomed as the pilots were to life in the colonies, many of their contributions involved humans. The way they spoke made it seem like some of the humans were good and kind. Galen told of taking Nyros to meet Botha, and how Nyros had feared falling over the side of the human's boat. Imagining her brother, who hated even rainfall on his skin, splashing into a tidal pool almost jerked a laugh out of her. He never had learned to relax and enjoy the moment.

Her i'shin's display brightened in an array of color as he offered a memoir. Galen's empathic skills suited him to storytelling. She'd noted that when their relationship was beginning, but this was the first time she'd heard him relate an adventure in a group, the first time she'd seen him comfortable among others with his hands in constant motion to emphasize a point or illustrate a poignant bit of his Telling.

How long had they been partners now? Nine seasons? Ten? The exact moment she'd recognized his special role in her life might be lost. But she remembered with perfect clarity the first time they had made it physical. Since she too was now an outcast, no one would object to her partnership with one. And if the unammi went to Earth and accepted the underground city she'd found, there would be plenty of room for the pilots to stay somewhat segregated in the beginning for the comfort of the other survivors yet remain close enough to allow gradual reincorporation into communal life.

She scanned their faces. Empath, glamourer, intuitive, healer, pusher, reader—such talented individuals, each one committed to frem service even at the high price they'd paid! What would the council do with them, given that they had no further need for pilots beyond escaping Iridos? For that matter, what would they do with *her*? With Lurien gone, they needed a harvester. Maybe Alira could use this to negotiate for the pilots. Rakalesh couldn't afford to lose Alira. Alira didn't want to lose Galen. And Galen wouldn't stay without the other pilots.

When the stories at last slowed and stopped, Tiral stirred as if to rise. "We should go back to our duties. We still have no news to give the council."

Alira's brow furrowed. "What kind of news?"

"They've tasked us with finding a new home world for the unammi before we're lost."

"Because of the sickness, yes."

"It's more," Galen explained. "The council fears that in manipulating our own bodies to be immune to the radiation, we may have evolved ourselves into sterility."

Sharp white patterns skittered across her display. "*What?*"

"We'll need to get away from here for a while to know with certainty. The condition may reverse itself."

"But it is possible?"

The pilots nodded.

"When did they task you with this?"

"Last cycle." Tiral shrugged. "We haven't made much progress, I'm afraid."

"Why not?" Teal veins snaked across her limbs. "Didn't they tell you—"

"Tell us what?" Galen asked, his head tilted.

Red replaced Alira's other colors by slow degrees. She could understand the council keeping her find quiet until they could further investigate. But it should have at least been shared with those who had been charged with this task. Even in the shadow of this horrific possibility, could the councilors be that intractable?

you knew this about them. why are you surprised now?

She closed her eyes, grumbling. Of course. Silly question. For them, there was only one way—theirs. But now Alira had opened a door, one she couldn't easily close.

She looked back to her fellow outcasts who had been asked to bear this burden even knowing they may not be welcomed in the unammi's new home. Images of the Earth city flashed through her thoughts. It had felt safe, comfortable, as though it had been waiting all this time for them to permeate its halls once more with the excitement of home. Her passengers protested, but she ignored them. Earth was a viable candidate, damn it, and worthy of consideration.

"I told them I'd been to Earth."

"The humans' old home world?" Galen asked, his entire body gray.

"Yes. It has everything the unammi need to sustain us, even to thrive," she said. "Underground living space, plenty of water, fertile ground, safety from the humans, room to grow our families again. No radiation." She ticked off the details, raising a finger for each.

"What about the Iri?" Tiral asked. "Would they thrive there?"

She considered the question. "I can't imagine why they wouldn't."

One of the other pilots leaned forward. "What did the council say?"

"They wouldn't hear me," Alira said. "They fear I'm using this tragedy to further my own position."

"Are you?" Tiral asked.

"My find is suitable, even ideal, for a number of reasons. But... maybe. Probably."

"Why?"

Her discoveries stirred, whispering in her thoughts. Words of that revelation formed in her throat and pressed against her lips, struggling to be shared. They councillors had forbidden her to do so, yes. But what would they do—what *could* they do—if Alira disobeyed their command? Kick her out of the city? Make her outcast?

The people deserved to know. And weren't they there for a Telling? This was a story of their beloved dead, after all.

"I'll answer your question with another story, but it must remain between us for now. The council knows, and they are still deliberating whether to share the news with the others. Will you agree?"

The others nodded.

"Good enough. I'll begin by calling the name of our honored ancestor, Elias Sullivan."

chapter 63

ALIRA STEPPED ONTO THE SURFACE by the monument. She looked up at its sheltered face, comparing it to its smaller kin at the outpost. This had to be the ship that brought the Founder and his people here. She kept the thought to herself.

Galen stopped beside her. "An underground city. I'm still trying to imagine it. Did it occur to you that you were the first person to walk there since the remaining humans died out? The only person on the entire world?"

She laughed like Ijydin would have, freckling Galen with gray. "I did think about being first after maybe thousands of seasons, but not the rest." Her expression sobered at the thought of what Skalar would have done to Earth's beauty, had he known it was safe.

Galen's colors hinted at curiosity.

"You speak well of them," Alira said. "The humans. But they're so violent, always hurting or killing or torturing or using one another as if they aren't all connected to each other, as if their actions don't rebound back on themselves in the end. If they aren't doing it to one another, they're doing it to other creatures, or to their worlds with no thought to the harm imposed. They treat everything as if it belongs to them.

it does, squib, raw material there to profit whoever finds it first.

shut the fuck up, crow.

"They care nothing about sharing or fairness or the next generation. They take and give nothing back to complete the cycle. I don't know how you abide living among them."

Confusion colored Galen with veins of blue and lavender. They listened to the wind for a while before he replied. "You haven't told me everything."

Alira glanced away. Even without the turmoil displayed in her skin, he would sense it in her. She owed him an explanation, but how could she tell him of the others she carried in her head? That the sh'toi she despised lived there too, with no way for her to escape them? That they whispered their poison into her thoughts at every opportunity? That she wrestled with the shadows they cast?

In her peripheral vision she saw his frown deepen. "Not all humans are like the Traders," he offered, his tone almost too quiet to hear over the wind. "Most of those I've met have been more balanced."

She heard the admonishment, even though he gave it no voice. But he was right. He knew more about them than she did. She closed her eyes with a sigh. "Like Botha."

"Yes, or any of the villagers there. For the most part, humans are cruel when they are given justifiable cause—"

"Justifiable cruelty. There's a topic for endless debate." And there it was, her unthinking step into hypocrisy. A short, sharp bark of laughter escaped her lips before she could stop it. He paused, and she could almost feel him trying to understand what had upset her. "I'm sorry. Please continue."

"I know you'll tell me when you're ready, but it feels like your experience with the Traders turned noxious."

"You could say that."

Galen flickered with mild amusement. "Your words sound like something Ijydin would say. My point is that humans can be fickle but they can also be caring, kind, compassionate. The trick is in learning to recognize the signs for both. I have complete faith in you, but it was a huge risk for you to go to Harajüd so unprepared, much less to take on the Consortium. I'm amazed you weren't killed."

he's amazed YOU weren't killed? what the actual—

"So am I," she murmured.

"Before, all I could think about was how tragic it would be if you never came back, just when our paths to each other had been cleared."

If she never came back. In a way, she hadn't. The Alira who had left for Harajüd wasn't the same one who'd come back.

His touch brought her back to the moment. "Is everything all right?" He paused, his cheeks freckled with lavender backed by streaks of blue. "I expected we would resume our relationship as before, and that you would be as happy about it as I am. Did I assume too much?"

Alira gripped his hand. "No! No, Galen, I want a shared life as much as you."

But he would need to be told.

no! alira, you can't tell.

i'm not listening, cesar. this is my choice, my life.

If she and Galen were going to be long-term i'shin, if there was any chance of younglings in the future, he needed to know who she was, what she was, what she could do.

"But?"

She pulled him down on the sand in the crook of the lee and told him all of it, everything from the moment of Cesar's death to her return to Iridos. She spoke for a long time, purging as much as informing, giving voice at last to the experience she'd kept inside because who would possibly understand? When she finished, the wind's keening filled the void. She tried to read his reaction. But Galen was the empath, not her. She drew random patterns in the sand, darting glances at him in between.

"So that's how you did it."

Alira looked up. "Did what?"

"You—harvested? is that the term? You harvested Ijydin, and *she* told you how to fly the ship? How to act in New Canaan?"

"More or less. It wasn't a seamless process."

Amused sparkles reflected in the sand beside him. "Now I understand why you talk like Ijydin, why you have Nyros' little wrinkle between your brows, why you seem so much more confident. With Cesar's wisdom to guide you, how could you not be? And isn't that Cesar's coin I saw you holding a little while ago?"

She grunted, nodding. "So now I twist your own question around: do *you* still want *me*? The Alira you knew is gone. I can't tell you, yet, who I'm becoming. And with every harvest, I'll change again, over, and over as I adjust and assimilate and blend all the voices together into a cohesive whole. You'll never be sure who you are with from cycle to cycle. I have no way of knowing whether the process will drive me mad or even take my life. It has been known to happen, so you need to think about this before we go any farther."

She didn't try to guess his mood this time. Instead, she watched him watching her until at last he took her hands in his.

"I've always known you were unpredictable. How would this be any different?"

chapter 64

THE LANDING CAVERN STILL BUSTLED with activity when they emerged from their reunion. Mitigants, miners, and nutritionists alike joined forces to fill Alira's ship. She and Galen joined in, lifting and carrying and storing for some time before they were relieved by new workers. Together they moved through the tunnels, helping where they were needed, staying out of the way where they weren't, until a summons through the joinedmind brought Alira's feet to a stuttering halt.

Galen stopped a few paces ahead. "What is it?"

"The council has called me."

He nodded, his face calm, but his fingers intertwined in front of him. "Do you want to talk after?"

"No." She grasped Galen's hand. "I want you to come with me now."

He flushed gray. "Alira, they asked for *you*."

"Then come with me and wait outside."

Galen regarded her, seeming to consider the request, then he let out his breath all at once. "Let's go."

At the chamber door, Alira touched her forehead to his, then went inside.

Rakalesh spoke without a greeting. "You told him."

"You tasked the pilots with finding a new world. I thought it relevant."

Rakalesh sighed. "Come in here, Galen."

Galen entered and stood near Alira.

"We've given a great deal of consideration to this Earth."

"And?" Alira asked.

Confusion and displeasure punctuated Rakalesh's response. "None of us wants to go there." She turned to Galen. "Have the pilots found an alternative?"

"No, Na'ama. We discussed Alira's discovery, though, and reviewed the readings she took there. It is a viable option."

"Then we've no choice but to take our chances there," Rakalesh said. "At best, we'll find it a perfect home. At worst, it can provide a stepping-stone to widen our search."

"Good to hear," Alira said. "What of the rest?"

Rakalesh shot a glance at Galen, then back at Alira.

"If we stay on Earth, it would be a matter of time before someone went to its satellite and found this news. We would rather they hear it from us." Rakalesh heaved another sigh as if the thought wearied her. "We'll call a gathering to inform the others."

"Take care, Councilor," Alira said. "The Traders still use that base. Visits from unammi would raise the specter of attack again."

"The council is aware of the danger."

hoity squib has no fucking clue.

netzyl, when i don't make it back to harajüd, the consortium crew you sent home will go back. once they find me....

i know. i know.

"Of course," Alira replied. "Do we have enough ships to take everyone and all our supplies?"

"Not in one trip," Rakalesh said.

"There are other unammi ships at the outpost," Alira said, eager sparkles dancing across her skin. "Once we deliver the survivors and the essentials to Earth, perhaps the pilots and I can retrieve a few more ships and come back for the rest."

"We can address that at the gathering."

"What of my entreaty before the council?" Alira asked. "Will you lift the taboo on emotional expression, allow our people the freedom to access their natural gifts?"

"Gifts?" Rakalesh pulsed red. "Our mitigants say they're a curse—"

"What do you expect?" Alira pressed. "You have given them no choice."

"Zhachi!" Rakalesh shot to her feet, her display flaring with red.

With a jerk, Alira felt herself snatched again into Musju's coursing Flow. Its peace washed away her annoyance and she stood hip-deep in the water, waiting for what she knew would come. Where she stood, the current ran strong and true, its surface pulled taut.

Rakalesh heaved forward against the churning current that splashed white foam against the councilor's red, red skin. She reached Alira, lips parted to deliver the usual censure—

Until the voices joined in. Alira reached out to restrain them

no, stay back—

but it was too late. Their ethereal bodies surrounded Alira and Rakalesh, Cesar with Nyros and Ijydin in the Flow while Crow and Skalar stood on the shore, all talking at once.

> *rakalesh, no!*
> *who the fuck does she think—*
> *alira, don't let her—*
> *sister, why do you insist—*
> *netzyl, who is this pushy—*

Rakalesh aborted her advance, staring at the sudden noisy crowd so unexpected in this sacred space, all her red drained to white. At last, she looked to Alira, the question in her expression unmistakable.

Alira gazed back, a touch of rebellion in her stance, but unashamed for the first time in her life. Whatever happened, Rakalesh had forced this revelation. She would have to deal with the consequences.

A wave of change washed over Rakalesh, distorting her features into a mask of uncertainty. Alira marveled at the transformation. Who would have thought?

The council chamber reappeared around them. Galen stood where he'd been, lavender swirling in his face and arms.

"Leave us," Rakalesh commanded.

Gray raced through the others. The councilors frowned. Before they could demand an explanation, Rakalesh relented. "Please. We need privacy."

When they had gone, Rakalesh gestured to the cushions, then sat by Alira. "They're with you? In your mind? All the time?"

"Yes. They are part of me now."

Rakalesh frowned. "I didn't know."

"I thought Lurien discussed these things with you."

"She did. But hearing about it and seeing it firsthand are two different things. All those voices! Even sh'toi—" The elder shook her head. "But I never saw Lurien's harvests in Musju. Why can I see yours?"

"I'm not sure yet. Maybe it's because you...." Alira hesitated to provoke further hostility between them. She chose her words with care. "...caught me by surprise? Whatever the reason, this is yet another piece of evidence to support my claim. If humans weren't kin, could I have harvested their pithasias? Would they show up on the banks of Musju?"

"Now I understand why your mother feared the harvesting madness," Rakalesh said, after a long hesitation. "I can't imagine living like that, even with five voices. Lurien had hundreds. Maybe more."

A chill ran up the back of Alira's neck. "Are you saying the madness is taking me?"

"Not that I can see. Not yet. But you need to get those reapings under control."

"How?" Alira asked. "Should I try to force them to be quiet? I thought I was supposed to listen to their advice, though with hundreds of voices...."

"No," Rakalesh said. "To be honest, I don't know the answer. I do know you need to assert control of your mind, your actions. Force them to take a supporting role, rather than a controlling one." She regarded Alira. "You were right before. I don't much like you, but I acknowledge your courage."

"Thank you."

"I couldn't have done what you did. None of the council could have, not even Lurien."

Gray patterns skittered over Alira's skin. Every step of her journey, plotted by guesswork, could well have been her last.

The elder regarded Alira through narrowed eyes. "You've changed, daughter of Lurien, blossomed toward fullness. But you're never going to conform, are you?"

"No."

Rakalesh nodded, her shoulders slumped. "I'm tired of us being at odds. If you're content, I'll convince the council to let you be. But you are no longer a suitable harvester for our people."

"Because of my human memories?"

"Yes. You've taken a path the unammi can't follow. Those sh'toi should never be passed on to another of our kind. No matter how much you deny it, we don't fit with them, and the humans don't fit with us."

A weight lifted from Alira. "I agree. We were already starting over. I can still provide you with an heir, teach them the knowledge and share with them Tellings from the unammi harvests I've collected."

"I'll hold your offer in trust, but we won't know if it's necessary until we can assess the damage to the vault. If Lurien's samples are still viable, we'll use hers."

Amusement flitted through Alira's chaotic display. "Mine might produce unpredictable offspring?"

"Just so." Rakalesh sighed, flickering with lavender veins. "I've been thinking about what you said. About how now would be the best time to change our way of doing things. Start directing the survivors into multiple fields of study and expertise. I must admit I don't like the idea. It unsettles me. We've always done things a certain way and the prospect of additional change, especially now when our whole civilization is on uncertain ground, fills me with dread. No one else will welcome the idea either. They'll want to cling to known expectations. They'll need familiar structure and boundaries if they are to cope well with all that lies ahead of us."

"But?"

The councilor shook her head. "You may be right. We must replace the knowledge from the lost guilds, which won't be easy. Maybe it's best we start now, while so much else is in transition. By the time the next generation comes through their rites, perhaps they'll dedicate to two or three guilds. One primary and two alternates. I don't know yet. The debate on implementation rages on in council, but they at least agreed to cross-train. I thought you'd want to know."

Finally! Alira wanted to shout, to express her relief. A smattering of yellow speckles raced across her limbs and vanished, subsumed by green.

"Is that why you got so angry? You didn't want to agree with me but felt you had no choice?"

Red flashed in Rakalesh's cheeks, then faded. "Perhaps. Or maybe you were being yourself."

"Regardless, thank you for telling me." Alira pressed her advantage in the moment. "What will happen to us? The outcasts?"

"I don't know," Rakalesh said, rubbing her forehead. She seemed tired. "Reintegrating you all into the rest of the survivors won't be easy for any of us. We're still debating this."

The councilor had a point. If Alira wasn't to be a high cleric or the harvester, what place was there for her in unammi society? Her lifelong struggle to fit in now felt like a youngling's dream, never achieved but no longer important in the larger context. What was left? For that matter, the same would be true for the pilots. Yet, as long as the unammi upheld those traditions, outcasts would be expected to work in their chosen guilds. Awkward didn't begin to express the ripples that would cause.

Unless....

Flecks of yellow skittered across Alira's skin. If they—

"What is it?" Rakalesh said.

Alira dragged her focus back to the councilor, mind racing. They'd never go for it. They might even forbid it.

But it would solve everything. For all of them.

She raised a trembling hand to touch Rakalesh's arm. "I have an idea."

Alira laid out her nascent plan for the councilor, speaking quickly so she could complete the thought before Rakalesh refused. As she spoke, the elder's display peppered with gray, then white. By the time Alira fell silent, red splotches had joined Rakalesh's other colors.

"Have you lost your mind?" Rakalesh gaped at her through wide eyes.

"You said you didn't think the madness had taken me yet." Alira peered at her. "Can you convince the others it's a good idea?"

"How can I do that when I don't believe it's true? You've offered some insane proposals in the past, but this one tops them all." Rakalesh squinted at her. "You can't possibly think you'll ever convince those sh'toi you are who you say you are."

"You wouldn't have believed I could do any of the other things I've accomplished since I last left home, either." Alira tilted her head. "What say you now?"

Rakalesh's expression softened into doubt.

"You've already said you didn't think I would ever fit in with the others." Alira shrugged. "This way I'll be in a better position to ensure our people's safety. And what better way is there for me to serve?"

Rakalesh sighed, then nodded. "Very well. I'll convince the council. You convince *him*," she jerked her chin toward the draped doorway, "to go with you. You'll need someone with a more level head nearby to ensure you don't kill us all."

Restraining her enthusiasm, Alira rose and went to the door to find her i'shin, the green and white iridescence in his skin coloring the nearby corridor walls.

"I heard," Galen said. "She's right, you know."

"What do you mean?"

"You're mad. But then you always have been. It's one of the many things that drew me to you in the first place." His mouth curled up at the corners. "When do we leave?"

chapter 65

<u>**Earth**</u>

ALIRA TOUCHED HER SHIP TO the surface, the smoothest landing she'd yet made. All the practice she'd gotten of late showed in her skill. Voices murmured in her mind, and she silenced them with a thought.

Galen's voice sounded from the doorway. "Can I let our travelers out of their seats and off the ship?"

She finished locking down the ship. "They're eager to see their new home, then?"

His head wobbled from side to side. "Eager, anxious, trepidatious…depends who you ask."

"And you?"

He glanced at the viewscreen, then back at her. "Yes. I haven't even seen it yet, and I wish we could stay. With our people."

"We would never be one of them. Ae'staani te Musjuva." We are in The Flow. She held out her hand.

"I know. Still." He touched his fingers to hers, then gripped them in his own. "Frem asal. I serve." He pulled her to her feet. "Show us this wondrous new city, then."

Together they led the people off the ship and onto the surface where they reacted much as she had. They'd never seen that much sky. They squinted in the piercing light of this world's brighter star. And all the sand stayed beneath their feet. Such a marvel!

"We don't want to stay on the surface for long. This star's light may be too strong for our skin," Alira said. She showed them the opening in the cliff face. "There. That's where you go in. No, leave your things behind. Explore first. You can come back later."

Galen gazed at the landscape, his inner lids closed over eyes huge and round, pupils slitted in the bright light. "It's enormous. We'll be like raneals here, tiny and insignificant."

"Raneals aren't insignificant," she said. "They have a place on our world." She caught herself, corrected her words. "On Iridos."

His gaze came back to hers. "Will we help them get settled before we leave?"

"No." She drew a steadying breath. "The other pilots will have to do that before they go back for the rest of the people and supplies. You and I need to take a few of the pilots to their new home, show them where it is and how to operate it before we change ships and finish our journey."

He nodded. "Where will they be staying?"

She looked up, shading her eyes. "It isn't visible now. You'll see it on approach." She touched his hand. "I would like to show you the new city though, if you want to see it before we go."

"I thought you would never ask."

Alira led Galen through the tunnels she'd found in her exploration of this place. It seemed so long ago! Everywhere they went, unammi scurried here and there, scouting the passages and rooms, noting the wells and ventilation shafts, practicing with the door block stones. Rakalesh's ship had arrived first. Her crew, already hard at work, unpacked in specific chambers that had apparently been designated by the council.

After a while, they emerged onto the surface to see that their ship was being unloaded. The sun had shifted toward the western horizon, throwing shadows across the plain. Alira sent word to the few pilots who would accompany them to the outpost, then she and Galen joined the others in unloading those items that would stay here, on Earth.

By the time it was dark, the planet's satellite hung huge, round, and pale in the sky. Alira gazed up at this beautiful sight. Galen soon joined her, followed by the sounds of others come to see. "That's where they'll be," Alira said.

"Will they be able to see the city?" Galen said. "Is there equipment there the pilots can use to keep an eye on our people?"

"The base is on the other side of the satellite," Alira said, "so, no. Until we set up additional equipment, they'll be limited to comm contact. I've advised Rakalesh and Tiral to keep that to emergencies only. No sense advertising their presence at either location."

Soon the first few pilots joined them, and they lifted off toward the outpost. The flight was short, but the lessons at the other end took longer. Alira mined the knowledge of her harvests, giving Tiral and the others a tour of the base, instructing them how to work the equipment, and showing them how to shield their ships from simple scans. Not that she expected any of those. Not yet. Maybe not ever.

fingers crossed, squib.

for once, we agree, crow.

After a brief rest, Alira shifted the necessities to the other ship with Galen's help, and soon they were on the last stage of their journey. She tried to squash her trepidation, but with all the messages awaiting their attention on the comm system, it was hard to do. Her passengers stayed quiet for a change, thank Na'staani.

Galen did not.

"What did the messages say?" he asked.

"They found the bodies I left in Northside district." The scene flashed through Alira's mind in vivid clarity and she rose to stretch her legs.

He sighed. "Does the Consortium know any of the unammi on Iridos survived?"

"They suspect some of the pilots survived." A few, at least. Purple lines of grief flittered down her arms and were gone. She gazed at her surroundings, half-present in the moment. Onscreen, space slurred by in a milky stream that mocked the pace of her own racing thoughts and the approaching point of no return.

"I confess, I'm not convinced this is a good idea," Galen said, as if he had read her mind.

She shook her head. Not him, too. "Why is it that no one ever thinks I can succeed, no matter what I set out to do?"

He came to lay a gentle hand on her own. "That's not what I meant. I have complete faith in you. But it isn't just about the two of us. There is so much more at stake."

She eyed him. "You think I don't realize that? I know what I'm doing."

no, you don't.

Alira pushed the voice away. "Do you trust me?"

"Of course!"

"Then stop doubting my plan. I'll need every shred of focus I can muster to pull this off, at least in the beginning. It'll get easier, I'm sure."

yeah. keep telling yourself that.

shut up, crow.

"I hope you're right." Galen shifted and they viewed the milky stream of interstel in silence for a moment. "Will Harajüd security stop you for questioning? After the Northside incident, I mean…."

"No. Walker said she cleaned it up, though Sa'abah oversaw the operation. I'm confident they left no trace." She hoped. "They'll never know I was there."

He turned to her. "You're sure?"

Blue uncertainty registered in her dermal display, and she shoved it out, pushing dutiful green into its place. Why couldn't she do that before? When it would have mattered?

She sighed. "One thing at a time."

chapter 66

On Approach to New Canaan, Harajüd
<u>Aboard the Nebula</u>

GALEN STIRRED NEXT TO HER in their shared bed. His tug on the blanket left a gap that sucked in a cool draft. Alira's skin pebbled before she could adjust her body's temperature.

"We should get ready," he said.

Instead, she pulled the coverings closer, and burrowed further into their nest. She didn't want to leave it. "Where are we?"

"Ten minutes to normal space." He bent closer, touched his forehead to her temple. "Last chance to change your mind."

Why did those words sound so familiar? She groaned and curled away from the pillow. She opened her eyes a slit to see him there, so close. He would probably follow her anywhere. This proved it. She'd give a lot to have stayed where they were, before she'd embarked on this crazy scheme. She hoped Rakalesh wasn't right about her, but Alira didn't dare show a scrap of doubt. "I'm committed, but you aren't. Not yet. Do you want to back out?"

He peered at her a moment, then continued as if she hadn't spoken. "Did you sleep?"

She grunted.

"That's too bad," he said. "Might not get another opportunity for a while."

She pushed the covering away and stretched, then sat up and slung her feet over the side of the bunk. "I'm fine."

The rustling of blankets and the sound of his feet on the deck told her he'd risen. "I hope you're right. Come on. We need to practice. I know you can do this, but it isn't going to be as easy as you think."

She stood. "It never is."

They ran through practice sequences, testing their disguises and voices, quizzed each other on relevant facts and details. Soon, far too soon, they passed the turning point and approached the planet. Alira drew a tight breath and let it out slowly. Pregnant silence weighted the air on the bridge as they awaited permission to enter Harajüd airspace.

Alira smiled. "Showtime approaches," she whispered, almost to herself. Rugrat would have laughed at that. The thought wiped the grin away.

Rugrat.

"Bravo six one," the voice said over the comm. "State your purpose."

As the flight controller spoke, Alira's body expanded from one hundred thirty-nine centimeters to a full one hundred ninety-three centimeters, shifting from her natural female shape to her new persona's male one, filled out to ninety-two kilos. Head and appendages resized accordingly to fit his memory. He touched his face. Thick, close-clipped beard. Thick brows. Dimples. Full lips. Check. Check. Check. To the side, Galen—Thrace Baldric. Galen was now Thrace Baldric—filled out a curvy female form. Brown skin, gray eyes tilted up at the outer corners, shiny black hair. All black, tight clothing.

"Ready?" he flung over his shoulder.

"Yes." Her voice carried an odd accent that would take some getting used to.

He squinted at her. "Yes what?"

"Yes, sir."

"Much better." He took a deep breath. "You have to play this role to the fullest or they'll never believe us."

"Got it. Sir."

"Bravo six one," the comm voice said again. "I repeat. State your purpose."

"Very well," he said. His own deeper voice felt odd in his throat. It rumbled in his chest.

skalar, you're up.

stand back, netzyl. i'll show you how it's done.

no, alira! you can't—

netzyl, you must. i'm the only one who can get you through this.

okay, but if you step out of line even once, i'm resuming control.

watch and learn.

"Here we go."

He touched the comm system. "This is Admiral Skalar of the Consortium, piloting the Nebula. I am en route to my New Canaan base." The tower knew whom they addressed, or so they thought, anyway. Why they felt it necessary to play this game escaped him. It also annoyed him.

In the pregnant pause, Thrace eyed him across the bridge. He saw but did not reciprocate.

"Acknowledged, Nebula. You are cleared to approach on your usual vectors. Tower out."

"TICS, resume programmed flight."

A soft chitter confirmed his order, and they flew for a few moments in silence. It had been a while since Alira let Crow out for a run back on Harajüd, before her whole outpost debacle. Now, the oddity of having not just voices but a copilot inside her head

his head.

his head threw him off balance. Simple things, like the view of the enormous planet filling the screen as they approached, were dichotomous and confusing. So many memories of this place, few of them her own.

his. his own.

Right.

"Five minutes," Thrace said.

Skalar regarded her. "In the past," he said, "you've had little faith in your own ability to cope with a dangerous situation. Yet you never once hesitated to take on this challenge with me."

"Rakalesh was shocked, I think."

Skalar shook his head. "Maybe. But I know you. You're stronger, more courageous than you believe."

She huffed. "You say that now only because you can't see the white in my skin." She checked their position. "Coming up on the base."

Skalar felt the niveym spread its wings in his chest. Thrace was right. He offered thanks to Na'Staani that no one could see his true skin, either.

The Nebula descended from its flight path and into base airspace, then into the landing bay. Skalar shut down the engines and sat in the relative silence. This might be the last private moment he had with Thrace for a while.

She did not let him enjoy it. "Ready, sir?"

He sighed, nodded. "Let's get this over with."

The moment he stepped from the Nebula's hatch, Commander Walker descended on him. Her team stood nearby alongside Captain Sa'abah. It would seem that the commander had been conferring with the chief of security. Probably Sa'abah's doing.

"Welcome back, sir. We were beginning to worry about you, and thought we'd have to declare you missing. I'm glad you finally responded. Is everything okay, sir?" Walker rattled, her gaze going from her C.O. to the stranger beside him.

Is everything okay? Skalar stared at her. Nothing would be okay again. At least not the way it had been. Before their world collapsed and they'd been chased from their home by humans. *These* humans.

Walker blinked, waiting another moment before she cleared her throat and offered a TICS pad. "I've followed all the orders you commed, prepared things the way you instructed. I've done my best to maintain order and to keep business running at peak efficiency, with security's assistance of course."

He made no attempt to take the device. "Report."

Walker blinked, lowered her arm. She glanced at Sa'abah.

"Well, sir, as I said in my message, Captain Crow commed to say he'd gone offworld on faction business. The landport later said his jumper had been left parked in a restricted area. When we retrieved it, one of the managers at the land port confirmed that Crow had taken one of the squib ships on your orders."

Skalar's fists clenched.

calm down, netzyl. leave this to me.

But Walker wasn't finished. "It wasn't until one of his contacts commed here asking for him that I knew something was wrong. Apparently, he'd entered one of the flats more than ten days before to take care of something, but had never checked back in with her as he usually does. We took a team to the flat and found two bodies."

"You didn't identify them in your comm." Skalar steeled himself.

"No, sir. Captain Sa'abah advised against doing so." She took a deep breath. "It was Captain Crow and a squib. I'm sorry for the loss of your second, sir. I know you'd been working together a long time."

Skalar ground his teeth together.

stop fighting me, netzyl.

"After I commed you," Walker said, "security removed the bodies and scrubbed the flat. I think medical wanted to dissect the squib, but decomp had progressed too far for that to be useful."

"Go on."

"Corpgov does have an audio record of Captain Crow requesting departure clearance in one of the squib ships on the same date as his comm to me. But the timeline doesn't fit. Medical estimated he must have been lying in that Northside flat since about that same time. It looks like he never left after all, but if he didn't, then where's the squib ship? And if he did, how did he leave and get back so quickly? Why didn't New Canaan air control log his return? We don't know the exact sequence of events, sir. But medical autopsied his body."

"What did they find?" Skalar interjected.

he was fucked, sir.

"Medics put it down as massive organ failure, but they found no pathogens or evidence of external trauma. It was almost like he…imploded, sir."

"Surveillance?"

"Captain Crow's contact took care of the feeds before he went in, sir. They went live again a little over two hours later, but she said she scanned the first two hours of the vids once they picked up again. She found nothing incriminating."

"Good. Is that all?"

"No, sir," Walker went on. "Relays in Iridos orbit reported four pings, one just after you left here and three others a couple of weeks ago."

"Only four?"

"Yes, sir. Relays went dark a while later, sir. No further signals from any of them. Apparently, we didn't get them all." Walker licked her lips. "I wanted to send more ships to finish them, but Captain Sa'abah suggested I wait to confirm such an action with you, Admiral."

"Very well. Anything else?"

"Small stuff, sir." The commander made another attempt to offer the TICS pad, but Skalar shifted his attention to Sa'abah.

"Is your investigation concluded?"

"No, sir, still ongoing."

"Very well. Keep me informed. I want to know who killed Crow." Skalar turned to the woman beside him. "Captain Thrace Baldric, you are hereby promoted to my second in command. Congratulations."

Captain Baldric nodded. "Thank you, sir."

Pushing past the stunned commander, Skalar pressed toward the lift, Thrace two steps behind him.

Walker's voice rang out. "Admiral Skalar, I protest!"

Heat rushed up the back of his neck. Skalar stopped, pivoted, and took a step toward her. "Excuse me?"

Sa'abah squinted. Walker's personal crew fidgeted despite their attentive stance, looking at the floor, the ceiling of the hanger, the opposite wall, anywhere but at the admiral. Vandana Walker, however, stood tall, her back to the ship.

"You may not know, sir," she said, "but Captain Crow made me his second after Harley died. We were still on the Iridos mission, sir, aboard the Leonid, and I've done a damn fine job. Right after we got back, both you and the captain disappeared. I held the base together, managed to reach you, followed your orders to the letter. I thought I was working my way into a respectable position in the faction."

Walker waved toward Captain Baldric. "Now you promote this untried stranger ahead of me? With all due respect, I thought the chain of command ran from you to Captain Crow to the captain's second. That means I'm next-in-line for his spot, not this…person. Sir."

He took another step toward her, grinding his teeth.

don't do it.

if you want to pull this off, you must be ruthless. step aside. let me handle it.

And another.

i won't let you kill her.

if you don't, these crewmen will never follow you. they'll assassinate you at their first opportunity.

Skalar moved toward the protesting officer, debating his options until

netzyl, don't hesitate. you'll get us all killed.

there are other ways. watch and learn.

his hand shot out, latched onto Walker's throat, and pushed her back against his docked ship. Her TICS pad clattered to the floor. Gagging, she clutched at his fingers, nails digging into his skin

don't you dare heal those scratches!

while he lifted her off the floor, her eyes wide, feet now thrashing in an effort to kick herself loose. Skalar's thoughts reached into hers, *pushing* her toward unconsciousness, and—

—nothing happened.

what the actual fuck?

Wait…oh damn, he should have remembered. Walker had taken longer than the others to succumb to the bryse that day in the canyon when the humans first came to Iridos. She resisted! How?

His fingers squeezed tighter, his thoughts pushed harder until at last, Walker's struggles weakened, then went limp.

kill her, netzyl. while you still can.

His other hand joined the first and slammed her head against the ship. He dropped her at his feet and turned.

"Any other objections?"

Most of the gathered officers faced straight ahead. Only Sa'abah had the nerve to speak up.

"Of course not, Admiral Skalar," she said, voice rock steady. She stepped closer and dropped her voice. "Shall I screen a new crew to replace those you sent home from the outpost, sir?"

"No. That is covered. But put this," he toed the commander's unconscious form, "in the brig. Leave her there until further notice. Also, contact Rubene's transport officials and inform them Captain Baldric left her rented jumper on Ynysbedd Island. The Consortium will pay for whatever charges or fines she incurred."

"Yes, sir." Sa'abah blinked. "What reason should I give them for having left it there?"

"Tell them whatever you wish. I'm not in the habit of explaining myself, Captain. Dismissed."

"Yes, sir." Sa'abah gestured to the crew to get Walker out of the admiral's way while Captain Baldric stepped up beside him.

When the others were out of earshot, Thrace eyed Skalar. "You know I support you, whatever happens. I'm curious to see how far you can go now that no one is holding you back. But you do know that there's going to be far more to this plan than you expect."

"Yes."

no, netzyl. you don't.

Thrace stepped closer. "Don't you find it ironic that you spent your entire frem life fighting for the freedom to be authentic and now you can't even wear your own face?"

"I have many masks. They all reflect who I am." Echoes of Elisul's similar words rang through his mind, and Skalar shook it off. He looked at Thrace. "What about you? Are you sure you can do this?"

"I'll manage. It's the pilots and the mitigants I worry about."

"Tiral will take good care of them. They'll be fine. Better than fine," Skalar pointed out, "away from all the criticism and disapproval of the others, with a new way to serve. They'll be an added layer of security for the new city, a 'Consortium' crew specially selected by Admiral Skalar to run the facility, even though I don't think they'll need to worry. Earth is taboo to the humans. Unammi know how difficult it is to ignore a taboo."

"Difficult, perhaps," Thrace murmured. "Not impossible. You've proven that."

Skalar grunted. "If other Consortium crewmembers show up, I'm confident Tiral can manage it. The biggest change will be that they're no longer alone. They have each other and the mitigants for company. And who knows? Maybe some of the others will join them after a time."

Thrace seemed to consider this. "Do you think they'll provide adequate protection for the survivors?"

"The Consortium is a huge faction. With the resources at our disposal now, the unammi...." He lowered his voice. "They'll be safe there for a long time."

Thrace nodded. "And what of us, Alira?"

He turned away. "Skalar. The name's Skalar."

Did you enjoy this book? Please leave a rating and/or comment wherever books are reviewed and help others find and enjoy it, as well!

Sign up for Drema's newsletter!

You'll get articles, project updates, garden pictures, and cat news.

You'll also be the first to receive announcements about upcoming releases, cover reveals, and other juicy tidbits from Niveym Arts.

https://niveymarts.com/newsletter

Want to follow Drema's process on her indie publishing journey? Subscribe to Drema's blog and/or follow her on social media.

Blog: https://www.dremadeoraich.com
Facebook: https://www.facebook.com/NiveymArtsLLC
Instagram: https://www.instagram.com/dremadeoraich
BlueSky: https://bsky.app/profile/dremadeoraich.bsky.social

Acknowledgments

This book has been in the works for a very long time, and would never have made it into print without the assistance and guidance of many other people, to whom I owe my deepest gratitude:

To the teachers and organizers of the Hampton Roads Writers Conference, where I first learned that 800K words just might be a bit too long for a single novel (unless you're Brandon Sanderson).

To the teachers and volunteers at The Muse Writers Center, where I learned how to hone my craft into something others might actually want to read.

To my social circle and friends, who listened to me talk about TFS *ad nauseum* for years and were patient with my long silences and distractions whenever I retreated into my story's worlds.

To the many individuals who contributed to my research: Tom, William, and so many others! There's a piece of you in these pages.

To all my beta readers from every single draft: Becky, Dylan, John, Lillith, Lily, and Vince, who helped me tighten the plot and stop showing off all the research I'd done to write this book.

To my editor, Lauran Strait, who loved my characters almost as much as I did, and helped me tell their story in a cleaner, clearer way.

To my proofreader, Stephanie Brannick, who hunted down every last error or glitch in this manuscript and smoothed out the last few wrinkles. Any remaining errors in this book are on *me*, not Lauran or Stephanie.

To Francis and the team at 100Covers, who listened to my ideas and created the perfect cover in record time.

Last, but not least, to B, who scanned my badly hand-drawn maps and refined them into something publishable, whose faith and belief in my ability to tell this story never once wavered, who ran our household while I worked on the manuscript, who ensured I ate at semi-regular intervals, and who made sure I took tree breaks when I needed them. I love you, Silly Man!

About the Author

Drema Deòraich is a writer of speculative fiction that sometimes asks big questions. Her short stories have been published in numerous online journals, as well as a few semi-professional zines. Her short story "Upshot" won an honorable mention in the Writers of the Future contest in 2018, and later went on to be published in the international magazine, Mithila Review.

Drema's debut novel "Entheóphage," a medical sci-fi/climate fiction novel, released on October 14, 2022. "Phagey" (as it is affectionately known by its fans) is currently available in paperback, ebook, and audiobook.

Her membership in multiple writers groups surrounds her with other creatives, both indie and traditionally published, who understand the special craziness that comes with being a writer. When time permits, Drema blogs about writing, ideas from Life that inspire her, environmental issues, ways to live more sustainably, and whatever else captures her fancy. Follow her writing posts at www.dremadeoraich.com, and her environmental posts at www.niveymarts.com.

Currently, Drema is hard at work on the next book in the Founder's Seed trilogy with plans to release later this year. When not writing, she helps her legal-eagle boss save the world one case at a time, pets her husband's cats, or spends time in Nature, surrounded by flora and fauna.

Also by Drema Deòraich

Entheóphage
https://books2read.com/Entheophage

Coming Soon:

Broken
The Founder's Seed Book 2

Driven
The Founder's Seed Book 3

Appendix A

Characters List

Alira (ah-LEE-rah)—Unammi. Female frem dedicated to the clerical guild, though she tends to study many subjects, and knows a little about many trades.

Amadi (ah-MAH-dee)—Unammi. See Patel, Amadi.

Baldric, Thrace—Unammi. Female human persona of Galen.

Botha (BOI-tah)—Human. Beloved male elder in the village of Bregaina on the human colony world Bejami. Called "Baba" by some outside his village.

Cesar (say-ZAHR)—Unammi. Male elder in the historical guild. Councilor on Iridos. Special unammi gift: reader. Could see into people's intentions and motivations, enough to predict likely outcomes.

Cohen, Mira—Human. Female crewman in The Consortium Trader faction.

Companion—Other. The ethereal multifaceted entity that represents the hive mind of all the Iri, not just on Iridos, but everywhere; appears to Alira as Guide and Advisor. Only she can see him/them. See entry for "Iri" in Appendix B, Glossary.

Crow—Human. Male captain and second in command of the Consortium Trader faction.

Dawa, Tenzin (DAH-wah, TEHN-zihn)—Unammi. Male human persona of Galen.

Dodger—Human. Female agent sent by another Trader faction to find a source for slave labor. Captured by Skalar's people and held prisoner in the Consortium.

Dyson—Unammi. Male councilor on Iridos. Special unammi gift: intuition.

Elisul (ee-LIE-suhl)—The name given to The Founder by all unammi. It was Elisul who brought the unammi to Iridos generations ago to escape a catastrophe on their homeworld.

Enfili (ehn-FEE-lee)—Unammi. Female youngling in Alira's clerical class.

Galen (GAY-lehn)—Unammi. Male frem in service to the trade guild; pilot and outcast. Has multiple human personas, all genders. Galen is Alira's i'shin. Special unammi gift: empath. Can sense/feel and, sometimes, influence or manipulate emotions of those around him.

Ijydin (ee-JEE-dihn)—Unammi. Female frem in service to the trade guild; pilot and outcast. Special unammi gift: truthseer. Can tell with a great deal of certainty whether an individual is telling the truth.

Kipa (KEE-pah)—Unammi. Male youngling in Alira's class.

Kobe (KOH-bee)—Unammi. Male frem in service to the security guild on Iridos.

Logan—Human. See Roucharde.

Lurien (LOO-ree-ehn)—Unammi. Alira's mother. Female frem in service to the clerical guild; serves as high cleric and as a counselor.

Malcolm—Human. See Skalar, Malcolm.

Mira—Human. See Cohen, Mira.

Nyros (NEE-rohs)—Unammi. Alira's brother. Male frem in service to the trade guild; pilot, and outcast. Special unammi gift: projection. Can "push" a thought, desire, or idea into the mind of another and make it seem like it originated in the mind of the target.

Patel, Amadi (pah-TEHL, ah-MAH-dee)—Unammi. Male human persona of Ijydin.

Rakalesh (rah-KAY-lehsh)—Unammi. Female councilor on Iridos. Frem in service to, and head of, the trade guild. Special unammi gift: projection. Can "push" a thought, desire, or idea into the mind of another and make it seem like it originated in the mind of the target. Rakalesh can also drag/pull another unammi into muñara.

Rizzo—Human. Female. Known to a rare few as Turizomi. Admiral of The Syndicate Trader faction.

Ronan—Human. Male captain of the *Treasure Chest* for The Consortium Trader faction.

Roucharde, Logan—Human. Male chairman of the board of directors for Harajüd House Unlimited. See glossary entry for "Harajüd."

Rugrat—Human. See Skalar, Amelia.

Sa'abah (sah-AH-bah)—Human. Female captain and head of security in The Consortium Trader faction.

Skalar, Amelia (skah-LAHR)—Human. Female. Also known as Rugrat. Malcolm Skalar's beloved little sister.

Skalar, Malcolm (skah-LAHR)—Human. Male admiral of The Consortium Trader faction.

Sufamel (SOO-fah-mehl)—Unammi. Female elder in the horticultural guild. Mentor to Alira. Special unammi gift: empath. Can sense/feel and, sometimes, influence or manipulate emotions of those around her.

Tenzin—Unammi. See Dawa, Tenzin.

Thrace—Unammi. See Baldric, Thrace.

Tisalan (tee-SAH-lahn)—Unammi. Female frem in service to the horticulture guild.

Tiral (tee-RAHL)—Unammi. Male frem in service to the trade guild; pilot and outcast. Has multiple human personas, all genders. Special unammi gift: sensory enhancement. Can heighten any one of his senses exponentially.

Trumo (TROO-moh)—Unammi. Male youngling in one of Alira's classes, one with whom she feels a strong kinship.

Van, Vandana—Human. See Walker, Vandana.

Walker, Vandana—Human. Female captain in the Consortium Trader faction.

Appendix B

Glossary

acusjal (ah-cyoo-ZHAL) *Unameze*—indigenous to Iridos. Small, androgynous low-growing plant. Forms a crusty tube on its exterior surface that can slice through skin; inner parts are tender. Plant extends these outside the tubes only to expend oxygen and take in other gases. Carnivorous. Feeds on sub-surface sand beetles and grubs that venture into their electrified root systems. Bioluminescent. Grows in clusters.

Adjustment—a physical process performed by unammi healers at a new frem's Rite of Decision; intended to "nudge" the brain/mind/persona to help the new frem be content with their chosen role and serve without doubt.

aes (AY-ehs) *Unameze*—are; can also be and often is merged with another part of the sentence (most often the adverb which qualifies or gives focus to the verb).

Ae'staani te musjuva (AY-eh-stah-AH-nee teh moo-ZHOO-vuh) *Unameze*—We are all in the Flow.

Aes te nalya (AY-ehs teh NAH-lee-yah) *Unameze*—We are one.

Aggregate—refers to Saacharis Aggregate Mining, the corporate governing body on the human colony world Saacharis.

ama (AH-mah) *Unameze*—genetic dam; mother.

ani (AH-nee) *Unameze*—light.

anita (AH-nee-tuh) *Unameze*—rainbow. (Literally "play of light.")

apa (AH-pah) *Unameze*—genetic sire; father.

asa (AH-sah) *Unameze*—I.
Forms of use:
       asal (AH-sahl)—I am.
       asad (AH-sahd)—I was.
       asatu (AH-sah-too)—I will.
       asabi (AH-sah-bee)—I have.

asabilen (ah-SAH-bih-len)—I have been.

asi (AH-see) *Unameze*—me.

atlish (AHT-lihsh) *Unameze*—indigenous to Iridos; large serpentine predator that can move from the tree-top muñise communities to hunt creatures beneath the surface of the sand. Thick, dark, iridescent skin that sheds to allow the animal to grow.

Ba'nostade puda ba'tujhur (bah-NOH-stah-deh POO-dah bah-too-ZHOOR) *Unameze*—Your deeds write your fate.

Ba'riba asatu'lan (bah REE-bah ah-SAH-too-lahn) *Unameze*—I will speak your name. Traditional words of honoring at the vigil for someone who has died. (Plural: ba'riba te'lan.)

Baba (BAH-bah)—Father; a term of respect used by many humans as an honorific for tribal and village elders.

bala (BAH-lah)—indigenous to Bejami. A tall (127-130 cm) wading bird found along equatorial riverbanks and deltas. Feeds on fish, crustaceans, and reptiles found in water or marshy areas. Bright green feathers on back and wings, sky blue belly and undertail, reed-yellow legs. Long sinuous neck is iridescent blue-green, face is black with bright red crest feathers that stand up when courting or fighting. Long, spear-like bill. Bright red eyes.

balé (BAH-lay) *Unameze*—you.
Forms of use:
> **basut** (BAH-soot)—you (plural).
> **ba** (BAH)—your (possessive).
> **basu** (bah-SOO)—your (possessive plural).
> **basute** (bah-SOO-teh)—yourselves.

basu'tao (bah-SOO-tuh-ow) *Unameze*—exclamation; be still; be quiet. Literally "still yourselves." (See tao.)

Bejami (beh-JAH-mee)—one of twelve human colony worlds. Governed by the Bejami Trust. Located on a moon in orbit around Orta, a gas giant in the Emlacha star system (same as Rubene), though the Bregainans call the star Lynju. Home to the Mandoslóna prison continent. Equatorial regions are all wild, untamed. No spaceport. Single landport located in the capital city of Bel-rhovan.

bejhe asal (beh-ZHAY ah-SAHL) *Unameze*—I am empty; expression of frustration, end of one's wits, out of patience.

bejhur (beh-ZHOOR) *Unameze*—full, complete, ready.

bejhur asane (beh-ZHOOR ah-SAH-nay) *Unameze*—I'm not ready.

Bel-rhovan (behl-ROH-vahn)—Bejami's capital city. Located on the continent of Dorucuin in the northern hemisphere.

bh'tati (buh-TAH-tee)—indigenous to Bejami; oceanic fruit of enormous sea lily forests in Dairnen Bay on the west coast of Dorucuin. Savory, salty, juicy. Center of the fruit is eaten raw or in stews. Pulp from layer between edible center and skin is used in pigments for tattoos, paints, dyes, etc. Rubbery skin is soaked in other fruit juices and allowed to ferment; makes an alcoholic mead-like drink called úta. Fruit is harvested by divers.

Bregaina (breh-GAY-nuh)—second largest village (not city) on Bejami. This is Botha's home. All buildings situated on platforms raised above the delta so that the tide can ebb and flow beneath them.

bryse (BREE-suh) *Unameze*—to "nudge" or gently "push" someone or something (at the cellular and atomic level) toward a desired outcome. Forms of use:

    brysedin (BREE-suh-deen)—nudging.
    brysedun (BREE-suh-duhn)—nudged.
    brysedu (BREE-suh-doo)—a nudge or push.

canara (cah-NAH-rah) *Unameze*—flute-like instrument used on Iridos. Made from roots or thick stems of the odasen plant.

chauf (CHAWF) *Unameze*—indigenous to Iridos. Sub-surface dun-colored beetles whose eggs and grubs are found around roots of many surface plants. Parasitic. When the unammi find these grubs around their own indigenous food or other resources (bashir, dozhan, rufesh, etc.), they harvest and include the fat, juicy grubs in their food.

chithe (CHEE-thay) *Unameze*—no direct translation; familiar pet nickname for a youngling; acknowledges connection to and concern for the child.

Clan, The—Trader faction located on the human colony world Danua. Run by Admiral Tsurin; no current second in command.

comm—common term used for messages or communications sent via TICS system or by wristcom.

Consortium, The—Trader faction located on the human colony world Harajüd. Run by Admiral Skalar and second in command, Captain Crow.

corpgov—human slang term. Refers to corporate governments on the human colony worlds. Sometimes morphs into similar slang specific to a particular world, i.e. Danuagov.

chur (CHOOR) *Unameze*—gender-neutral pronoun; used in place of he or she.
Forms of use:

> **churen** (CHOOR-ehn)—gender-neutral possessive pronoun; used in place of her or his.
>
> **churte** (CHOOR-teh)—gender-neutral pronoun; used in place of her or him.

cycle—unammi measure of time on Iridos, analogous to "day" in human vernacular. One cycle = .8 standard days. As Iridos is tidally locked to its star, it has no sunrise/sunset to determine day/night length.

Danua (DAN-yoo-ah)—one of twelve human colony worlds. Governed by Danua Textiles. Located in the Restelys star system. Home to the Danua Clan Trader faction. Three small moons. One spaceport. One landport.

dedicant—unammi younglings who have completed their education, but who have not yet chosen a guild.

dermal display—colors that appear in washes, veins, and patterns on an unammi's skin as a reflection of their emotional state. Though the unammi visual perception exceeds that of human visual range, basic color references are:

> * Blue: uncertainty, angst.
> * Brown: sexual tension.
> * Copper: sexual attraction.
> * Coral: disappointment.
> * Cyan: tension.
> * Gold: gratitude, joy.
> * Green: duty, obligation.
> * Gray: surprise.
> * Lavender: general unhappiness.
> * Lime: relief.
> * Olive: calm.
> * Orange: healing.
> * Pink: annoyance.
> * Purple: sadness, grieving.
> * Red: anger, frustration.
> * Sand: amusement.
> * Tan: affection, devotion.
> * Teal: confusion.
> * White: alarm or pain.
> * Yellow: excitement, happiness.

deshtanta (deh-SHTAHN-tah) *Unameze*—to visually display erratic and confused dermal flashes of color and light beginning at the time of physical death and continuing for several cycles.
Forms of use:
>**deshtandes** (deh-SHTAHN-dehs)—displays.
>**deshtantin** (deh-SHTAHN-tihn)—displaying.
>**deshtantun** (deh-SHTAHN-toon)—displayed.
>**deshtant** (de-SHTAHNT)—the death display of an Iridosian.

dozhan (DOH-zhahn) *Unameze*—indigenous to Iridos. Long, fibrous, bioluminescent leaves that grow in clusters in and around muñise tree communities. Harvested for use in making clothing and other textiles, as well as sold to human colonies.

educator's house—one of the guilds on Iridos. At the age of nine or ten seasons, all younglings move from the familial house to this guild, where they are educated and guided on unammi social customs, given basic lessons from all guilds, and provided with the knowledge and support that will help them to become productive members of unammi society.

ELF radiation—extremely low frequency radiation.

equilinus (eh-kwih-LIE-nuhs)—a.k.a. smooth ride. Product of The Federation Trader faction on Rubene. Recreational. An herbal capsule holding a compound of natural herbs and flowers. Not enhanced. Makes the user feel calm and easy about almost anything. Smooths out the emotions. Taken with alcohol, can have strong soporific effect.

Estobael isja yetandu (Eh-STAH-behl EE-zha yeh-TAHN-doo) *Unameze*—Where the mind finds a need....
>*Response:* **Sintuna ba fojenas** (sihn-TOO-nuh bah foh-ZHEH-nahs) *Unameze*—...the heart opens a way.

familial house—one of the guilds on Iridos. This is where all new mothers live with their offspring, other mothers and younglings, and other frem dedicated to this guild.

fasju—(FAH-zhoo) *Unameze*—no direct translation; closest meaning is "renew" or "restore," to be made whole.
Forms of use:
>**fasje** (FAH-zhay)—renews.
>**fasjin** (FAH-zheen)—renewing.
>**fasjun** (FAH-zhoon)—renewed.
>**fasjtalen** (FAH-zhtah-lehn)—renewal or state of being, having been renewed.

fealle sprite (FEEL sprite) *Unameze*—indigenous to Iridos. Surface-dwelling, four-legged animal with short dun-colored fur and skin that blends in well to the sandy background for camouflage. Huge, double-lidded eyes. Powerful hind legs. Short, wide, stumpy tail. The animal's hearing is poor, but its eyesight is keen. It can spot the slightest move nearby and will instantly leap into the air to escape potential threats. The wind then carries it a short distance before it lands, scurries away, and burrows under the sand to wait out the threat.

Firstrite—marks a youngling's move from the familial house to the educator's house, where they will begin their training and start working toward guild membership and frem service.

frem (FREHM) *Unameze*—adult in service to the unammi; the opposite of youngling.

fuj (FOOZH) *Unameze*—life; experiences; personal history.

Gadney (GAD-nee)—one of twelve human colony worlds. Governed by the Gadney Farm League. Located in the Biziar star system. One small moon. One spaceport. One landport.

ground car—personal ground transport vehicle. Operates on electricity. Friction from contact with the ground makes a crackly sound; motor makes a moaning sound. Some older models whine. No emissions.

ha (hah) *Unameze*—bright.

ha'ani (hah AH-nee) *Unameze*—dayside; perpetual sunlight and heat on side of Iridos always facing its star.

Harajüd (hah-RAH-joohd)—one of twelve human colony worlds. Governed by Harajüd House, Unlimited (HHU). Located in the Lakaya star system. Seven moons, all small, icy; the largest holds medical isolation facilities under a pressurized dome. Harajüd is the largest and most affluent of all the human worlds. Home to The Consortium Trader faction. One of the first three exoplanets to be settled by colonists from Earth. Five space ports, as well as one space-based shipbuilding port and one space-based repair station (Orbital Repair Station). Two land ports.

hematium (heh-MAH-tee-uhm)—metal found only on Iridos; holds unique qualities, like the ability to shed a radioactive charge, which make it essential in contemporary shipbuilding.

HHU—refers to Harajüd House, Unlimited, the corporate governing body on the human colony world Harajüd.

holo—short for holographic; often used in place of the term "holographic."

holocam—holographic recording device.

holodisplay—playback device capable of projecting holovids from TICS devices or holocams.

holovid—holographic visual output.

hoverbus—large public transports that do not make physical contact with the ground to move. Intracity transport only; limited to short-distance travel. Free passage to any traveler. Motors make a deep thrumming sound near the lower end of human hearing spectrum.

i'betser (ee-BEHT-zer) *Unameze*—a strand of three beads hung around a dedicant's neck during the rite of achievement: one gold for the debt to one's teachers, one copper for the duty to one's people, one obsidian for the connection to the All (see Na'Staani).

Intercolonial Charter—an agreement drawn up and signed by governing bodies of all twelve human colony worlds. Initially drafted and confirmed by the first three human colonies to be settled in Earth Year 2687, the Charter governs the vast majority of human interrelations between the colonies, as well as what is acceptable and legal on any one of those worlds, including (but not limited to): ecological sustainability, intercolonial time measures (standard day/week/month/year), weaponry, languages, the sanctity of the Contract, citizenship, rights and privileges due all citizens, responsibilities of all citizens, medical and other systems of law, population growth, extradition, governance, etc.

interstel craft—interplanetary and interstellar flight capable. Some come in small personal craft size, but most are mid-sized or larger and belong to Trader factions or colonial governments. Smaller and most mid-size craft can dock at landports; larger craft may only dock at spaceport.

Iri (IH-ree) *Unameze*—subquantum beings that live in the rocky surface of the caverns on Iridos, as well as many other places in other realms, other worlds. It is thought that they are hive-based entities, and that they and those with whom they find a connection, like the unammi, live in symbiotic relationship. For the unammi, that symbiosis produces the irolium crystals that grow in three places inside the unammi city. (See irolium.) The Iri "sing" in nearly subliminal tones that all unammi can hear, and they communicate with most unammi through guided "feelings."

Iridos (IH-rih-dohs)—the only known world inhabited by sapient beings who are not human, the unammi. Gravity is 2.1 that of Earth Standard. No moon. Tidally locked with its small, unnamed star. The unammi, along with most known plant and animal life on Iridos, dwell in the liminal zone where extremes from the dayside (ha'ani) and nightside (ne'ani) are in balance. Constant chilly climate. Strong surface winds. Due to high moisture and dust in the atmosphere, stars are not visible from the planet's surface. Wherever irolium is located, there are slightly elevated levels of low-level, non-thermal magnetic radiation. Not a signer of the Intercolonial Charter, thus not considered a colonial world. No ports; unammi prohibit human presence on their world. Unammi city does have one landing bay that is hidden, known only to unammi pilots and citizens.

irolium (ih-ROH-lee-uhm)—blue crystals that encrust the surface of the temple cavern on Iridos, as well as the training cavern and a space inside the Founder's Monument called "the vault." The stones emit low-level, non-thermal magnetic radiation. It is rumored among the unammi (especially the younglings) that exposure to the irolium is what gives them their special abilities.

i'shin (ee-SHEEN) *Unameze*—familiar pet name for a beloved friend or lover, any gender; a shortened combination of "my heart."

Isja riba unammitu'lan. (EE-zha REE-bah oo-NAH-mee-too-lahn) *Unameze*—loosely translates as "My people will speak my name."

joinedmind—the hive-like shared consciousness utilized by the unammi; differs from muñara in that joinedmind is more purposeful, more action-driven.

jumper—usually small (though can be mid-sized) personal transports. Atmospheric craft capable of flight within a single planet's atmosphere. More functional than stylish. Makes a small whining sound.

LADRAS (LAH-drahs)—stands for Limited Area Dispersal Radiation System. LADRAS missiles are illegal, as are all radioactive weapons, by the terms of the Intercolonial Charter.

Levyron (leh-VIE-ruhn)—one of twelve human colony worlds. Governed by the Levyron Institute. Located in the G'laudis star system. One small moon. Levyron has an axial tilt of 157°, and a retrograde axial rotation. Sun rises in the West and sets in the East. Visible in the night sky is the Finbeck Galactic Arm, which extends beyond Levyron. Home to The Order Trader faction. One spaceport. One landport.

Livuce'ba wenaes bujhul (lih-VOO-chee-bah wee-NAY-uhs buh-ZHOOL) *Unameze*—traditional saying at a Rite of Mourning. No direct translation; closest meaning is "By your loss we are diminished."

Mari Bay (MAH-ree BAY)—large bay located to the west of New Canaan, Harajüd, between the Syrinaia coastline and Shamashu Island.

medfac—common human term for a medical facility.

mitigant—an unammi frem who has repeatedly proven to be problematic to unammi society in one way or another and has undergone the process of mitigation.

mitigation—a physical process undertaken by healers on Iridos to reprogram a frem's entire brain. Intended to "fix" frem who cannot adjust to a life of service, or whose mental and neural connections go awry due to some unforeseen problems in their physical makeup. It is also used to "fix" those who have difficulty in conforming, or who refuse to conform, to unammi social expectations, and is seen as a tool to bring troublemakers into line so that they do not foster discontent in others.

muil (MWEEL)—indigenous to Bejami. A small wading bird found along shorelines in equatorial regions; eats insects, small fish, crustaceans, worms, etc. Small-bodied, stands up to 38cm tall. Dull greenish gray backs and heads, pale gray bellies, mottled faces. Brownish yellow legs and bills, orange eyes.

muñara (moo-NYAH-rah) *Unameze*—meditative communion with each other, or with Na'Staani. Shared mind/awareness; differs from joinedmind in that muñara is more meditative, more spiritual.

muñise tree (moo-NYEE-suh) *Unameze*—found only on Iridos. Tall, stately. Sturdy trunks with crusty, scale-like exterior surface (thicker on the windward side) to withstand sand and wind. All limbs are found at the top quarter of the tree, above the winds, and all angle up. Tiny flowers are bioluminescent, and star shaped. Large, thin-skinned fruits feed the treetop community of animals and birds, which then drop the skin from the canopy. The seeds embedded in the skin germinate new seedlings. Roots from new seedlings latch onto and grow *into* the older, mature roots before even breaking the surface of the ground. A muñise grove is a true communal organism; all the trees in a grove are connected in and by their massive, shared root system. Gives them more stability in the winds, greater chance of survival.

Musju (MOO-zhoo) *Unameze*—no direct translation; best approximation is "the flow" or "The Flow of Things As They Are." Comparable to the old Earth concept of the Tao. The unammi envision it in meditation or dream as a river or a stream, a body of water that has currents and eddies.

It is the way of the Universe, of the Great Mind. Also used as a proper name given to the part of Na'Staani that directs the Flow.
Forms of use:

> **Musjuva** (moo-ZHOO-vuh)—in the flow.

Na'ama (nah-AH-mah) *Unameze*—see "napi."

Na'apa (nah-AH-pah) *Unameze*—see "napi."

Nalena t'staani (nah-LAY-nah tih stah-AH-nee) *Unameze*—One is All; proper response to "Aes te nalya."

nanopanel—large plaz panel chemically treated and infused with nanotech. Can be clear, like a window, or be set to project colored pattern displays, specific scenes from historical or contemporary vistas, or any visual that the programmer or user can adequately define.

napi (NAH-pee) *Unameze*—to respect.
Forms of use:

> **Na** (NAH)—respected.
> **Na'ala** (nah AH-lah)—respected elders, plural, genderless.
> **Na'ama** (nah AH-mah)—respected female elder.
> **Na'apa** (nah AH-pah)—respected male elder.
> **Na'frem** (nah FREHM)—respected non-gendered adult (see "frem").

Na'Staani (nah stah-AH-nee) *Unameze*—The Great Mind, The Sacred All, The Universe, the unammi concept of All-That-Is, or the Divine.

Na'Staani bu bale (nah stah-AH-nee boo BAH-lay) *Unameze*—Na'Staani take you.

nawhúd flowers (nah-WUUD) *Unameze*—pale blue flowers that nod and bob even when there is no wind to push them. Fruits are small, prickly pods that pop open when ripe to expose the papery seeds to the wind. Delicate plant. Grows only on Iridos in the twilight, sandy soil, and protected rock crevices.

ne (neh) *Unameze*—no, not.

ne'ani (neh AH-nee) *Unameze*—no light; refers to the nightside of Iridos, which is always facing away from its star.

netzyl (NEHT-zul)—an unflattering, slang term for someone who causes problems or whose actions generate upheaval; a troublemaker.

New Canaan (noo KAY-nahn)—capital city on the human colony world Harajüd; located on the west coast of Syrinaia near the equator. Largest human city on any human colony world.

niveym (nih-VAY-uhm) *Unameze*—indigenous to Iridos. Large, delicate white bird; never comes to the surface. Lives its entire life in and above the very tall muñise trees. Bird's body is slight, long, and slender, but wings are exceptionally long and powerful, as is its tail, to aid in flight.

nosta (NO-stah) *Unameze*—deed; action.
Forms of use:
> **Nostade** (NOH-stah-deh)—deeds; actions (plural).

odasen (oh-DAY-sehn)— dioecious plant native to Iridos; male parts live on the night side (require cold for their pollen to ripen); when pollen pods are "ripe" they burst out of the male plant, and roll/bounce/blow along the ground or low near the ground toward the day side; in the brighter area, nearer the warmth and brighter light of the day side, the female plants thrive, growing low across the ground where they can catch any pods that happen by. When germination is complete, heavy female spores fall to the ground to grow alongside other female plants. Feather-light male spores are expelled up into the winds, where they are carried through the wind cycle back to the night side where they are weighted by cold and drop to root.

passenger carriers—large capacity interstel ships run by corpgovs for transporting tourists, workers, migrants, and sometimes prisoners between worlds. Can only dock at space ports. Inside and outside the spaceport, they make no sound. Inside the ship, they produce a slight low, resonant rumble that is more felt than heard. Usually offer sleeping bunks stacked atop one another in a dormitory fashion.

Pidai'ba livitu, ba'riba t'ujhendun (pee-DAY-ee-bah LIH-vih-too, bah-REE-bah tih-oo-ZHEN-duhn) *Unameze*—no direct translation. Closest meaning is "Your body is dead, but your name lives on (is remembered)."

pithasia (pee-THAY-zhah) *Unameze*—no direct translation; similar to human concept of spirit; that portion of the Great Mind that is eternal, but which is tied to the DNA in a living physical body. Upon the death of the body, the bond is broken and the connection between the eternal and the mortal is disentangled, freeing the pithasia to reblend with the Mind, carrying its collected experiences and data for assimilation into the whole.

pithe (PEE-thay) *Unameze*—no direct translation, related to pithasia; similar to dreaming, when the awareness leaves the mortal tie during sleep to communicate with Na'Staani more deeply than is possible during meditation.

Forms of use:

> **pithes** (PEE-thays)—dreams.
> **pithin** (PEE-thihn)—dreaming.
> **pithun** (PEE-thoon)—dreamed.
> **pithele** (pee-THAY-lay)—a dream.

plaz—a non-toxic, plastic-like polymer used in place of glass on the human colony worlds. Used in windows, doors, furniture, artwork, anywhere glass could be used.

raneal (rah-NEE-ahl) *Unameze*—indigenous to Iridos. A natural scavenger. Very timid, small reptile, no danger to the unammi. Good climbers, very quick beneath the sand, found almost everywhere the unammi range on the surface. Raneals are eaters of dead flesh, scavenged eggs, tidbits left by other creatures, etc.

recreational(s)—herbal or pharmaceutical substances used for recreational purposes. Mostly legal in all twelve human colonies; only a few are banned for serious safety reasons or because the botanical substances necessary to produce them are endangered.

Rite of Achievement—the unammi ceremony held to mark the completion of one's training, and entry into a period of isolation; takes place between ages 28 and 29 seasons.

Rite of Decision—the unammi ceremony held to mark an individual's choice of guild in which they wish to serve; can happen almost immediately after Rite of Achievement or can be delayed by as much as several cycles; changes an individual's status from youngling to frem.

Rubene (roo-BEE-nuh)—one of twelve human colony worlds. Governed by Rubene Holding Company. Located in the Emlacha star system (same as Bejami). No moon. Home to The Federation Trader faction run by Admiral Georgeanne ("George") and her second-in-command, Claudio. One of the first three exoplanets to be settled by colonists from Earth. This is a "green" world, heavily focused on sustainability and eco-system friendly practices. One spaceport. Two landports.

rufesh (ROO-fehsh) *Unameze*—indigenous to Iridos. Opportunistic epiphyte that entangles tubers in the root systems of other plants and trees on Iridos. Flesh is savory, juicy, and crisp, but skins are rough, prickly, and inedible. If the tuber is ripe enough, squeezing the skin will pop out the flesh. Whole epiphyte has a dull indigo color, dimly bioluminescent. Edible; harvested by the unammi.

Saacharis (sah-KAH-rihs)—one of twelve human colony worlds. Governed by Saacharis Aggregate Mining. Located in the Nadisa star system. Two moons. Home to The Syndicate Trader faction run by Admiral Rizzo and her second-in-command, Captain Bailey. One of the first three exoplanets to be settled by colonists from Earth. Closer to its star than would normally be habitable for humans. Nadisa is also larger and brighter than the star of old Earth. Yet the planet's thick upper atmosphere reflects much of the harmful radiation and heat. The surface of Saacharis is dimmer, darker than other colonies. Two large spaceports. Two landports.

season—unammi measure of time on Iridos, used to denote a complete circuit of the planet around its star.

sedolyn (SEH-doh-lihn)—indigenous to Harajüd but farmed on several human colony worlds. Recreational. Safe herbal relaxant made from leaves and flowers of the *sedolinis* plant. Usually smoked but can be taken by capsule or ingested in food or drink. Small dose is mild, not sleep-inducing. Larger dose with alcoholic beverage can have soporific effect.

Shamashu Island (SHA-mah-shoo)—large island off the coast of New Canaan, Harajüd. Mountainous on the western coast.

shuttle—small version of a passenger carrier; ferries passengers and travelers back and forth between the spaceport and the landport, or from one planetary city to another.

sh'toi (shih-TOI) *Unameze*—no direct translation. Lowest form(s) of unintelligent life; derogatory, insulting.

skimmer—small personal craft same size and class as a jumper (though skimmers don't come in mid-size). Faster, sleeker, more elite. Stylish, functional, greater capacity for speed and distance. Still limited to atmospheric travel. Quieter than a jumper.

squib—derogatory term used by some humans to describe an unammi.

staani (stah-AH-nee) *Unameze*—all.

standard time—colonial measure of time created to standardize business practices between the various colony worlds, which all have varying natural day, week, month, and year lengths. Hours, minutes, and seconds remain the same as old Earth time measures.

> One standard day = 30 hours.
> One standard week = 6 standard days.
> One standard month = 30 standard days (5 standard weeks).
> One standard year = 15 standard months (75 standard weeks).

stunner—up-close weapon. Smaller versions must touch the target. More expensive (and illegal) ones can fire from short distances. Depending on the setting, the weapon can simply stop the target, or render it unconscious.

tao (tuh-OW) *Unameze*—still; Ex: basu'tao—be still.

TICS (tihks)—Tachyon Interlink Communication System. Used for inter- and intraplanetary communications, computer controls, personal memo systems, and numerous other purposes. Voice activated/controlled.

Traders—loosely organized groups of independent businesses modeled after Earth privateers; Traders operate outside corporate law and the Intercolonial Charter, with the tolerance of the corpgovs. Factions also run legitimate businesses on their own corporate worlds, as well as engage in business on other worlds with the agreement of the resident faction. At the time of this story, there are six extant Trader factions, each on a different colony world.

unammi (oo-NAH-mee) *Unameze*—the Iridosians' name for themselves.

visaug (VIH-zawg)—visual augmentation gear standard in human space suits.

wristcom—personal communication device linked to the larger TICS system on a Trader base or a planetary communications system. Worn around the wrist.

youngling—young unammi between the ages of birth and the age of 28 or 29 seasons; once their education is complete and they choose a guild, they are considered frem.

Zebalu (zeh-BAH-loo)—one of twelve human colony worlds. Governed by The Zebalu Association. Located in the Rasuka star system. Three moons, one large with some atmosphere. Home to The Cartel Trader faction run by Admiral Bellamy and her second-in-command, Captain Hannah. Three spaceports. Two landports.

Zebalu Association—the corporate governing body on human colony world Zebalu.

zhachi (zhah-CHEE) *Unameze*—adamant command: no direct translation; its closest meaning is "Stop!" or "Get out!" or "Get away!" Serves as a warning.

www.ingramcontent.com/pod-product-compliance
Lightning Source LLC
Chambersburg PA
CBHW072001190726
48293CB00001B/112